mr. charming

Piper Rayne

Cover Design and Illustrator: Buerosued

1st Line Editor: Joy Editing

2nd Line Editor: My Brother's Editor

Proofreader: My Brother's Editor

about mr. charming

Three years ago, I swore to myself we were done.

Since then, Tweetie Sorenson has embraced the professional hockey player bachelor lifestyle—his social media is a highlight reel of clubs, friends, and a never-ending stream of different women.

It's hard to believe he's the same man who stole my heart the very night we met. With him, everything felt wild, spontaneous, and absolutely perfect. I thought he was my forever.

Then, he broke my heart. Or maybe we broke each other's. Either way, it was over.

I've moved on—new city, dream job—until my boss throws me back into Tweetie's world. I'm sent to Chicago to manage the Falcons' social media, which means working alongside the one man I never truly let go of. *FML*.

Mr. CHARMING

one

Tedi

"I don't know, maybe Gill has a talent none of us appreciates." I drop the pictures from the Chicago Falcons social media campaign on the conference table.

Mindy, my assistant, picks them up and scans through the player photos. "What exactly would that be? It looks like the Falcon players work on the board of an insurance company."

"Exactly! Anyone who can get Tweetie Sorenson to look like he's knocking on your door to give you a complimentary quote on life insurance deserves some credit." I slide his picture across the table toward the other members of my team, not wanting to look at it any longer.

When the national league promoted me to put together a social media campaign for each franchise—hoping to improve attendance across all arenas, increase social media engagement, and improve viewership—I was thrilled. This is my opportunity to shine and show them what I can do, even if I know that my new position was formed because of the commissioner's ego. His brother is the commissioner of the football league, and they have a sibling rivalry going on. In the interview, my mission was clear—make every hockey team and player household names to ensure there are more hockey fans than football fans.

As I sit in a plush chair in a conference room that overlooks the Manhattan skyline, living a dream I never even envisioned for myself, my stomach sours as the picture of Tweetie gets passed around, each one of my team members commenting about how well he cleans up.

The thirteen years since we first met don't seem to have aged him, only made him more handsome. Of course it did. Meanwhile, I'm hunting down every face serum and lotion that promises to keep my youth intact.

No one in this room knows my past with the man who is still the best left wing in the league except, for Lyric since we've become close friends. It's a past so twisted that just seeing his picture makes that almost healed crack in my heart fracture again.

"No offense, but none of these guys look fuckable." Mindy slides the pictures back in front of me. Thankfully, it's Tweetie's teammate Rowan's picture on top.

"Yeah, we need them looking rough and tough," Jasmine says before sipping on her green smoothie.

"Exactly. They need to look like they can pick you up over their shoulder and drag you into the bedroom," Lyric says next to her. "I get that Henry Hensley is a dad, but damn, he looks like he works a nine-to-five and wears black socks and sandals mowing his lawn in the summer. We want a daddy, not a dad."

We all laugh.

I knew Gill wasn't the norm of who I usually hire, but finding thirty-two people to put out in the wild on their own was a challenge. We had lots of applicants, but I had to make sure they weren't going to be fangirling or fanboying over the players. Or in it just to try to springboard the job into furthering their own social media following. They were hired to do a job. The last thing I need is to have to tell the commissioner that one of my hires is sleeping with a player.

"Look at the Florida Fury. Aiden Drake doesn't look like the old man in the league here."

I stop the sliding picture Lyric pushes across the table at me, and I bite down my smile. "I'm not going to ogle my best friend's husband, but yeah, Aubrey did a great job on their campaign. Slide over the others."

After I have them in my hands, it occurs to me that maybe I purposely sent Aubrey to Florida because they'll always have a special place in my heart.

"Warner looks good too." Seeing him and Aiden and even Kane as the coach reminds me of what they all have. We all started there together, and somehow, I'm still the single one with no kids, ovaries drying up by the minute.

"Aubrey is the best." Mindy looks at me. "You played favorites with that one."

I drop the pictures. Mindy's not wrong. And I have a sinking feeling that I did the opposite to the Chicago Falcons for personal reasons as well.

"Well, we have to fix this. They're positioned to win the Cup this year." Jasmine leans back in her chair. "Want me to go over there and straighten Gill out?"

I examine everything Gill sent me. The meet-and-greet photos that look like a grade school class picture, the videos that look as though they belong on a ten-year-old's lip-synching social media account. I could easily send Jasmine and wash my hands of this. She'd do a great job. She's young and vibrant and has the eye to make the Falcons the "it" team in the league.

"Knock, knock."

We all swivel in our chairs to find the commissioner, Mr. Herington, in the doorway.

I straighten in my chair. "Mr. Herington, good morning."

He steps into the room. My boss, Calvin, follows, cringing behind him. What does that mean? Are my entire team and I about to be fired?

Mr. Herington takes the seat at the end of the long conference table. He's tall and lean and intimidating as hell. Not at all what you'd think the league commissioner would look like. His piercing blue eyes land on me. "Tedi, I received a phone call yesterday."

Calvin cringes again as he sits. So, it wasn't a good phone call, I take it.

"Oh?"

"Bud, the GM over in Chicago, called. Usually I'd send something like this down to Calvin, but Bud and I go way back. He saw some of the other campaigns and feels as if theirs is lacking."

At least he's being polite. Gill's campaign is god-awful and certainly wouldn't make me want to find out more about the team or watch or attend any games.

"Who do we have there?" he asks.

"Gill Gregory."

He looks at Calvin.

"He was an editor or something for the website, if I remember correctly," my boss says.

"He was a copy editor but looking to venture out," I say.

"I think we can all agree that he might be a better editor than promoter." Mr. Herington leans back in his chair, and his gaze falls to the papers in front of me. "What are you all discussing this morning?"

"It's funny you ask. We were going over some of the campaigns," I say.

He rolls his chair closer to the table, his elbows landing on top, and waves his hands toward him. "Great, let me see what Gill Gregory is doing over there in Chicago."

My stomach sinks. I do not want him to think I was sleeping on the job. As if I wasn't already about to address the situation with Gill and the Falcons.

"Okay." I push the folder to Calvin, who passes it to Mr. Herington. "We were just talking, and I think we should send Jasmine to Chicago. Give Gill some tips on how to make the campaign more of what we're looking for."

Mr. Herington doesn't look up at me, and Calvin has little beads of sweat lining his hairline. His anxiety only raises my own.

"Jasmine?" Mr. Herington looks up then around the table.

Jasmine lifts her hand, sucking the last of her smoothie from the straw and making the sound echo through the room.

"Hmm," he says, his long, thin fingers riffling through the images. "Bud does have a point. I think my granddaughter could do better." He shuts the file and passes it to Calvin. "Did you know that the Falcons are favored to win this year?"

"Technically, they were last year too," I say.

Calvin coughs or chokes on his saliva, I'm not sure. Either way, I probably shouldn't have said that.

Mr. Herington laughs. "Very true, but I heard the chemistry is good over there. That Tweetie Sorenson has stepped up as a real leader."

I school my nonverbal reactions since they usually have a mind of their own when it comes to the topic of Tweetie.

"Bud and I were in the same frat way back in college, and he did me a few favors back in the day. I owe him one. And since the Falcons are the team to watch this year, they need the best person on their campaign."

His gaze lingers on Jasmine.

She's young, but that's who has an eye nowadays. The

only thing I worry about with her is whether she'd be too intimidated by the players to ask them to do certain things.

She sips her smoothie—out of nervousness, I think—and the air coming through the empty straw makes that terrible sound again.

"I think it's all gone, Jasmine," Mr. Herington says.

Jasmine flushes.

"This is your ship to steer, Tedi, so I think you should go to Chicago. This whole experiment is new, and we need to really know if it can get the results we want."

The way he reminds me that this is an experiment is no accident, I'm sure. If it doesn't pan out, all my people and I are out. I didn't come this far to not make a name for myself in the hockey realm. But at the same time, the angry, heartbroken girl inside me is screaming that she doesn't want to go to Chicago.

"Me?"

Calvin's head whips around, and he widens his eyes at me. "Save the sinking ship, Tedi." His voice is cool and on the edge of demanding.

"It's why we hired you to run the program. Go up there and make us proud. Show your team what needs to be done and how to do it. Plus, with the right campaign and them winning the Cup, we'll easily turn people into die-hard hockey fans. Chicagoans alone will think to themselves, who are the Grizzlies?" Mr. Herington stands and straightens his suit jacket. "I'll call Bud and let him know you're coming. Have a good day." He nods to the rest of us and walks out of the room. "Calvin?"

Calvin scrambles to get up, almost falling off his chair. "I'll see you in your office," he says, rushing after Mr. Herington.

"So, you're going to Chicago?" Mindy asks.

I stand from the table. "It appears so." I attempt to keep the dread from my voice.

Lyric gathers all the folders, but they slip from her hands, and Tweetie's picture slides across the table to me. She gives me an apologetic look, knowing our history.

His chin-length blond hair, his devilish blue eyes, and defined jawline. God, I hate the man, but just looking at him still makes my core ache.

two

Tweetie

I'm in the back of an Uber on my way to our morning skate, scrolling through my phone to pass the time, when Aiden's name flashes on the screen.

I slide my thumb over and bring the phone to my ear. "How's the fam?"

I played with Aiden back in Florida. We're roughly the same age, both refusing to hang up our skates. Thankfully, we're still performing, but there's no doubt our time is coming.

"Good," he whispers.

"Why are you whispering?" I whisper back.

"I'm in the closet, packing my shit for an away game. Saige is on the phone in the bedroom."

"Man, you're taking whipped to a whole new level. You practically live in a mansion, and you can't find a room to talk in where you're not interrupting her?"

He scoffs, and I can't help but laugh.

"Hey, I'm putting myself on the line right now." He

pauses. "Yeah, I'm almost done packing," he calls out to who I assume is Saige.

I shake my head. "What's going on with you?" A quick glance out the window tells me we're getting closer to the rink.

"Saige is on the phone with Tedi."

A knot forms in my throat. The moment has come, the one I've been dreading for years. Tedi's engaged or maybe already married. Maybe even pregnant. Aiden's whispering makes more sense to me now. Ever since Tedi and I were finished, we don't discuss her when Saige is around. Tedi is Saige's best friend, her ride or die, and to her, I'm the asshole who broke Tedi's heart.

"Yeah?" I try to keep the dread and despair, the anger of envisioning her with someone else, out of my fucking tone.

"It's not good," he says softly, and I hear the sound of a zipper.

"Who is he?" I try to make it a little easier for Aiden because he's a great friend to warn me before the news travels and people start looking at me with fucking pity.

"No, that's not it."

I straighten in the back of my rideshare, gripping my phone tighter. If it's not about another guy, then why is Aiden in a closet, whispering, hiding whatever he's about to tell me about Tedi so his wife doesn't overhear?

My mind flashes to a million different scenarios. Is she hurt? Is she in the hospital? Is she sick? Fuck, last I knew, she worked for the national league out of New York. Did some asshole—

"Did she get hit by a bus?" I ask.

My rideshare driver looks over his shoulder at me in a panic.

"That's where your mind goes?" A door closes behind him.

"What do you expect? You're being all vague and shit." My

anxiety is at an all-time high, and pretty soon I'm going to have to ask the rideshare driver to detour to the hospital if Aiden doesn't fucking spill.

"I think you should address this issue. I can hear the panic in your voice." Aiden is talking normally again. Why didn't he shut the door to begin with?

"Just fucking tell me," I grit out.

The rideshare driver pulls to the curb, and I give him a nod of thanks, grab my bag, and get out. On the curb, the cold wind of Chicago seeps into my bones. Fuck, Florida and Nashville definitely had better weather compared to this frozen tundra.

"No one's reached out to you yet?" he asks.

"Fucking hell, Shamrock, just tell me already." I linger outside, not wanting anyone else to see my reaction to whatever he's about to tell me.

"Okay. Okay. Well, you know this new program with the league and how she heads it. Actually, did you know that? Shit, man, I should've told you, but things got crazy around here—"

"I know. Jagger told me," I interrupt. My agent sent me a text message the night we all went camping before the season started, and it was a gut punch I wasn't prepared for. I was on fucking pins and needles until Gill Gregory showed up to our campaign. I thanked the universe for small favors that day.

"Okay, good, so you know she got that job and is in charge of the entire program?"

"Yeah, yeah, I know. Unlike you sitting in the warm sun, I'm freezing my nuts off, so just tell me whatever you have to."

He laughs. "Shit, man, as a Wisconsin boy, I can't even imagine being back in those cold-ass winters."

"Fuck you and your sun and your palm trees and your shorts in February."

"My blood has thinned out—"

"I don't give a shit, why are you calling me?"

He laughs but sobers quickly. "I'm sorry, man, but your guy isn't cutting it there, so she's coming up to handle the Falcons' campaign herself. She's hopping on a plane tonight."

My mouth opens, my bag sliding off my shoulder to the crook of my arm. "Meaning?"

"Sorry, babe, I'm coming. Just got a call quick. Yeah, I know..." Aiden continues talking to Saige in the background while I process what he just told me.

I thought I was in the clear. I thought I wouldn't have to see her.

"You there?" Aiden asks, whispering again.

Saige is going to kick his ass if he keeps acting all secretive like he is now.

"Yeah. Thanks for letting me know."

"That's it? Do you want to talk about it?"

"Nah, it was ages ago. Surely we can coexist. We're adults, right?"

"Sure." The doubt in his tone matches what I'm feeling right now. "But—"

"Thanks, Shamrock. Knock 'em dead tonight."

"Hell, I'm going up against Cory, I need all the luck I can get, but seriously, Tweetie, if—"

"I'm good. Go."

He lingers on the line for a second. "Let's get together after the season. A bunch of us are thinking about going tropical—"

"Maybe. We'll see. I gotta get inside, I think there's an icicle hanging off my ball sac." I open the door to the arena and step inside.

He laughs. "God, I miss you."

I don't say anything because I still have hurt feelings about my trade so many years ago. "Of course you do. Now go fuck your wife so good she's not worried about how cagey you're being by whispering in the closet."

"Kids are home."

"Sounds like a drag." I nod toward the security guard, Mike.

"Does anyone up there know about your past with her?" He changes the subject because he's concerned.

All of our friends are concerned anytime we might be thrown together. I already bow out of anything Aiden and Saige have because that's Tedi's domain. She tends to give me the same respect when it comes to Ford and Lena. She can have Kane and Jana since they screwed me over anyway with that trade from Florida. Tedi and I haven't been able to coexist with our Florida friends since the demise of our relationship.

"A few, but they'll be quiet about it." Although our relationship was never a secret. For all I know, people are talking about it behind my back all the time. "I gotta go. Give Cory my best. Ever since he got out from under you, he's had the star power."

"No one made him stay as long as he did, and I don't see you announcing your retirement."

"They'll have to drag me off the ice."

Aiden laughs. "You, me, and Warner."

"Fuck, we should do a trio one year. All of us go in one shot."

He laughs. "You know someone will just come in and take over our spots."

"They'll never be as good as us."

"Definitely not." The phone muffles. "I know. I know." He returns. "Okay, I'm here, and so is Ford and all the other guys if you need us. I know this isn't going to be easy—"

"Bye." I cut him off.

"Tweetie." His voice sounds as though there's so much more he wants to say, but he can't fix this situation for me.

I hang up and pocket my phone, chewing over the fact that my ex is going to be working with me. I haven't seen Tedi in years, and I have no clue how this is going to work.

three

Tedi

I GET SNUG IN MY FIRST-CLASS SEAT WHILE THE SUN descends and grab my tablet to do some work during my flight. I need to figure out how I'm going to turn this around in Chicago. Scanning through what Gill has done so far, my finger stops on a picture of Tweetie laughing with the men I think are his closest friends on the team. He always makes friends so fast, so it doesn't surprise me how close he is to the other three key players on the Falcons.

"You a Tweetie Sorenson fan?" the woman in the seat next to me asks.

I tilt the tablet toward the window and turn to look at her. She's about my age, with red hair cut in a cute short style I'd never be able to pull off, but it looks great on her. Her smile is wide and welcoming.

"Sorry." She cringes and raises her hand. "Huge Falcons fan."

"It's okay." I lower the tablet, allowing my defenses to subside. I have no claim to Tweetie anyway.

"If my husband was sitting where I am, he'd be talking your ear off about that Trifecta."

I smile politely. The Trifecta. The name used for Tweetie, his center, Rowan, and right wing, Henry. Coined by his agent, Jagger Kale, the person whose brain I should probably be picking about how to sell these guys. It's a name he purposely used a few times, then bam, it stuck, and now they will always be referred to as the Trifecta. After Conor Nilsen joined last year as their goalie, it's now "The Trifecta and Pinkie are unstoppable."

"They are something."

She looks at the tablet again. "Go back to whatever you were doing. I'm sorry for interrupting."

My vision lingers on the line of people still boarding. I could sit here and allow my anxiety over what I'm about to do to keep ratcheting higher and higher the closer it comes to the plane's wheels leaving the New York tarmac only to land in Chicago, or I can distract myself.

"Are you from Chicago?" I ask.

She nods. "I was just here for business. It's new for me to be traveling, and I can't wait to get home. They say it's so easy doing this career and family thing, but it's hard to be away."

"My best friend struggled with that for a long time."

"The struggle is real, but I think I'm a little hormonal from still breastfeeding. Lugging around a pump isn't ideal for self-confidence. Petrified you're going to leak in the middle of the conference room."

She talks about how bathrooms don't have specific rooms for nursing mothers and how she leaked in front of her boss this week. All things I know nothing about. I wasn't always sure I wanted to have kids, but the older I get, the more I worry that that stage of my life is passing me by.

"Forget what I'm saying." Her hand on my arm pulls my

thoughts back to the present. "Let's talk hockey since you're clearly a fan." She nods toward the tablet on my lap.

"Oh, it's for work…" Shit, I regret opening my big fat mouth right away when her eyes light up.

"What do you do for work?"

Crap. Crap. Crap.

"I work for the national league, but I'm heading to Chicago to do some social media stuff for them."

Her mouth gapes open. "You're so lucky. That sounds exciting. So, you're going to, like, meet Tweetie and the rest of the players?"

"Yeah, I can't wait." I smack on a smile I'm sure doesn't reach my eyes.

"God." She looks around and leans in closer. "Do you know Tweetie's real name?"

I don't say anything at first. Not that I'm surprised she's asked. But he's only ever used his initials, and now everywhere that mentions him only says Tweetie.

"Um…" *Just lie, Tedi. You'll never see her again.* "No. Just the initials. He keeps that top secret." I shrug.

She sighs. "My husband and I throw around ideas all the time for what we think the J stands for." She rocks her head back on the headrest and turns to me. "I bet there's some girl out there who knows. Someone special."

My stomach lifts from the memory of the night he trusted me enough to tell me.

"From what I hear, he's kind of a ladies' man." The words feel like shards of glass leaving my lips.

She nods. "Yeah, me too, but you just know it's because some girl broke his heart." She shrugs. "My husband says I'm a romantic and I conjure up these things out of nowhere."

"It's sweet." I have a feeling if she heard the story of Tweetie and me, I'd be passing her tissues.

"He's the last man standing." Again, she leans in close to

me. "I probably shouldn't admit this, but I kind of stalk them all on social media. Did you know that Pinkie got married this past weekend? Some blonde started showing up in his socials this past fall, and then bam. Married." Her hands rise, and her fingers are spread as if it's the hottest gossip.

I hadn't actually heard this rumor, and I wonder if it's true. Whenever those dark nights come and I search Tweetie's socials, Conor's usually with him at some club or another.

"They say when you know, you know."

I swallow past the lump in my throat.

The line of passengers has cleared from the aisle, and the flight attendant is pushing down the overhead bin doors.

"I'm not trying to be rude, but I have some flying anxiety." She pulls out her AirPods.

"Oh, no problem." I smile and put away my tablet, digging my own AirPods from my bag.

We both put our AirPods in, and I stare at the ground crew doing all the things they need to so we have a safe flight. My heart skips a beat when I think about being face-to-face with Tweetie again.

At some point during the pull back from the gate, on our way to the runway, I remember our first night together.

four

Tedi's Journal Entry
Thirteen years ago
Florida

To my older self,

Tonight was one of the best nights of our life! I know... I've written that before, but I'm serious this time. Tweetie Sorensen from the Florida Fury knocked us over with his charming smile and big dick. God, his dick... magical. I'm not even exaggerating. The man knows what equipment he has and how to use it. The only sad thing is we'll never experience it again. The two of us didn't exchange numbers. Mostly because we snuck out of his house after our third time when he was passed out. I know, I know... one of these days, we'll be the one left naked and alone in bed, but Tweetie knew the score before we hopped in the rideshare. Just in case we ever forget how tonight feels, I'm going to recap it here because believe me, older Tedi, we don't want to ever forget tonight.

All the Florida Fury hang out at this restaurant and bar named Carmelo's, and I scored an invite thanks to Saige (so if she's sitting in the wheel-chair next to yours right now, give her your Jell-O at dinner).

Sure, I had to endure a conversation with Ford Jacobs (that guy is so full of himself), but eventually the torture was over when Tweetie appeared at the table, sliding into the side with Aiden. Ford finally left (thank God).

Tweetie had given me the eye all game. Winking, smiling, waving... and he made promises with his eyes as soon as he got in the booth.

Of course I wasn't going to just let him keep his distance. I'm not one of those shy girls who waits for the guy to come to them. I take what I want. Tonight, I was going to check "sleep with a profes-sional hockey player" off my fuck-it bucket list, and Tweetie was said hockey player.

I got out of my side of the circular booth and went over to his side. Saige left, Aiden following her (if Saige married Aiden, remind her he was smitten for her even then). Thank you to them because then I had Tweetie all to myself.

It didn't take long for me to end up in his lap and flirting before he whispered the magic words in my ear, "Come home with me."

I practically leaped off his lap.

Neither one of us said goodbye to anyone as his hand found mine and he escorted me out of the bar and into an Uber a minute later.

In the back seat, I climbed into his lap again, straddling him this time. He didn't push me away. He actually welcomed me. His strong hands on my hips tugged me closer, and through my thin pants, I felt his promising bulge. Let me say, I grinded pretty hard on him during that Uber ride. His lips found mine, and my hands dove into his hair.

Tweetie wasn't worried about the Uber driver at all. I had his whole attention, and oh my, it was amazing. Like the two of us were in our own little bubble. Up until today, no man has ever made me feel the way Tweetie did. As if I was his already and he didn't want to be apart from me as much as I didn't want to be apart from him.

He took me to his house since I don't bring guys to mine (I'm sure you remember the drill).

He was smooth. Never letting my hand go. Leading me up his walkway with a few glances over his shoulder as if somehow my body wasn't attached to my hand and he was afraid I'd take off. He tight- ened his hold on me every five seconds.

Tweetie lived in a house on the beach. It wasn't

huge, but he wasn't the "it" player on the team. If I wanted a guy to take me to a mansion, I would've chosen to go home with Ford since he's the trust fund baby of the group.

After he unlocked the door, he released my hand only to hold out his arm for me to walk in first. It felt like trust, as if he was telling me he didn't have any demons to hide.

I stepped into his world, and the entire place smelled like him. It was the same scent I was already addicted to. The one I wanted to rub all over my body, hoping I could still smell him the next morning. Yeah, I already had it bad for him.

"Want something to drink?" he asked, leaning along the open staircase at the bottom of the stairs with a mischievous grin as if he was only asking to be polite.

I turned around and walked over to him, ignoring the butterflies in my stomach, and stood right there in front of him. I've gotten good over the years at masking the vulnerable girl inside.

Tweetie's hand cradled my head, and I leaned into his touch. Something happened in that moment when I tilted my head and locked eyes with him. He was staring at my lips, and I felt something shift inside me, but I'm not sure what.

"No drink," I said.

"Good." His hand fell from my face, and he

squatted down, running his hands over my ass before picking me up by the thighs with the finesse of a professional athlete. He turned and walked me up the stairs.

"I haven't seen the rest of your house."

"There's only one room you need to see."

A minute later, I was through a door and pressed against a wall. "I like this."

"I thought you would."

He grinned, then his lips crashed to mine, and his tongue didn't wait more than a half second before it was in my mouth. He tasted so delicious, and all I wanted to do was strip down and tell him to do whatever he wanted to me as long as the big dick I'd already felt the outline of in the Uber was part of his plan.

We were barely able to stop kissing to undress, but somehow in the midst of dirty talk, sloppy kisses, and laughter, we undressed one another. The jokes, the lines, the easiness of Tweetie was surprisingly hot.

Still, he never took me to his mattress. He kept a hold of me, walking over to his nightstand, and took out a condom. For the first time in my life, I wanted to ask a guy to go bare, but thankfully, the chemistry between us hadn't knocked all the sense out of me.

He brought the package to his mouth, tearing open the foil wrapper, then hoisted me up on a small chest of drawers.

"God, you're so hot."

I didn't mean to let that internal thought out, but Tweetie only glanced at me through his long eyelashes as he rolled the condom down his impressive length with one hand. It wasn't anything he didn't already know.

"You almost ruined my game tonight," he said.

"Why?"

His hands found my hips before sliding down to my ass and plucking me off the dresser, then walking us back over to the wall. "I couldn't take my eyes off you. The way you were cheering and hitting the glass. Fuck, I wanted to ditch the game and fuck you right there in the middle of the arena."

My entire body needed this man. What was he doing to me? He was just supposed to be a check-mark in a box and nothing more. "Well, you can fuck me now."

"Just so you know, once isn't going to be enough."

"You saying you have the stamina to fuck me more than once tonight?" I gave him a challenging look, and he chuckled.

"You have no idea the ride you're about to have."

"Let's see what you got, hotshot." Then I laughed until he slid inside me, filling me completely and shutting me up.

But no worries, Tweetie knew exactly what he had,

and he was right, once wasn't enough. Nor was twice. It took three times and many positions before we both collapsed on the mattress.

Don't worry, it was a great night, but I snuck out right as dawn hit. Check mark accomplished.

five

Tweetie

Ever since I hung up with Aiden, my mind has been in a tailspin and unable to straighten.

Tedi is... I can't even fathom what it will be like to see her again, let alone work alongside her. What if one of these dipshits hits on her, or worse, she starts dating one? I shake my head, trying to engage in the bullshit locker room talk going on around me, which lately consists of my three best buddies talking about what they did with the loves of their fucking lives the night before.

I'm the odd man out now. Conor and Eloise disappeared all weekend, and I've started going out with the Chipmunks. Every night I feel older than the last when I say my goodbyes and they continue down to the bar that's open the latest.

Now with Tedi coming here, I'm a complete and utter mess.

Conor pushes open the locker room doors, causing all of us to stop dressing and turn and look at him. He's late. The last one to arrive.

He drops his bag and raises his hands. "I have an announcement to make. I'm a married man!" He shows off his left ring finger that's tattooed with a giant E.

"What the hell?" Rowan walks over to him.

"Beat you to it," he says, then points at Henry. "Beat you too."

"You got married?" I ask, fully turning around, not understanding why he's marrying someone he's only been with for a matter of months.

"And you didn't invite us?" Henry scowls at Conor.

"Three-day trip to Vegas," he says.

Yeah, I knew they weren't home, but they're always crossing something off those damn bucket lists of theirs. I never thought it would be getting married.

Coach Buford comes out of his office. "What's going on out here?"

"Pinkie got married," Alvin says. He's a nice enough kid, though maybe I just think that because I've been spending way too much time with him. But he's always in the know and has the gossip.

Coach trains his gaze on Conor for a moment. "Congratulations," he deadpans. "The rest of you, listen up. There's been a development with this whole social media thing the league is pushing. Gill just got the axe, which I think we can all agree is a good thing for him and us."

Everyone laughs. The guy didn't have a clue what he was doing, so I wasn't surprised that he didn't work out. I really tried to help him so that I wasn't in the situation I'm about to be in, but the guy wouldn't listen. I mean, I dated Tedi for years, and she handled my social media the entire time. I have an idea of what sells tickets, but Gill thought he knew best.

"Since there's no one else waiting in the wings, and the season is already underway, and we're one of the favorites to win the Cup, they're sending in the boss. This Tedi Douglas is going to use us as an example to show others what's possible, so get ready to put those hockey smiles on display, boys." He walks back into his office without another word.

All of my asshole best friends turn their attention to me. Right now, I wish I'd never told them about her. Since they're all living happily with their wives or soon-to-be wives, they think Tedi's the one who got away. I don't know, maybe she is, but our time to try to figure it out ended years ago. We've moved on from one another. Not to mention, who wants to feel that fucking pain all over again when we fuck up our chance another time? Not me, that's for sure.

"Fuck off and go play Monopoly." I stalk toward the bathroom, throwing the dig that after you're with someone for a long time, you end up playing boring board games because the bedroom turns into a barren wasteland, cold. Not that my bed with Tedi was ever cold.

I go to the urinal to take a piss, but really, I just want to be away from everyone. It's bad enough that these three know. I don't need the entire team talking about my situation with Tedi.

"Shit, man." Conor speaks first. He probably knows the most about my past with her.

"Do you mind? I'm taking a piss." I don't bother looking over my shoulder.

None of them step forward, but they don't leave either.

"Are you okay?" Henry asks.

I flush the urinal, tuck myself in my underwear and pants, and go over to the sink to wash my hands. "I'm fine."

"But—" Rowan starts, and I cut him off with a hand in the air.

"Listen, I appreciate this whole 'bros got my back' thing between us. And I was happy to talk you assholes off the ledge when it came to the women you love, but Tedi and I have been over for a long time. I'm sure she's moved on, as have I."

They all share a look.

"The last thing I want right now is to have this gossip fill the locker room. I don't need everyone looking at me the entire time she's working here. So, just keep it to yourselves, and if I need your input or advice, I'll seek you out."

I walk by them, and they part, allowing me through, whispering to one another behind me.

I circle back around. "We're here to play fucking hockey. It's not a therapy session."

God knows I had enough of those when I was younger to know that these three are not qualified to deal with my bullshit.

"Speaking of therapy, that brings up a good point..." Rowan lifts his finger, and I want to break it.

They all start laughing, and the tension leaves my body for a second.

"Cool, so we're ignoring the problem." Henry pats my shoulder as he passes me. "Good to know."

"Sweet, this was putting a downer on my whole wedding news anyway." Conor hits my chest a few times, following Henry.

Rowan doesn't move. He gives me that look as if saying, "Come on, man, you can't keep bottling this shit up."

But he's wrong. I can. So I turn around and head to the dressing room.

"If we're gonna win the Cup, your asses should be on the ice," I bellow.

The guys left in here scramble to get their stuff and stop talking, each of them filing out. Conor gets dressed in record time and leaves without saying another word to me.

Finally, I'm alone as I tie up my skates.

Coach Buford comes out of his office, but he doesn't walk out the door.

Fuck. Fuck. Fuck.

"You know this Tedi Douglas?" he asks.

I glance up, wondering if he's asking because he's heard about our past or just general curiosity. As usual, his face gives away nothing. I could easily lie. Who Tedi is—or was—to me doesn't matter, but if something comes out, then he'll see me as a liar.

"I do, through Aiden Drake." I grab my helmet and wait for the next question.

"She gonna make you guys run around doing bullshit media tours and crap?"

I walk toward Coach, chuckling. "Yeah, she is."

"I thought so. You know, I didn't mind Gill that much. He was shit at his job, but at least he wasn't interrupting my plans and my time with the team."

I liked Gill too. He was hard on the eyes and didn't make me regret all my life decisions.

"Well, it's good for the team, right? What's good for the team is good for us?" My line is complete bullshit.

"Don't throw that optimistic crap at me. Go get on the ice. I have to keep you in shape before our new drill sergeant comes to town." He smacks me on the back, and I head out.

As my skates glide onto the ice, only one thought comes to mind—what will it be like to be in Tedi's orbit again?

six

Tedi

I'm a rip-the-Band-Aid off kind of girl. Always have been. So I get Tweetie's address—which isn't hard since he lives at The Nest, a condo building he shares with his teammates on the north side of Chicago that has a bar underneath called Peeper's Alley.

It's a well-known destination for all the puck bunnies that, from the rumors around the league, Tweetie likes to entertain. It's embarrassing how much he's gotten around since we broke up. Embarrassing and heart-wrenching, not that I'd ever let anyone know that second part.

I tip the Uber guy on the phone and walk across the side-walk. They're off today, so I assume he'll be home, sleeping off a hangover. My attention is drawn to a sign written in girly script with a black Sharpie that reads, The Nest, that's been fixed to the gate. God, it's worse than I thought. Notes are taped to the sign with phone numbers and promises of a good time, all fixed with pieces of chewed gum. How can he even live here?

I press his buzzer, which just has the number for his unit, no last name. So, it's okay for every warm-blooded female to know that three of the Falcon players live here, but they can't know which condo they're in? Men.

No one answers. I try to sneak a peek through the security gate, but it's pretty well blocked with thick black mesh. So I press the button again and wait, looking around the area.

At least he chose a pretty awesome area to live, right by the Colts' stadium and all the bars.

After a bit, I pull out my phone to check the time. I'm not going to leave here and think about this inevitable meeting between us all night. My first day to report with the team is tomorrow, and I want to deal with the awkwardness between us before then.

I press the number two buzzer. Surely one of the other players will let me up.

Still no answer.

Finally, I press the number one, but that's a failure too.

I grunt, annoyed that Tweetie is making even this difficult, regardless of if he knows or not. My gaze veers to the sign above the bar. Fuck it, I'll have a drink and hope he's back by then.

I open the door of Peeper's Alley to find a typical sports bar with televisions lining almost every inch of wall space. At least the inches where the Chicago sports team paraphernalia isn't hung, most of which is the Falcons. I dodge examining Tweetie's jersey and head right to the bar.

"We're not open."

I thumb toward the door. "But it was unlocked."

The older red-haired woman puts her hands on her hips and looks me over. "It's really sad, you know."

"What is?" How could I have possibly offended this woman when she just met me?

"That you allow your hormones to take over your

common sense. Do you see them in here? No. They don't sit in a bar in the middle of the afternoon." She points at the door. "I open in fifteen minutes. Go wait on the sidewalk or go back home, I don't care." She turns away from me.

I huff. I could listen to her—she's definitely a "I'll take you down if you cross me" type, but so am I, so let's get scrappy. But first, I'll kill her with kindness.

"Listen, I'm sorry, but I think you're mistaking me for someone else. I'm not here for one of your employees. I just need to have a drink and wait for one of the residents upstairs to get home."

She groans. "They're all taken."

My stomach swoops. "I'm sorry?"

"The Falcons. You're late, they've been snatched up by other women. Women not like you."

My fingers point at my chest as if I'm not hearing her correctly. I want to say not all of them unless Tweetie was the one who got married in Vegas this weekend and not Conor.

God, stomach, stop with the reactions. We don't need him in our life.

"I'm not here to date them or sleep with them."

She finally turns around from wiping down the liquor bottles. Her gaze coasts over me again, and she hums. "You are older than the usual ones."

"Thanks," I deadpan.

She studies me further. Just when I think she's going to escort me out by my arm, she pats the bar in front of her. "One drink."

I smile, take off my coat, and slide up on the stool. "Rum and Coke with a lime."

She nods. "At least you can order a good drink."

She busies herself pouring my drink, and I cross my legs, observing. I'm pretty sure under that harsh exterior is a woman with a heart. After all, if she's so protective of the guys, she must care about them.

She places my drink on a napkin. I figure she'll go back to the liquor bottles, but she slides another stool out from behind the bar and sits across from me. "So, who do you want?"

"I already said I don't want anyone."

"You're looking for someone?"

I nod, sipping my drink before setting it back down. "Tweetie."

Her head rocks back, and she studies me again. I've never felt so scrutinized by anyone. She doesn't say anything, but there's something in the way her lips almost tip into a smile that I don't understand.

"It's business-related," I clarify.

For a woman who speaks her opinion on every turn, she's awfully quiet.

"We knew each other a long time ago."

"What did you say your name was?"

I have no frame of reference on how well she knows him. He lives upstairs, and it's not out of the realm of possibility for him to be close to the bartender in the same building he lives in. Tweetie makes friends with everyone. Plus, she's protective of them. The one thing I have on my side is that Tweetie keeps everything superficial with people. He's not one to tell a story about how he's been hurt. Then again, I'm not sure he was even that hurt when we broke up.

Shut up. You know he was. Just as much as you. You just like to deny it.

"Hello??" She waves her hand in front of my face.

I blink. "Sorry. Tedi. Tedi Douglas." I extend my arm.

She stares for a moment before shaking my hand. She still doesn't say anything, and it almost comes across like she does know my name, but there's no way.

"And you are?"

"Ruby." Her hand slides out from mine. "I own the bar."

"I figured."

Light filters into the bar from behind me, and her gaze veers over my shoulder. A small smile creases her thin lips. "Hey, boys."

I have no idea how I'm able to feel that he's entered the room, but I do. He's here, and we're back to sharing the same space. The hairs on my neck rise, or maybe it's just my anxiety.

Game time. Do not let him see how much this hurts you.

After my version of a pep talk, I pick up my drink and swivel around on my stool.

All four of them are here. The Trifecta and Pinkie. Tweetie's head is buried in his phone. As the other three stand with their jaws on the floor, he's clueless. Conor elbows Tweetie and he glances from his phone to him, then Conor nods toward me at the bar.

Do not feel hurt that you felt him enter the room, but he didn't sense you.

Tweetie's head turns in my direction, and I swallow the lump in my throat until our eyes meet. I refuse to give him the satisfaction of a reaction from me.

So I bring my drink to my lips with a smile as if to say I'm perfectly fine. "Hello, boys. If you'll all excuse us, Tweetie and I have some things to discuss."

Tweetie's phone slips from his hands and topples to the floor.

Ruby laughs behind me. "Back room," she says, and I hear her feet hit the floor. "The rest of you, what can I get you?"

As if she's their mother, the other three walk over to the corner of the bar, as Tweetie stands in place. I'm pretty proud of myself. I'm doing a bang-up job of acting as if my heart isn't pounding out of my chest. I deserve an Emmy for this performance.

Until his gaze falls down my body and rises back up at a sloth's pace. His eyes are like a caress, and it's impossible not to remember when his hands used to travel the same path.

God, no other man has ever incited the desire he can from just one look.

seven

Tedi

I DOWN THE REST OF MY DRINK AND PLACE IT ON THE bar, acting as if his teammates aren't slyly looking at me the entire time. I slip down from the stool and point at the door to a back room I noticed earlier.

"In there?" I ask Ruby.

She nods, opening a water bottle and handing it to Rowan Landry.

Without glancing at Tweetie, I walk across the bar and into the back room that has a large round table along with some smaller tables for two on the wall, giant televisions, a dartboard, and a pinball machine. I don't bother turning around when the door clicks shut behind me.

"You look good."

I clench my jaw, gather my confidence, and circle around. "You always were an ass man."

"When it came to you, I was an everything man." His eyes dip to my chest.

Why does he have to be better-looking than when I first

fell for him? It's so unfair how men become more handsome as they get older.

"You can tone down the flirting. Save that for your next victim."

He widens his stance, crosses his arms, and chuckles. "Victim? I don't remember you screaming for help when you were under me..." He cocks his head. "Or over me for that matter." He shrugs.

"Listen, I'm sure you've gotten wind as to why I'm here."

He saunters over to the table and slides a chair out for me before taking the one next to it. Is he delusional? I'm not going to sit that close to him. So I leave one chair between us, and he laughs. "Damn, I almost forgot how stubborn you were."

"Almost?"

He lifts one shoulder. "You're hard to forget."

I inhale what I hope is a cleansing breath. "Let's just get this over with. Who knows about us here?" I lean back and cross my arms.

"And what if I said no one?"

I roll my eyes. Games. Always fucking games with Tweetie. "I wouldn't be surprised."

He chuckles, but it's not a real laugh. He finds no enjoyment from my words. His forearms fall to the table, and he slides his chair closer. "You know I'm a private kinda guy."

"Really? Because from what I hear, you like to share your privates with a lot of people. Women specifically."

That damn smirk that annoys me and turns me on all at once creases his lips. "You know how good that certain part of my body is. It would be a tragedy not to share."

I try not to outwardly show my irritation or jealousy. "Enough of the games. I'm here to sell tickets, ad spots, and merch so the league can afford to keep you all playing. You do know the oldest players go first, right?"

His smirk falls, and I don't feel an ounce of satisfaction because of it. "Throwing shots? That's how you want this to play out?"

"Just..." I hate that he can get me so flustered. This isn't a good sign for what's going to happen tomorrow when I'm trying to get all his teammates to respect me. "I want to be prepared. Who knows about our past?"

He turns away from me for a second before his eyes meet mine again. "The three guys out there."

"That's it?"

He nods.

"Coach Buford?"

He shakes his head. "Not really. I told him I know you through Aiden."

"Then I'm sure you can make some kind of deal with those three to keep their mouths shut."

He chuckles again, leaning back in his chair. Using his foot, he slides the chair between us out of the way. "Why would I do that? I'm not ashamed that you're my ex."

My mouth sours at the word ex. There was a time I thought I'd be his forever. "So, you want everyone to know you're not against monogamy? You want to answer questions about what happened between us and who broke whose heart and—"

"Fucking hell," he says and runs his hands through his chin-length hair. "You know I don't like my personal shit everywhere."

"Neither do I, so how about you turn off the persona you use to make everyone think you're someone you're not, and let's just have some real talk?"

His eyes bore into mine, and I blink, the intensity in his gaze unnerving.

The door opens, and Ruby stands there with two drinks. "You've been in here so long I thought your mouths must be going dry." She places another rum and Coke in front of me and a beer in front of Tweetie.

She squeezes Tweetie's shoulder and leaves after we both murmur our thanks.

He eyes my drink but doesn't say anything. "The guys won't tell anyone."

"Good. This job is really important to me, so I'd appreciate their discretion. Tomorrow when they introduce us, act like you've never met me, and I'll do the same."

His jaw hardens, but he doesn't argue. "Fine." He tips back his beer. "Is that all?"

I sip my drink and stand. "Yeah."

"You didn't have to ambush me. You could've called me."

"I don't have your number," I say, heading toward the door.

"I never changed it."

"I don't have it because I deleted it." My hand lands on the doorknob, and I remain there with my back to him.

He huffs, and the chair skids along the floor as he stands. "You really think we can do this?" I hear him walk over to me, and I really wish I had my drink to coat my dry throat.

"Do what?"

"Coexist? See each other and not touch each other?" I don't have to be facing him to know that his gaze roams down my body again. "You still..."

He leans forward, caging me between the door and his body. I hear him inhale, smelling me, and goose bumps travel up my arms.

"We just need to be professional and keep our distance," I mumble, too affected by his chest along my back.

Goddamn it, Tedi, move!

"That's the problem, though. You're the one thing that ruins my self-control. You're the one person I can never stay away from." He slides my hand off the doorknob.

"You've done it for three years, you can do it for the rest of the season. Goodbye, Tweetie." I open the door and bolt.

Four sets of eyes turn in my direction before looking over my shoulder at Tweetie.

"Boys," I say. "Thank you, Ruby." I nod, walking across the bar to the door, trying to keep my steps even so it doesn't appear as though I'm rushing.

As soon as I'm outside, I keep walking until I turn a corner, then I press my back to the brick wall, close my eyes, and inhale deeply. I pull my phone out of my purse, dialing Saige.

She answers on the first ring. "How did it go?"

"Not good. I need to figure out a plan and fast."

"I knew it was going to be hard on you, but I was thinking, how can we make sure he knows you're off-limits?"

I laugh, look to my left, and start walking as far as I can away from him. "I am off-limits."

She scoffs.

"What was that for?"

"You know when Tweetie is involved, you lose all your willpower. It's okay. I'd be the same with Aiden."

"He's your husband," I say.

"I meant if we had your type of relationship."

"Okay, I'm going to hang up now. I feel very insulted."

"Come on. You know I'm right. Anyway, you need a man in your life." I hear a child screaming in the background.

"Thanks. You make me feel so good, bestie."

"That's not what I meant. Hold on." The receiver is muffled, but I still hear her arguing with her two girls about something. "Okay, I'm back. I mean, you need to find a boyfriend and make it seem serious."

Her idea isn't horrible, but where am I going to find a guy? I can't pick up some random on the street.

There's another scream. "Sorry, I have to go, but think about it. Plus, maybe it will help you finally get over Tweetie."

I want to tell her that based on the reaction he just got from me, I'm probably going to want him on my deathbed. "All right. Go."

"I'll call you later." Another muffled sound. "Girls!" she screams. "You got this. If there's anyone who can do this, it's you."

"Thanks for the vote of confidence. Now go handle your shit."

She laughs. "Bye. Love you."

"Love you."

I end the call and people-watch for a minute, wondering if all of these people have their lives figured out. No way I'm the only screw-up.

eight

Tweetie

"YOU LOOK LIKE YOU JUST GOT THE SHIT BEAT OUT of you," Conor says when I step out of the back room at Peeper's.

I feel like it, but like hell if I'm gonna tell them. "We just had to clear some shit up. You dipshits need to keep your mouths shut tomorrow. No one on the team can know she's my ex."

Rowan's eyebrow quirks. "You really think that's not going to get around?"

Ruby watches me the entire time I walk over, then grabs a shot glass and fills it with whiskey. She slides it across the bar, and I grab it, downing it. The burn does nothing to soothe my aching heart after seeing the only woman I've ever loved again.

God, she smelled good. I could've stayed there with her between the door and me forever. I didn't even have to touch her, I just wanted to be near her again.

"It has to stay between us. This job is really important to her," I say.

Henry smiles, and when I narrow my eyes, he chuckles into his beer. Asshole.

"We're not going to say anything, but"—Rowan puts his hand on my shoulder—"you okay?"

I nod. "It's just weird. It's been three years since I've seen her in person."

"Yeah, when Jade returned, it was a shock," Henry says. "All those feelings come rushing—"

"It's been over for a long time." I slide the empty shot glass Ruby's way.

"Yeah, but anyone can tell there are lingering feelings there. Maybe the door isn't completely closed."

I really wish Henry would stop comparing Tedi and me to him and Jade. We're different.

"Do you want to finally tell us why you broke up?" Conor leans his weight on the bar top.

I could talk to them. They're some of my best friends, and none of them were tangled up in the situation like all my Florida teammates. Even when I've broached the subject with Ford a few times, he somehow ends up saying something that makes me feel as though he sides with Tedi, and we end up in an argument. I finally just stopped talking about it with him. Now it's been so long since I've discussed Tedi and my relationship that I can almost pretend it never happened. But seeing her today... it took everything I had not to pull her into my arms.

"There isn't much to say. We were on for a long time. We dated for years, and then I got hurt... got traded... and we were off... then Ford retired and had a party, and we were back on briefly before we were done for good."

There's so much between those events. We were a couple I'd be jealous of today. But we were young and felt as if we had our entire future in front of us. Now, I'm struggling to stay relevant in my career, and she's finally made it to the big leagues like she wanted.

"It's over now. So, just help me get drunk these next few months, and if I'm around her, detour me away. That's all I ask."

Ruby pours me another shot, and I down it. She hasn't said anything, and I know she'll corner me at some point, but she won't do it in front of all of them.

"That's how you want it to be? Just get through it?" Rowan asks. I can tell he's not judging, he's only asking.

I shrug. "It's the only way."

Henry raises his eyebrows and glances at Conor, who shrugs.

"You don't think it's going to affect your game?" Conor asks.

It's something I gave each of them hell about when they were having problems of their own in the love department. "Nah, I realized a long time ago that Tedi Douglas isn't mine to keep."

They each take a sip of their drinks, and the door opens. I'm thankful for the distraction. All I need to do is center myself again and pretend we're not sharing the same city.

"No dogs!" Ruby scolds, pointing at the girls.

"He could be your mascot." Eloise, Conor's now-wife, holds their new dog, Wilbur.

"You're screwed, buddy. You just got replaced," I say to Conor, who stares with so much love at Eloise.

"No mascot. No dog." Ruby narrows her eyes.

Kyleigh looks around the space. "No one else is here." She walks over to Rowan and wraps her arms around his waist.

He kisses the top of her head. "How was the park?"

She rests her cheek on his chest and stares up at him just like Tedi used to look at me in the early days. "Turns out dogs are kind of a dick magnet."

Rowan's smile slips from his lips.

She laughs. "Don't worry, Bodhi made sure to tell them we were all taken."

Rowan lifts his hand, and Henry's seven-year-old, Bodhi, jumps up to slap it.

"Can I have a kiddie cocktail?" Bodhi asks his dad.

"Ask Ruby," he says, pulling Jade over to him.

Bodhi climbs up on the stool next to me. He doesn't even have to ask Ruby before she's dropping three cherries into the drink. "There were all these birds at the park. I thought they flew south in the winter?" Bodhi says to Ruby.

All three of my teammates are coupled up, and I'm definitely the odd man out, but that's the way I want it. Don't I?

I gave up the hope a long time ago of having what they have, but I can't deny that after seeing Tedi today, the ache in my chest stings a little more than usual. Which tells me I'm gonna have a helluva time keeping my distance from her.

nine

Tweetie's Journal Entry
Twelve years ago
Florida

To my teenage self,

You'd be so proud of me, man. We've got a girlfriend. Yeah, I asked Tedi to be my girlfriend, which sounds really juvenile now that I'm in my twenties. Things are coming around for us, though. She's different than the other girls. She's like us. Crazy, wild, and spontaneous. But let me tell you how it all went down...

Our season ended, so I booked us a flight to stay in one of those huts over the ocean. The water was so clear, the sand so white, and the sky so blue. It was the perfect place for us to decompress after all the traveling during the season. (We've come a long way.)

She changed into a bikini right after the bellhop left our private hut. Damn, she looked so good. She already had a bronze glow since we live in Florida, but somehow under the sun there, she was even hotter.

Tedi walked up to me and slid her hands under my shirt and up my chest. I love her hands on me. "Come on. The water is begging for us."

I let her push up my T-shirt, and I helped her shed it from my body. She cast small kisses along my collarbone as her fingers manipulated the button of my shorts.

"This is amazing, Tweetie."

I just watched her, still amazed that she was mine. I rested my hands on her waist, wanting so badly to pull the strings at her hips and watch the flimsy fabric float to the wooden floor. "You like it?"

"What's not to love?"

We hadn't said the words yet. The three words I've never told anyone because of my fear of abandonment. (Yeah, we still have that problem.) Even though I haven't said them, that doesn't mean I don't feel them. I do. She's changed me, and all I see and want is her.

"Aren't you hungry?" I asked.

She pushed my shorts down, leaving me in my boxer briefs. "I'm not hungry for food. What I want is to jump into the ocean with you. Don't you want to feel me all wet?"

Fuck yeah, I did. "Give me a minute."

She rose on her tiptoes and placed a kiss on my lips. "Hurry."

I placed my hand on the back of her head to keep her with me, and she slid her tongue into my mouth. I'd never grow tired of her forwardness and the way she took what she wanted from me. The trust she gave me was addicting.

I patted her ass after we closed the kiss, and she gave me one quick peck before sauntering over to the water's edge.

Not wanting to be away from her, I hurriedly changed into my swim trunks. When I reached the deck, she was still standing at the edge, looking down at the water. I was surprised she wasn't already neck deep.

"What's the matter?" I asked, wrapping my arms around her and nuzzling my head into the crook of her neck. It was my favorite position with her, feeling as though I was offering her shelter and protection. Plus, she smelled so damn good.

"I thought if a shark came and ate me, you'd think I ran away with another man. So, I figured I'd wait."

I laughed and tightened my arms around her. "I think I would have noticed the bloody water, and I'm hoping you would have screamed so I could be your hero."

"What if he just swallowed me whole and you spent the rest of your life without me, thinking I'd found some man who swept me away? That'd be sad."

I kissed the nape of her neck, and she put her hands over my arms. "Want to tell me the real reason?"

She sighed. We were so alike, always trying to hide our real fears. "What if there really is a shark and you weren't here to save me?"

"I'd sacrifice myself so you could live."

"But what if the shark only wanted me because I'm cute?"

"Are you saying I'm not cute?"

She circled in my arms, and I clung to her tighter. "You're the cutest, but you're hairy, and maybe the shark doesn't want hair in its teeth."

I lowered my hands to her ass. "Let's get in the water, babe."

She rested her head on my chest. "The sun feels good."

"The water will feel better." I wasn't about to let her not enjoy the water because she was scared of sharks.

"Maybe I'm in the mood for that food you promised me now." Her hand wedged between our bodies, and she ran her palm over my dick.

"Hey." I placed my finger under her chin and raised her head to look at me. "You trust me?"

She nodded.

So I walked us to the edge, picked her up, and

jumped toward the water.

"Tweetie!" Her scream was quickly garbled from the water.

When we emerged, she wrapped her body around mine, her eyes frantically searching the water.

I laughed. "I swear I would never imagine you'd be scared of sharks."

She reared her head back. "Have you never seen Shark Week? Or Jaws?"

I laughed harder. "I figured you were more the kind to learn exactly where to punch the shark to make it go away. That you'd be protecting me."

She pushed my hair away from my face. My face was clean-shaven since the season had ended, and she seemed to enjoy my clean face. "I would. I'd put myself in harm's way for you."

I kissed her. "I know, but then we'd be wrestling one another to see who could save the other."

She giggled, and her legs tightened around my waist. "And we'd both be eaten."

"Or the shark would think we weren't worth the trouble." I kissed her shoulder. I didn't ever want to leave this water, and I feared every day I might lose her. I didn't want this to end.

She came into my life on a whim. It was supposed to be one night. I was supposed to be a checkmark off her fuck-it bucket list that she better have retired now, otherwise, I might morph into that asshole kid I was when I was younger and beat the shit out of every person she propositioned.

She tilted her head back, and I admired the way the sun soaked her skin. She was so beautiful, I could stare at her all day.

"Be my girlfriend?" The question came from the fear of losing her, but it was what I wanted.

Her head sprang up, and she stared at me. I opened my mouth to explain that I knew I was changing the game, but...

A small smile formed on her lips, then it grew. "You want to be my boyfriend?"

I drew in a deep breath. "Yeah."

"Okay," she said and went back to laying her head back, feeling the sun on her skin.

A moment I was so scared of was over, and we were officially a couple.

She made it so easy, but that was Tedi. She didn't dissect situations or scenarios, she lived her life in the moment.

She laughed in my arms.

"What?"

Picking up her head, she looked into my eyes. "It's just funny. You're my fuck-it bucket list turned boyfriend." She shrugged. "It's funny." Her face grew serious. "But also amazing."

I captured her lips with mine, and we didn't end up swimming for long before we tried out the bed.

ten

Tedi

I ARRIVE AT THE ARENA EARLY TO MEET COACH Buford so we can talk and so I don't mess with his schedule and what he has planned with the players. Usually, coaches aren't on board with the distraction social media can have on their objectives, so I want to assure him I'm here to work with him and make his program more successful. I'm here to fill the seats, sell merch, and hopefully get more rabid fans who can't get enough of the sport he loves.

The door behind me opens, and he rounds the small table in the room I was put in to wait for him. Coach Buford is known as a no-nonsense coach, but like any good coach, he cares about his players. Otherwise, the top players in the league right now would be doing anything to be traded. A coach's worth is usually seen through the players they coach, and Chicago is no different.

"Miss Douglas," he says, folding himself into the chair across from me. "Thank you for meeting me before I introduce you to the guys."

"Of course." I straighten in my seat. "I did want to discuss a few things. Set some expectations."

He quirks an eyebrow but doesn't interrupt me.

"You tell me times that are off-limits. You don't want me at practices? Done. Games, I'm happy to sit in the stands. I'm not going to interfere with what you have going on. After all, you helping the Falcons to win the Cup only makes my job easier."

He nods, and the tips of his lips rise. "I appreciate that."

"And please, call me Tedi."

"Okay... Tedi. I know Bud called his frat brother or whatever about Gill. I feel bad for the kid. He was a little out of his league, but—and I'm biased." He raises his hands. "There's a great group of guys in that room next door. Easy to market. Guys who put everything on the line for me and this team, this city, and their fans. All I ask is that you don't make them out to be some kind of sex symbol. I couldn't stomach the thought of these stands filled with hormone-crazed women only here to see their warm-ups. This team is a once-in-a-coach's-career dream come true, and they need to be appreciated for their skill and mastery on the ice."

I blink, surprised by his candor, but happy at the same time. "It's my job to gain loyal fans. Loyal fans who stick by your side even in the droughts. Sure, those men in there aren't hard on the eyes, and their faces will get them a certain amount of attention, but I'll do my best to make sure it's about their athleticism and not their weekend activities."

He nods. "Well then, it's a pleasure to work with you." He sticks out his hand and stands from his chair. I shake his hand. "Come on and let me introduce you to the guys. They weren't thrilled with Gill, so hopefully you have better luck. If any of them give you any real problems, all I ask is that you come to me before Bud."

"Deal."

"I heard good things about you, so I'm excited to work alongside you." He holds his arm out for me to go out the door first.

"Oh, you heard about me?" I tilt my head, really hoping it doesn't have anything to do with Tweetie.

"Tweetie Sorenson. He said if anyone can do this, it's you."

My feet falter, and I stumble forward. Coach Buford grabs my elbow, and I put up my hand. "I'm good. Thank you. My heel must have gotten caught on the carpet."

He offers me a kind smile, but I fear there's something underlying it. I'm probably just paranoid that everyone knows our story. But no one knows us here. What was left of us remains in Florida.

Reaching around me, he opens the door, and I step out into the hallway, running straight into a man. His hands grab my elbows, and before my gaze lifts to see his face, I already know it's him. Tweetie.

"Sorry," he mumbles.

"Tweetie, you know Tedi, right? I was just telling her how much faith you have in her." Coach Buford stands next to us.

I swallow down my parfait from this morning that's coming back up.

"Yeah, we knew each other back in Florida. Tedi is a friend of Saige Drake, Aiden's wife," Tweetie says.

It sounds so believable, as if we ran in the same circles a few times. Ran into one another at a baby shower or wedding or something.

"I tried to get Drake here years ago, but he said he'll be retiring in Florida if they'll let him." Coach Buford shakes his head and pats Tweetie on the shoulder. "Thank goodness the Burrows let this one go so we could eventually get him."

Tweetie puts on a brave face, a fake smile to say he couldn't be happier to be in Chicago, but I remember the day he was traded to Nashville from Florida and how cutting that felt to him. Sure, he's ended up in a great place here, but there will always be hurt feelings.

"Which way is the room with the guys?" I step back from Tweetie.

Coach Buford pats his pockets. "Damn it, I forgot my phone in my office. Do you mind if Tweetie shows you the way?"

Tweetie isn't saying much, and I doubt this is his usual behavior around here. He's going to give us away if he keeps staring at me as though he can't believe I'm here.

"If you just give me the directions, I can find my way," I say.

"Nonsense." He pats Tweetie's shoulder. "Show her the way, and I'll be right there. You're in good hands, Tedi."

I smile softly, but when Coach Buford turns his back to his office, my smile drops. "I can find it myself," I murmur, walking down the hall like a spoiled teenage girl.

"Good luck then." Tweetie leans against the wall and crosses his arms.

The hallway is long, and there are a lot of doors. Surely one is marked conference room or something. I turn in the direction of where Tweetie was heading, figuring it has to be that way.

His chuckle rings out down the empty hall. I turn around, and he pushes off the wall. So damn dramatic.

He places his hand on my elbow and turns me down another hallway that I wouldn't have guessed. I shrug out of his hold, and he turns right, opening a door into the room I need to be in.

"You're welcome," he says, holding the door open for me.

"You could have just given me directions."

"That's not what Coach asked me to do." He nods, and I step into the room.

All of the players are in there, talking and laughing.

"Tweetie!" a player they call Alvin shouts but stops when he sees me. "Who are you?"

I narrow my eyes at him, walking down the stairs to get to the bottom of what reminds me of a lecture hall from college. I sit in the first row and cross my legs, waiting for Coach Buford.

"Hey, Tedi." I look over my shoulder to see Henry Hensley behind me.

"Hi." I don't know Henry, but he seems like a nice guy.

"Where are you going?" I hear that same guy who made a spectacle of Tweetie walking in as if he's the it guy in high school, and they're trying to befriend him or kiss his ass.

A big body walks by me and sits next to me.

Snickers from the row behind me have the hair on my neck rising.

"What are you doing?" I whisper to Tweetie.

His elbow falls onto my armrest. I elbow him back, and I'm not sure if it's Henry or someone else who laughs when Tweetie's arm falls off.

"Believe me, I don't want to sit here either."

I lean forward, looking past him to a few seats down the row that are unoccupied.

"Kick my ass or tell me off later, but I'm not gonna let you be ogled in a room full of athletes," he admits, and I can tell from the tic of his jaw that he wishes he hadn't.

"I can handle myself," I whisper.

"Deal with it, Tedi."

I turn in my chair and glare at him, but his gaze remains forward, pretending we're not having a conversation. "You know what your problem is?"

"I'm sure you're gonna tell me."

His calmness drives me crazy, and he knows it. That's why he's doing it.

"We're not a thing," I seethe through my teeth. "Let them ogle me because it doesn't matter, we're not a couple." I wave my finger between us.

"I'm doing it for your own good."

I scoff.

Henry leans in, his head between us. "You're worried about us, but you're giving yourselves away."

Tweetie doesn't turn around, but when I look at Henry, I see some curious expressions on the other players' faces as they pointedly stare at us.

I huff and straighten in my seat. "Why do you have to be so... you?"

Tweetie chuckles. "I'm sitting in a chair. You're the one who has such a problem with it."

"Well..."

"What, Tedi?" He crosses his arms, not glancing at me at all.

"I'm not sure my boyfriend would appreciate it." I almost gasp and cover my mouth. Where did that lie come from? But somehow, I manage to remain calm, at least on the outside.

Tweetie's head whips in my direction, his eyes dark and pissed off.

I open my mouth to say something, but the words don't come.

"Sorry, guys." Coach Buford jogs down the steps and taps me on the shoulder, nodding his head for me to join him. "We have our new social media manager with us today."

I'm frozen, staring at Tweetie as his jaw locks and his chest rises, but he faces forward again. Then all the tension disappears, and he raises his hands, clapping and smiling at me. What the fuck?

"Come on up here, Tedi," Coach Buford says.

The entire time Coach Buford tells them about me and my objective for the Falcons, all I can think about is how I promised Tweetie I'd never lie to him. I kept that promise until right now. But does it really count when we're not a couple anymore?

Somehow, it feels like it does.

And it's not as though he ever has to meet my fake boyfriend.

eleven

Tweetie

A BOYFRIEND? SHE HAS A FUCKING BOYFRIEND? What the fuck, Aiden? He tells me she's coming to Chicago, but not that she's seeing someone? Not that it matters. We're not going to be anything anyway. It's over for us, but fuck, she killed me with that information, and she knows it. I hate that she saw my reaction.

Now she stands up there with Coach, and I'm front and center, but I'm not the only asshole in this room who's staring at her. The only difference between me and the other unattached guys here is that I've had her. My hands have slowly unbuttoned her out of blouses and pants like she's wearing today. I've taken her heels off after a long day or night and kissed my way up her legs. And I was the lucky asshole who found her wet and wanting.

"So, no one give her a hard time. If you do, you have Tweetie to answer to." Coach saying my name pulls me out of my maze of memories with Tedi.

"Oh, I can handle myself. I don't need a bodyguard." She smiles at Coach and shakes her head.

Her laugh dies quickly, and it's not hard to see she's uncomfortable, which is not very Tedi-like at all. Maybe I'm the only one who sees it.

"I think I speak for all of us when I say welcome, and we look forward to helping you make this program a success." Coach smiles at her. "She's going to be meeting with each of you in the coming days, but I'll let her explain it some more. The floor is yours, Tedi."

Coach stands to the side, and Tedi takes the center stage.

"I've done a random selection, so you'll all receive an email from me later today. If the time I selected is a conflict for you, just let me know. I'm pretty flexible."

The doors in the back shut, signaling someone just walked in. Rustling in the seats sounds as the players turn to see who's joined us.

"My dream team. Good morning." Bud Caldron walks down the steps, patting a few players on the back, stopping at Rowan and telling him how great he looked the other night. When he reaches the bottom, he extends his hand toward Tedi. "I haven't had the pleasure. Bud Caldron, GM."

Tedi shakes his hand. "Tedi Douglas. I was going to stop by your office after I was finished here."

He laughs because he's kind of a goon. He nervous-laughs at things that aren't even funny. Plus, he tends to only look at and appreciate the guys on the first line. Whoever is selling the most jerseys is always his favorite. The word team doesn't seem to be part of his vocabulary, and he makes you feel about as dispensable as a napkin.

"No need. Here I am." He holds out his hands.

Bud is tall and thin with a small beer gut that hangs over his belt. He dresses as though he never left the nineties, with wide-legged slacks, loafers with tassels, and huge sports coats. I really don't like the guy, but he was the one calling me in Nashville, promising me he was putting together an unbeatable team, and he hasn't been wrong. I'm at the tail end of my career, and I want to win again, not just play.

"Tedi was just telling them about the interview process," Coach says.

"Yeah, that Gill wasn't worth his weight in—" Coach clears his throat, and Bud waves off his comment. "Anyway, I'd like to talk to a few players and Tedi. I have some ideas. Do you mind?" Bud looks at Coach.

Coach sighs but reluctantly nods. "Fine, but I need them on the ice in a half hour. Who do you want?"

Bud turns to me and nods. "Tweetie, Rowan, Henry, and Conor."

A few guys groan. I'm sure it's because we're seen as the best on the team, but we couldn't win without everyone here.

Tedi's back straightens. I'm sure she's pissed off that he's taking over her agenda, but since Bud called in the favor to get her here, she's smart enough not to make waves. I hate that my heart still hurts when she hurts.

Bud holds out his arm for Tedi to go first, and she leads the way up the stairs. All of us have our heads down because it's like being the teacher's pet and everyone hates you when you're singled out like this.

In the hallway, Tedi's jaw is hard, and her eyes have that fire they do when she's trying to hold in her anger.

Bud walks toward the same room she was in with Coach earlier, and now there are refreshments on the side table. Fruit, juice, coffee, water, and some bagels. What the hell is this, a timeshare meeting?

"Please help yourselves to something to eat." There's already a bagel with cream cheese and a coffee in front of a chair Bud sits in. Seriously, what's it like to be a GM?

We all take a seat. My friends and I cross our arms,

extending our legs, all of us on the same page with not liking Bud. Tedi also sits and doesn't take anything to eat or drink.

Bud takes a bite of his bagel, looking around to see we're all waiting for him to tell us why we're here. He laughs and swallows. "No one else is hungry? Okay then." He turns to Tedi. "There's really no need to focus on the entire team. I've decided to center the campaign around a select few."

Tedi's eyebrows scrunch, and she stares at him as if he told her he doesn't want to win the Cup this year. "Excuse me, Mr. Caldron, but—"

"We did it your way, Tedi, and you sent us Gill." He shuts her down quickly.

Her face turns red, and I'm actually scared for Bud's balls for a second.

But it seems she's found a way to school her nonverbal cues when she's mad, because with a blank face, she says, "Actually, I think I'll grab a coffee."

"I figure you're our stars." He looks at all of us. "You're who's going to bring in the fans."

My gaze diverts to Tedi, whose hand is shaking as she pours coffee from the carafe. She's trying to center herself, and it's taking all my restraint to keep my ass in this chair. She picks up a creamer, and it drops to the table. She huffs and picks it up again, fidgeting with the foil on the top.

"That's a lot on our plate if we're doing the brunt of the social media," Conor says.

"If you want us to be fresh on the ice to win games, we can't spend all our time on camera and doing photoshoots," Rowan chimes in.

"My kid isn't going to be a part of any of it," Henry says.

As Bud tries to calm them, I rise from my chair, silently cursing myself the entire time. I step up to her side and take the creamer from her hands. She wrestles it back, so I stay at her side as her fingers steady, and she peels back the foil, then dumps the creamer into her coffee.

"We're going to have a dinner. Get to know one another better," Bud says.

Tedi and I turn around so fast, her coffee spills all over my shirt. Fuck, that's hot. I grab the edge of my shirt and pluck the fabric away from my skin.

"Oh, I'm sorry," she says.

If it was only her and me, I'd strip it off just to show her what she's missing out on. Fuck it, why am I second-guessing my instincts? I pull off my T-shirt, and her eyes widen at my abs.

I might be old according to the league, but there's nothing old about my defined chest and abs.

She clears her throat and shifts her attention back to the table.

"What are you doing?" Conor says with a scowl. "Put your shirt back on."

"The coffee was hot," I say, and my three friends roll their eyes.

"There's no reason I can't get to know the players here," Tedi says, abandoning her coffee and turning her back to me.

"It's a distraction when they should be practicing, just like Rowan mentioned. So, let's do a dinner. You guys bring your girls." He looks at Tedi. "I'm sure you have a boyfriend, bring him. We'll make it a casual thing. Once you know one another, Tedi can have a better vision for what's going to work."

"I actually have a vision already," Tedi says.

"Well, it will only help it then." He picks up his plate with the bagel. "I'm really excited about this. Once Candice makes the reservations, she'll let you know." He stops by me. "Tweet-ie." He laughs. "Let me know if you'll have a plus one. Surely you can scrounge up a girl to come, but only one, okay?" He pats me on the shoulder, laughing as he walks out.

The only thing that could make this dinner more awkward is if I brought a date, so that's not happening.

After he leaves, Tedi huffs and closes her eyes.

"We're not that bad. We'll make dinner fun," Conor says. "And Eloise was upset she didn't get to meet you the other day."

"Yeah, Ruby had good things to say about you, which is a small miracle in itself," Rowan adds.

Tedi stares at the door.

"Can you excuse us, guys?" I say.

They all get up from their chairs, talking about Bud in not the kindest terms and how he's going to be screwed when our line isn't on top, which we all know can be one injury away.

They say goodbye to Tedi, and she tries to follow them out, but I lightly grasp her upper arm. "Hold up."

She doesn't turn toward me.

"I know this isn't the way you work, but from my experience with Bud, he'll give up on this in a week when some new shiny idea pops in his head."

She yanks her arm out of my hold. "I don't need you to make me feel better. I'm fine."

"Well, I'm excited to meet him." I change the subject since she's going to keep that wall up around her.

"What?" She spins around, and her face is twisted in a "fuck you" expression.

"The boyfriend. I can't wait to meet him."

Her shoulders sink. "Put a fucking shirt on. What do you think this is, some *Magic Mike* audition?"

She storms out the door.

Now I have to decide if I want to find a date to bring or make Tedi's boyfriend my sole focus for the night.

twelve

Tweetie's Journal Entry
Twelve years ago
Florida

To my teenage self,

We did it. We opened the door and allowed her in. Tedi knows all about our fucked-up past now, buddy, but it's for the best because trust me, she's the one. The one we can trust with our heart. Just wait until I tell you how great she was when I told her what a piece-of-shit Dad was.

It was a lazy Sunday morning. I got home from a late game the night before to find Tedi already asleep. I showered, crawled into bed, and cuddled up to her. I really tried to let her sleep, but I'd missed her.
She must have felt the same because she was

responsive to my roaming hands. Her back arched into me, offering herself. We had some of the best sex we'd had in a while. Our schedules had been hectic, only seeing one another for a few hours here and there.

She and Saige had been having to travel for work too. I always felt a little territorial when she'd have to go entertain other professional athletes in hopes of being hired for their social media. I didn't want some other guy to steal my girl. Not that I don't trust Tedi—she'd probably kick them in the nuts if they ever tried anything. I just don't like to think about her having to deal with some guy making advances at her.

The next morning, she was sprawled halfway over my back, her arm around my waist and her cheek on my shoulder blade. We were both stomach sleepers.

The sheets rustled, and I felt her roll over and get out of bed. I was still so out of it, I fell back to sleep. I'm not sure how long I stayed asleep, but when I woke up, she was kissing my shoulder and running her hands over my back.

"Breakfast, babe," she whispered.

I tightened my hold on my pillow and groaned. I'd taken some pretty bad hits the night before, and I was sore as shit. But the smell of bacon and eggs was enough to rouse me. I'd had a late snack on the plane last night, but I was starving now.

Rolling over, I sat up in bed and kissed her. "Good morning."

"Good morning. Great game last night." She snuggled closer to me, the tray at the bottom of the bed. "Thanks."

"That pass to Ford in the second couldn't have been more perfect."

One thing about Tedi was that she always complimented me after a game. Even after a shitty game, she'd find something I'd done right to comment on. Leaning forward, she brought the tray up to rest between us. Watching her ass in her silk pajama shorts teased my morning wood.

My phone vibrated next to us, and I reached for it as Tedi turned on the television. It was my mom, and if I didn't answer it, she'd just call me again.

"Hey, Mom," I answered, putting it on speaker. "Tedi's here too."

"Hi, Tedi." But I heard it in her tone. She wasn't calling me to tell me, "Good game last night."

"Hi, Melody."

We exchanged a look, and Tedi nodded. I loved the way we could speak to each other without words.

I took the phone off speaker and got out of bed. "What's up?" I asked my mom, walking into the bathroom.

"Please tell Tedi that I'm sorry for not chatting, it's just... um... Georgia is here too."

"Hey, JD," my sister said.

My mind went to thinking about how quickly I could get home, because something was very wrong.

"What's going on?" I asked again, hoping one of them would stop being so vague.

"Your dad died last night," Mom said, and my phone almost slipped from my grasp.

It felt like a blow to the chest. But he wasn't in my life anymore, so it shouldn't matter. Plus, I'd been preparing for this day for a long time. In some ways, I felt how I did when I was a kid and he'd flake on me, and I'd tell myself I didn't give a shit.

I cleared my throat. "And?"

"JD," Georgia said.

"I don't give a shit what happened to him." And I didn't. Maybe some small part of me did a little, but I would never admit that to anyone. Because I shouldn't care. He'd never cared about me.

"Don't be like that," Georgia said.

Tedi came into the doorway, silently asking if I was okay. I waved her over to me and widened my legs so she could sit in my lap as I sat on the edge of the tub. She laid her head on my shoulder, offering me the silent comfort she thought I needed.

"Fine. How'd it happen? Although I can guess."

"Suspected overdose." Mom's voice didn't crack. "They called Georgia since she's next of kin."

"All right, well, thanks for calling. I gotta go. Love you both."

My mom sighed, and Georgia called my name, but I still clicked End.

I placed the phone on the side of the tub and wrapped my arms around Tedi. "I'm starving. Come on." I patted her hip, and she rose, walking into the bedroom without asking me anything.

We'd touched on our pasts before, but I hadn't told her about my dad. When she met my mom and sister, I explained his absence by telling her he just wasn't part of my life, and she'd never pried for more.

I barely ate any of the breakfast Tedi made, and she kept stealing glances at me. I knew I could trust her, and it was time she knew how fucked up my dad was. I wasn't sure if there was a funeral for the son of a bitch or who'd have to pay for it. I wouldn't go for him. I'd go for my mom and for Georgia, but not for him.

Since it was only a matter of time before Tedi would be privy to the fact that my dad had died, I might as well get it over with. She was the woman I'd fallen in love with, and she deserved to know everything.

"Hey," I said, running my hand down her arm until her hand was in mine.

She looked over and squeezed my hand, giving me encouragement and confirming silently that whatever I told her would stay between us.

"I'm going to tell you why my mom called, but I don't want you to be upset or sad for me because I'm not, and I'm going to tell you why. Just don't hug me or feel like I need to be treated with kid gloves, because

I don't."

She pushed the tray back to the end of the bed and turned to face me, her tanned and toned legs crossed and my hand tight in hers in her lap.

"My dad died last night."

She schooled her reaction. She didn't hug me or tell me she was sorry.

"Probably overdosed, but I don't really care." I shrugged.

She made it easy for me to open up because she didn't make me listen to bullshit excuses or platitudes about why my dad never chose me over drugs, how addiction is a disease, and so on and so forth. When you're a kid and your dad constantly disappoints you and puts you last, none of that matters.

"My dad was a drug-addicted asshole who weaved in and out of my life at his own convenience. He only ever thought about himself and never cared if we had food or a roof over our heads. He'd tell us he was coming to visit, coming to one of my games, whatever, and almost always left us disappointed. Then he'd show up out of the blue and ruin a perfectly good day. I love my mom, and she was trying to save us from him in her own way, but she never denied him a visit whenever the urge struck him, even when he was strung out."

She scooted a little closer, and her knees brushed my ribs. I slid my hand out of hers and wrapped my arm around her, wanting her close. She was my future, and I was no longer that kid looking for love or validation from him.

"You know how I only go by my initials on the rare times anyone calls me anything other than Tweetie?"

She stiffened and lifted her head. "You don't have to tell me if you don't want to. Honestly."

I stared at the woman who held my entire heart in her hands. I had no idea if kids were in our future, but if they were, I didn't want any secrets between us. "I want you to know."

She nodded.

"My dad was adamant that I was named after him. My mom said when he found out I was a boy, he really wanted a junior. Mom got to name Georgia, so she felt it was only fair. But good ol' Dad wasn't around when she went into labor. He was off on a bender or something, and she couldn't get a hold of him. When it came time to fill out the birth certificate, rather than putting in the full name, she just filled it out as JD Sorenson. Sure, the J stands for his name, but no one has ever called me that but him."

She kisses my shoulder. "And now everyone calls you Tweetie."

"Which I made sure of. As soon as I was given that nickname, I started introducing myself as Tweetie to get rid of JD altogether."

She picked up her head. "And what do you want me to call you?"

"Anything but..." I told her what the initials stood

for. The name I shared with my dad. "Please don't ever call me that."

She nodded. "Okay. I promise." She sat up, straddled my lap, and placed my head in her hands. "I'm not pitying you, but I am sorry you had a shitty role model for a father. Thank you for trusting me with that knowledge. I'll never betray that. Your secret is mine to hold just as close as you do."

My hands rose from her hips and up her back, urging her to come down and hug me. As she sat on top of me, I buried my head in the crook of her neck and tried to center myself. I'd moved on from him, and he had been dead to me long before his heart stopped.

Tedi was my future. She represented everything good I'd done after I'd freed myself from him. And a huge weight was lifted off me from sharing it with her.

"If there's a funeral, will you come with me?" I whispered.

"You don't even have to ask. You know I'll be there." She kissed my cheek, and we went back to hugging.

After I demanded that we didn't give my dad any more room in our happy life, we went back to eating, and Tedi told me about her own upbringing with a mother who'd left her family in search of another one.

We already had a fucking great relationship, but that morning, it turned and shifted, making me even more afraid to ever lose her.

thirteen

Tedi

"You what?" Saige asks me, the sound of chaos behind her.

"You're the one who gave me the idea." This really is all her fault. The boyfriend thing wouldn't have been in my head in the first place while I was all tongue-tied, trying to act as if his protectiveness over me wasn't as endearing as I thought it was.

"I meant you should actually find a boyfriend. Go on dates and get Tweetie out of your head. Not lie and tell him you're seeing someone." I hear a knife chopping, and Saige sighs. "God, I hate cooking."

"Um... you're married to one of the best centers in the league, hire a damn chef."

"*One* of the best?"

"Way to protect your man."

She sighs again. "You know I didn't grow up like that, and I don't want my girls thinking that life just hands them everything."

"So listening to their mom whine about cutting up vegetables is better?"

"They need to learn that suffering makes you grow. Yes."

I plop down on the couch in my short-term rental. The stark white walls and drab artwork make this place feel clinical. "This couch sucks." I wiggle my ass, but it's so stiff, there's no way to relax on it.

"Buy a new one," Saige says. "Fuck! I just cut myself."

"Mom swore!" one of the girls says in the background.

"If I buy a new couch, I can't suffer in order to grow." I make fun of her, hearing a faucet running. "Is it bad?"

"No. Just annoying. Screw this. I'm ordering pizza. Aiden's away tonight, and I'm calling it girl time."

The girls shout in delight in the background.

I laugh because that's totally my best friend. "Way to suffer. What was that? Two point two seconds when you were really drowning there."

"Hey, leave me alone. You have bigger problems. Where are you going to find this boyfriend before your dinner in two nights?"

She's right. I had hoped I had more time. Hopefully find some willing partner online and go on a few dates before asking him to do me a solid and go to a work meeting where he pretends to love me and acts as though he can't live without me even if he knows barely anything about me. But then Candice, Bud's assistant, emailed me and said dinner is in two days' time at some fancy restaurant in a private room. So much for keeping it casual, Bud.

Throw me into Lake Michigan, why don't you?

"I have no clue. I think I'm going to say he's sick or had to work late. Surely a guy like Bud Caldron will understand a man who wants to work his way up the ladder."

She scoffs. "God, you know he came to our house once? Kind of slimy. He was all over Aiden like some fanboy, telling him how great he was and how Jana didn't see the player he could be. The minute Aiden told him that he was staying in Florida, he just went to Cory and said Aiden was a half-talented player who was screwing him over by not retiring."

"Yeah, I figured he wasn't exactly a good guy. First, he goes behind my back, and then he's trying to take over my job. The only reason that locker room isn't a mess is because of Coach Buford. He's a great guy, I really like him." I scoop from my quart of cookies and cream ice cream, scrolling through my streaming services to find something worth binging. I'm going to have a lot of quality time in my apartment these next few months.

"Regardless, he's the GM, Tedi," she says it in her "I hate to tell you this, but..." voice.

"I know."

"And he knows Mr. Herington. It's like a double whammy."

I dig another scoop of my ice cream. "So you're telling me to get off the phone with you and get on a dating app, hoping I can bribe someone to be my pretend boyfriend for a night?"

She giggles but sighs right away. "I'm sorry. But you figure it's one night. After that, you can just mention him by name, and then you'll be back in New York, or you can lie later and say it's not working out. Once you're really over Tweetie. If I knew anyone, I'd send them up to you. But you're hot. You could go down to the coffee shop and pick someone up."

"I'm afraid Tweetie will know. I mean, he's still so fucking in tune with my feelings. I hate it."

Like today when I was getting coffee. He knew I was upset and came over to help me. Why does he still do that shit?

"All the more reason why you need to do this. You need to put as much space as you can between the two of you. Oh!" she shouts. "I know who your pretend boyfriend can be."

My forehead wrinkles as I spoon more ice cream into my mouth. "Who?"

"Decker Davis!"

"Unless you know another Decker Davis, that would be a hard no." I shake my head.

My twin brothers' best friend who was practically a third brother to me? No thanks.

"It's perfect, and you know he'll do it. Plus, it's the offseason for him."

"I don't think he even stays in Chicago during the offseason."

"Fine, take your chances on some serial killer through a dating app then." Saige huffs.

I put her on speaker and search him on my socials.

Decker Davis, third baseman for the Chicago Colts. Honestly, I never would've thought he'd make it this far. Way to go, Decker, annoying little runt, although he's not really little anymore. He's kind of cute, in a clean-cut, not-my-type kind of way, but maybe Saige has a point.

"You're welcome. I need to order pizza, and you need to call Decker. Love you." She hangs up.

I'm still scrolling through Decker's socials to see if he has a girlfriend, but there's more pictures of him with my brothers than with any women. Some things never change.

I blow out a breath, and because I love to torture myself, I leave Decker's profile and search up Tweetie. How will I ever get through an entire dinner with him next to me, let alone all these months? I know us. Something will happen, and it will send me into a tornado of despair. I have to keep repeating to myself that he's not the one, that we just had a really long relationship, so of course we know each other so well. That's the only reason there's still this pull inside me to him.

I scroll, seeing Tweetie tagged last week at a club with that damn kid they call Alvin, two girls flanked at his sides.

Fuck it.

Here I come, Decker Davis, my new boyfriend, even if I have to blackmail you into it.

fourteen

Tedi

Thankfully, Decker agreed to meet me for dinner. I'm his best friends' older sister, and I think he was always a little scared of me when he was younger.

He suggested the restaurant, and I thought for sure I would end up at a wing place or a sports bar, but it's a cozy Mexican restaurant nestled in a quieter part of the city.

The hostess seated me by the window after I gave her Decker's name. As I wait for him, I admire the string lights and decorative paper banners hanging from the ceiling. The walls are painted in hues of orange, turquoise, and yellow, and there are rustic wooden shelves filled with clay pottery and small succulents. The smell of warm tortillas fills the quaint space.

I order a pitcher of sangria because I'm going to need a little alcoholic encouragement to ask my little brothers' best friend to do this favor for me and to keep it a secret. I do not need my brothers involved in my business. It's bad enough that every time I go home, my brothers go on and on about

Tweetie, asking how he's doing in the league. Like, read the room.

Decker walks in at exactly the time he told me to meet him here. He says something to the hostess, and she laughs, pointing him in my direction. He rocks his head back in greeting, thanks the hostess, and breaks the small distance to me.

"Tedi," he says, stopping at the end of the table and opening his arms.

Okay, we're gonna hug? I stand and hug him, my head buried in his chest. His cologne is a nice, crisp scent. Much better than when he was in middle school and I'd choke every time he walked by.

"Hey, Decker." We break apart, each taking our seats. "This is a great place."

He looks around as if he hasn't ever been here, but smiles and waves to the older woman making the tortillas in the corner. "I love it. Found it right after I got picked up by the Colts. Not a lot of fans, and it gives me a little bit of privacy. Plus, the food is delicious." He picks up the pitcher and pours some sangria into his glass. "Gotta love the offseason."

After his glass is filled, he lifts it in the air, and I do the same, clinking our glasses and both of us saying, "Cheers."

He sips, and I sip, and it's a tad uncomfortable if I'm honest. We both begin to talk at the same time and laugh, and Decker signals with his hand for me to go first.

"I thought maybe you'd go home during the offseason." I pick up a chip and dip it in the salsa.

"I did for about a month, but I got bored. Your brothers are busy with work and Mason, and I figured I should get used to this city, so it feels more like home."

"It's hard being an adult in a new city. Making new friends and stuff." I don't anticipate making a lot of friends while I'm here. There are practically no women in the office, and it's not as if I'll become new BFFs with the girlfriends and wives of the players. I represent their biggest fear—I couldn't lock down the hockey player in my grasp.

He shrugs, leaning forward and picking up a chip. "It's not terrible. The single guys on the team kind of all stick together. Easton Bailey is a good friend, but he's back in his hometown in Alaska right now."

"It's weird to hear you talk about all these huge athletes. Well, I guess you're one." I lean back and laugh, remembering when he tried to play hockey with my brothers but couldn't stand on the skates. I guess cleats were more his thing.

"It's still a little surreal. I mean, I've been in the league for a while, but it's still weird when someone stops and says my name, wanting a picture or an autograph." He picks up another chip, scooping the salsa. "Enough about me. So, why are you in Chicago?" He places the chip in his mouth, and I debate if I should get on with it or bide my time some more.

"I'm working for the national league, down here doing a social media campaign on the Falcons. Trying to recruit all those baseball and football fans into being hockey fans."

He laughs. "Hey, with the way our season went, I'd say you shouldn't have a hard time. Especially since the Falcons are killing it right now. Their entire first line is insane." He immediately realizes what he's said, and his shoulders fall. "Sorry, I mean everyone but the left wing. He's a complete disaster out there. Like a baby fawn on ice."

I laugh at his attempt to make me feel better. Maybe this will be easier, since he knows at least a little of my history with Tweetie. "It's okay. He's still a great player, just not meant to be someone's forever."

His lips thin, and I hate that pitying look. Fuck it, I'm not going to ease him into this. I've got bribery in my back pocket. He did a lot of shit as a kid that I'm sure he doesn't want made public.

"Speaking of... are you in a relationship?"

Decker's eyebrows scrunch, and he picks up his glass of sangria. "No."

"Good."

"Good?"

I wave him off, grabbing a chip and breaking it apart in pieces, distracting myself for a second. "I need a favor."

"So this wasn't just a friendly catch-up while we're in the same city?" He sits back, waiting for me to continue.

"It is. It's really good to see you, Decker, but um... I need you to be my fake boyfriend tomorrow night."

Silence.

Dead air.

Zero expression on his face.

"You what?" he asks after I gobble up three more chips.

"Well, like you mentioned, Tweetie is a problem. So, I need someone to pretend to be my boyfriend so he keeps his distance from me."

His eyebrows raise, and I think maybe he's been doing some tweezing to get that shape. "You can't just tell him to leave you alone?"

I tilt my head, and he nods.

"God, you two and your games."

"Excuse me. There are no games. We're just like magnets and can't get unstuck. You're going to be the paper between us."

"Me?" He points at himself.

It's time to lay it on thick.

"Please, Decker. I have no one else, and what would my brothers think if I had to resort to sorting through a bunch of creeps on the dating apps?"

"You're playing the best friends' sister card?"

I smile at him over my glass of sangria. "Do you want to see my boobs?"

"Fuck, Tedi." He looks around to make sure my question didn't draw any glances.

"Well, you wanted to see them when you were in the seventh grade. Remember when I caught you spying on me?" I laugh.

He leans over the table, lowering his voice. "Because I got a hard-on and didn't understand what was happening to my body. And I've apologized for that, like, ten thousand times. You can stop bringing it up."

"It would be a shame for that to end up on SportsVerse."

His expression blanks, and he drills his gaze into mine. "Now you're resorting to blackmail?"

"I'm a desperate woman." I finish my sangria and reach for the pitcher. "I'll get you tickets to the games. First row, best in the house."

He seems to think about it. Maybe I should've started with the hockey tickets. I just assumed with his income and connections, he could get a ticket to any game he wanted.

"What do I have to do?" he asks, watching me pour another glass. "And just so we're clear, it doesn't entail me carrying you back to your place tonight." He eyes my full glass.

"Okay, Decker, let's remember who's older here. I can handle my alcohol. Do I need to bring up the time you threw up in the middle of the family room during my party?"

His cheeks flush. "Jesus, your memory is like a catalog of misdeeds. You can just dive in and pluck out every embarrassing thing I ever did."

"It's a gift. Maybe if you do this favor for me, the Decker Davis catalog magically gets erased?"

He groans, and I smile at him. The waitress comes over and takes our order. After she walks away, he's staring at me again.

He crosses his arms. "I can't believe I'm saying this, but

you seem pretty desperate, and Toby and Theo would probably kick my ass, so... what do you need me to do?"

I almost drop my glass when I yelp. Decker looks at all the other tables staring at us.

I get up and hug him, kissing his face. "Thank you! Thank you!"

He stiffens but doesn't fight me. "You're making a scene. People are going to think you're actually my girlfriend."

"Should I sit in your lap? If someone snapped a picture, it'd be all that more real."

"Tedi..." His voice sounds drained, so I go back to my seat, not wanting him to change his mind.

"So tomorrow night—"

"Tomorrow?" He leans in. "Thanks for the notice."

Our dinner arrives as I explain to him that it's only one dinner, then he'll be free and clear.

fifteen

Tweetie

I SHOW UP AT THE STEAKHOUSE BUD PICKED FOR this dinner. Not surprising. He's an old-school guy. Not that I go to dinner with him often, but when he came to Nashville to talk about me moving to Chicago, he picked a steakhouse there too.

I head over to the hostess, unsure if anyone has arrived before me.

Laughter coming in through the circular doors tells me some of the other guests are arriving. I turn to see Conor and Eloise. She's laughing at something he's saying, and he's staring at her as if all his happiness is wrapped up in her. Pathetic.

"What a surprise. A steakhouse." Conor lifts his eyebrows. I'm sure it was the same with him when Bud visited him before his trade.

"Hey, Tweetie, can't wait to meet your girl tonight." Eloise rises on her toes and hugs me.

"She's not my girl."

"And she's bringing her boyfriend, right?" Conor's smirk is so wide I want to punch it off his face.

"Oh yeah, I forgot. I'm sorry. I heard about that." Eloise gives me her sad eyes and sad mouth. Whatever.

I really need to shake off this shitty mood I'm in tonight.

I circle around, ignoring the topic of Tedi. "Caldron. Private room?" I tell the hostess, and she smiles at me. Actually, she gives me that smile that says she'd meet me in the coat room or the bathroom later if I wanted.

"You're the first to arrive. Do you want to be seated or wait here?"

She's cute but too young for me. I should give her one of the Chipmunks' numbers.

"Hey," I hear Eloise say after another cold gust of wind seeps into the warm restaurant.

"I think we have more who just arrived, give us a second." I hold my finger and turn around to see Jade and Henry being hugged by Eloise. Couple number two has arrived.

Couple number three, Rowan and Kyleigh, come in soon after, but there's still no sign of the only person I want to see tonight. And I'm not even sure why. Is it because if I see Tedi with another guy, it will somehow solidify that there's no future for us?

I turn back to the hostess after we all say hello to one another. It used to be handshakes, maybe a pat on the back, but ever since the girls have infiltrated our group, it's all hugs and kisses on cheeks. They've taken what should be a one-minute process and made it into a fifteen-minute ordeal. "We're ready."

"Great." The hostess looks over my shoulder, pulls the menus, and whispers something to a coworker who's come up to the hostess stand. She tries to be sly about it but fails as she checks us all out. But neither of them says anything directly to us about being Falcons players.

"Decker?" I hear Rowan say as we're stepping away to head to the private room.

We all stop, and I place my hand on the hostess's arm to tell her, "Sorry, we just have to say hello to a friend." She smiles wide and looks at the other girl. Definitely way too young for me.

Henry's shaking the hand of the third baseman for the Colts as I head that way.

"Decker Davis, shouldn't you be on a beach or some shit?" I put out my hand, and we do the whole man-hug thing.

Decker is one of my agent's clients, and we see him at our shared gym courtesy of Jagger.

"Yeah, it's your offseason." Conor shakes his hand. "Let me introduce you to my wife."

The guys all do the introductions to the loves of their lives since we don't see Decker often. Our seasons are during opposite times of the year for the most part, and he doesn't seem to be a club guy. At least not the ones I'm hanging out at.

I actually don't know much about Decker, but there is one thing I know about him—he's Tedi's twin brothers' best friend. I met him at her brother Toby's wedding years ago when he was just a rookie. Now, Decker's one of the best players in the baseball league.

"So tell us again why you're not on some beach right now," I say.

He huffs a small chuckle as if it's an inside joke. "Eh, I decided not to this year."

I snap my fingers and point at him. Maybe he knows something about Tedi's boyfriend. He can give me a little intel, so I'm prepared for who's going to walk through the door. "Did you hear that Tedi's in Chicago?"

My friends grow quiet, and I can just imagine them leaning in closer as soon as they heard me say Tedi's name.

He nods. "I did."

"She's supposed to join us tonight. She's working here for a few months."

"I heard about that."

Did Theo and Toby tell him he can't talk about Tedi in front of me? Why is he being so vague? She's clearly reached out to him since she got here if he knows everything I do.

"She's bringing her boyfriend. Do you know him?"

He looks uncomfortable and opens his mouth to respond.

"Shit, never mind. I'm not going to put you in the middle. I mean..." I shake my head. "What do I care? But can I ask you one thing?" I lean in closer and block off my friends, giving them my back.

Decker's back straightens. I hate putting him in this position, but if he gives me the answer I want, then it'll be much easier to take a step back, hands up, and leave her behind.

"What?" he asks, voice breaking.

"Is she happy?"

His shoulders fall, and a small breath falls from his lips.

Another blast of cold air hits us all from the circular door, and we turn as if it's the person's fault, but my gaze locks with Tedi's. She stops cold, the door hitting her in the back, and she stumbles forward. I step over, catching her elbows, and our eyes meet.

"Thanks." She's quick to stand up straight.

When she looks over, I expect her to be surprised to see Decker. I expect her to squeal and run over, wrap her arms around his neck, and probably pick on him about something from when they were younger.

But Tedi doesn't do any of that. She slides her arm through his, rises to her tiptoes, and kisses his cheek. "Hey, babe."

Decker stiffens, his eyes on me the entire time.

"Fuck," Conor whispers behind me.

A hand lands on my back and rubs up and down. I don't

know which one of their girls felt compelled to try to soothe my pain away with the comforting touch.

"Your boyfriend is Decker Davis?" My eyes narrow, and my stomach clenches.

Tedi smiles bright and wide, almost too wide, as if she's lying. Then again, there's a smugness to it too. As if she's saying, "I didn't need you, Tweetie, I've got myself another pro athlete."

"Was that the next item on your fuck-it bucket list? A baseball player?" I regret the angry words the minute they're out. I want to drag Tedi into a corner and apologize profusely, but I don't.

Her smile falls, and her jaw hardens.

"Tweetie!" Kyleigh hits me in the back.

"We apologize on his behalf." Jade peeks around my shoulder and extends her hand. "I'm Jade, Henry's fiancée."

Tedi steps away from Decker and shakes her hand. "You don't have to apologize for him. Jealousy looks kind of good on him, don't you think?"

She walks over to the hostess stand, dragging Decker with her. He's now giving me an expression like, "Sorry, man." He shouldn't be stealing my girl. Okay, he didn't steal her, but I didn't see this coming.

I'm so stunned and pissed off at myself for saying what I did to her that I don't register that they've all started following the hostess until Henry slaps me on the back. "Come on, man."

I inhale deeply and follow the group, counting the minutes until this dinner is over so I can go wallow in pain.

sixteen

Tedi

I'm so pissed at Tweetie, but I won't give him the pleasure of seeing me react to him throwing in my face how we met. He used to brag about how he was supposed to be a one-night stand, then made me fall in love with him.

Decker looks like a scared cat in a tree waiting for the firefighters to show up. He needs to loosen up and show me some affection if we're going to pull this off.

The hostess, who has thoroughly enjoyed gawking at all of the guys, shows us to a room down a hallway from the main dining room. The table is a large round one, snuggled in between draped walls and a fireplace.

"Man, hockey players are some high rollers, huh?" Decker says next to me.

"Whatever, you guys have the highest salaries." I let go of his arm and sit at the farthest side of the table with the hopes everyone else will fill in and Tweetie won't be anywhere near me.

Everyone files in, taking the chairs to my right, Decker on my left.

Tweetie stops the hostess before she can leave the room, touching her elbow, and she turns around with hearts in her eyes. He releases his hold, running his hands through his hair. "Thanks. I know we filled up your waiting area for a while."

She sighs and follows his hand as if she's envisioning running her own hand through his hair.

I groan and place my napkin in my lap.

"You're welcome. If you need anything, just grab me." She sticks out her tits.

I pick up my water glass and look away.

"You're so thirsty, babe." Decker puts his hand on my wrist, giving me a look like you cannot throw that glass at her.

"Sure am, babe."

Rowan side-eyes me from the seat next to me. I'm going to have to tone down using the pet name.

I should make an appointment at the dentist now because my teeth are going to be ground down to stubs before this night is over.

Tweetie keeps his back to us, watching the hostess leave. She does have an amazing ass, and no doubt he's noticed. I hate the sick feeling that swirls in my stomach.

As Tweetie is about to finally join us, Bud Caldron walks in with a woman I'm fairly sure isn't his wife. What the fuck?

"Ky," Rowan says, his hand slipping under the table to grab her thigh. When he looks at her, she narrows her eyes at Bud and the youngest woman in the room on his arm. I get the feeling there's something behind Kyleigh's reaction, but I have no idea what, beyond the same amount of disgust I have over him so openly cheating on his wife.

"Tweetie," Bud bellows, and a shiver runs up my spine at the sound of his voice.

"Bud." Tweetie shakes his hand, then extends it to the woman. "Tweetie Sorenson."

She puts her hand in his. I'll give her credit, she doesn't let her gaze shift from his eyes. Then again, Tweetie has great eyes. Big, blue, and dreamy. Bastard.

"Is that, like, your real name?" She laughs, and Bud joins in with her.

I grunt, and Rowan glances at me again.

"Your attention should be on the front of the class." I circle my finger in the air.

Rowan snickers and turns to watch the scene playing out in front of him.

"No one knows Tweetie's real name. He keeps it close to the vest," Bud answers for him.

The night Tweetie told me his given name flickers in my memory, but I swallow it down, pushing it as far back as I can. Decker was right, my brain is like a catalog, and I wish it would lose all the entries with Tweetie in them. It would make my life a lot easier.

Bud walks his girlfriend, or date, or whatever she is, to the table, and Tweetie's gaze pauses on me as if he's remembering that I'm one of the only people who knows the truth of his name. Everyone stands and shakes hands with Bud and the girl who is named Mila. Decker and I are the last couple to be introduced to her, and Bud's eyes widen when he sees Decker next to me. Maybe I should've found an average Joe to draw less attention.

"Nice to meet you, Mr. Caldron." Decker sticks out his hand.

Bud looks at me while shaking Decker's hand. "Decker Davis? That's your boyfriend?"

I slide closer and rest my cheek on his shoulder. "He is."

Bud nods as if he's impressed I can score such a catch. Asshole. He finally turns his attention back to Decker. "So happy you could join us, and sorry for how your season turned out this year. Tough one."

Decker nods. "I think we'll turn it around next year." Their hands drop, and Decker shifts his gaze to Mila. "Nice to meet you, Mila."

She nods frantically. Although I have no interest in Decker, I'd appreciate it if she didn't look at my fake boyfriend as though she wants to fall to her knees and suck him off.

I tighten my grip on Decker's upper arm and clear my throat.

"Let's sit." Bud interrupts our silent catfight.

Everyone goes back to their seats, but Tweetie takes the one right next to Decker, immediately engaging him in conversation. Decker doesn't help with all his fawning over the Falcons and how exciting they are to watch.

"If you want tickets—" Tweetie says midway through appetizers.

"Oh yeah, Tedi said she could get me some." Decker nods, leaning back in his chair as we wait for our main course.

"If you don't mind sitting in the wives and girlfriends section, I can get you in there. Tedi will be on the bench with us, scoring pictures for social media." Tweetie smiles at me.

I grip the stem of my wine glass harder. "God knows you don't ever use your tickets in that section."

Tweetie chuckles. "Keeping tabs on who I invite to games?"

"I just figured you find your entertainment after the game, and then they're gone before the next one." I shrug and sip my wine again.

"Man, that calamari was really good. What did you think, Tweetie?" Decker tries to change the subject.

Tweetie's narrowed gaze doesn't veer away from mine. "Like I said, keeping tabs on me?"

"I don't have to. I hear the rumors. Your extracurricular activities are talked about more than your slap shot."

Rowan chokes on his bread, and Kyleigh asks if he's okay as he reaches for his water glass.

"Oh, that's right, you believe everything you read, right?" Tweetie picks up his drink.

Decker puts his arm around my shoulder. "The weatherman said it was going to be freezing this week. I had to go to order a warmer jacket. I guess that's why they call it the Windy City, huh?"

"Based on my experience, there's always some truth in what gets reported." I purposely lean in closer to Decker's chest, and Tweetie glares at the movement.

He quickly turns his attention back to Decker, though. "Come to our home game next week, and afterward we can all go out."

When I place my hand on Decker's thigh, his leg flinches, then freezes. I give Tweetie a syrupy, sweet smile. "That sounds great. I'm sure you have some great club you can get us into. Those velvet ropes probably just open up when you arrive since you're a regular and all."

"Rowan, what is going on?" Kyleigh asks when he chokes again.

"Yeah, well, you know for yourself that I'm well versed in how to show people a good time."

I sip my wine and try to school my features. "Can't say that's the rumor I've heard."

Rowan chokes again, and now Kyleigh smacks him on the back.

"You're really not supposed to do that," Mila says from across the table.

She goes on to inform us that she was a lifeguard in high school and tells Kyleigh the best course of action if someone is choking. Tweetie's gaze holds mine the entire time, challenging me, but I lean in closer to Decker, setting down my wine and putting my hand on his chest.

The problem comes when Decker acts like a fucking scarecrow and doesn't reciprocate any of the affection I'm giving him. He's going to need to sell this. It's then I realize that I have to get Decker to agree to another performance after this week's home game.

seventeen

Tweetie

WE'RE IN WARM-UPS BEFORE THE GAME WHEN BODHI knocks on the glass, waving to us. Jade, Kyleigh, and Eloise are all standing by him, each in their man's jersey. Even Bodhi has on a small version of his dad's.

The entire team takes turns skating over and smacking his hand in a high-five against the glass. I head in that direction, smiling at the little man I consider myself an uncle to, until I spot Tedi walking down the staircase with Decker Davis right behind her.

She's not wearing my jersey, of course she's not, but for a moment, a memory flickers in my head of when she used to. Hell, she had my number all over her fucking body. A necklace, earrings, painted on her face. One time when I came home from an away game, she had my number painted between her breasts in chocolate and whipped cream. It got me going, and I always had better games when she was in attendance than when she wasn't.

I give Bodhi a slap on the hand through the glass and skate

away, ditching my stick and getting down on my knees. My buddies follow suit shortly after.

"You sure are stretching hard there," Conor says next to me, going side to side in front of the goal.

"Trying to make someone jealous?" Rowan does his hip flexors next to me.

"She did always love my warm-ups."

"Let's remember who has the nickname Magic," Rowan says.

Henry gets down with us. "I'm not sure you're playing this whole thing the right way."

Fucking Daddy and all his sage advice. I don't want his deep fucking thoughts today.

"I agree," Rowan says. "You guys at dinner the other night." He shakes his head.

"Magic almost didn't live to see today." Conor chuckles, getting on all fours with us.

"I was just pissed off," I admit.

I've been beating myself up about all the shit I've been saying and doing, allowing my self-control to slip like that punk-ass kid I was in my teens. I worked so hard to put that asshole in the grave, and now because she has a boyfriend, that version of me is being resurrected. I have no idea what the fuck to do.

"We know," Henry says.

"And now you want us all to go to this club," Rowan groans.

"Sorry to interrupt your Monopoly game with Kyleigh. Please tell me she at least has to take off a piece of clothing every time she ends up in jail?"

"Fuck you, Tweetie." Conor goes back to his goalie warm-ups. "That's my fucking sister."

"Get over it. Are you gonna think it's a miraculous conception when she's pregnant with Rowan Junior?" I don't have time for Conor's brother drama. I've got real problems.

I glance to where Tedi and Decker are sitting with Kyleigh. Conor's dad is talking to Decker while Tedi is throwing popcorn, and Bodhi's trying to catch it with his mouth.

That's one thing I always loved about Tedi—she fits in everywhere she goes. I never had to worry when I'd take her into a room full of people she didn't know. Hell, there were times I wished she'd stayed at my side longer, and by the time the night was over, I missed her so damn much.

"You gotta stop this whole 'I don't care' shit. It's bullshit and annoying." Henry gets up and grabs his stick, hitting the puck back and forth.

I follow suit, and so does Rowan.

Henry has no idea what he's asking me to do. Admit that I still want Tedi and suffer the consequence of rejection? I'm not sure I can do it another time. Three years ago, she broke me. I played like shit, couldn't get out of my head. I almost retired just so I could retreat to some piece of land off the grid and not have to deal with anything or anyone.

"He has a point," Rowan says. "Do you think they're the real deal?" He smiles and nods to Kyleigh when she blows him a kiss.

"I have no clue. I thought it was a joke because he's her twin brothers' best friend from childhood. But she's always touching him." I watch the two of them laughing and sitting next to one another. She feeds him a pretzel with cheese dripping off the end, and my heart feels as if it's shrinking with every smile she gives him.

"Why did you invite them to the club then?" Henry asks.

I shrug. "I don't know. To try to prove I don't care? Maybe I have some sick disease where I want to torture myself."

"There's another reason." Henry and Rowan chuckle to

themselves, then Conor joins in as if I'm the one on the outside. I never like being the one not in on the joke.

"What?"

"You invite him, she comes with," Henry says. "So you see it as torturing yourself, but in reality, you're giving yourself what you want the most."

"Time with her," Rowan says.

"Even if you say stupid, insensitive shit." Conor cracks his neck a few times.

"It's like you're the little kid being mean to the girl you like." Henry rests his chin on his gloved hands on top of his stick, giving me a smug look.

"Fuck you."

"Upset because we figured you out?" Henry raises his eyebrows.

"Just remember, it's never too late to change it." Rowan looks over his shoulder. Kyleigh's crooking her finger at him. "I'll be right back."

Conor glances up at the Jumbotron, then looks at me. "Did you at least pay someone to make sure they don't end up on the Kiss Cam?" He skates away toward the girls, laughing to himself.

"I get it, Tweetie. I do. Sure, Jade wasn't attached to someone when she came back to town, but she had found someone while we were apart, and it killed me. I was pissed, but I realized something." Henry waits for me to nod like he does with Bodhi.

I scowl at him. "I'm not your kid."

He pats me on the shoulder. "I was mad at myself, not the guy, because he wouldn't have had a shot had I not messed up. Now, I don't know what happened with you two, but I'm sure fault doesn't lay just on one side." His gaze veers to Jade and Bodhi, a smile creasing his lips. Jade's got Bodhi in her arms and they're laughing. "It's not too late. If you want her back… fight for her."

Henry skates off. I watch my friends, remembering when I was that guy and Tedi was on the other side of the glass. Taking my chances, I look at her and find her looking at me while Decker is on his phone. I'm about to mouth to her that I'm sorry, but she turns her head, staring off at the stands before I'm able.

Does Henry have a point? I'm worried we drifted too far from each other to ever find our way back.

eighteen

Tedi's Journal Entry
Eleven years ago
Florida

To my older self,

Tonight was a hard one. We made a decision on the fly, and I'm unsure of it, but I think maybe it's the right one. Then again, maybe we'll read this entry again years from now and think we should've walked away. Either way, I'm going to give you a play-by-play of what happened so that if we ever want to recall this moment again because things go south with Tweetie, this might enlighten us to the first sign that we weren't meant to be.

Tweetie had been quiet for weeks. We'd still go out and be pretty much attached at the hip, but he was always staring off into space, and his quick wit had taken a hiatus. I'd known something was on his mind, and tonight after he got home from a late away game, I finally confronted him, my patience worn thin.

He walked in, stopping inside the door, surprised that I was still awake and on the couch.

"Hey, babe," he said, dropping his bag. He bent over the back of the couch and kissed me hello, but immediately went to the kitchen.

"Congratulations," I said since they'd won.

"Thanks."

I heard the fridge open. Since he was going to continue dodging me, I rose off the couch to meet him. We'd been dating for eighteen months, and I had never seen him like this.

He was making himself a sandwich, so I slid onto a breakfast stool and watched him. His movements were meticulous, and he didn't say anything or even glance at me.

Something was going on. That pit in my stomach grew. Had he found someone else? Someone more loving and more affectionate, someone hotter? I knew I was strong-willed and could be difficult at times, but we were good together, weren't we?

I hated this version of myself. Hated what my mother made me into by abandoning our family. I repeatedly told myself to be stronger and to never rely on anyone else, yet here I was, waiting for Tweetie to crush me.

"Tweetie," I said in a near whisper.

At some point during our time together, I allowed him to chip away at that wall around me. And thinking about us ending was crushing me.

"What's up?" He pretended he didn't hear the plea in my voice, but I saw his shoulders tense. We both were aware that something was going on.

"Don't make me a fool," I said.

He finally raised his gaze to meet mine.

I swallowed past the dryness coating my throat. The armor I usually protected myself with clinked back into place. I was strong enough. I could take this. He wanted to end it? Fine.

"I'm sorry," he said and stepped back from the counter but didn't round it to come to me. No, now he was farther away from me.

"It's fine." I stood from the stool and climbed the stairs into his bedroom without looking back at him.

Technically, I still had my place, although I was almost always at his.

I pulled out my bag and opened the drawers with my things, piling clothes inside the bag before going into the bathroom. When I emerged with my toothbrush, he was leaning against the doorframe.

He was still wearing his suit, minus the jacket, the

flaps of his button-down now wrinkled and out. His arms were crossed, and he watched me. "Where are you going?"

Tears pricked in my eyes, but I pushed them back. He would not get a reaction from me. "I'm going home."

I jammed my hairdryer in the bag. Over the months, I'd brought too much stuff. It wouldn't all fit into the bag, and the zipper fought me as I tried and tried again to zip it closed. "Oh, fuck it." I grabbed the straps, but when I turned, I ran right into Tweetie's chest.

"Can you give me a minute?" His voice was low, and without me answering, he took the bag out of my hands and placed it at our feet. He sat on the bed and took my hand, guiding me to sit next to him.

"Spare me, Tweetie. I don't need the 'it's me, not you speech.' We're done. I get it. Just please let me leave." I was holding on by a thread. A red alarm was blaring in my body that I was at max emotional capacity and couldn't hold it in much longer.

"God, I'm a fuck-up," he said mostly to himself.

"You think I want to break up with you?" His face looked stricken.

"Don't you?"

"God, no, but after I tell you what I'm about to, you might want to break up with me."

He'd cheated. That was my first thought. Of course he had the opportunity, he must have them all the time, but I had learned to quiet that voice inside me and trust him. Even when he'd go out with the guys, he'd take the time to message how much he missed me and couldn't wait to be by my side again. He'd cradled that seed of doubt in his palms and starved it little by little with reassurances. And now it was as if he'd put it in a pot with Miracle-Gro soil.

"And this is why you've been off?" I asked.

He nodded.

"Tell me. Just say it."

He turned to face away from me.

"You can at least look me in the eye when you tell me." My anger was rising even though I really wanted to put on a mask of indifference when he told me that he'd ruined us by sleeping with someone else. That wasn't something I could ever get past, ever put behind us.

He faced me and separated my fingers until he held just my left ring finger. His two fingers ran up and down it, his eyes studying it. "I'm not ready. I know we've been dating for a while and the guys have been giving me hell, and you make me so fucking happy, but I just can't."

I tilted my head, allowing his words to run through my mind again. "I don't understand."

He dropped my hand, rose from the bed, and

walked over to the window that looked out at the Gulf. It was dark, but the stars were out with a half-moon hanging in the sky. "You know how screwed up I am from my dad. I wish I was one of those guys who could just say fuck it and fall on bended knee. Take my chances. You deserve a guy like that." He circled back around. "I'm not him."

Tweetie had confessed a few things to me over the years about his youth. How his dad would weave in and out of his life until he just stopped coming around altogether. How, as a result, Tweetie lashed out when he was a teenager, unable to process the anger inside him. But he'd gone through therapy and found an outlet, but I guess not all of his demons were dead and buried. How could I fault him? I had demons of my own.

"That's all well and good, but I don't understand what changed between us. Why have you been so distant?"

He broke the distance between us and fell to his knees in front of me, wrapping his arms around my waist and putting his head in my lap. "I don't know how to keep you."

I closed my eyes, my fingers weaving through his hair. "Why would you lose me?"

He picked up his head and rested his chin on my thigh. "I can't marry you, Tedi. I tell myself that it's no different than what we're doing now, but then this fear rises up and says if I marry you, I'll destroy us."

One tear came and then another until I couldn't hold them back. His arms grew tighter. I hated to see him hurting so much.

"It's okay." The words flew out of my mouth before I could really process them. "I don't need marriage."

He peeked up at me, hope filling those gorgeous baby blues, and I wasn't lying. I didn't know what I wanted either. I had my own hangups. "You don't?"

I shook my head, and he rose to his knees again.

"I just need you," I said, and all that worry and torment washed from his eyes.

"Really?"

I nodded.

"Because I do love you, Tedi. I love you so fucking much."

I knew he did, and I trusted that everything he could give, he gave me. I loved him just as much, and I didn't want to lose him either.

We didn't need a marriage certificate to prove our love to anyone, but even as he kissed me and toppled me to the bed, situating himself between my thighs, one thought haunted me—would his hangup about marriage eventually be the end of us?

nineteen

Tedi

IT'S ABOUT THREE-QUARTERS OF THE WAY THROUGH the third period. I told Coach Buford I wouldn't interfere during the game, but I need to get some footage when they're coming off the ice.

I lean over and whisper to Decker, "I'm going to go, thanks again. I'll call you this week."

He nods, more enthralled with Rowan skating down the ice, passing to Henry than with what I'm saying.

Tweetie skates by, and I decide to get the hell out of here. He already scored two goals, and I don't want to see him get a hat trick in the first game of his I've been to in years.

I'm halfway up the stairs when I catch everyone's eyes glued to the ice with expressions of awe. Unable to stop myself, I circle around as Tweetie shoots the puck and the buzzer goes off. The entire arena is on their feet, cheers and roars and screams blaring. They chant Tweetie over and over again, all the fans throwing their hats onto the ice.

I watch him on the ice, celebrating with his teammates,

and I smile because I do love to watch him play even if I hate it just the same. His enthusiasm is infectious, and he's worked so hard to be so prominent this far into his career.

I turn back around and run up the stairs, unable to watch. His love for hockey is part of the reason we didn't work out. It's hard to remember that, though, when I see him on the ice.

With my pass, I get into the back tunnel, and I'm ready with my phone as the third period ends, and the Falcons win three to one.

They all file through the tunnel, ecstatic from their win. It's the different reactions that I love capturing as they pass me —the goofballs on the team always sticking out their tongue or saying something into the camera, while the quieter guys just give me a nice smile and keep walking. The Trifecta and Conor are the last to come off the ice, and they're all congratulating Tweetie on his hat trick.

"I think that solidifies our theory," Conor says.

"Definitely, your best game of the season." Henry draws back when he sees me holding my phone up for a video, but he smiles and nods, continuing to walk.

"I've had plenty of good games this year," Tweetie says, stopping altogether when he sees me.

"Just admit it, you wanted to—" Rowan stumbles into Tweetie's back, and I wonder what this theory of theirs is.

"It was just a good game. There was no other reason for it. It's dedication and hard work," Tweetie says, eyeing me and not the phone. "I was bound to get a hat trick this season with all my offseason work, unlike you slackers."

He continues walking, and Conor dips his head at me with a small smile.

There goes that footage to use on socials. I can't show Tweetie calling his teammates out for being slackers.

I stop the video and pocket my phone, walking down the hall. The locker room is loud and boisterous, and I continue my trek down the hallways, having learned my way around a little more this last week. As I'm about to leave and go back to my lonely apartment, the wives and girlfriends and Decker step off the elevator.

"Hey, I bet they're so happy." Jade beams. "Did you get some great footage?"

They start down the hall the way I just came, so I walk with them. "Um... a little. I'm sure there's something I can use."

"Did you see Tweetie?" Bodhi asks me.

He is so adorable.

"I did." I feign excitement.

"He stopped smiling when he looked at the stands and you weren't there. Did you tell him good job?" He rises on his toes and lowers his voice. "He hasn't scored in three games." His cringe makes me smile, and I ruffle his hair.

"I guess his luck is turning around." I ignore the idea that maybe Tweetie was upset I didn't see his third goal because that's not anything I'm ready to dissect just yet.

"Daddy says it's not good luck," Bodhi says. "It's practice."

Jade wraps her arms around Bodhi, and he squirms out of her hold before running over to a little girl standing with her mom on the other side of the room.

"Is this the girlfriends' and wives' room?" I ask Jade.

"It's the family room. Welcome." Eloise envelops me in a hug.

"I was just about to go." I peer over her shoulder and give Decker a "what the fuck" expression.

We'd both already planned to sneak out of here and not have to go to the club with them. The only reason I got Decker here was for the game, since I can get him that close to the glass.

"No, we're going out," Eloise says.

"Yeah, if I'm going, you're going." Jade points from me to her. "We just have to drop Bodhi off at my parents'."

"I say we suggest going to Peeper's Alley. The last place I want to be tonight is a club with loud music and a bunch of girls trying to get into our VIP section because they want our men. I'm not in the mood." Kyleigh looks really tired.

"Don't mind her, she's cranky. There's a bride at work who's giving her hell." Eloise thumbs in Kyleigh's direction.

"Oh, what do you do?" I ask.

"I'm a wedding dress designer."

"She has her own shop and everything." Eloise puts her arm around her friend's shoulders, looking so proud.

God, I miss Saige so much.

"Oh, I'd love to see it. Not that I'm getting married." I laugh, and they all smile but don't say anything. Okay, tough room.

"You're welcome to come anytime. I'll give you the address." Kyleigh gives me a warm smile.

We talk a little more about what the rest of them do. Eloise is a stylist, and it's a new venture for her. Jade is a photographer. I suddenly feel like the least creative of the bunch. How do I fit in? Then again, I don't have to. I'm not Tweetie's girl, so it doesn't matter. Maybe he'll find himself a baker, and they can all live happily ever after.

Okay, I'm bitter. This isn't good.

"Excuse me," I say, heading over to Decker, who is standing against the wall with his phone in his hand. "Why are you here?" I whisper. "You were supposed to leave."

He glances up. "They're like a cult. They wouldn't let me even go to the bathroom on my own. They were waiting for me when I finished. And then Bodhi talked to me the entire time about my baseball season, asking me about Easton Bailey and stuff. I couldn't sneak off."

"Then I guess we're going out with them," I growl and lean along the wall with him.

"I'm not sure I understand this charade you're putting on. I mean, you two were at each other's throats the other night at dinner. If you don't like each other, don't be around each other, then I can go live my own life."

"Boo hoo, Decker. If you don't know what that fight at the table was really about, then you've obviously never loved anyone. Just play along."

"I'm done with this. You want to let out my secrets? Go ahead, I was a kid." He pushes off the wall.

"Okay, how about the time you stole the good rum from my dad's bar? The one he got in Mexico and couldn't replace?"

He narrows his eyes at me.

"Right now he assumes it was Toby or Theo. But maybe I will enlighten him." I shrug.

"Your dad wouldn't care. I'll get him a case and send it to him to make up for it."

I hum and shake my head. "You could, but then my dad thinks you're a thief. Your reputation will be forever tarnished."

I almost feel bad because Decker is an all-around great guy, and he cares what people think about him. And now I'm using that against him. But I need him. I'm a desperate woman.

"This entire thing is demented." He huffs next to me. "This is the last thing I'm doing."

We stand in silence, and I bury my head in my phone, replaying the footage on slow speed to see what parts of it I can make work. I pause the video right as Tweetie came off the ice. There's no anger, almost happiness to see me there, but it vanishes right away into a hard glare.

"I think he still wants you," Decker whispers, knocking his shoulder to mine.

I look up at him. His whole face softens when he looks at me. "No, he doesn't. Our time is over."

"The other night at the restaurant, he asked me about your boyfriend before he knew I was him."

"Of course he did." I roll my eyes, but Decker's face only shows sincerity.

"He asked me if you were happy."

Warmth spreads through my body, and my heart picks up pace. I have no idea what to say, but I don't have a chance because Tweetie and the guys burst through the doors, and everyone claps, congratulating them on the win.

"Next time, don't tell me things like that." I hate that I'm taking it out on Decker, but I don't want to know that Tweetie wants me happy. It just makes everything harder.

"I just—"

I shake my head. "Let's just get tonight over with."

I watch Tweetie pick up Bodhi, swinging him around, and I ignore the pull in my ovaries that says it could've been our son he was swinging around the room after a great game, but that wasn't our destiny, and it never will be.

twenty

Tweetie

I GOT OUTVOTED. OF COURSE I DID, BECAUSE ALL these couples want a chill night at Peeper's Alley rather than to go to a club.

Which leaves me in the back room, sitting at a table and watching Decker and Tedi play darts against the reigning champs, Jade and Henry.

There are pitchers of beer on the table and glasses of wine sprinkled around. It's casual, and no one is getting drunk.

Tedi winds her arm around Decker's neck, hugging him to her body, and the urge to grab a bottle of whiskey and find a dark corner is greater than ever.

Ruby comes in and eyes me sitting here and not really talking, but she detours over to the smaller tables, picking up the empty cups. Decker is in her way, and she stops and glares at him. "Why are you here?"

He laughs and draws back. "I'm Decker," he says, holding out his hand.

She just stares at his outstretched hand, then looks at me,

then at Tedi before her gaze settles on Decker only. "I know who you are. That wasn't my question."

"He's my boyfriend," Tedi answers for him, leaning her head on his shoulder.

She used to do that to me all the time, and it sometimes made me feel like a childhood stuffed animal she could never part with.

"Boyfriend?" Ruby clarifies.

Tedi nods. "Do you want me to help you clean up the empties?"

"Be nice, Ruby," Kyleigh singsongs from next to me.

Ruby can be protective. She knows who Tedi is to me. I got drunk one night and spilled my guts to her about the one who meant the most to me, who I couldn't keep. So when Tedi showed up here, Ruby already knew who and what she was to me, so her back was already up. I almost feel sorry for Decker. Almost, but not quite.

"I take offense to that, Kyleigh." She never looks in Kyleigh's direction, keeping her eyes on Decker. "You're the new guy, so you get to help me clean up. Take some glasses."

Decker glares at Tedi, and she looks back at him somewhat sheepishly. What the fuck? I hardly ever got that look from her.

"I'll help," Tedi says.

"No, you won't. He plays the hot spot well. He can surely handle a few glasses." Ruby turns around without saying anything else.

Ruby is like a bossy grandma, and it's just easier to do what she wants than to argue. Decker must realize that, so he picks up the empty pitchers and a few glasses, following her out.

Tedi watches him as though he's on his way to the electric chair. What the fuck is that about? He can handle himself. She doesn't need to baby him.

"Come and sit here," Eloise says, patting the spot next to her at the table.

Tedi grabs her glass of beer and sits down, purposely avoiding any eye contact with me, though I know she can feel my gaze on her.

"So, tell us a little about you. You live in New York?" Eloise leans back, allowing Kyleigh into the conversation.

Soon, Jade kicks Rowan out of his seat, and the four women are all talking to one another.

This is the problem with the back room. It's too quaint, too close of quarters, so now I have to hear about Tedi's life as an eavesdropper rather than her telling me alone over an intimate dinner like it used to be.

Decker comes back holding a tray of shots and sets them down in front of us. He sees there's no chair by Tedi, so he takes the open one between Conor and me.

"Is she always so pushy with the shots? She just made me do two at the bar. Said it was some ritual because I'm new?" Decker looks between the two of us.

Conor laughs. "You never know with Rubes." He smacks Decker on the back. "She warms up eventually."

"Well, she wants us all to take a shot." Decker picks up the shots and passes them around. "She said this is for you, Rowan." He puts one that was set away from the rest on the tray in front of Rowan.

"Why are we doing shots?" Henry asks. "I have a kid who's going to wake my ass up at six tomorrow morning."

"Just do the shot," I say, lifting my shot glass.

All the girls pick up theirs.

"Welcome to Peeper's, Tedi and Decker," I say.

We all clink and down the shots. I probably love the burn a little too much. To be honest, I would love to numb my mind tonight, so when Ruby comes back through with another tray of shots, I don't groan and complain like the others.

"Fuck, I feel like I'm at my twenty-first birthday," Decker says, picking up his beer.

"You should feel honored. She didn't do this to me when I joined the team." Conor shrugs.

Tedi is making all the girls laugh with her stories, as she always does.

Wanting to crawl out of my skin, I head to the bathroom. Peeper's isn't busy, since it's a weekday night, so there's no line and no women waiting to get a glimpse of us when we leave the back room.

Ruby flags me down at a table she's cleaning. "I have another round of shots for you guys."

I stop and cross my arms, staring at her. "What are you doing, Ruby?"

She shrugs. "Did you know she had a boyfriend?"

I shake my head.

She sets the glasses back on the table. "You've been dodging me. Haven't seen you since she showed up here." Sliding a chair out to sit down, she eyes the chair across from her.

"Sorry, Ruby, you haven't given me enough alcohol to sit here and pour my heart out again."

"Okay. Don't forget to get the tray on your way back in then." She stands, picks up the glasses, and walks away.

I go to the bathroom, and on my way back to the room, I grab the tray of shots off the bar.

Henry sighs when he sees the tray in my hands. "Fuck this. We're out."

Jade joins him, grabbing her purse. "We're leaving, but let's plan the shopping trip maybe Friday night. I'll get a babysitter." She hugs Tedi. "You don't mind, Decker, do you? Us stealing your girl on a Friday night?"

"You can have her Saturday too." Decker's eyes are a little glazed over, and I'm pretty sure he's on his way to being drunk.

"Stop joking, Decker," Tedi practically growls, and Conor eyes me. "Friday sounds great."

"We're out too," Rowan stands.

"Don't let him bully Boardwalk away from you," Conor says, and I laugh. Decker looks confused.

"Snatch up the railroads and utilities," I say, and Conor laughs harder.

"Fuck you both." Rowan flips us off.

Kyleigh puts on her jacket before hugging Eloise and Tedi goodbye.

They've really welcomed Tedi into their friend group. It was probably a mistake to ask them to come out tonight. I should have kept Tedi away from my friends. Did I learn nothing in Florida?

"I have to use the restroom." Decker gets up, wobbling for a second before he straightens.

"Want me to take you?" Tedi asks. "Jeez, how much have you had?"

"Why don't you ask the bartender who's been feeding me drinks all night for whatever reason?"

"It's okay to possibly offend people and say no, Decker." Tedi rises from her chair, but he puts his hand in the air.

"I'm good."

She sits back down, and we all watch Decker leave.

Eloise gives Conor a look, then he's sliding his chair out from the table. "I'm beat. See you tomorrow. Tedi, it was nice spending time with the one who..." Eloise cuts him a look. "You. It was nice spending time with you."

Eloise whispers something in Tedi's ear, and Tedi waves off whatever she said. "I've got to get Decker home. I think he's had too much anyway."

Conor nods at Tedi before he and Eloise leave the room, shutting the door behind them.

Now, it's just the two of us. I either do this now or never.

I swallow hard. "I'm sorry for my comment I made at the restaurant."

She meets my gaze, and I see the tension lining her body. "Nothing you said was untrue. Fucking a baseball player was on my list."

I pick up the last lonely shot on the table and down it. "I assume you can get him home?" I stand and grab my coat.

"I'll be fine."

I nod and push through the chairs toward the door. My hand clenches around the metal doorknob.

Just leave. There's nothing else you need to say. This is for the best. The more she hates you, the easier this will all be.

"Thank you," she says so quietly that I wouldn't even hear her if other people were in the room. "I'm sorry too."

I turn around and our gazes meet. How did we ever get here?

"I don't want this," I admit, waving a finger between us.

"Me either, but..."

I nod because she doesn't have to say anything else. I get it. I understand exactly what she's thinking.

"We can do this, can't we?" I ask.

She shrugs. "We were never just friends."

I huff. She's right, we never were. "Maybe that's what we were meant to be?"

A painful expression crosses her face, and I regret my words. If I had to do it all over again, I'd change a lot of things, but never allowing myself to have her as more than a friend in my life is not one of them.

"I'll try harder," I say.

"Me too."

The door opens, and I step out of the way before it hits me. Decker comes in looking white as a ghost.

"I'm leaving. Are you coming or not?" he asks Tedi.

She stands quickly, grabbing her coat. "Yeah, let me get you home, babe."

My insides clench with the pet name.

She walks by me, giving me a soft smile.

"You sure you got it?" I'm ready to help her, though leaving her at his place would kill me.

"Yeah. We're good."

Decker gives me a nod and a wave before they leave.

I pick up all the empty glasses and take them to the bar, continuing to dodge Ruby, before heading up to my place to try to get Tedi out of my head and not think about her and Decker sharing a bed tonight.

twenty-one

Tweetie's Journal Entry
Ten years ago
Florida

To my teenage self,

I can't believe I'm about to tell younger me this, but we did the one thing we always said we'd never do—we tattooed a woman's initials onto our skin. Yeah, I know, we said that was some lame bullshit that doesn't mean shit, but I kind of like it. Like a brand that she'll always be mine. I admit, I felt a little pressured, but I'm glad I did it. This is how it all went down...

We were hanging out with everyone, and Cory decided he was going to get a tattoo of Ande's name on his chest. The guy is next level and makes me look even more like a schmuck who won't commit.

Ever since I had that conversation with Tedi about never wanting to get married, things have been good. Great, actually. She never brings it up. Now that we're living together, maybe that's really enough for her.

Suddenly, Cory saw a tattoo shop, and it was like he was hypnotized, walking toward it and forgetting all of us.

"How romantic," Tedi said, hitting me. "What about you?"

"I love you, Tedi, but this is other-level shit."

"Seriously?" She crossed her arms.

I was pissed at Cory for putting me in this position. This was like facing my demons head-on with an audience, and I wanted to stomp my foot and say "fuck you all" and storm out of there.

Tedi gave me the cold shoulder, but her I can deal with.

"You know what? Make that two." Tedi walked up to Cory's side. "You might not believe in us, but I do." She poked me in the chest.

She had me, she knew she did. I wasn't going to let her tattoo my name on her skin and not do the same.

I ran a hand down my face. "Fuck. Make it three." Tedi smiled in Cory's direction.

Thankfully, it was a slow night, and they were hockey fans because they squeezed us all in.

I settled on getting Tedi's initials only because it felt safer to me than her entire name. I got it on my shoulder blade because Cory got his over his heart, and I didn't want to copy that sap. She looked a little annoyed. Especially since she got Tweetie tattooed along her right rib with a heart.

I felt like an asshole.

After we got home and were lying in bed, I knew I had to tell Tedi why I didn't want to get the tattoo at first. She was curled up on her side, turned away from me, and I was staring at the ceiling with a hand resting behind my head when I took the plunge.

"My dad has five different women's names tattooed on him," I said.

Tedi didn't turn around, but I knew she was listening. And I knew the demons I was still haunted by were chipping away at our relationship once again. She was probably so tired of my shit.

"My mom wasn't the first tattoo, and she wasn't the last. He never got one removed and would make these awful jokes that he still loved them all." I took a deep breath to fight against the tightness in my chest. "I swore to myself I'd never get a woman's name tattooed on me because it's not romantic. There's nothing romantic about how my dad made them feel special, then went on to steal from them, beat them, or leave them. He fooled so many women and left a sea of broken hearts behind. I wanted to carve my mom's name off his skin, hoping it would free her of him."

I had such a hard time talking to anyone but my

therapist about my issues with a drug-addicted dad who couldn't get his shit together. A man who was supposed to lead by example but would come in and out of my life without a care for my well-being. The first time I opened up to Tedi about him, she gave me that pitying look I hate, but I was okay with it. But I didn't tell her all of it. I didn't want her to see how fucked up I was and have her run away and leave me.

She rolled over and tucked her hands under her chin, staring at me. "You didn't have to do it."

I gave her a look because I'm not usually a guy who feels pressured to do anything I don't want to do, but with her, sometimes I feel as if I'm disappointing her. So for her, I did it.

"Sorry," she whispered.

I cradled her cheek with my palm, running my thumb under her eye. "I like it, though. And I know it's not your name, but to me it might as well be."

"I think I got caught up in the whole thing."

I smiled at her because I did too. "I don't want you to think I don't like it or that I regret it. I love that you're my girl. I love that you understand me and get me, and I'm honored that I get to be the guy who tattoos your initials on me. But I don't want you looking at it and thinking that I didn't want it. I might not have at first, but I was wrong. I'm not my dad, and sometimes I have to take a step back and remember that fact."

She scooted closer to me, and I wrapped my arms

around her, careful of her tattoo.

"I love you, Tedi. So fucking much. And this tattoo is just a symbol of what you mean to me. Of our unbreakable bond and how you'll always be my girl."

She nodded into my chest. "I love you so much."

It turned out to be a great decision. Maybe I need to hang around Cory more.

twenty-two

Tedi

I'M IN THE BENCH AREA, INSTRUCTING FLETCHER, the cameraman who's been assigned to me, on what shots to get at practice this morning since Coach Buford said he was fine with me getting some raw shots and videos. I've planned a photoshoot next week to replace the shots Gill got.

After the other night at Peeper's, I'm really trying to have a better attitude when it comes to Tweetie. All this animosity between us isn't good for the team or for me. I don't really hate him, and I do want to see him succeed. It's just a struggle when there are so many deep and hurt feelings between us.

"He's got limited time left," someone says behind me.

I stop directing Fletcher where to shoot, wanting to hear whoever it is since I'm fairly sure they're talking about Tweetie.

"His contract is up this year. What are you going to do?" someone else says.

"Last week I was ready to send him packing, but his hat

trick this week was promising. We'll see how he does this season."

I recognize the one voice now. Bud Caldron. Slimy asshole.

The man has no shame. Openly talking about one of his players within earshot of other people. Bringing his mistress to dinner. When I asked some of the guys at dinner about it, they told me he's always been that way. Apparently the rumor is that his wife knows about his cheating and just turns a blind eye. Even so, just because you can doesn't mean you should.

"He's all over the blogs and socials. The fans love him after that game," the other guy says, and I can't place that voice.

I fight my urge to turn around and give them both a piece of my mind. Tweetie is the best left wing in the league, and they'd be fools not to sign him to another contract.

"He's inconsistent. Which is why I came down here today to have a look. He'll have one good game, then three bad ones."

God, I fucking hate Bud.

Fletcher eyes me because he must hear them too. I really wish their conversation would be held somewhere more private and not feet away from the person they're judging.

Tweetie steals the puck and skates down the ice, dodging and deflecting, shooting it to Henry, who passes it back to Tweetie before he circles the net and shoots it in.

Conor shouts, "Fuck you!"

Tweetie laughs, and he and Henry do a bit of a celebration on the ice, throwing their goal in Conor's face.

Take that, Bud Caldron.

The team takes a break to get a drink, and Coach Buford and the rest of the coaching staff instruct them on the next drill. Fletcher and I sit on the bench, waiting for things to start up again.

I pull out my phone, ready to film some amateur videos to put on socials. They've been going well. Everyone loved seeing

Tweetie coming off the ice after his hat trick. I took off the sound, and a bunch of the female fans commented on the look he gave the camera.

"Getting good stuff?" Bud sits down next to me. He's not in a suit today, but in jogging pants with a matching zip-up sweatshirt.

"Yep."

"Good. Good. You'll send it to me. I saw your video from the other night and all the comments it got. You've got an eye for this stuff."

Does he expect me to say thank you over his judgmental comment that he's shocked I can do my job? I bite my tongue, having learned a long time ago that if I keep fighting upstream, I'm not going to get anywhere. I need to swim with the current if I want to make progress here.

"So, I was thinking," he says, and I inwardly groan. "Let's narrow the field even more. Base the social media around Tweetie. Everyone loves him."

"And just forget the rest of the players?" I try to keep the skepticism out of my tone, but this man makes it impossible with his ludicrous ideas.

"Think about it." He puts his hands in the air as if a video is about to play.

Is he sane?

"The oldest player in the league."

"He's not the oldest player in the league."

Bud sneers at me. Okay, I don't need a call up to Mr. Herington, so I zip my mouth.

"As of right now, he doesn't have a team to play for next year."

I feel the first roar of the lion coming to life inside me. "You'd be an idiot not to sign him again."

He turns all the way in his seat to face me. "Do you think

you're more qualified than me to say who should play for the Falcons?"

I grab my coffee, my hand tightening as I tell myself that I cannot throw it in his face. "Sorry, go on with your vision."

He smiles like the popular girl in high school who just got her way. "Everyone loves an underdog."

"Underdog? Tweetie?" My voice gets a little too shrill, and some of the players and Coach Buford look in our direction.

Swim with the school of fish, Tedi. Swim downstream with them.

"Perhaps I should make a call up to headquarters. Maybe we need someone else who can see my vision."

He's threatening me, and I mentally calculate how much savings I have in the bank if I tell him to go fuck himself and be done with this job. It's costing me my mental stability anyway. But if I tell Bud to go screw himself, my name will be blacklisted all over the league, and this is what I love, so I swallow my pride.

I give Bud a smile I hope seems sincere. "I'm just saying that I think having the fans getting to know all the players is better for the team's long-term success."

He waves me off. "All you younger generations bounce around to whatever's hot at the moment." He moves to put his hand on my knee, but I slide it away from him before he has the chance. He pulls back his hand. "I have faith that next year, you'll have a fresh idea on what kind of campaign we should do, whether Tweetie's here or not."

There go my teeth grinding again.

"So, just Tweetie. Forget your entire first line."

He shrugs. "You can do a little on them, but make Tweetie the main focus. People will be either rooting for him to get signed or wanting him to go."

"And are you signing him?"

He chuckles and points at me. "Trying to trick me, huh? I

don't tell people what I'm doing until I do it." He turns his attention to the ice, staring at Tweetie. "Anyway, you should schedule a meeting with him, so he knows what way we're going with this." He stands.

"Me?" I squeak.

"What's with the confusion, Tedi? You're the social media person." He shoves his hands in his pockets. "Oh, and good catch. Decker Davis. Look at you, surprising me at every turn."

My mouth is too open to respond as he walks away, telling Fletcher to make sure he gets a lot of pictures of Tweetie today.

I stare into my lap.

"He's such a prick," Fletcher whispers when Bud stops by Coach Buford, saying something to him before he laughs and walks away.

"I'm not crazy, right? What is he thinking by gambling with Tweetie's contract for next year?"

Fletcher shrugs, and we both look out at the ice.

They're doing skating drills, and Tweetie is first every damn time. Even faster than Rowan.

"You're definitely not crazy. He's playing a game of chicken, and I'm pretty sure Tweetie is the type of guy who will call his bluff."

Fletcher is right. Once you wrong Tweetie, there's no getting back in his good graces. Just ask Jana and Kane Burrows.

twenty-three

Tweetie

I WALK DOWN THE AISLE OF THE PLANE TO THE usual seats I sit in with Conor, Rowan, and Henry, hoping to catch some sleep because I've slept like shit the last couple nights.

"Hey, Tedi. Welcome," Coach Buford says.

There goes my nap.

"Thanks, Coach." She walks by our row and sits two down by the window.

I fight my body's reaction to ditch my friends and go sit next to her. Rowan sits across the aisle from me, eyeing me as though he's waiting for me to do just that.

"Listen up," Coach says, as everyone finds their seats. "Tedi's joining us for this away game to get to know you guys better. So, if you got an email from her about meeting with you, you adhere to her schedule and be cooperative in the interviews. She's doing this as a favor to you, so you don't have to give up any personal time with your family when you're at home."

"Thanks, Tedi. Jade and Bodhi thank you too," Henry says to her as he slides into the seat next to Rowan.

"Kiss-ass," I murmur.

"I'm appreciative." He buckles his seat belt and pulls out his phone, no doubt messaging Jade how much he loves her.

Conor is scrolling through his phone beside me, then unbuckles his belt and slides past me. "I'm first up. Sorry, Tweetie, you'll have to find someone else's hand to hold during takeoff." He laughs and walks down the aisle, taking the seat next to Tedi. "How's Decker doing?"

I slide over to the seat Conor was just in and shift to stare out the window.

"I'm sorry you didn't get picked first," Rowan says.

I flip him off.

"Seriously, don't hurt Conor. We need him." Henry pockets his phone as the flight attendants close the door, readying us to leave.

I didn't get an email, so I guess she's not going to get to know me. Then again, she knows everything there is to know. I haven't changed in the three years we've had no contact.

The plane pushes off from the terminal and heads toward the runway.

Now I know the anxiety people feel on a plane. The suffocation that makes it feel as though you can't breathe. Because I'm on this plane with her for the next two hours, and I have to try to pretend everything is normal.

After the plane barrels down the runway and we're in the air, I try to rest my head on the small pillow. I wiggle to try to get comfortable, but when Conor slides into the seat next to me and I see McCormick take his place, I forget trying to sleep.

"Message for you, sir." Conor drops a piece of paper on my lap and fastens his seat belt.

"What's this?"

He shrugs. "I don't know. Sally asked me if you like-liked Tedi during study hall and said to give it to you."

Rowan and Henry chuckle, their eyes on the note now in my hand.

Why would Tedi send a note to me instead of just talking to me? Have we really lost our way that much?

I open the letter, and my gut twists at seeing her hand-writing again.

My room after check-in. Room 532. ~ Tedi

"Hmm... looks like being an asshole is working for you." Conor looks at the guys. "Our little boy got an invite to her room," he whispers.

"Now hopefully he doesn't blow it." Henry picks up his phone again.

"Doubtful. He refuses to grow up." Rowan picks up his phone, doing the same as Henry. They're probably playing some game on an app and competing with each other.

"You guys can all go fuck off," I grumble.

The plane lands, and when I get into the terminal, I can finally breathe, being away from her. We file onto the bus, and Tedi sits up front with Coach Buford, thanking him for letting her do the interviews during the away game. The note burns a hole in my pocket.

What could she possibly want with me? There's no way she... nah, she's not looking to hook up with me. There's no way. But if she was, would I want to? Fuck yeah, why did I even think twice about that? Sex with Tedi was always off the charts. I've missed it over the years. More than I care to admit.

Basically every other girl I've fucked since her, and there

have been a lot, was in an effort to get her off my mind. To find someone else who measured up. But they never did. They never even came close.

We get our room keys, and I head up to the room I share with Conor. He drops his bags and plops on the bed as soon as we get in the room.

"Now, honey, remember, abstinence is the best form of birth control." He finds the remote and turns on the television. We have about two hours before we have to show up to the rink.

"Screw you." I walk out of our hotel room and find the hallway completely empty.

Taking the elevator down to the fifth floor, I follow the signs until I'm outside her door. I lift my hand to knock but lower it. What am I doing? This is a really bad idea. Tedi and I in a hotel room?

My stomach is a riot of nerves and anxious energy as I lift my hand again, my knuckles ready to knock on the door when it swings open.

"Jesus, Tweetie, what the hell are you doing?" Tedi walks away, and I put my foot out to stop the door from shutting.

She's changed out of her dress slacks and blouse and into tight-ass workout pants and a T-shirt. She looks fucking hot, and I really wish this was a booty call even though it would fuck with my head even more.

The farther I get into the room, the more I see, and I realize that she's got a suite.

"How did you know your room number?" I ask.

"Because I booked it myself and checked in on the app. Why does it matter?"

"It doesn't, but I was curious."

She sits at a small table, and my gaze shifts to the door that must lead to the bedroom area.

"Why do you want to see me?" I ask, ignoring all my

instincts when it comes to her and sitting across the table from her.

"I didn't want to tell you this on the plane."

My body goes into high alert. My gaze flies to her left ring finger, but it's bare. Then again, maybe they eloped or went to city hall or something and didn't have time to get a ring. "What?"

She's quiet. Whatever she has to tell me, she doesn't want to. It's written all over her face, and her body language screams it.

I'm thrust back into that hotel room three years ago when things between us fractured for the last time.

"Bud wants me to center the campaign around you," she says.

I don't really see why that's bad until she continues.

"He wants it to be portrayed as this is your last year with the league. Like, will you get signed for next year or not?"

My blood boils. "You've got to be fucking kidding me." I bolt up from my chair and turn, pushing a hand through my hair.

"He's an asshole, Tweetie." She's behind me immediately, her hand on my back. "If he doesn't know what he has, then he shouldn't be a GM."

I can't even listen to her try to pick up my spirits.

"Did he say that he isn't going to extend my contract?" I circle around, and she's quick to shake her head. Slight relief soothes my blood.

"No. I asked him point-blank, and he wouldn't tell me, but he made it seem like he's..."

"Just fucking say it, Tedi." I prop my hands on my waist.

She swallows and her eyes glisten with wetness. "He seemed like he was on the fence."

My head falls back. "Fucking hell."

She places her hands on my arms. The impulse to wrap my

arms around her and pull her in is a living, breathing entity inside me.

"He's probably playing a game," she says. "I don't trust him, and neither should you."

"I have to go." I step back, and her hands fall off me. As much as I hate it, it's necessary if I'm going to keep my head on straight.

"Just wait. Let's talk about this." She follows me to the door, and when I put my hand on the knob, her hand covers mine. "Don't leave."

I close my eyes to center myself, but her chest to my back feels so good, so right. All I want to do is push all this pain away by sliding into her. To let her soothe the unbearable anger rising up inside me.

Fuck Bud Caldron.

I turn and rest my back on the door. Both of our hands slide off the doorknob.

"I'm so pissed." I scrub my face with my hands.

"I know. I was mad for you, but you need to channel it into your game tonight."

God, she looks so good. I've been starving for the sight of her, and my gaze dips down her body. I swear I hear a slight moan slip from her lips. My hands fall to her hips before I can stop myself.

"Tweetie." Her voice is barely a whisper, her eyes wide.

I step forward, turning her so her back is to the door, then I rest one arm above her head and keep the other one on her hip. "You know it's always been you, right?"

I don't know why I say it. It's the truth, no doubt, but why I'm confessing it to her here, I don't know.

She shakes her head and puts her hand on my chest. "You're just upset."

"I'm fucking so pissed off that I could tear this room

apart." My gaze doesn't leave hers. When I lean down, her hand falls from between us. "Tell me to stop."

I'm practically begging her to save me from myself before I cross this line I'm not sure I'll make it back from. Her chest rises and falls, but her eyes never leave mine.

I'm millimeters from her lips, and I can taste her breath. Her breasts brush my chest with each deep inhale, and I want this more than my next goal.

"We can't." She pushes me back.

I blink several times, and my stomach sinks. "Fuck, Decker."

"Yeah... Decker." Her head shakes as if she were as lost as I was.

"Yeah. God, sorry." I run my hands through my hair and step farther away.

Kissing Tedi behind Decker's back would be really shitty. I'm a lot of things, but I'm not that guy. And I know for a fact that Tedi's not that girl.

"I'm gonna go. Thanks for telling me." I open the hotel room door so I won't say fuck it, pick her up, and take her to the bedroom.

"I'm sorry. For what it's worth, I think he's crazy."

I nod, step out, and walk down the hall.

I don't hear the door shut behind me, and I feel her eyes on me the entire way to the elevator, but I never turn around for fear that my self-control will crumble.

twenty-four

Tweetie's Journal Entry
Eight years ago
Nashville

To my teenage self,

It fucking happened, buddy. My worst nightmare—
we've been kicked off the team, and yeah, I'm more
than pissed. I get it, I do, three injuries back-to-
back. First, my shoulder, then my groin. I thought
we'd done enough exercises using that part of our
body that I couldn't strain it, but fuck, now my
knee. But don't worry. Jana and Kane might not
really believe that we can come back from this, but
we will, and we'll be a champion again. Here's how it
went down...

When the owner of the team, Jana, and her husband, who's the coach, came to visit me as my sorry ass was stuck on the couch with a pillow under my leg, I knew right away what it was about. I planned on working my ass off to get back to being the player I'd been before the next season started, but I could tell I wasn't going to get that chance.

"Hey, guys." Tedi answered the door and let them in. "How are you two?"

I heard Jana say things were good, then she asked how things were here. Things hadn't been good, and I was to blame. I'd been distant, lost in my head over this injury, knowing that changes needed to be made. We're not the same Florida Fury that conquered their competition three years in a row. Tedi swore they'd never get rid of me, but that visit said she was wrong.

Part of me knew it. I knew I'd be the one to go. So when I collided into fucking Nick Lipstein and couldn't get up, I could've signed my trade papers right then and there. Still, it didn't make it easy. My life had been here since the beginning of my career. I took the back seat when Warner came on the roster, happy to be a team player. Sure, it was an ego check, but I loved playing on Cory's line too. Now, I'd made those sacrifices in vain—stayed true to the Fury instead of hopping over to another team where I could be on the first line—only for them to come here and fuck me over.

"Hey, man." Kane squeezed my shoulder as he walked by. "How's the knee feeling?"

"Great. Physical therapy is helping." I was exaggerating since physical therapy hurt like a son of a bitch. Might have had something to do with me being in a shitty mood that I had to be there in the first place.

"That's good to hear."

"Do you guys want anything to drink? Hungry?" Tedi asked.

I wanted to tell her to let them starve, we didn't need to host them anymore.

"No. No, we're good. Thanks, Tedi." Jana sat down next to Kane on the couch.

I could barely look at either of them. The feeling of betrayal was already seeping in.

Tedi leaned over the edge of the couch. "What about you? More water?"

I shook my head and crossed my arms, waiting for them to deliver the blow.

"I have some work to do, so I'll just be outside on the deck." Tedi wound around me, but I grabbed her hand to stop her. Let her see what backstabbers our so-called friends were.

"Stay," I said, staring at Jana and maintaining eye contact.

I'm not sure what I expected, but Jana had no reaction. She could be cold like that when she wanted, but I guess she had to be a tough, business-minded person to run a professional hockey team.

Tedi sat next to me and put my hand between hers. Kane cleared his throat, shifting in his seat. "Listen, Tweetie, first, we know you're going to get through this injury."

"And second?" I raised an eyebrow.

Tedi squeezed my hand, her silent way of telling me to calm down.

Kane opened his mouth, but his wife put her hand on his thigh and spoke instead. "We're sorry, Tweetie, but we're trading you to Nashville."

There was the cold, cunning owner of the hockey team.

She had to be, because Kane was a player first, coach second. He knew what being traded felt like, especially after what our team had achieved together. What we'd won. They'd probably had some conversation on the ride over where she told him she'd do the talking.

I nodded, and Tedi sighed.

"I'm sure you understand, this is just business." Kane inched closer to the edge of the couch, as if he just wanted to get out of here.

"Of course." I shrugged as if I didn't care. They wouldn't get the satisfaction of a reaction out of me.

"We'd love it if this didn't affect our personal relationship." Jana's gaze veered to Tedi, then to me.

"No. We understand." Tedi was quick to put the "we" in there.

This affected her too. Her work was here. Her best friend. Her life. Sure, we lived together and said we didn't need a marriage certificate, but what was going to make her want to upend her entire life and come with me to Nashville? We were either looking at long distance or she moved with me. And her following me wasn't a guarantee, which was one of the reasons I'd fallen in love with her. She had a mind of her own, goals of her own.

Jana studied me as if she knew the hatred that was filling my veins. My hatred for her, for Kane, for the fucking Florida Fury now. I'd given them everything, and they'd just slammed the door in my face without so much as a conversation beforehand.

"Thanks for coming by," I said, hoping they'd take the invitation to leave.

Kane went to stand, but Jana put her hand on his thigh again. "Tweetie, please don't take this personally," she said.

Tedi shook her head. "We understand, Jana."

What did she have to understand? She wasn't the one who hit the ice with a hundred and ten percent every game. Who swallowed his pride when he got put on the second line and stayed faithful because he believed in what they were building. So Tedi might understand, but I didn't.

And Jana knew I didn't understand. She knew I was pissed, and this changed our personal relationship with them forever.

"We should go." Kane took his wife's hand and stood. "The paperwork will all be signed later today. You'll have the entire offseason to find a place there." He ran his hand through his hair. "You have time." His gaze shot to Tedi. "You guys don't need to rush anything, is all I'm saying."

I had never seen Kane uncomfortable like this. He had been the old man on the team before he became the coach, so to me, he'd always been a mentor. Someone I looked up to.

Tedi stood. "Yes, that will give us time to figure out the logistics."

Tedi was pissing me off. I wanted to see the unfiltered version of her. I wanted her to tell them to go fuck themselves because I was going to make Nashville the best team in the league. But she didn't. She seemed like she was trying to make them more comfortable while they stuck a knife in my back and twisted it.

Kane walked up to me, putting his hand out between us. I didn't want to shake it, but I did. Not for today's bullshit, but for all the years that came before it. The mentorship, the coaching that made me a better player, the friendship that was now over.

I was going to return to the ice and make it clear to them that they should've never gotten rid of me. Jana approached right after Kane, and I shook her thin, soft hand. I looked into her eyes so she could reflect on this moment next year when I had the

Cup in my hands. When I was the winner, and she was the loser with whoever she'd gotten in the trade.

They left, and I heard Tedi tell them we'd plan a dinner soon.

The door shut, and she came over to me, crawling on the couch and wrapping her arms around my neck. "I'm sorry, babe, but maybe this will be better. You can get on the first line again. You can be a star there."

"Are you coming?" I asked. It was the only question in my head.

I was going to Nashville and leaving the Fury. I could figure out all the details of where and when I would leave Florida and where I would live in Nashville, but whether she was coming or not was the only thing I wanted to know in that moment.

She sat back on her heels and stared at me. "We don't have to talk about it right now. Let's just deal with this first." She motioned toward my knee.

And there it was. She wasn't coming with me. Something cracked in my chest. Part of me knew I couldn't expect it, but I really wished I didn't feel like she shut me down without even considering it.

She was quick to get off the couch. "Do you want to order dinner? Or I can go to the store and make something?"

"I don't care."

"Why don't we just get Cubans? We can binge that new show you've been wanting to watch. Have a night in and just relax."

She didn't wait for my answer and went about it.

I felt like I did when I was a kid and my dad didn't show to pick me up. My mom would fawn over me, giving me everything I wanted. Tedi was doing the same, but I wasn't a naive seven-year-old anymore. I was a grown man, and I knew when someone was trying to pacify me because they wanted to spare my feelings.

So, I prepared myself for Tedi to end things.

twenty-five

Tedi

Tweetie's been playing so well—I hope Bud Caldron is eating a big fat dick sandwich.

There was another away game tonight, and even though Bud told me to center everything on Tweetie, Coach Buford has let me interview a lot of the players so I can get things together and ready to go for when Bud's whole plan goes to shit. Either that, or what I'm really hoping for—which is what Tweetie said about Bud finding another shiny toy to mess around with.

I'm sitting in my usual seat on the plane. It's nighttime, so most of the players are sleeping. We're going to get in late, and I'd rather stay awake so I can really crash when I get home. There's nothing going on tomorrow, so I figure I'll have a lazy morning, treat myself to a bagel with cream cheese, and work a little from my bed.

A big body falls into the seat next to me, and from scent alone, I know it's him.

"Couldn't sleep," Tweetie whispers, buckling the seat belt.

I swear, airplanes seem to be the only place where Tweetie follows all the rules.

"I'm sorry?"

"I saw your light on, so I figured I'd come back here. I was thinking."

"Is that a new thing? Thinking?"

I armor myself for whatever he's about to tell me. I really hope it's not about our almost kiss. It took all my self-control to push him away, and when he brought up Decker, I was honestly like, Decker who?

He shakes his head, but a smile reaches his eyes. It was a middle school joke, but it was all I could think of to make sure he doesn't think I'm remembering his body caging me against the wall in my hotel room.

"Let's do it. Fuck Bud. At least if you showcase me, then another team will see what they can get."

I'm disappointed I didn't think of that angle or how he could benefit from Bud's stupid idea.

"But you'd have to leave Chicago," I whisper.

He nods, looking so sad and disappointed that I want to crawl into his lap and hold him. "Yeah, that sucks, but..." He shrugs and frowns. "Not much I can do about it. I doubt Bud is leaving, and I don't want to play for someone who doesn't believe in me."

It feels like déjà vu from when Jana and Kane tried to get him back after they'd traded him away. He's being proud, but I don't know, maybe that's not such a bad thing like I thought it was back then.

"Well, if you're serious, I have a lot of ideas."

He nods, and for the rest of the flight, I tell him what I've sketched out. I show him some of the stuff I have, and he chimes in with some good ideas too. That's the thing with Tweetie, he's always been really good about his social media. I suppose it's easy when you're Mr. Charming. I used to handle it for him when we were dating, but most of the time people just loved him because he's such an authentic person. You can try to hate him if you want, but you'll end up loving him all the same. Which is exactly my problem.

The plane lands, and Tweetie doesn't leave my side as we file off, but I get my bag first, so I go outside and order a rideshare.

I'm waiting at the curb when he walks out of the airport with Conor and Rowan. Tweetie glances in my direction and stops as Conor and Rowan wave goodbye to me and slide into their waiting vehicle.

"Hey, you're alone?" he asks with a frown.

I hold up my phone. "Car is five minutes away."

He looks around and holds out his hand. "Can I see your phone?"

"Why?"

"I just want to see where they are." His hand inches closer, so I hand my phone to him. He presses a button, hands me back my phone, then grabs the handle of my suitcase. "Let's go."

"Excuse me?" I ask, not moving.

He's walking toward the black SUV Rowan and Conor already got into. "You're not staying out here at two in the morning waiting for a fucking rideshare. You know who probably drives those things at this time of the morning?" He doesn't stop or even turn around.

"Tweetie!" I follow, glancing at my phone to see that my rideshare has been canceled.

"Bad people drive those things in the middle of the night, Tedi. You need to take your safety seriously." He pats the back of the SUV, and the back door lifts.

Rowan and Conor are in the third row as if they knew this would be the result of Tweetie coming over to me. "Hi, Tedi," they say in unison, looking over their shoulders at us.

"I'm out of your way. I can wait," I say to them.

"Do you live in Chicago?" Conor asks.

"Yes."

"Then you're not out of our way." He turns back around.

"And Kyleigh has a mean streak. She'd kill me if we didn't give you a ride," Rowan says.

Tweetie smiles at me. "See? Get in."

I hesitate.

Tweetie shuts the back door and steps around to me. "Either you get in or I pick you up and put you in, but standing on this curb waiting for some creep to pick you up isn't an option."

"I'm pretty sure they get background checks."

"Maybe, but you're not going to be the headline story tomorrow morning." He opens the back door. "Get in, so we can all go get some sleep."

I walk over to Tweetie, stopping before climbing in. "Thank you."

He smiles at me. A true smile that I haven't seen directed at me in years, and my heart pitter-patters, remembering what it felt like to be on the receiving end of that smile for so long.

I climb in and slide all the way to the window. Tweetie sits on the other side and shuts the door.

"We have one more stop to make," he tells the driver, and I give him my address.

The driver doesn't seem to have a problem with the added stop. Rowan and Conor are arguing about some play from the game, and Tweetie remains so still I wonder if he fell asleep sitting there, until we reach my apartment and he opens the door.

"I'll be right back," he tells the guys.

Tweetie grabs my bag and walks me into the lobby of my apartment building. "I'd like to walk you all the way to your door. You know, so I can sleep tonight."

"Believe it or not, I've survived this long walking myself home at night."

He runs a hand through his golden locks. "It would give me peace of mind. I need a really good night's sleep if I'm going to play well in two days and make your job easier."

I chuckle. God, it feels so good being around him and just being able to be ourselves.

"Are you gonna make me beg?" he asks.

"Fine." I press the button on the elevator.

He doesn't say much on the way up, and I shouldn't be sad that he really is just making sure I'm okay and doesn't have a hidden agenda. But still, I wish things were different with us. It was like old times on that plane, working together on his social media, bouncing ideas off one another, no thoughts of the past and all the hurt and disappointment that lay between us.

We file out of the elevator and down the hall toward my door. I insert my key into the lock and step inside. He places my suitcase just inside the door.

I spin around, arms out at my sides. "See? All safe."

"I'd come in and check for monsters, but I'm afraid I wouldn't be able to leave."

My shoulders sink, and I'm bowled over by a wave of loss. "Don't say things like that."

"You know I don't have a filter." He holds my gaze.

"I know," I whisper.

We stare at one another, and the tension crackles between us. How easy would it be to open the door wider, to step out of his way, and welcome him in? I could break the distance, press my lips to his, and take what I want right now. But I can't. Because the aftermath will only destroy me like it did once before.

So instead, I say, "Thank you again. Get home safe."

He nods but doesn't move. "Always, Tedi."

I inch the door closed, and he steps away from the doorframe. "Good night."

"Sweet dreams," he mumbles.

I shut the door, flicking the lock as a failsafe against myself and the poor decisions that wait on the other side of the door. My back hits the door, and I rock my head back and forth, squeezing my eyes shut.

I feel it, just as I did at Ford's retirement party back in Florida three years ago. That chemistry mixing and bubbling between us until eventually we both lose control and succumb to the inevitable.

twenty-six

Tweetie

MY FEET DRAG ALONG THE CARPETED FLOOR OF HER building's hallway. I force every muscle in my legs to keep walking toward the elevator and not turn around to go back to her apartment.

Tonight on the plane was the first time since she came to Chicago that I wished all that bullshit wasn't in our past. That we were just two strangers meeting. But we aren't.

So I take the elevator down to the lobby, walk out the front doors, and hop into the black SUV to head back to my condo—alone.

"How was that?" Conor asks from the seat behind me.

"It looked really rough," Rowan says.

I want to tell them about Bud's plans, that he doesn't know if he wants to keep me. Even if I know what they'll say —that he's crazy, that I've still got it, that I'm not going anywhere. I could tell Conor and Rowan, but it won't do any good. In this industry, you have to be worried about yourself, as sad as that is.

I once thought differently, until I was traded to Nashville. Sure, my teammates felt bad for me, but they all stayed in Florida. I don't blame my Florida friends for staying loyal to the team. It just really sucked to feel so left out, the one left behind. Reminded me too much of my childhood. Being the one who was pushed out never sat well with me. So if it happens here in Chicago too, I might as well retire. Fuck, just thinking about that six-letter word causes my heart to beat erratically.

"Thanks for letting me take her home and for waiting," I say.

Rowan puts his hand on my shoulder. "You don't have to thank us."

"First you sat by her most of the flight, then you took her home. Are you changing your plan?" Conor asks.

"What plan?" I frown.

"Well, first you tried to hate her, then you decided to act like you were five years old on the playground, and now you're being protective."

I can't say Conor doesn't have a point. "There's just this past I can't erase between us, and it fucks with my head."

"My ceiling has been really quiet," Rowan says, his sly way of saying I haven't brought anyone home with me.

"For how long?" Conor asks him.

"Funny thing, since that brunette we just dropped off arrived in town." Rowan leans forward, so he's right next to my ear. "What do you have to say about that?"

I shake my head at the shit they're insinuating, but they're not wrong. "I can't."

"I think it's more that you don't want to." Rowan leans back in the seat.

"It's okay. But you have a boyfriend to contend with," Conor says.

I think about it for a second. He's right. Decker Davis feels like the death of me right now. But even if he wasn't in the picture, I'm not sure Tedi would let me in again.

"What do you want?" Rowan asks, voice serious. "From her."

I sigh. I've never been good at talking about my feelings. Hell, it's the reason I put Kane out of my life the minute he traded me. I couldn't show him how hurt I was by that decision. Stupid or not, trades happen, yes, but they felt like family to me. My therapist from when I was younger and Tedi are the only people I've ever felt comfortable knowing how fucked up I am.

I think about Tedi. Besides my mom and sister, she was the first woman to come into my life and love me for me—all the messed-up pieces included. I want her to find happiness, even if I'm not the guy. Even if it feels like a twisting knife in the gut.

So, I answer truthfully. "I want her to be happy."

"And if Decker Davis makes her happy?" Conor asks.

"Well, I'm not going to go stop her wedding or anything like your dumb ass."

Conor and Rowan grunt from my need to always deflect with an insult or humor when I don't want to face something.

"Then I'll survive. If Decker Davis is the one she wants, I'll step aside."

They might not understand my decision. They probably think I should fight for her. But why would I upend her life, put her in turmoil, and ruin her happiness? If I did that, then I never really loved her in the first place.

Neither of my friends says anything, but I don't care.

I mean it, if she's happy and I'm not, I can live with myself knowing she is.

twenty-seven

Tedi

THE SCHEDULE HAS BEEN GRUELING, AND I'M ABOUT done with this travel thing. I remember it being hard when Tweetie traveled and how much he didn't want to go and craved being home. I understand it on a whole different level now.

By the time we get off the plane after the Washington game, another flight coming in well after midnight, I just want a bed and soft blankets.

I'm walking out with Tweetie, Conor, and Rowan, but I planned ahead this time and ordered a car that should be here when we walk out. This way I won't have the temptation of inviting Tweetie into my apartment when he insists on getting me home.

"You coming with us?" Rowan asks as the sliding doors of the airport open for him.

"Fuck, it's cold." Conor zips up his jacket and rushes over to their SUV.

"No, I scheduled my own ride." I lift my hand. "See you guys later."

Rowan and Conor wave, but Tweetie stands outside their SUV as if it's not below zero with the wind.

I walk over to the car with the license plate number pulled up on my phone. For a moment, I think Tweetie's going to stop me and make me go with him, but the sound of a car speeding down the road draws my attention. It stops right in front of my driver's car. What the hell?

I glance over my shoulder, and Tweetie nods at whoever the driver is and puts his bag in the back of the SUV.

Decker climbs out of an expensive-looking car and rounds the back. He goes to the driver's side of the car I hired and digs out his wallet, passing the driver cash before rounding the back of the car. The car I reserved drives away, and Decker takes my suitcase from me.

"Why are you here?" I seethe through my teeth.

"Ask your overbearing ex," he whispers, opening his trunk and putting my suitcase in.

My gaze lifts. Tweetie's still standing outside the passenger door of the SUV. I try to figure out why he's watching me, but he climbs into the SUV. I miss his gaze on me immediately.

"If you haven't noticed, it's fucking cold out. Get in the car," Decker says.

I shift my attention to him holding open his passenger door. The black SUV pulls into the traffic lane and speeds off since they're one of the only ones on the road.

Mindlessly, I walk to the car.

"By all means, take your time. I don't need my hands to play baseball or anything."

"I don't understand."

"Just get in the damn car, Tedi." He waves as if I need directions.

"I like this bossy side of you. Don't be afraid to show it in the bedroom," I joke.

He gives me a saccharine grin. "No worries, honey, your seat warmer is on, and I've blasted the heat for you."

"That's so sweet. What did I do to deserve you?" I put my gloved hand over his cheek in a playful way.

"You blackmailed me, remember, sweetheart?" he says through gritted teeth.

I climb in, my ass falling into whatever low-slung sports car he's driving. He slams the door before I can even reach for my seat belt.

Then he's in the driver's seat, swearing and complaining, putting his hands in front of the heating vent. "We need to talk."

After he blows into his hands and rubs them together, he slides on his seat belt and puts the car in drive.

"This car is a little excessive, no?" I ask, looking around at the stitching and leather and the lit-up screen. Maybe I'm just used to Tweetie, who never really splurged on anything like this. I mean, he lives in a two-bedroom condo when he could easily be overlooking Lake Michigan. But that's Tweetie, and one of the reasons I fell for him.

"Am I asking you to make the payment?"

I turn my body toward him. "Decker Davis, I'm seeing a whole new side of you."

"This is me at one thirty in the morning, having to stay up to make sure I pick up my fake girlfriend because leaving her to be picked up by a rideshare driver is inconsiderate... let me think of what else he said." He pulls onto the highway.

"Who?"

He glares before speeding to get in the far left lane. "Your ex."

I grab the holy shit handle. "Tweetie?"

He groans. "I'm hoping you don't have any other exes who

are going to call me up and school me about how I'm treating you."

I bite my lip to stop the smile from emerging. Tweetie called Decker to tell him to pick me up?

"Oh god, look at you." He shakes his head. "You guys are, like, next-level demented with the games you play. First the guy acts like he wants to beat my ass, and now he's telling me to pick you up at the airport, and you're going gaga over him."

"I am not." I cross my arms, but in truth, I kind of am.

Decker aggressively passes another vehicle, jerking the car to the right lane, then back into the left.

"Are you trying out for Formula One or something?"

"No, I want to get home. Speaking of which, where do you live?"

I tell him what exit to get off on.

"Honestly, Tedi, this is absurd. Why are you doing this?"

I shrug. It was a really good idea at first. "You don't get it. And I've hardly asked you for anything. I'm sorry about you having to come get me, but I didn't know anything about it. Do you want me to buy you some donuts or something?"

He takes the exit toward my apartment, and his shoulders fall at the stoplight. "A glazed donut isn't going to fix this."

"What about one with sprinkles? You always loved the sprinkles." I smile wide and act excited as if he's four years old and I can bribe him.

He blows out a breath. "I have no idea how you manage to get me to agree to everything."

"I know I'm abusing being the older sister of your best friends, but I have no choice. Like tonight, having you pick me up saved me from the temptation of Tweetie taking me home. It's not easy not giving in where he's concerned." I rock my head back. "But I do feel bad about you coming to the airport, so let me buy you a donut or two."

The light changes, and he turns left toward my apartment. "Help me understand why I'm putting myself through this?"

I stare at the city, quiet at this time of night. The homes lining the street are dark. "Have you ever been in love?"

He sighs. "Once."

"Then maybe you get it. Tweetie and I are 'all in' people. We don't do things halfway, so when we fell in love, we fell hard and fast. But we came down just as hard and fast when things ended. We know we should stay away from one another, but there's this invisible string still tying us together that only we can feel. You're like my buffer, forbidding him from getting too close. I know it doesn't make sense—"

"It makes perfect sense." Decker pulls into the donut shop just down the road from my apartment.

"Thank you." I cover his hand on the gearshift. "I really appreciate you doing this."

He doesn't say anything. "You're buying me a hot chocolate too."

He turns off the car and gets out, shutting the door. He waits for me at the front of his car with his hands stuffed in his pockets, and when I climb out and meet him, he falls in line with me, knocking me with his shoulder.

We don't say anything and find a place by the window where we eat our donuts and drink hot chocolate without asking the other one any questions about our past loves, but I see it in his expression, why Decker understands—someone from his past still haunts him.

twenty-eight

Tedi's Journal Entry
Eight years ago
Nashville

To my older self,

Tweetie being traded while still recuperating from his knee injury and him having to sit on the bench for a new team isn't helping us remain as connected as we usually are since he moved to Nashville. The situation is stirring up a bunch of shit for me, and I worry we're about to ruin everything. There're so many questions, so many what-ifs hanging in the air around us. But I feel all my abandonment issues nipping at my heels, sending me running faster and faster toward our doom. Before you judge, future me, let me remind you exactly what's happening.

I decided to surprise Tweetie in Nashville. When I told him I couldn't uproot my life and my goals to follow him to Nashville, he said he understood, but I know he didn't. Maybe he did a little, but not enough. It was so hard to say no—so hard—but I felt like I owed it to the little girl who said she'd never hang her life on a man, that she'd always have her own money, her own dreams, her own sense of self.

I went to the condo he rented in downtown Nashville and sweet-talked the doorman into letting me up and into his place. Thankfully, I was on the approved visitor list, but the doorman went above and beyond by unlocking the apartment for me after I showed him a ton of photos of the two of us through the years.

I scattered flowers along the floor, leading to the bedroom. Then I turned off the lights and used the battery-operated tea lights to light the path. I opened a bottle of champagne, pulled out two glasses, and changed into the new red lingerie I'd bought for him.

Tossing more rose petals on his bed, I waited until he should've been on his way home, then I sank down in the middle of the bed, posing in my best sex kitten position, and waited for him.

I was going to make this work with him. We were so good for so long. Right after he left, our video chats were awesome. Little texts would be sent to each other with I miss yous and I love yous. But in recent weeks, things had changed. Video chats weren't happening, being replaced with good morning and good night texts. I hadn't gotten a vulgar dick pic from him in a month. That should've been my first sign.

After talking to Saige, I decided we needed this weekend together. He was off and it would just be us, reconnecting and finding our way back to one another. Finding our way back to being the best couple I'd ever known.

I waited for a half hour after he should've been home, and the condo door never opened. I grabbed my phone from my nightstand, anything to keep my mind from wandering to a worst-case scenario, and scrolled through my emails from work. After an hour had passed, I shot him a text.

> Call me when you're on your way home.

The three dots never popped up.

My heart sank. I kept repeating to myself nothing was going on, he was just delayed, maybe stopped at the grocery store or to grab something to eat. But I could feel the panic and the anxiety setting in.

I probably should've told him I was coming. I should've given him the heads-up to be here, then surprised him with the candles and the roses and the lingerie.

My first mistake was going to the blogs after I'd checked my work emails. I used to stay off them. Never wanted to be sucked into rumors and gossip that most often weren't true. But I had to know if Tweetie was making me a fool. Was I lying in his bed while he was out with someone else? Although I hated myself the more my thumbs scrolled, it didn't stop me.

Then I found something. A picture of him with a blonde at some club. Comments about how funny and down-to-earth he is. Innocent enough, but my eyes only zeroed in on the girl's hand lying flat on his stomach. I read through every comment, and from what people were saying, it sounded like Tweetie was at the clubs an awful lot. A lot more than he had told me. And it was women who were commenting. Suddenly panic and fear had me in their grip, and each comment I read felt like a bullet through my flesh.

He's so nice.

He's so friendly.

He made me laugh so hard I almost peed myself.

He bought me and my friends a round of drinks.

Thank goodness Florida gave him up.

He was born to be a Nashville boy.

Thank you, Florida.

Welcome, Tweetie.

My new favorite player, Tweetie Sorenson.

I closed out of the app before I screamed so loudly

someone thought I was being murdered. Tossing my phone on the rose-petal-covered bed, I threw on one of his sweatshirts and went into the family room, knowing what I was going to do.

I hated myself the entire time I scoured his apartment, almost wanting to find something just to prove my demons right. He was out with another girl right now. He'd found someone here in Nashville to replace me and was just afraid to tell me.

At some point, I lost control of myself. That little voice that said I was crazy to think he was cheating on me vanished, leaving only the voice that was certain he was done with me as I searched his things like a trained FBI agent.

I covered every inch, and I found myself almost wanting to get one piece of evidence so I could be waiting in the dark when he returned home. It all played out in my head—I'd be holding the piece of evidence, shining a flashlight to reveal myself and the evidence, and watch his face pale. I'd already have my bag packed, but I'd leave the roses and candles to show him what he could have had tonight. I'd leave him without giving him a chance to try to get me back. It was like a movie playing out in my head.

A key hit the doorknob, but I wasn't prepared. I didn't have anything to yell "aha" and confront him with.

The sun had already descended, and his apartment

was masked in an orange glow from the stupid tea lights I'd set out.

I stood to the side so he couldn't see me, hoping she was with him so she could see what kind of guy he was. But no woman's voice came as I heard his bag thud to the floor.

"Tedi?" he called.

The tension in my body fell at the hope I heard in his voice. At him seeing the rose petals and candles and assuming I was here because no one else would have gotten into his apartment.

I walked around the corner, and his face lit up. God, what was wrong with me? I was being crazy. He broke the distance, his eyes soaking me in with so much desire, I thought I'd burst into flames. "I love it when you wear my clothes." He picked me up, and I wrapped my legs around his waist. "Babe, what are you wearing under my sweatshirt?"

I gripped him harder, and he let the question go. He didn't kiss me right away but buried his head in the crook of my neck. And then it happened. First the sting of tears. Then the painful closing of my throat. Third, a rasped apology. "I'm sorry."

He pulled back and stared into my tear-filled eyes. "What's wrong?"

He walked me over to the couch, sitting down so I was still straddling him. I kept my face in his neck, not wanting him to look at me. He'd see what I had done and how I'd failed to trust him and how certifiable I could be.

He wouldn't let me hide, though. Instead, he nudged me to look at him. "What is it?"

"I'm a horrible person." More teardrops fell down my cheeks, but he didn't brush them away.

He froze, staring at me, waiting for me to explain.

"I just searched your entire apartment."

He didn't say anything but stared into my eyes.

"I thought you were out cheating on me when you didn't come home."

He nodded, but still nothing.

"I have no excuse. I'm a horrible human being." I rested my forehead on his collarbone.

He chuckled and ran his hands down my hair. "You're not a horrible human being, but did I do something to make you think that I was being unfaithful?"

I shrugged.

He said my name with the same patience and understanding he almost always had for me. This was the Tweetie who got me over this fear all these years together. And in that moment, I found myself upset with Jana and Kane for trading him, because they were making me into a nutcase and ruining my relationship with the best guy in the world.

I pulled back, and he cradled my cheeks in his hands. "I just..."

"Talk to me."

"Things are changing. We barely talk. We barely text. You don't send me dick pics anymore." A wail slipped from my throat, and I tried to hide my face, but he wouldn't let me hide from him.

His laugh bounced around the half-empty apartment. "So what you're saying is that you miss my dick?"

"I miss you."

He laughed harder, and his smile grew. "I know. I was joking. Okay, so we suck at this long-distance thing. Noted."

His thumbs dried my tears. "I'm sorry."

"It's okay. When you said you were a horrible person, the same thought came to my mind, and I just about keeled over. I know I've been lost in my own head since the trade." We held one another for a few minutes, and he kissed my forehead. "Funny that you're here. I was going to surprise you, but I had to meet with the trainer first, then I was coming here to pack my bag."

Maybe if I had waited for him to come to me, this feeling of guilt wouldn't be invading every cell in my body. I hate the version of me that just made an appearance, and I hate that this trade made it come to the surface like some parasite lying dormant in me all these years.

Tweetie's hands slid under his sweatshirt. "Lace, silk, and skin. As much as I love it when you wear my sweatshirts, can I see what's underneath?"

I sat back in his lap and grabbed the hem of the sweatshirt, peeling it off my body.

"Fuck, how did I get so lucky to score you as my girlfriend?"

Without saying anything else, he picked me up and walked me into the bedroom. He didn't ravish me but took his time, as if he was savoring my body, my very presence. We stayed up talking about how we would get through this until we figured out a way for us not to do a long-distance relationship.

I was back in my familiar, blissful state with him until a woman knocked on his door the next morning, accusing him of impregnating her. All at once, I was back to being the insecure, anxious woman I'd been twelve hours before.

twenty-nine

Tweetie

"WHO INVITED TEDI?" I ASK, SEEING HER AND Decker in the stands for Bodhi's game as we make our way around the rink.

I fist-bump Bodhi on my way to the seats with Rowan and Conor.

"The girls asked them to join us. Surely, you don't mind since you're all Team Decker, now that he makes Tedi happy?" Conor claps me on the shoulder.

"Is this the same fucked-up shit you did to Henry?" I grumble.

Rowan laughs. "Nah, we know better than to try to force you to do anything."

Tedi's in a huddle with the girls, and Decker sits next to her, but he's on his phone again.

Rowan and Conor sit closer to Decker, so I do the same.

"Hey, Decker," I say, putting out my hand.

He shakes my hand, then Rowan's, and lastly Conor's. "Hey."

"When's the last time you've been to a novice game?" Conor asks.

"Since I was a novice," Decker says. "Ice hockey isn't my thing."

"Is field hockey?" Rowan asks, laughing.

Tedi's ears must perk up because she turns in our direction, her hand immediately seeking out Decker's leg.

You can do this. She's happy. Look at her fucking smile.

"Decker's not really good on the ice," she says, shaking her head and smiling.

"Thanks, babe." Decker stretches his arm out around the back of Tedi.

Would anyone notice if I ripped his arm off?

"Come on. You admitted it yourself. That's why you're a baseball player." She pats his leg and leans in.

I turn my head before I have to witness her lips touch his cheek.

If I gave him a bloody lip, she wouldn't be able to kiss him.

"That's because hockey is the hardest sport." Conor puts his hands on Decker's neck and squeezes.

"You think so, huh?" Decker asks.

"We have to skate, control a small puck with a stick, and body check. It's not easy, my friend."

"Last time I checked, you sat your ass in front of a net and had a huge stick and pads to block the pucks. Doesn't seem that hard." Decker picks up his coffee from whatever café he and Tedi stopped at before this, since they have matching cups.

What a couple-y thing to do.

"You sit your ass in the dirt and wait for a ball to dribble over to you," Conor argues.

I keep my eyes on the rink, waiting for this game to start so it can be over and I can leave. They can all do whatever they want to do afterward. I'll find something else. I don't have to witness her being happy every damn time I'm with my friends.

"Dribble? You try catching a ball going one hundred miles per hour and then throw it to first before the runner gets there."

Conor laughs. "And what was the Colts' record last year? I'm thinking you missed a lot of those hundred-mile-an-hour balls."

Decker shakes his head, but there's a smile on his lips. "I didn't get the Golden Glove award two years ago for my mediocre skills."

"Relax, boys, both of your sports are hard in different ways." Tedi smiles, and our eyes catch for a second before I turn back to the ice.

Jade and Henry join us, Jade heading to the girls and Henry over to us.

"There's open skating after the game if anyone wants to join us." Jade sits down in the row in front of the women and rests her elbows on her knees, watching Bodhi.

"Jade, come back here. He's fine," Henry says, but she shakes her head without turning around.

"We're here!"

I turn to see Jade's teenage twin brothers rushing over. Owen and Waylon pound on the glass when they reach us.

"Go, Bodzilla!"

Bodhi must hear them because I see his head move in their direction, but the cage on his helmet blocks most of his face. He lifts his hands in a wave.

"About time. He's been asking about you guys all day," Jade scolds them as they shake our hands and hug the girls.

"Why are you here?" Owen asks, pointing at Decker.

"And who are you?" Waylon points at Tedi.

"This is Tedi, she's Tw—" Henry says, but Tedi interrupts.

"I'm Tedi, and I work for the national league, and this is Decker, third baseman for the Colts." She sticks out her hand.

Jade's twin brothers shake her hand.

"Are you together?" Waylon asks.

Tedi leans in and pats Decker's thigh but thankfully doesn't leave her hand there. "Yep."

They nod. "Cool."

Decker sits up. "You guys are twins, huh?"

"I guess you have twenty-twenty vision, huh?" Owen says with sarcasm.

Jade slaps his arm. "Sit and watch your nephew." She leans back in her seat and looks at Decker. "Yes, they're twins. You are too, right? Henry was telling me the other day."

Decker sits up. "Yeah."

I don't know what the deal is, but he certainly doesn't sound like he loves the fact that he's a twin.

"It's how Decker became such good friends with my twin brothers," Tedi says. "Although Decker and Foster are fraternal, not identical. But our moms were in this twins' parent group when they were younger since we all lived in the same town."

"I didn't know you guys have known one another since you were young," Kyleigh says.

"She's robbing the cradle," Decker says, and Tedi elbows him in the side.

"So, you're the older one, Tedi. That's cute. Did you want Tedi when you were younger, Decker? Was she the hot older sister?" Eloise asks.

Jesus, is this a fucking background check Eloise has going here?

He looks at Tedi, and they both laugh as if they have some secret inside joke.

I rub my hands down my thighs, antsy as fuck.

"You could say that." Decker picks up his drink, and thankfully, Tedi doesn't kiss his cheek.

"Go, Bodzilla!" Waylon and Owen scream, interrupting the *Newlywed Game* Eloise and Kyleigh have decided to play with Tedi and Decker.

Jade jumps up with the cheering. "Go, Bodhi, go." Her hands are up in the air.

Bodhi is skating toward the net, no one around him. All of us rise to our feet, and I wonder what the other parents think about us having ten people cheering for one kid.

We're all shouting, "Go. Go. Go."

Bodhi shoots at the net, and the puck goes in to the sound of all of us cheering.

Jade glances over her shoulder at Henry, and they share a smile. That's what I've always wanted. Coming from a family with two parents who were never at my games together, I was always envious of my teammates who had parents who would fawn over their kids. The look Henry and Jade just shared is pure happiness for their kid. They have the real deal. Maybe I'll find it one day.

I turn back to look at the ice and find Bodhi doing my celly dance like I do when I score. My mouth drops open, and my chest pinches.

Everyone stares at me.

"He's been practicing it all week," Henry says, seeing me bewildered.

"Seriously?" I ask, and my chest warms. It's an honor to have an uncle role with Bodhi, and it's made me wonder what it would be like to be a dad one day. Although that day isn't anywhere near, because if anything good came from my childhood, it was figuring out that who you have kids with is one of the most important decisions you'll make in your life.

"Remind me to show Bodhi what a real celly should look like after the game," Rowan says.

Tedi glares at him, and I chuckle.

Why so protective, Tedi?

We continue to watch the game, and I feel slightly bad for the other kids because Bodhi is the best by far. Whether that's because we've been his playmates for so long or he's just naturally talented, who knows, but by the time the game is over, everyone on our side is happy.

"Man, what a cheering section." A woman approaches us wearing tight yoga pants, a small top that reveals her stomach, and an open fluffy pink jacket. Her hair is styled perfectly in a ponytail, and she's wearing a decent amount of makeup. She's not at all what I think of when I think "hockey mom."

"Hi, Maci," Jade says. "Kale played great."

"How are you, Jade?" Her eyes linger on Henry. "Bodhi was just amazing. Must be his dad's genes." She smiles extra wide.

No one tells her Henry and Bodhi don't share genetics, that Henry adopted Bodhi.

The girls all stand, seeming ready to get out of here.

"Tweetie, right?" She puts her hand out in front of me. Her long, manicured nails scratch my palm when I shake her hand.

"Yeah. Who's your kid?" I ask.

She doesn't glance away from me. "Number thirty-three."

"Left wing. Best position." I wink.

"I know. He loves you."

My eyebrows raise.

"You know, in that he looks up to you. You're his idol. Would you mind meeting him and taking a picture? It will just take a minute."

I shrug. "Sure."

I'm not going to be the asshole who denies a kid a picture and a quick greeting.

"Great, I'll go get him." Her gaze roams over the group,

then she giggles. "The single one, huh?" She places her hand on my shoulder. "Me too. The only single mom in the bunch, can you believe it?"

I smile politely, knowing that this isn't just some innocent woman. She knows exactly who belongs to whom in this group.

"We're single!" Owen raises his hand, and Waylon follows.

She laughs. "Sorry, boys, I'm too pretty for jail."

"Oh, look, the boys are coming off the ice." Jade walks down, and Henry follows.

Maci follows them. "Come on. He's going to be so excited." She loops her arm through mine. "You don't mind escorting me, do you? I'm always so scared I'm going to fall with these boots."

The heels of her boots are about four inches high, and I'm wondering who she planned to pick up at her kid's hockey game. Because I'm pretty sure a woman like Maci is looking for a husband or a plaything everywhere she goes.

I entertain her to be nice to her kid, biding my time before I can get the hell out of here and stop torturing myself.

thirty

Tedi

"Good thing you don't have lasers that shoot out of your eyes," Decker whispers.

I blink. "She's all over him. Look at her. It's embarrassing."

"I know," Eloise joins in. "I hate how these women just assume our players are single." Her wedding ring sparkles from the lights above.

"I'm sorry, *isn't* he single?" Decker asks.

"Good for Tweetie. He deserves to get some," Waylon says.

Kyleigh smacks him across the back of the head.

"Hey," he says, but she gives him a look that makes him stop arguing.

They're all so close. Even to Jade's brothers. They're like a family, just like we were in Florida—before Tweetie and I ruined it for all of us. I mean, they all are a family still, and then once in a while, either Tweetie or I are thrown in there.

"Who wants to skate?" Kyleigh asks, already walking down the stairs.

"I hate rentals," Rowan whines, following her.

"You probably want to leave, right?" I whisper to Decker, but Conor peeks his head into our conversation.

"Come on. You go in net. I bet I can score against you."

Decker glances at me, and I see it in his eyes—the competitive juices are flowing. Tweetie used to get that way too. Competitive right down to their bone marrow. How many times did I witness Tweetie throw down with someone just to say he won? Poor Mr. Hawkins didn't know what happened to him after he told Tweetie that he'd be lost putting a puzzle together after he finished the border. We ended up winning the annual Veteran's Hall puzzle competition. Tweetie displayed that sad little trophy for a year.

"Have fun," I say.

Decker grabs my hand. "If I'm going, so are you." His expression threatens to out me, so I reluctantly follow.

It takes a half hour to get our skates, and I haven't seen Tweetie since he was taking a picture with the Kale kid. Maybe he left. I hate the disappointment that sinks my stomach with that thought.

Jade joins us as we're walking away from the rental counter. "That Maci just drives me insane. She wiggled her way into a picture with Tweetie, and I'm pretty sure her hand is on his ass."

Decker glances at me but says nothing.

I grab my skates, and we're coming through the tunnel when I see Maci talking to Tweetie. I swallow down that jealous green monster inside me because Decker is right, Tweetie's single. He can take her home, or get her number, or go on a date with her. Whatever. What do I care?

"Come on," I say.

Decker groans, following me. "Why do I feel as if this isn't going to end well?"

"You're the one who made the bet with Conor." I stop

and turn around. "Actually, you never even put a wager on it. You're just doing it to say you did it."

I circle back around and draw back because Tweetie's right there.

He reaches out, grabbing my hips to steady me. "Sorry. I was just going to get some skates."

"It's okay," I say, glaring behind me at Decker.

"You let Conor get to you, huh?" Tweetie pats Decker on the back and walks out of the tunnel, laughing.

"Why didn't you catch me?"

Decker holds up his skates and his drink. "How? My hands are full."

I blow out a breath and shake my head. "No wonder you're single."

"Let's remember who's doing who a favor here."

We sit on the benches to put our skates on, Decker practically growling the entire time.

"I do appreciate you," I say, and he glares at me.

After everyone gets laced up and heads onto the ice, Conor gets Decker set up in the net. "I'm not going to injure you, so I'll take it easy on you."

Decker scoffs.

All the boys huddle around and make their rules. Somehow, they've found a helmet and pads for Decker, but it's not a goalie's helmet, so there's no visor.

"Are you sure about this?" I ask him.

"Afraid we're going to injure your boy?" Tweetie skates around me. "You're doing pretty good there." His gaze falls down to my skates.

Tweetie is the one who got me skating again. I grew up skating, but after years of not doing it and living in Florida, I was really rusty. The night he got me back on the ice, we went home, and my god... after having his hands on my hips the entire time and feeling so close to him, the sex was explosive.

One of our top ten highlights for sure. Which is probably why he's bringing it up.

"It's his choice." I shrug.

Conor gets ready at the center line. The kids who have stayed are cheering him on. It's clear they want any of the hockey guys to win and Decker to lose.

"Just remember that in the spring, you're going to be at third base," Decker calls.

"Bring it." Conor grins at him, dropping the puck onto the ice in front of him.

"Conor, this is a little juvenile, no?" Eloise asks.

"Watch your husband, baby." He puffs out his chest.

She rolls her eyes, and I skate over by the girls.

Conor stick-handles the puck for a bit. "Count me down."

Tweetie skates up next to him. "Three. Two. One!"

Conor starts skating, and I'm fearful for Decker, although he doesn't appear to be afraid in the least, grinning the closer Conor gets to the net.

Conor circles behind the net, and Decker loses sight of him, allowing Conor to skate around and just tap the puck into the net. Conor raises his arms and does a celly I've never seen him do. I wish I had my phone out so I could get some footage of this. Conor laughs as Decker takes off his helmet and tosses it on top of the net, shaking his head, but still has a smile on his face.

"My turn!" A little boy is already skating toward Decker.

He tries to grab his helmet, but the kid is fast.

"No!" Rowan skates toward the kid to grab him, but he's too late.

The kid swings his stick back, hitting the puck, and it all happens in slow motion. The puck in the air. All of us yelling no. Decker's shocked expression right before the puck hits him square between the eyes.

Rowan swings his arm around the kid's waist, swooping him up. Decker falls forward, his hands covering his face.

"Oh my god." I skate over there, but Tweetie beats me to Decker.

He squats, and everyone circles around us.

"Let's see," Tweetie says.

Decker lifts his face, and everyone groans at the blood streaming down his face. He seeks me out, giving me a look to say, "I'm done."

thirty-one

Tedi

WE'RE IN THE EMERGENCY ROOM, DECKER AND I behind a curtain, waiting for the doctor.

"It doesn't look that bad," I say even though it looks very bad. He has two black eyes forming, and I'm fearful his nose might be broken.

Decker just gives me a pissed-off expression, and I don't blame him.

"You're the one who accepted the challenge."

"Well, I wasn't prepared for a kid to go rogue." He rocks his head back, closing his eyes.

"At least it was only a kid." I try to offer a little positivity.

"Would you like to be sitting here? You are aware that the way I earn a living is based on how well I can see the ball, right?" He glares.

I sink down in the seat. "I said I was sorry, like, a million times."

He picks up his head and sighs, not looking at me. "I get it, Tedi. I get that it's hard for you with him."

I stare at my lap.

"I see the way you look at each other."

I shake my head, still not meeting his gaze.

"Yes. You know, it's funny. I always had this crush on you when we were younger."

"What?" I look up, and he's nodding.

"I'd say it's just the best friends' older sister thing. And don't let your ego inflate too much, because it died quick once I started dating."

"Gee, thanks. Way to pop my balloon."

He chuckles. "I remember when you brought Tweetie to Toby's wedding. You guys were the talk of the night. More so than Toby and Carrie. Everyone said how perfect you two were together. You suited each other so well."

"We were good together, but that doesn't mean that—"

"It was the end of the evening, and Foster was drunk, as well as Theo. The two of them were trying to prank Toby into doing something stupid. I walked into the venue, and a lot of the guests had already left. And you and Tweetie were on the dance floor. Your head was on his chest, his arms tight around you. The twinkle of the lights was scattered over the both of you and all over the dance floor. It was the first time I realized that's what I wanted. You guys were something." He shakes his head a little, then cringes.

My nose tickles, but I suck back the tears. "Why are you telling me this?"

"Because I don't think ignoring the pull you two have toward one another is the right way to deal with this. It actually surprised me when you asked me to be your fake boyfriend."

"Why?" I frown.

"The entire reason I had a crush on you when we were younger is because of your ability not to take any bullshit. To meet every bend in the road head-on. To never shy away from what you want. I know when your mom left, you took on a role you probably didn't want to."

I stiffen. I don't want to talk about my mom, or any of this actually.

"Where is the doctor?" I stand and peek out of the curtain.

"We're in the emergency room in Chicago, it's going to be a while." Decker is so calm. He's the opposite of Tweetie.

I wonder if Tweetie's questioned why I picked someone so different from him. If he were in that bed, he'd be making some jokes and probably blowing up the plastic gloves. I smile to myself, missing that part of him so much.

I sit back down in the chair. "I understand if you want to tap out."

He sighs as if he's thinking about it. "Just not ready yet, huh?"

I shake my head.

"Then I'll keep up this stupid charade," he groans.

I'm not sure why Decker has a soft spot that has him helping me so much, but I rush to the bed and hug him. "Thank you. Just a little while longer. And I'll try to keep you from being swindled into joining the group."

"Sure, you will." He pats me on the back as though he's appeasing me and wants me off him.

"In my defense, I thought it would be an easy two hours. We watch kids play hockey, and then we leave. We showed our faces together. I never imagined it would be this." I grip his hand.

"Oh, sorry."

I glance over my shoulder to find Tweetie emerging from behind the curtain.

"I didn't mean to interrupt, I was just checking on the patient." Tweetie looks uncomfortable and shifts in place.

"Right now, the patient's hand hurts." Decker slides his

hand out of my grip, flexing and stretching his fingers a few times.

"We're waiting for the doctor. You guys should go. You don't have to stay," I say.

Tweetie sits in the chair on the opposite side of the room. I guess he's not leaving. "Jade and Henry took Bodhi home. The rest of us are out there feeling like a bunch of assholes." He sets his gaze on Decker. "I'm sorry, man."

Decker shrugs. "It's not your fault. No one saw that kid coming."

Tweetie cringes.

I tilt my head because he knows something. Decker doesn't see it, but I do.

"What?" I ask Tweetie, and his eyes meet mine before he stares at his hands in his lap.

"Well... fuck, this is awkward." Tweetie blows out a breath. "You guys don't really know Bodhi, but when Jade came back to Chicago last year, he tried to set his dad up with her. And it worked. They're engaged and living together." He side-eyes me, and a floating sensation fills my stomach.

"What does this have to do with today?" Decker asks.

"What can I say? The kid looks up to me. He loves me." He laughs at his attempt at humor. "Jeez, okay." His shoulders slump a bit. "I guess Bodhi heard Jade and Henry talking about Tedi and me the other night and thought you were the reason we weren't together." He glances at me. "So, that was his friend, Micha, who hit you with the puck. They kind of planned it."

"What?" I gape.

Tweetie raises his hand. "They weren't intending for this to happen. They were actually going after your... lower half." He cringes again.

Decker's hands go between his legs as if he needs to protect his manhood.

"They're kids." Tweetie's shoulders lift. "But shit, I'm sorry, man."

Decker narrows his eyes at me. What does he want me to do here?

Tweetie stands and pats Decker's leg. "I'll give you two some privacy."

I don't miss the way his eyes linger. It's clear Tweetie feels like an idiot when this entire situation is on me.

"Thanks, Tweetie, and I hope Bodhi isn't in trouble," Decker says right before he leaves.

Tweetie chuckles. "Well, I think he's off his video games for a little bit, but that's more because he had zero regrets for what he did." He shakes his head. "Someone needs to tell him that I'm not the one he should idolize." Again, he glances at me.

It's nearly impossible not to rush over to Tweetie and throw my arms around him and tell him how wrong he is.

"I'll see if I can get the doctor to come in." He smirks. "Use the clout of being the best Falcon and all."

Decker chuckles at his attempt to inflect humor, but I can't find it in myself to laugh. In fact, I feel like the worst person in the world.

He leaves, and I hear him asking a nurse when the doctor will be in to see Decker. Tweetie throws his name out and says he can get some tickets to whoever can fix Decker up and get him out of here the fastest.

"That was nice of him to check on you," I say.

Decker's eyebrows rise.

"What?"

"He didn't come in here for me. He was here for you."

I look down at my lap.

"It's coming, Tedi. Pretty soon, he's not going to be able to keep his distance."

I don't look at him.

"Because when a man loves a woman like he loves you, there eventually comes a point where he doesn't give a fuck who or what's in his way. He's going to fight his demons *and* yours to win you back."

Thankfully, the curtain opens, and a doctor comes in, so I can try to ignore the fact that there isn't enough armor in the world to protect myself from Tweetie.

It's one of the things that keeps me up at night. The knowledge that if he does come for me, wanting a real second chance, I don't have the fight in me to stop us from making another mistake.

thirty-two

Tweetie's Journal Entry
Eight years ago
Florida

To my teenage self,

Our worst nightmare just came true, and I'm not sure where we go from here. I want to apologize, buddy. I fucked up and understand if you never forgive me. A part of me doesn't even want to write this down, but another part of me needs to purge what happened onto the page to see if I can make sense of it myself.

It's like someone put the biggest dark cloud over me, and it refuses to move on no matter how much I beg and plead.

First, my injuries.

Next, my trade.

Then, Tedi.

I was used to the gossip. Used to fans, both men and women, saying shit that wasn't true and had no basis in reality. Okay, it was mostly the women. Especially when I was single. But once Tedi and I got together, the blogs turned my way. Reports of how happy I looked and how they liked seeing us together. And slowly, I saw that wall lower around Tedi. Brick by brick, she tore it down until I didn't feel the need to reassure her all the time, to make sure she knew I wasn't going to ever cheat.

So after the trade, I took it for granted that she knew that still held true. I was so hung up on my injury, on my trade, that I didn't put her first. Things got to a crisis point, and as I held a crying Tedi in my arms and saw her fear of losing me, I promised myself I wasn't going to wallow anymore. I wasn't going to be pissed off that she didn't move to Nashville with me. We talked it out that night, and I made love to her over and over again so that by the time she got on the plane back to Florida, she would be assured I wasn't going anywhere.

But with the way my life had been going, I should've been prepared that that wasn't the end of it.

So the morning Tedi opened the door to find a tall blonde who looked vaguely familiar, though I couldn't put my finger on why, I didn't realize that was the beginning of the end. I wasn't even sure how the woman got into the building, let alone knew where my apartment was.

"Who are you?" she said to Tedi as if Tedi was a girl I was cheating on her with.

I came up behind Tedi, holding the door open and only wearing my pajama pants and no shirt. Tedi was wearing my shirt, just how I liked it.

"I'm sorry? Who the hell are you?" Tedi's back was up immediately. She didn't look to me to see why a woman was standing outside my door, and I stupidly patted myself on the back for the job I'd done being an excellent boyfriend the night before.

"I'm the one he got pregnant," the stranger said.

"What?" I shouted.

Tedi took the door from my grip and slammed it shut. Turning around, she crossed her arms. "Please tell me she's delusional."

"She is," I affirmed, panicking.

Tedi swung the door back open.

The woman turned as if to walk away, but then she stopped.

Fuck, that moment will haunt me for a long, long time. My heart stopped, worried that Tedi would believe her.

It took weeks, but a hefty lawyer's bill and a blood test freed me from the woman who had falsely accused me. I'd never even slept with her. The investigation I launched revealed that she was dating someone in my building, and I'd run into her and him in the elevator a few times. He was a big hockey fan and always chatted me up.

The woman wouldn't admit that she'd never slept with me, and I saw the doubt that lingered in Tedi, although she came to every lawyer's appointment with me. She stood by my side without asking me every day if I was telling the truth. All of it took a toll on Tedi and me, and I didn't know how to undo the damage.

In the end, the woman said that she had been hoping that I was alone in the apartment that morning to try to seduce me to get back at her boyfriend. But when Tedi opened the door, she didn't know what to do, and she panicked, then it all got out of hand.

She blew up my fucking life because she didn't know how to rein in her false accusations. I was beyond pissed and retreated into my apartment, then went into overdrive with Tedi to make sure she didn't think I would cheat, but I felt everything we'd built crumbling.

I knew it was bad, but I didn't know how bad until I returned to my Florida house when I had a two-day break and walked downstairs to find Tedi crying.

She'd had plans with Saige the night before, so I'd hung with Aiden and Ford. I'm pretty sure she told Saige all of our problems, and I told Aiden and Ford my version. I didn't love the advice the guys gave me, and Tedi had come home in a worse mood than when she left.

So tonight was our only night alone together, and I wanted to take her out and make it special.

As my feet hit the main floor, I heard the sob from the kitchen. Tedi's back shuddered, and she was trying to catch her breath.

I broke the distance and wrapped my arms around her from behind, sorrow and frustration and fear filling me. "What's the matter?"

"I can't do it." Her voice was a raspy whisper.

I looked over her shoulder to see the phone on the counter. Her screen was black, and I didn't want to see what I'd uncover if I opened her phone. I didn't want to know that she was still checking the hockey blogs. But I was the delusional one, because I honestly didn't know it had gotten this bad between us.

"Babe, we've talked about this. It's all bullshit."

She nodded and slid out of my grasp.

I shouldn't have given her the space from me, because she grabbed her phone and threw it across the room.

"Tedi." I'd never felt weaker than that moment. I didn't know what to say or do that I hadn't done already.

She walked over to the couch and sat down, burying her head in her hands.

When I joined her, her body stiffened.

As if some other creature emerged, her back straightened, and she lifted her gaze and set her eyes on me. "I don't even know who I am anymore." Her words crushed me like a hit from behind into the boards. Sure, she was different, we both were. But it was all temporary, and we'd get back to who we were.

I couldn't find the right words to say.

"See? You know it. God, Tweetie, you know it too."

"It's just all the shit we've been dealing with. It will pass. All of it will pass." I didn't know if I was trying to convince her or myself.

She shook her head, and when I felt the devastation of that one small movement sink into my soul, my walls went up. I couldn't deal with the feeling of abandonment I knew would follow if she did this. I'd been ignoring that creeping feeling since I went to Nashville, thinking that if I didn't give it room, it couldn't grow, but it did. Like a slow creeping vine, it had been winding its way around us, and we didn't notice until it choked the life out of us.

"Say something. Please." She looked at me with as much devastation in her eyes as I felt inside.

"It's all my fault." My voice didn't hold any emotion as I mentally prepared the walls around my heart. This was it. We were ending this right now, right here, and I knew in that moment I would never have with another woman what I had with her. I'd never even be able to sit in my family room again without envisioning Tedi's tear-stricken face.

"It's not either of our faults. But we can't go on ignoring it. I loathe myself. I'll convince myself one day that everything is good, we're happy, then the slightest thing will set me off and this version of myself that I loathe comes out and I want to book a flight to Nashville so you can reassure me everything is fine." She cried into her hands, deep, racking sobs. "I can't do it anymore."

My body went cold, and I went numb. I had no idea what to do, how to change this. Suddenly, I was that twelve-year-old kid again, sitting on the step and waiting for my dad to show up. Not worth anyone's time. Anyone's attention. Not worth sticking around for.

"So that's it. It's over?"

Her head popped up. She narrowed her eyes at me.

I didn't know what she wanted me to do to fix this that I hadn't already tried. It was my fault we were in this position. It was my injury, my trade, my job that had fucked this all up. All the hockey blog bullshit was because of me and my need to be the center of attention and Mr. fucking Charming all the time, and it wasn't going to go away anytime soon.

Then my earlier conversation with Aiden and Ford ran through my head.

"If you want her, you have to show you're serious. You're asking her to give up everything for you. You need to give up something too."

They were two men I'd looked up to. Two men who

had found and kept the women they loved. I looked up to them as examples of great men and hockey players.

So I did the only thing I could. I fell to one knee and grabbed her hands.

"Tedi, will you marry me?"

thirty-three

Tedi

"Easton!" Conor shouts across the bar.

Decker told me he was bringing reinforcements today, but I didn't think it would be a teammate. Last I'd heard, Easton Bailey was in Alaska.

All the guys shake hands and do that man-hug thing.

"I thought you were back home with the moose," Tweetie says to Easton, sitting down next to him.

"Hey, babe," I say to Decker, and he actually bends down and kisses my cheek before sitting next to me.

"How are the hips? Holding up, old man?" Easton jokes with Tweetie, and everyone laughs.

"His hips will be the last thing to go. Too much conditioning," Kyleigh says.

The guys all huddle together on one side of the table, and the women do the same on our end.

"You've been busy, huh?" Eloise asks me.

"I'm trying to get this campaign to be successful with all the roadblocks the GM has put in my way. And the traveling takes more out of me than I thought it would." I sip my wine.

I somehow got on a group text with the girls, and they do a lot of things together. With and without the guys. I declined the last three meet-ups, not wanting to put Decker through the paces and not wanting to be around Tweetie by myself. But I figured a quick meal would be okay. I told Decker to meet me so he can leave early if he wants, but it just keeps it in Tweetie's head that I'm off-limits. Although he's not trying to win me, so maybe this is all for nothing. Maybe this is all for me and not him.

I don't want to examine that thought too hard.

"Well, I loved what you did the other day at his endorsement deal, and you did that whole 'how do you make a hockey player go from rough and tough to handsome and polished' thing. Who would've thought Tweetie cleaned up so well?" Kyleigh, the one who seems to be the hardest on Tweetie's lifestyle, says.

"Yeah, the women loved it too." Reading the comments on the posts reminded me of the nutcase I had been back in the day, and it only made me want to accept their invitation tonight just to make sure I never see that pathetic version of myself again.

"I hate those comments, right?" Eloise rolls her eyes.

"Hey," Jade says and looks at Decker then back at me. "I'm really sorry about the whole puck-in-the-face thing. Bodhi just—"

"It's fine." I wave off her concern and look at Decker.

There was a light fracture. He has to go back for a few scans in the coming weeks, but you'd never guess it by looking at him.

"I felt horrible. Like the worst mother when he admitted what he'd planned." Jade blows out a breath and shakes her head.

I place my hand on her arm. "It's kind of cute." Which it was. All three women peer over at me, so I'm quick to correct myself. "That he tried to get you and Henry together."

"The verdict is still out on which one of us got them back together." Kyleigh elbows Jade.

Eloise holds up her hands. "I wasn't in the picture for that. So I'm as much in the dark as you."

"I thought it was cute how he tried to get Decker out of the picture," Jade whispers, and I sigh.

"Just so you guys all know, there is no chance of anything happening between me and you know who."

They all kind of look at one another and raise their eyebrows.

"I'm serious." I double down.

"Okay," Eloise says in a singsong voice.

She and Kyleigh talk about something else, and Jade places her hand on my arm. "I get it. The past can be really hard to overcome. If you ever want to meet for a coffee or anything, I'm here."

She's so sweet. Just like Saige. It would be easy to drag Jade to a corner and tell her all of our shit, but what good would that do?

"Thanks, I appreciate that."

She nods but doesn't push me for more, which makes her even more sweet.

"Shut up, you're doing it?" I hear Easton and look down the table.

"Yeah, I've always been able to handle a lot of spice." Tweetie stands, glancing in my direction for a second before he approaches some woman in the corner.

"What's going on?" Eloise asks.

Conor puts his arms around the back of her chair. "Tweetie's entering the hot wing contest."

"Who bet him?" I point around the guys.

Easton slowly raises his hand. "Guilty."

I shake my head.

"Hey, we need one more," Tweetie shouts to the guys.

"Does he think we're stupid? I'm not playing tomorrow night with my throat burning." Rowan shakes his head.

"Come on!" Tweetie holds his arms out at his sides. "East, man, you're from Alaska."

"Which has what to do with me eating a hot-ass chicken wing?" He chuckles.

Tweetie's quick to move on. "Decker, my guy, let's go."

"I've had about my fill of trying new shit." Decker eases back in his chair.

"I thought you loved this shit," Easton says to Decker.

Decker shakes his head.

Tweetie comes back over to the table. "The lady says if one of us wins, we get a free T-shirt and our picture on the wall."

"Oh yay, a T-shirt." I roll my eyes.

"What about you?" Tweetie asks me.

"No way." I shake my head.

"We need one more!" the woman says over the microphone.

"What is this even for?" Decker asks.

"They have some new flavors or something they're trying out. It's a publicity thing." Tweetie shrugs, like, *who cares what it's for? It'll be fun.*

Easton eyes Decker. "You need better press. Do it, and I'll snap some pics, put them on my socials. You know, to help you out and all."

Decker flips off Easton.

Decker does have a pretty shitty social media game.

"I will say"—Tweetie holds up his hands—"connecting with the town you're playing in is part of the game."

"Not the way you connect, Tweetie," Rowan says with a laugh, obviously referring to his philandering.

My stomach clenches at the reminder.

Tweetie is right, though. I noticed it when I started doing his socials in Florida. He was so easy to deal with because he always wanted to explore the city and take pictures in obscure places. People feel as though he's their friend. Sometimes they think they're more than his friend, unfortunately.

"I can grab some pictures if you want." I offer, but I don't want Decker to feel forced.

Easton raises his eyebrows in a challenge. Just like at the hockey rink, Decker stands. Can none of these men not have something to prove when they're challenged?

"I'm in," Decker says.

"We got one, Gwen!" Tweetie puts his arm around Decker's shoulders and walks them over to the table at the front of the bar.

I pull out my phone.

"This is interesting," Henry says with no other explanation.

I ask a table in front if I can borrow a chair they're not using.

It's Tweetie and Decker, one other guy, and a young girl.

Before the contest even starts, everyone is cheering for someone at the front, and our table is no different. I've never seen Tweetie lose any competition he's entered, so this should be interesting.

The taller middle-aged woman with jet black hair gets on the microphone. "Okay, we're gonna start you off with something mild. Just to get your palates wet."

A young kid comes by and places a wing in front of each contender.

"You have ranch or blue cheese in front of you if you want and some water. If you grab the glass of milk in front of you, you're eliminated. You have one minute to eat each wing. Everyone understand?"

They all nod.

"Ready. Set. Go."

Everyone cheers, and Tweetie and Decker each pick up their wing, both finishing it in way under a minute.

We go through three more rounds, and everyone is still in.

"Way to go, you two at the end, competing with a pro hockey player and a pro baseball player. Impressive." Gwen puts her hand on Tweetie's shoulder, and I want to roll my eyes, because of course she does.

I set my phone to video to film a clip.

"This is where we find out who has hair on their chest." She looks at the one female at the table and winks at her. "Sorry, sweetie."

The young kid dishing out the wings puts one down that just looks spicy. The guy next to Decker starts off well, finishing the wing before he blows out his breath as sweat beads on his forehead.

"You can do it, Dad!" a kid shouts from behind me.

"Yeah, Phil!" a woman shouts.

Phil looks as though he's going to pass out. He tries the water, but you can see that gives him no relief. Somehow, he stays in, and Gwen keeps it going.

I will say whoever picked her to do this contest, they did well. She gets the crowd going. And I'm all Team Gwen until she stops the contest to ask them all personal questions.

She goes to the young girl first. "Tell us why you came out today on this cold Chicago evening."

The girl says she's here with her family, who came to see her at college. They all hoot and holler for the school she attends.

Next is Phil, who answers that he's here with his family to celebrate his wife's birthday. Gwen gives him a little hell for ruining her night when he's throwing up later and she's eating her birthday cake alone.

Then it's Decker's turn.

"And you. Is one of those special ladies yours?" She points toward our table.

"She's right there." He points at me.

Gwen tips her head and nods. "Front and center. She must really like you. But." Gwen pretends to whisper, but she's still got her microphone in her hand. "She's been taking more photos of this guy to your right. Maybe she's more of a Falcons fan than of the Colts." She cringes, and the room laughs. "Oh, I'm just kidding. Gotta keep the competition alive and well, you know?"

Decker glares at me, but hey, he signed up for this.

"And you, Mr. Charming, something tells me that none of those women are yours."

Tweetie smacks on his usual smile. That easygoing casual one that women fawn over. "Nah, I haven't found a woman who could tie me down."

My jaw clenches.

A bunch of women raise their hands, and the word "me" comes from multiple women around the bar.

"He'll be taking applications after he wins." Gwen goes back to her place at the side of the table.

The next round, poor Phil can't even finish his wing before he gulps down his entire glass of milk.

Gwen escorts him back to his family, and his wife kisses his cheek and hugs him. His kids all tell him it's okay, he did a great job.

I'm still smiling at the display of familial love when I turn back around, and my gaze collides with Tweetie's. Clearly both of us were admiring the family.

The girl drops out after another wing, leaving just Decker and Tweetie.

"So what will it be, cute brunette in the first row? Whoever wins gets a date?" Gwen doesn't wait for me to answer before waving. "Just kidding. But did I get your competitive juices flowing, Decker Davis?"

Decker smiles but doesn't say anything.

Tweetie forces a smile. Maybe I'm the only one who sees it, but his back straightens, and he positions himself at the table as if he wants to ensure he wins.

Which I'm sure he does. That's how he is.

"All right, two more, boys. If you both hold off, then I'll have to come up with something else, and I kind of want to go home, so one of you drop out, please."

The boy comes by and places the wings in front of Decker and Tweetie.

They're both eating much slower and taking deep breaths between each bite now. I think Decker's hand might be shaking. It looks horrible from here, and I abandon my phone, too enthralled with who is going to win.

Both make it through that round, taking us to the next. "Only a minute, boys."

Tweetie smiles at Decker, but it's the same look he gave Mr. Hawkins when he had the last piece of the puzzle that time. Oh boy, sorry, Decker.

The two of them take a bite and then another one before resting. They look as though they're in so much pain.

Tweetie closes his eyes and gobbles up the last of the wing, but he still has to chew and swallow. Which he does, while Decker takes it slower, his eyes on the clock the entire time.

Tweetie is inhaling and exhaling, each breath more painful than the last from the look of it.

Decker has the sauce all over his hands and keeps the wing between his fingers, taking one small bite at a time. I feel as if the way they eat this wing is demonstrative of the way they live their lives.

Tweetie stands and accidentally knocks Decker's arm,

which makes the wing slip from his grasp, flying up and hitting him in the eye.

"Fuck!" Decker shouts.

"We have kids in the room, Mr. Davis," Gwen scolds, because she doesn't see what we do.

Decker is blinking over and over. The wing drops to the table, and he presses his palm to his eye.

The timer goes off, and Tweetie raises his hands in victory, practically pouring the glass of milk down his throat.

Despite Tweetie's victory, everyone is looking at Decker.

"I can't see," Decker says, face contorted in pain.

I guess it's back to the hospital we go.

thirty-four

Tweetie

"H_EY, THE_ U_BER IS HERE._ R_EADY?_" I _GO OVER TO_ where everyone is trying to help Decker since he still can't see out of his one eye.

Tedi took him to the bathroom, washed his hands thoroughly, and sat him in a chair while everyone tried to flush out his eye, but he said it still stung. Since it's his vision, we figured off to the emergency room we go.

"Yeah." Decker rises, and Tedi holds onto his arm. "I've got it," he says, and she backs off.

"See you guys later. Thanks for another fun night," Tedi jokes.

I chuckle, although I feel bad that it's at Decker's expense.

"Thanks for helping me reach my deductible this year." Decker waves.

Tedi's at his side, Easton and I behind them. Easton takes the front seat, leaving me to take the seat next to Tedi.

She reaches to shut the door, and I grab a hold of it. "What are you doing?"

"I'm coming with," I say, wedging myself between the door and the car.

"Why?" she asks, still holding the inside door handle.

"Because it's my fault, and I want to be there for him."

"Can we please just go?" Decker asks, obviously annoyed.

His tone makes Tedi let go of the handle, slide to the middle seat, and I slide in next to her.

"This is fun," Tedi says, her arms squeezed in on both sides.

I shift to move my arm and wrap it around the back of the seat, and she sinks a little into my side. The smell of her shampoo reaches my nostrils, and I close my eyes briefly, inhaling a little deeper. I've always loved the way she smells, no matter what new scent it was.

"You're complaining? My career is over."

Easton turns around from the front seat. "That's a little dramatic. They just have to flush it out properly, and you'll be fine."

I tap his shoulder. "I really am sorry. The T-shirt is yours."

"Oh, thanks. Multi-million-dollar contract gone. But I get a T-shirt that says I won a wing contest. Yay." Decker groans, and I don't blame him. I'd probably be the same.

Tedi pulls her phone out and punches something into it. "It says that you should be fine. I'm sure the doctor will help."

Decker doesn't say anything, and I feel like an asshole that I'm at fault.

We get to the hospital, and all four of us file out and head inside.

Decker registers himself with the help of Tedi. Seeing them act like a couple sends a shooting pain through my chest. Her digging into his wallet to get his insurance card. Her making the little jokes with the woman registering them. Her touching him and whispering something.

"I don't get this," Easton says and takes a seat next to me.

"What?" I don't take my eyes off of them. That was me at one point. I was sitting where Decker was, and I was one happy son of a bitch.

"So, Tedi was yours?"

"Yeah." I don't ask who told him. It could've been anyone at this point. Decker knew about Tedi and me before.

"And you're okay with him dating her?"

My jaw tightens. "What can I do?"

Tedi makes the woman laugh again, and I lean forward, resting my forearms on my thighs as if I want to be in on the joke too.

"I'm not saying do something, but how can you hang around them all the time?"

I tip my head in Easton's direction, giving myself time to form the right words. "With the hope it helps me get over her?"

His eyebrows shoot up to his hairline, and he rocks his head back. "Fuck."

"Fuck what?"

"Fuck that you want the girl my friend is dating. Fuck that I think she wants you too. Fuck that we already had a shitty season, and now if Decker is all heartbroken, there isn't much hope for this coming season." Easton shakes his head.

"She doesn't want me. She's clearly happy." I nod in their direction.

She seems like it. Sure, she's different with him than she was with me, but that's to be expected, isn't it? No two relationships are the same. I think. I've only ever had one with Tedi.

Sometimes I think I see her almost second-guessing her decision to touch him, but maybe their relationship is newer. I have no clue. And I wasn't about to call Aiden and act like I cared, letting it get back to Saige, who would definitely tell Tedi.

"Is she?" Easton sits up and rests his arms on his legs, mimicking my position. Both of us look at them. "The first thing I noticed tonight is how he stiffens a bit when she leans her head on his shoulder."

Tedi does that all the time. She used to do it to me, but I was so annoyed every time she did it to Decker, I never noticed his body language.

"See." He nods, and sure enough, Decker's back goes up as Tedi lays her head on his shoulder. "She didn't fawn over him in the car."

I shrug. "He was in a shit mood."

"What woman do you know wouldn't feel so bad they'd be asking nonstop if you were okay?"

My mind travels back to when I was injured and how Tedi was constantly asking me if I needed anything, if I was in pain. At one point I told her to sit down, I was good.

I huff and meet Easton's gaze. He nods as if his point is made.

Could Decker and Tedi be in trouble? In danger of a breakup? I curse the moment of hope I felt there because I don't want Decker to break Tedi's heart. I hate seeing her in pain even if I wasn't the one who caused it.

Tedi and Decker come over and join us.

"He should be called in soon," she says, sitting down and pulling out her phone.

"Make sure you keep the group updated," Decker sneers.

"They're worried," she says.

Decker nods and doesn't say anything.

Easton must know him well because he doesn't say much else. Maybe it's best to leave Decker alone when he's in a shitty mood.

A few minutes later, a nurse comes out and calls Decker's name.

He stands and Tedi follows, but Decker stops. "I'm going to take Easton with me."

Tedi freezes, and her eyes widen. "Why?"

Oh shit, is he going to break up with her right now? My hands fist at my sides. I step closer as if I could shelter her from the pain that's coming.

"Here? In the waiting room of the emergency department?" I ask Decker, pissed off that he's being so insensitive about this.

Easton doesn't say anything.

"What?" Decker scowls at me.

The nurse calls him again, and he puts up his hand.

"I get that you're mad, man, but this isn't cool. The puck thing was Bodhi, and this is me. Tedi doesn't have anything to do with this." I step up, but his eyes remain on Tedi.

She shudders a breath.

Easton still doesn't say anything, and Decker's gaze doesn't leave Tedi's.

"It's time," he says to her.

She nods and tips her head down.

The nurse calls him again, but Decker doesn't go to her. He walks over to Tedi and places his hands on her upper arms, and she looks up.

What the hell is going on? They have some kind of conversation without words, and I hate that they're able to do that. I used to be the one who could do that with Tedi.

The nurse calls his name again, but before she can finish, Decker says, "I'm coming."

He turns and walks toward her, Easton cringing at me but following.

"Hey!" I call, and Decker stops. "How big an asshole are you?"

"Just talk to her, man. Ask her." Decker walks away.

Easton lingers in the doorway, a smile tipping his lips. He

nods to Tedi, who is standing in front of me twisting her purse strap around her fingers.

They disappear through the doors, and I notice people looking at us, waiting for the show to begin.

"I gotta go," Tedi says and races out of the waiting room and into the street.

Oh, no, there is no running today. I wanna know what the fuck is going on.

I follow her, catching up to her at the corner. "What am I missing, Tedi?"

She shakes her head. "Nothing. We just broke up." Instead of crossing, she circles back, going the opposite way as if she just needs to be away from me.

My legs are longer, so I keep pace with her, weaving around people. "That's not what I just saw."

She shakes her head, pulling her coat tighter around her neck because we're headed into the wind.

"Tedi." My voice is a mix of desperation and confusion.

She stops and looks at me, tears in her eyes.

My stomach clenches.

"Fine." Her arms fly out to her sides. "It was fake. All of it."

"All of what?" I'm so confused.

"Me. Decker. Us. We were never a couple. I asked him to pretend to be my boyfriend so you would stay away from me."

"Seriously?" I can't mask the hurt in my tone. She did all that so that I would stay away? Does she really hate me that much? "I don't understand."

"Yes, you do." She turns and walks down the street.

I don't follow, still processing. She and Decker were never a thing? She did it all because she wanted me to stay away from her? It takes me a minute to get it... she didn't do it because she was afraid of me or because she hates me. She did it because she feels what I feel.

I jog to catch up to Tedi, but when I reach the next corner, I can't find her. I turn right and then left and then straight. She couldn't have gotten far.

I smile because this entire time I thought I had no shot, but maybe I was wrong. And I'd like to thank Decker for being a shitty fake boyfriend who didn't pick her up from the airport, so now I know where she lives.

There's no hiding from me now, Tedi. We're far from over.

thirty-five

Tedi's Journal Entry
Three years ago
Ford Jacob's Retirement Party, Florida

To my older self,

*Oh, Tedi, we'd never been so scared in all our life—
we had to see Tweetie again tonight. Ford was the
first one to retire from the Florida Fury. He's a
trust fund baby, so he won't be hurting. I am
surprised, though. I thought he had a lot more
years to go. I don't know why I'm rambling on
about Ford after everything that went down with
Tweetie. I'm sorry, but we caved for a hot second,
but don't worry, we're back on track without him.
Please read this again whenever you need a*

reminder that Tweetie Sorenson isn't the one for us.

Ford's party was in full swing, although it wasn't anything like the parties we all used to attend. Instead, there were kids running around with sticky fingers and cake all over their faces. It was just another reminder that I wasn't in the same place in my life as they were. That my future had stalled out years ago and not seemed to get back on track.

I was anxiously waiting for Tweetie to walk through the door. I knew he and Ford were still close. That's what happens when you're roommates with someone for the years they played together. Still, I wasn't sure if he would show tonight. Although he'd proven Jana and Kane wrong, knowing him, he'd want to be here to rub it in their faces a little. He'd gone to Nashville, healed, and returned to the ice stronger and faster than before, becoming the leading scorer on his team. And Nashville had won the Cup this year.

I hated to admit it, but I was looking forward to seeing him. Sure, our breakup wasn't great. Are any? But we didn't separate because we didn't love each other. We split because we loved each other and couldn't make it work and kept hurting each other.

After we'd been apart for about a year, we had an

awkward run-in at Ford's daughter's birthday party, and he requested to follow me on my socials the following week. I accepted and followed him back. We hadn't texted or called, but I was so happy for him when Nashville won.

I walked up to the bar to get a refill on my wine, and Mr. Gerhardt, Jana's dad, was there getting a scotch.

"Mr. Gerhardt," I said, placing my tip in the jar. I gave him a kiss on the cheek. "How are you?"

"Good." He nodded and smiled. His eyes scoured the immediate area, as if he was looking for someone.

"That's great." I sighed. "For me, it felt like it was over when Tweetie left, but now that Ford is retiring..."

It was like the end of an era. The team had ridden high, and although players were leaving and new ones would come, there was something special about those years. This event had taken me on a long trip down memory lane, and I was feeling particularly vulnerable.

"Have you talked to him?" he asked, clearly not afraid to broach the subject.

"Not really. We're Instagram friends and sometimes we DM one another, but that's about it. He seems happy in Nashville, though." Although I missed Tweetie a lot, time does start to heal, even if it's just to take the edge off the pain so you can carry on.

"Good. Is he coming?" No sooner was the question out of his mouth than Tweetie walked in.

My back stiffened. His blond hair was longer, and the beard he'd grown all season until Nashville won the Cup two weeks ago was now shaved off. He looked stronger, healthier, and a force to be reckoned with. I watched as Tweetie searched the room, and when our eyes collided, a slow, easy smile formed on his lips.

"Excuse me, Mr. Gerhardt," I said in a whisper, already heading toward Tweetie.

We broke the distance at the same time, but as soon as we got closer, we fumbled and stumbled into one another with a hug that probably looked as awkward as it felt.

"Congratulations," I said first.

A slight blush landed on his cheeks, and he nodded. "Thanks. It was a great season."

I'm sure he was there to support Ford, but I know there was an extra dose of satisfaction to have Jana and Kane see him in the best shape of his life with another Cup win under his belt. He always harbored such hurt from that trade.

"You look really good," I said.

His gaze fell down my body, and it felt like a caress. "You do too."

We stood there, and I'm sure more than a few sets of eyes were watching us. We were the couple who didn't make it. The ones who should've made them all appreciate what they had even more.

"God, I hate this," I admitted.

He ran a hand through his hair. "Are you happy?"

There was a lot I could cover in my answer, but I went the simple route. "Yeah. You?"

Tweetie shrugged. "I can't complain."

"Tweetie!" Ford shouted from across the room.

Tweetie didn't look up right away. Instead, his eyes stayed on me. I knew his unsaid words because I felt them too.

How did we get here? How the hell did we end up like this?

I didn't have an answer.

He cupped my elbow and held my gaze. "We'll catch up later?"

"Sure. Go." I nodded toward Ford.

Tweetie studied me for a second before his hand left my elbow, and he crossed the room. All of his old teammates huddled around him, congratulating him on winning the Cup.

Saige came up next to me, holding a sleeping Nora. "You okay?"

"It's good to see him smiling and happy."

We watched them for a while before Aria, Saige's other daughter, barreled into my legs, winding around to my back.

"Hide me," she said. "Xander is chasing me."

For the rest of the night, I'd catch Tweetie with his

eyes on me, but he was the life of the party as usual. That hadn't changed in the years we'd been apart. He was on the dance floor with all the kids or at the bar with his teammates. Part of me was happy watching the old Tweetie in action, the one from before all the shit that went down four years ago. I didn't need anything more than that, but I should've been prepared, because with the way he kept looking at me, it made it clear he wasn't going to just leave it at the quick conversation we'd had when he arrived. So as the night dwindled down, he asked me to dance, and I didn't have it in me to refuse.

He held me close, our entwined hands between us, his hand never leaving my lower back. I didn't lean my head on his chest as I once would have, and he didn't kiss the top of my head. But that invisible string that always pulled us together was still drawn tight, alive and present.

I'm not sure how it happened. I think he asked me to share a ride, and in the back of the rideshare, our pinkies met, and then he was holding my hand.

"Will you come back to my hotel?" he whispered.

That's why I'd tried to keep my distance these past four years. Something in my gut told me we weren't over. That maybe the timing wasn't right the first time around, but at some point, it would be. Even though the idea of setting myself up for the unbearable pain if things didn't work out scared me, we were both in better headspaces, so I accepted.

"Okay," I said, meeting his gaze.

We calmly walked through the lobby, my hand in his. Everyone who saw us probably thought we were just any other couple. They didn't know our past and how big of a step we were taking.

I didn't know what to expect, but as soon as Tweetie had me in his room, my back was against the wall and his lips were on mine. It felt as if I'd been straining to breathe for four long years, and one kiss from him, and suddenly I could take a deep, cleansing breath.

"I've wanted you out of this dress since I saw you tonight." He found my zipper, and I unbuttoned his shirt, the last few buttons flying off because of my impatience. "Goddamn, how have I gone this long without you?"

After that, there wasn't a lot of talking as we fumbled our way to the bed. I should've known, should've been prepared—sex was never our issue. We'd always been able to connect on a physical, intimate level regardless of what was going on in our relationship.

I woke up the next morning, and it felt like old times. I was so full of hope and expectation, ever the fool.

Tweetie was sprawled out on his stomach, and I

inched my way over to him, laying my head on his shoulder blade, running my fingers over his skin like I used to, over the ink that marked me as his, but my fingers stopped when I saw what lay underneath them.

I picked up my head, and my body chilled seconds before my blood boiled.

I blinked to make sure I wasn't seeing things. There was no fucking tattoo on his shoulder blade. He'd gotten it removed.

My mind cast back to when he told me what the tattoo symbolized for him, how it meant that no matter what, I would always have a piece of his heart and soul. The visual reminder that those words hadn't meant what I thought they did to him was a crushing weight on my soul. He clearly regretted me, regretted us.

I slid out of the bed and grabbed my things, tiptoeing to leave without having to deal with him. This was a very bad mistake. One I knew I'd feel the sting from for a very long time.

I slid on my dress and was zipping it up when he peeked one eye open. "Where are you going?" He held out his arms, wanting me to get back in bed with him.

"You're an asshole." I couldn't help the words from escaping my mouth. I finished zipping up my dress and went to find my shoes.

"What?" he asked, either not fully awake or not

remembering that he might have wanted to tell me something. Before we slept together.

"Nice back. So clean and unmarked." I searched the room for my purse once I slid on my shoes.

His face paled, and I actually took pleasure in his reaction. "Shit. Let me explain."

"I don't need an explanation." My voice was getting louder. Shit. Why was I giving him the satisfaction of seeing my reaction? "I'm not surprised, I guess. You never could really commit. Go the distance."

He sprang out of bed, grabbed his boxer briefs, and put them on. "You're going to throw stones at me for not committing? I asked you to marry me." Anger and hurt laced his voice.

Was he serious?

"When you had nothing else good in your life! When you were at your lowest point! That's when you suddenly decided you were all for marriage. After how many years together? You just woke up with the epiphany that you wanted me to be your wife?"

He inhaled a breath and released it, as though maybe he was trying to control his anger. "Would you believe me if I said yes?"

I probably gave him a look. I don't know, but whatever my reaction was, he continued, throwing his arms out at his side.

"You wouldn't. So fine. Believe whatever you want,

Tedi. You always did."

I let the dig slide. "Come on, Tweetie. I'm not an idiot. You didn't even have a ring."

He ran his hands through his hair and let out a frustrated growl. "You want to know the truth? Fine. I wasn't planning on proposing to you that day."

"I knew it!" I pointed at him, feeling justified that I'd been right to turn him down and end things.

He rolled his eyes. "But I also wasn't planning on you breaking up with me. You just gave up on us. After all those years and everything we shared, you just gave up. And so I was a desperate man. A desperate man who only wanted to hold on to the one thing he hadn't lost."

"That's not why you ask someone to marry you. I don't want someone to ask me just because they're afraid to lose me."

"That's the entire reason why someone asks someone to marry them, Tedi." His tone made it clear that he thought I was the idiot for not seeing the truth of his words.

I quieted and stared at him. He just didn't get it. Probably never would. I understood his past and his issues with his dad and abandonment. Hell, I had issues too.

My voice was a mere whisper when I said, "No, Tweetie, that's not why you marry someone."

I picked up my purse and stood at the end of

the bed.

"Enlighten me then, oh wise one." The anger was still pouring off of him.

I shook my head. "That's something you need to figure out yourself."

I walked to the door, tears pushing at the corners of my eyes the entire time. He rushed to stop me, slamming his hand on the door and shutting it before I got a chance to open it fully.

"Don't go," he whispered. He caged me against the door, his chest to my back, and for a moment, my hand slipped from the doorknob. He leaned his head in close, inhaling me.

It would have been so easy to stop, turn around, and let him try to convince me that what we'd done the night before was a good idea. But the voice that had been decimated by the loss of this man was louder than any others inside me, telling me we'd just end up at the same place if we did. Lost. Hurt. Alone.

I placed my hand back on the doorknob. "I'm sorry. I can't."

He stepped back, removing his hand from the back of the door, and I walked out and down the hall, not allowing myself to shed one tear until I was out of the hotel.

thirty-six

Tedi

I have no idea how I outsmarted Tweetie, but I don't take a deep breath until I'm behind my apartment door.

My shaking hands squeeze into fists. It's all crashing down, the reality of the position I'm in. I've been living in a make-believe world thinking I could pretend to have a boyfriend, pretend that the memories of Tweetie and me didn't plague me every time he was around. I've been a total fool.

I shrug off my jacket and kick off my shoes, then open my freezer and grab my cookies and cream ice cream. I look out the windows that face Lake Michigan and try to figure out how I get out of this.

I could call Saige, but I'm not in the mood to dissect this with anyone just yet.

A spoonful of ice cream is almost to my lips when a knock sounds on my door. I freeze.

"Tedi!"

Tweetie. Fuck, how does he know where I live?

Shit. I'm a complete moron. He saw me home that night from the airport.

"Eventually, you'll have to see me."

I roll my eyes and stick my tongue out at the closed door.

"Put the ice cream down."

I grunt and roll my eyes again.

He knocks again. "Tedi, I know you're in there."

He acts as if he can smell me, like in one of those romance books with vampires and wolves and fae princes named Rowan Whitethorn.

"You're going to be up all night if we don't just settle this. All I want to do is talk." I hear a thud on the door and wonder if it's his forehead because he's as exhausted as I am. Exhausted from trying to outrun the past.

I stick the spoon into the quart of ice cream and slowly walk to the door and open it. Tweetie stands with both hands on the top of the doorframe, leaning forward. Jeez, why is that pose as sexy as it is?

He picks up his head with a shocked expression that I opened the door. "Hey." He says the singular word in his easy-going drawl that only makes me remember how much my love for this man never waned.

I step back, letting him in. I guess we're doing this.

"Good?" he asks, dramatically raising his foot, leaving it elevated over the doorway.

"Whatever." I roll my eyes again for good measure, walking away.

"Huh, I was right." He eyes the ice cream as I take the spoon out and put the lid on before dropping it back in the freezer.

"You're not a genius. You've known me for, like, thirteen years."

I lay the spoon in my sink and round the counter, heading over to the uncomfortable couch. He follows me, and soon, we're both seated. Sure, there's a cushion between us, but all I can think about is how little space that really is.

"I'm gonna be honest. I'm upset." He rests his forearms on his thighs, leaning closer than he needs to.

I sit back and bring my legs up, crossing them. For a little added protection, I hug a pillow to my body.

"Scared?" he asks.

"Deathly."

He chuckles, and I realize how much I've missed being in a room with just the two of us. "Me too. Just tell me why."

"Why what?"

He peeks up at me through his long eyelashes. "Why Decker?"

I shrug. "Well, he was easy and convenient. He wasn't going to get attached, and most importantly, he wasn't a serial killer."

He doesn't laugh at my joke, holding my gaze. "You know what I mean."

I inhale a breath. "Haven't you ever felt like this thing between us is just too big to ignore? I knew you'd never encourage me to cheat, so I figured it would keep you just far away enough that we'd get through my time in Chicago without making a mistake."

"A mistake?"

"I don't think this thing between us will ever go away."

"Do you want it to?" Before I can respond, he adds, "I don't."

"Oh, Tweetie." I squeeze my eyes shut.

He slides a little closer, but not all the way.

I clutch the pillow a little harder.

"Listen. I know we have a lot of shit between us. And I'm totally up for ordering takeout, sitting here all night, and dissecting everything that went wrong, but in the end, having you here, seeing you with him, Tedi..." His gaze rises to meet mine, and I swallow from the depth of emotion in his baby blues. "I want another chance."

"Oh my god." I drop the pillow and stand. "No." I shake my head over and over.

"No what?"

"No, you don't."

This is all my fault—having Decker pretend to be my boyfriend has made Tweetie think he wants me back. After all these years apart, he decides to be all in now?

He laughs and sits back on the couch, no longer rigid and uncomfortable. "You're telling me what I want now?" He relaxes into my uncomfortable sofa, one arm splayed around the back and the other one cast lazily over a pillow.

"Someone has to."

"I'm not joking, Tedi." And he doesn't look as if he's joking. He looks very, very serious. Which only scares me more.

"I get it. I was jealous of that mom at the ice rink. It's hard for us to see the other with someone else, but a second chance?"

He's shaking his head before I can even finish. "It has nothing to do with Decker."

"Really? I never saw you seeking me out after Ford's retirement party. I don't remember any missed calls or texts or love letters being sent to me."

He leans over and pats the couch. "Sit down. You're making yourself anxious standing there."

I cross my arms, taking a dramatic step backward. "I'm fine."

He sits up again and grabs a fidget thing my nephew made on his 3D printer, moving it around. He studies it for a second, fiddling with it while I wait.

"You were right," he says. "I was in a pretty shitty time of my life when I asked you to marry me. And when you said no, fuck..." He shakes his head and closes his eyes, his shoulders sinking. "You ruined me."

I don't say anything for a moment. I ruined myself. "I'm not sorry. You would have regretted that decision as soon as you were healthy and found your place in Nashville. You didn't want to be married, Tweetie. You were just tired of losing things that meant something to you."

He nods. "I told you, you were right. You don't need to rub it in even more." He lifts his gaze off the fidget toy and smirks. "I've had a lot of nights where I wished you were next to me."

I could easily throw it in his face that his bed didn't seem to ever be empty based on the rumors, but that will only take us backward.

"Days too. I missed you over these years, and if you want to know why I never came after you, it's because I wanted you to find someone better than me."

My shoulders sink, and I walk over to the couch, sitting next to him. I don't say anything. I don't reach for him. I just sit near him.

"But I was wrong, because no one knows how to love you more than me. Sorry, but it's the truth." His cocky smile lights up his face, and it's not an act. He actually believes it. Maybe I do too if I want to be honest with myself.

"We can deal with that later, but I have a question I want to ask." I gather my courage.

"Ask away."

"Why did you remove the tattoo? I know you never wanted it to begin with, but it gutted me to see it gone after you told me what it symbolized for you, Tweetie. Gutted." I grip my shirt as though I can feel the pain from that day again.

He doesn't look upset, guilty, or scared to tell me as that smile stays on his face. "If you would've stuck around, I would've told you, but first, can I have a drink?"

I narrow my eyes. "Yes, how rude of me. Allow me to serve you, my esteemed guest." I cross my arms and get comfortable in the corner of the couch.

He stands. "So you don't mind if I get it myself?"

I hold out my hand in a gesture of *have at it*.

"Do you want anything?" he asks, glancing over his shoulder.

"I'm good."

He busies himself in the kitchen, and I watch him move around my space. Not only getting a drink from the fridge but also searching my cabinets for snacks. It's nice to share a space with him again. I'm not sure what kind of answer he can give me on the tattoo removal, but I'll give him the chance to explain.

His arms are full of chips, a can of nuts, and two drinks when he returns.

"That's a lot of food." I rest my gaze on the assortment.

"You can't blame me for trying to stay as long as possible, can you?"

I blow out a breath. "Come on, Tweetie. Explain." I wave at him.

He opens the bottle of water and places it on a coaster on the table. "Why do you always get me to be all vulnerable?"

"It's called growth. Stop stalling."

He nods, inhaling a deep breath before he starts. "I wasn't strong enough..."

I have no idea what else he's going to say, but that statement alone already tugs at my heart. I'm pretty sure I can't possibly keep him at arm's length anymore.

thirty-seven

Tweetie

"WHAT DOES THAT MEAN?" TEDI ASKS.

I don't miss the skepticism in her tone.

I forget the snacks since they were really just a way for me to stall and figure out the words I want to say so I don't fuck this up. I've thought about it a lot over the years, knowing if we ever found ourselves back here, she'd ask me like she would have that morning in the hotel room if things hadn't escalated. Although I don't think it would have changed the outcome in any way. I was still so bitter about her not accepting my marriage proposal, and I'd let that resentment build over the years.

"You're not going to want to hear this, but it started with a woman asking me about it."

She huffs and looks away.

"I'm pretty sure you weren't celibate during our time apart."

"Do you really want to compare numbers?"

Yeah, I know I'd lose, but my list after Tedi isn't as long as some people like to think.

"Anyway, a girl asked me what the initials stood for."

"Did you tell her?"

I try to fight the smile, but I fail miserably because I love the note of jealousy in her voice. As if she wished I would've told the woman it was the initials of the woman I loved. It would have been the truth, but I don't open the gates to my heart and soul easily. Tedi knows that.

"No, I just left. Put on my shirt and left."

"Hmph."

"She was the first, but not the last to ask. And every time someone asked, it just stopped me in my tracks. All I could think about for weeks was you. I'd look up your socials, maybe call Aiden or someone else, and ask a few vague questions to try to dig up any information I could on you. I'd scroll through old pictures of us on my phone and torture myself remembering the good times. Think of all the ways I fucked up and what I'd do differently if I could. It made me miserable again and again and again."

A small smile forms on her lips, but she sucks in her lips to stop it from getting bigger.

"It's okay. You owned me. You can feel vindicated."

She sighs, and her shoulders sink. "Come on. You'd be the same way."

I nod. "True." My gaze seeks out her ribcage, and I wonder if she took my name off her skin after the night of Ford's party. Probably not. I'm the only schmuck in this situation. "It paralyzed me, Tedi. I didn't do it because I wanted to forget you, or because you didn't mean anything to me, or to hurt you. I did it because if I couldn't have you, then I didn't want to be reminded of you over and over again."

She grabs her water and opens the bottle, sipping it before putting the cap back on. All without a word.

"You were my first and only love. I just wanted to close myself off from the pain."

"Did it work?" she asks. "Removing the tattoo? Did it make you forget about me?"

Temporarily maybe. For a night with a woman I never cared about.

"No." My voice is hoarse as the weight of emotion crushes my vocal cords.

"Then what were you doing?" I know what she's really asking, and I hate the hurt in her voice.

"I just got numb after a while. And I know you don't want to hear about the other people I was with, but they were just hookups. I never dated anyone after you because I wasn't going to go on dates in some futile attempt to find someone else." I look into her eyes, and she meets my gaze. "It was always you, Tedi. Always. And if I couldn't have the real thing, I wasn't going to pretend with someone else."

She inhales a deep breath and covers her face with her hands. Her shoulders shake, and I finally break the space between us, putting my arms around her and pulling her into my chest. I inhale her scent, and something clicks into place inside me, as if my body knows we're home.

"This is hard, it is, but we were good together, weren't we?" I have no idea what else I can do to convince her to give us another chance. "You were always the one for me." I rub her back, squeezing her tightly. "The one who quieted the noise in my head."

She whimpers in my arms and draws back. Her fingers curl into my shirt and her gaze lifts, her gorgeous eyes searching mine. I loosen my hold. The warmth of her body along mine stirs up memories of when she was mine. I'd do anything for our past to stop pressing in on us. Leave behind all the regret and yearning and make her believe in our love again.

"Tell me it's not too late," I whisper.

I'm afraid to breathe, because if she says no and I walk out of this apartment, it's over. We're over, and there will be a finality to us that I'm not sure I can accept.

"No. It's not," she says softly.

The hell if I'm going to wait. I press my lips to hers, dragging her onto my lap. She doesn't fight me but straddles me, inching closer until we're chest to chest.

I stop our kiss before I get in too deep. "You sure?"

She nods, and I bring her mouth to mine again, sliding my tongue into her mouth. She meets me stroke for stroke, the intensity growing too fast. I want us to remember this moment.

I slow the kiss and make a path down her jaw. She lifts her head, tilting back, giving me access to whatever I want. God, how long have I waited for this moment? How many times did I dream of having her in my arms again? I can barely believe this is real.

"Can I take you to your bedroom?"

Her eyes soften, and she climbs off my lap, offering me her hand. I rise off the couch with her help, and she leads me down the small hallway to a bedroom with a queen bed, two nightstands, and a dresser. This space isn't her. There's no color or art on the walls. Everything is white, chrome, and blah.

"It's not the most comfortable," she says, looking at the bed.

I tug her to me, and she tilts her head to look up at me. "Babe, I'd make love to you on a porcupine."

She laughs, and it's one of my favorite parts of us, making her laugh. "I don't think the porcupine would like it very much."

"You don't think he's into threesomes?"

She shakes her head. "Shut up and kiss me again."

"Just remember, you asked for it."

I swallow her laugh with my tongue, and she jumps into my arms.

I'm not sure how I got so lucky for her to let me in again, but I'm not wasting any time dwelling on it because she's finally here in the flesh with me. And I plan to fully enjoy it.

thirty-eight

Tedi

Tweetie doesn't take long to get me on the mattress, and as I lie beneath him, my fingers tangle in his wavy blond hair. His weight presses me into the mattress, solid and familiar, and despite everything—the years, the distance, the heartbreak—I still fit against him perfectly, like I always have.

We pause, breathless, just long enough to stare at each other.

A slow smile tugs at my lips. "Are we accepting that we have zero self-control?"

He smirks, his calloused palm sliding up my thigh. "I like to think it's more that we're romantically fated."

I laugh. "So, our story will be you tripped over your own shoes and fell on top of me?"

"And you couldn't resist me as soon as you felt my impressive length snug against your stomach."

I give him a look. "Impressive?"

He grins like the cocky bastard he is. "Don't deny it. I bet you haven't had anything close since."

He's right. Tweetie is definitely gifted in that department, both in the equipment and how he uses it.

His hand skims under my shirt, fingers grazing my skin, and suddenly, the teasing isn't so playful anymore. His touch slows, as if he's memorizing my body all over again. "I missed you," he says, his voice raw and quiet.

My heart clenches. The air between us shifts, the weight of everything we haven't said, everything we still feel encroaching on us. I swallow hard, tracing my fingers along his sharp jawline. "I missed you too."

And then he kisses me deep and slow, stealing my breath the way he always has. His hands roam over me, strong and sure, as though I'm a map he's studied all his life. The heat between us flares, electric and familiar, as if no time has passed.

I'm lost in him. Lost in his mouth and his taste and his touch. How have I gone this long without this? He's pushing my arms up, stripping off my shirt while my hands run up his back to get his shirt off at the same time.

Thump.

We both freeze.

"Did something just fall?" I ask, lips still against his.

He sighs, forehead dropping against my shoulder. "I think I knocked your clock over."

I laugh. "So your hand-eye coordination only works on the ice."

He scoffs, lifting his head and narrowing his eyes. "I have elite reflexes."

I arch a brow. "Oh yeah? Then explain why you got hit in the face with a puck last season."

He hums and kisses me briefly before shedding my shirt, then his. God, his chest is even more impressive than it was three years ago. My eyes feast on his beauty, and when they meet his again, he's smirking. So arrogant.

"Just so you know, the puck in the face was an accident."

"Was it?" I quirk my eyebrow. "From what I heard, you were chirping at McIntosh so much he took a slapshot at your head just to shut you up."

His eyes narrow. "Good to know you've been keeping tabs on me."

I shrug. "It's my job."

He groans, shaking his head. "Keep telling yourself that."

I grin, sliding my hands over his broad shoulders, my fingers skimming his scars and bruises from the way he gives his all every game. "You love it."

His gaze darkens, lips quirking. "You know what I love?"

He flips us suddenly, lifting me on top of him with his ridiculous strength. My fingers run down the curves and valleys of his chest. His body is solid muscle, years of training carved into every inch of him. He watches me touch him, and as my eyes meet his, I see how much desire fills them, and I forget how to breathe.

I swallow. "Uh...what was the question?"

He laughs, shaking his head. Inching up, holding his weight on his elbows, his lips brush my jaw, slow and teasing, before trailing down my neck.

"You have no idea how many times I've thought about doing this since you got to Chicago," he murmurs against my heated skin.

I shiver. "And yet, you tried to act like you hated me."

"It's a defense mechanism. You know that..." He lifts his head, eyes locking onto mine. "If I recall, you weren't too happy with me either. Although I knew you wanted me. How much willpower did it take for you to walk out of that room in Peeper's that night?"

I hesitate. "None at all."

His gaze stays steady. "So that shudder down your spine was just a cold draft?" He drags a finger down my spine, and the same shiver racks my body.

I swallow, my fingers curling on his chest. "It's winter in Chicago."

He exhales slowly, brushing his nose against mine, breathing me in. "You knew we'd end up here."

Maybe I did. Maybe I've spent years pretending I've moved on, only to realize I never really had.

I bite my lip. "You still talk too much."

His smirk returns. "You love it." And before I can argue, he kisses me again, deep and exploring, but pulls back as it's getting good. "Admit it now?"

"Nope." I inch back and unbutton his pants. "You're wasting time when you could have me naked."

He flips me again. "You always were the smarter one of us."

As his pants are splayed open, I can see a glimpse of his boxer briefs as he sheds me of my leggings. He stands at the end of the bed, staring at me as though he still can't believe I'm here. He pushes his jeans down his legs, revealing his thickly muscled thighs and the bulge straining his boxer briefs.

"Tell me you have a condom or, even better, a box of them?" he says, putting his fingers on either side of his boxers, tugging them off his hips and down his legs.

I lick my lips, feeling like a starved woman from the first glimpse of his length in three long years. "Tweetie Sorenson doesn't carry a condom around with him?" I tease, and he lifts his eyebrows.

"The only woman he wants to have sex with had a boyfriend until about two hours ago." He puts one knee on the mattress and stalks up to me.

"I'll give you that one."

He laughs. "Figured you would." He kneels between my

legs, running his finger along my red lace panties. "I think someone was thinking about me when they got dressed this morning." He dips his finger under the elastic, and I shiver when his finger grazes my pussy.

"Maybe Decker likes red."

His eyebrows lift and his mouth thins. "Not funny, Tedi. Want me to deny you an orgasm?"

I chuckle and sit up on my elbows. "It was a tasteless joke. I apologize."

"Look how far we're coming already."

I fall back to the mattress and watch him take off my panties, dragging them down my legs.

"I'm going to try really hard to control myself here." He lowers to the mattress, sandwiching himself between my legs and placing my thighs around his shoulders. "But I can't make any promises."

"Still talking," I say.

He chuckles, then slides his tongue through my folds. My back arches off the mattress, and he laughs again. That was the shock factor because he lifts my leg, casting feather-light kisses along my inner thigh.

"I love these legs." He squeezes my calf with his large hand.

"You love them wrapped around your waist."

He peeks up at me. His long, dark lashes just add to his sex appeal. "Don't worry, babe, I'll fuck you up against the wall before the night is over."

"Another promise?"

He lays my leg over his shoulder, mimicking the kissing on the other leg before his face is between my thighs again. With the first twirl of his tongue, my head falls back, and my eyes close from the sheer bliss of his mouth on me.

He trails his tongue from my clit to my opening, the tip tracing my center as his hand winds over my leg to the apex of my thighs. His thumb plays with my clit as his tongue continues its pleasure-seeking path.

My hands fall to my sides, gripping the comforter. I can barely keep my eyes open, but I want to watch him. Those little glimpses he always gives me, as if he wants to watch me enjoy what he's doing, gets me even hotter.

The tip of his finger rims my entrance, and the fingers that were on my clit splay across my stomach, keeping me from moving around.

"God, Tweetie," I beg, needing more. Needing him to take me to the place only he can.

"Just God works."

I glimpse down, and his teasing blue eyes only get me there faster. I forgot how much I missed this.

He doubles down and sucks on my clit while two fingers plunge and play inside me. My hands grip the comforter until my knuckles ache. Without any more smartass comments, he works me so good that I'm on the edge in seconds and leaping over it minutes later.

Bliss scatters through my body as I cry out—a mix of his name and gibberish until I'm left panting and staring at the ceiling. Picking up my head, seeing my juices on his chin, I only want him more.

"Didn't anyone tell you to say thank you?" He laughs and crawls on top of me.

"You should be thanking me."

"Touché." He kisses me briefly. "Now where are the condoms? Otherwise I can't thank you properly for letting me go down on you."

I wrap my arms around his chest, not wanting to let him go. "Top drawer of the nightstand that you knocked the clock off of."

He wiggles out of my embrace and stretches across the mattress, opening the drawer. "Gonna be honest, don't love the easy access." I hear him tear from the strip of condoms. "And I see you haven't been with anyone with as impressive of a dick as me?"

He gets on his knees, and I watch him open the condom wrapper and roll the condom down his length. "Were you hoping for dust on the box?"

"Expired would have been better."

I place my hand on his thigh, and he weaves his fingers through mine, our gazes holding for a minute as if it sucks that we allowed all this time to pass while we were apart.

"Me on top?" He blows out a breath, deflecting the moment with humor. "My job is never done."

"Oh my god, just fuck me already."

He gives me a wicked grin and pushes open my legs. "I should make you ride me so I can suck on your tits."

"Next time. After we fuck against the wall."

He looks down at his dick. "Man, she's already got a honey-do list for us."

Then the humor fades as he moves over me. Leaning down, his lips brush along my collarbone, lingering for a moment before he moves lower. The softness of his lips on my bare skin feels like a secret he's savoring and discovering. I inhale deeply, my fingers finding their way into his hair, gently pulling him closer, silently urging him on.

Tweetie kisses a path down my body, his touch tender and slow. I can't help but melt under his attention. A shiver runs through me as his hands glide over my sides, moving with a steady rhythm that matches the pounding of my heart. He traces the tattoo of his name with one finger, and his gaze flicks up to meet mine. In his, I see nothing but the weight of the love that still lies between us.

He rises back just as slowly as he moved down until our faces are aligned. "You're beautiful," he murmurs.

His fingers dance along my body, and a soft gasp escapes

my lips. The way he touches me, so carefully, so deliberate, makes me feel as though I'm the only thing in the world that matters to him. With each kiss, each caress, I'm reminded of what we were together.

His tip pushes against my opening, and he slides in an inch before he kisses me and slides in another inch. Once he's fully inside me, he gives me the moment I need to adjust.

"Take a minute, I know it's a lot."

"Tweetie!" I exclaim, and he laughs, sliding out and back in.

He doesn't joke anymore as he falls into an easy rhythm in and out of me, casting kisses along my face, my neck, and my ears. His breath rattles in my ear, and I grip his shoulder blades, then lower until I grab his muscled ass and urge him to push into me harder.

He increases his pace, plunging inside me over and over. My breathing hitches when his mouth falls to my breast, taking my nipple into his hot mouth, and it's all too much. Him, the sensations all over my body. My orgasm comes again, swiftly and without warning, but I hit a crescendo so far gone, I wonder if I'll ever move away from this state of euphoria.

"God, I love watching you come. I love being the one to make you come." He crashes his lips to mine, and I hold his chest to me, never wanting this moment to end.

He thrusts into me over and over, whispering sweet things about missing me, being lost without me, and how he finally feels found again until he stills inside me and comes on a curse.

His breathing is jagged as he comes down, laying his weight on me and kissing me languidly without any rush. Minutes later, he lifts his head.

"Thank you," he says, laughing as he grows soft inside me. With a chaste kiss to my lips, he slides out of me and goes into the bathroom.

I follow him and wait for him to dispose of the condom and clean himself. He stands and waits for me.

"What are you doing?" I ask, waiting to go to the bathroom.

"What are you waiting for?" he asks.

"You to leave." I motion toward the door.

His forehead wrinkles. "Why?"

"So I can go to the bathroom."

He crosses his arms and leans against the counter. "Go."

I walk over and turn him to face the door. "Yeah, we're not there yet."

"I've seen you pee plenty," he fights me, walking forward.

I shut the door on him, flicking the lock. He laughs, and god, how I missed that sound so much. More than I've been able to admit to myself over the years.

I exit the bathroom a few minutes later, and he's got his boxer briefs on and his phone in his hand. "So, what do you think? Chinese or pizza?"

It's always zero to sixty in no time with us.

thirty-nine

Tedi

MY PHONE ALARM BLARES, AND I REACH TO GRAB IT from the nightstand, but the phone falls to the floor.

"Grr." I sling my arm over the edge of the mattress and reach for it, but I can't feel it.

"Cold." Tweetie tugs the covers back over him. "Turn it off."

"I'm trying." I finally feel the tip of the phone, and I slowly bring it closer until I'm able to grab it. I pick it up and right myself on the bed, turning off the alarm.

Sliding up, I rest my back against the headboard and put the phone back down on my nightstand.

Tweetie rolls over, wrapping his arm around my waist and dropping his head in my lap. My hands mindlessly run through his hair, and he practically purrs like a cat under my touch.

Last night was like we took a time machine back to so many years ago. Before the injury, before the trade and our inevitable breakup. We ordered Chinese food, binged a television series, but stopped when the lingering touches became too much and we couldn't control our libidos. He fulfilled his promise and fucked me against the wall, then I rode him right before we went to finally fall asleep.

I gaze down at him, grazing my knuckles along his strong shoulder blades. I run my finger over the spot where he got the tattoo removed, barely raised and noticeable now. He stiffens under my touch for a moment before I continue my lazy exploration. He tightens his grip on me, nuzzling his head further in my lap.

Being with him again feels so good. I'm not sure I realized how incomplete I felt all these years. As though I had a missing twin out there somewhere. But with the sunrise, my mind fills with doubts. Am I really ready for this? What happens with my job? Not much has changed, because in a few months when the season is over, I head back to New York. With Tweetie's contract up, he could end up as far away as Los Angeles, playing alongside Cory, for all we know.

"I can feel you thinking. Stop," Tweetie mumbles.

"That's an impossible ask."

He rolls over, keeping his head in my lap, staring up at me. "Do you regret it?"

I should've known. The man reads me better than my own father. "I don't regret it."

"But?" He runs his finger up and down along the back of my neck. It's sensual and loving and makes what I'm about to say that much harder.

"There's a lot to consider here."

"Nothing we can't handle."

I raise my eyebrows. He knows it, and I know it. "What about after this season when I go to New York and you go wherever you get signed or stay here? Long distance isn't really our thing."

He huffs out a breath. Not in anger but annoyance. "I think it could be different."

"How?"

The last person I ever want to be again is that crazed, insecure woman who convinced herself he was making a fool of her. The obsessed woman who thought she was one comment away from finding out he was a cheater. The hockey blogs are still alive and kicking and causing turmoil in good relationships.

"I'm not in the same headspace as when I was dealing with an injury and trying to find my place on a new team." He doesn't stop running his fingers through the strands of hair at the back of his head.

"Not now, but if Bud doesn't sign you, then—"

He sits up and rests his back along the headboard beside me, taking my hand. "Then I go to another team, and it's a little longer or it's an even shorter distance. Maybe New York wants me? There are a lot of what-ifs in those scenarios."

"I think that's what I don't like." I turn to face him. "Last night was great."

"Uh-oh, I feel the 'it's not you, but me' talk coming on."

I stare down at our joined hands. "Not at all. I just need to ground myself. If this is really going to work, I think we need to pump the brakes a little. Ease into this slowly. We've always played hot and loose with our emotions and actions."

He doesn't say anything for a moment, but he also doesn't pull his hand from mine. "I meant everything I said. I'm not going into this as the same man I left our relationship as."

"I know that. I do." I crawl into his lap, straddling him, needing to be close to him. To know that I'm not saying no, I'm just saying slow. "You still trust me?"

"You're still the person I trust the most."

I put my hands on his cheeks and rest my forehead against his. "Then trust me that with time, we'll be there again. You're like a race car, pedal to the floor, tires screeching around the corners, and I just think this time around, we might need to take the Sunday drive approach. We're going to reach the same destination, I'm sure of it, but it might take us longer than we're used to."

He swallows. "I'm gonna be honest. I'm not sure if I'm built for slow, but if I'm gonna try for anyone, it's you."

I smile, and his hands tighten on my hips. "Thank you."

"I have to know, does this have anything to do with the tattoo thing? Because I can book an appointment right now. And this time I'll get your full name right over my heart. Fuck it if Cory tells me I'm copying him."

I shake my head. "It doesn't have anything to do with the tattoo. You made up for that with what you said last night. It's actually kind of romantic in a very twisted and weird way."

"I lo—"

I place my finger on his lips. "Please. Not yet."

When I remove my finger and draw back, he looks into my eyes. "Me not saying the words doesn't make it untrue."

Both of our phones vibrate with a text, but we ignore them.

"All right, let's go through the rules then," he says.

I lean back on his lap and tilt my head. "We don't need rules."

He nods and holds his hands up. "I am not fucking this up this time, so you give me the rules you want to go by, and if we get to the point that I'm allowed to break them, you'll let me know, okay?"

"God no, I'm not your teacher."

"Tedi." There's no humor in his voice. He's serious.

"No more sleeping together." I cringe.

He stares at me blankly. And then he brings his hands back to my hips, picking me up and plopping me next to him. "Then you need to sit over there. And put on some underwear. Actually, go put on a snowsuit or something." He waves his hand as though I should go do exactly that.

"You okay?"

He nods. "Continue."

"No dinners yet. We can do coffee, walks, maybe a lunch."

His mouth drops open. "We can't eat dinner together?"

I shrug. "Okay, no romantic dates. Like, I'm not wearing a dress, we're not making reservations, and you can't get me flowers."

He crosses his arms. "I don't think you can mandate no flowers."

"Fine. You can get me flowers. But I can't promise I'm going to water them."

"That's just being a shitty human being. If I got you a dog, would you not feed the dog?"

"Don't get me a dog, Tweetie," I deadpan because I know this man.

"You're really making this whole wooing process difficult. It's supposed to be enjoyable and make you want to date me."

Our phones vibrate again.

"We don't have to put any rules into action, but I'm being serious. I want to take this slow."

He blows out a breath and puts out his hand. "Fine, Tedi Douglas, I promise to abide by your rules while I try to court you into falling in love with me all over again."

"Dramatic much?"

He wiggles his hand in the air. "Come on. The faster we agree on the terms, the faster I can work my way around your rules."

I have no doubt he will.

I shake his hand, then he pulls me in a bit closer. "Looks like me and you are best buds again."

I playfully push him, and we both laugh.

"Do we have a time limit here?" he asks, and I blow out a

breath. "I'm kidding. But can we at least seal this agreement with a kiss?"

"Sure." I lean forward and kiss him, but he places his hand on the back of my head, keeping me there. I wait for his tongue to slide into my mouth, but he keeps the kiss respectable.

Our phones vibrate again, and we pull apart.

"What the hell?" Tweetie says, both of us leaning over to grab our phones.

We've been added to a group message asking us to go to breakfast.

"Well, thank you, Jade." Tweetie fiddles with his phone. "I just scored your number. Unless that's against the rules. Can I text you, madam?"

"You may text me twice a day," I say in my best version of an English accent.

"I negotiate for at least ten."

I shake my head. "You can text me whenever you want."

My phone vibrates in my hand, and his response in the group pops up with his name.

He peers over to see. "Uh-oh, someone's a little liar. You didn't delete me."

I hold my phone close to my chest. "I needed it for work."

"Bullshit." He gets me on my back, tickling me. After I fall into a fit of giggles, he remains over me. "I'm going to win you back. You know that, right?"

I smile and put my hand on his cheek. "Maybe I'll win you back."

"Babe, you never lost me."

Tears well in my eyes, but I try to push them back. Could we really get to where we need to be? I hope I'm not crazy for believing we can.

"Will you let me take you to breakfast with everyone?" he asks.

"I don't know."

"Hey, you said we could do coffee. I'll starve myself and just drink coffee if that makes you happy. Plus, we'll be in a group. And you'll get to see Rowan's neurotic pancake routine. You don't want to miss that, do you?"

"Fine, but no hand holding, and you have to sit across the table from me."

He holds up his hands. "I'll be on my best behavior."

"Doubtful."

"Come on. Let's go." He gets up and holds out his hand.

This is going to be interesting. I hope I can handle the slow pace. Time will tell.

forty

Tweetie

THE GANG IS MEETING AT THE USUAL BREAKFAST place because Bodhi loves to watch the pancake guy make the pancakes through the window. Plus, they know us now and have a table reserved for us every Sunday. It's become our tradition as long as we don't have a game.

The rideshare stops at the curb, and I'm still in shock that Tedi's with me. But there's one thing we haven't talked about, and that's what we're telling the people inside this restaurant.

So after we climb out, I pull her to the side, out of the foot traffic. "How do you want to play this?"

"And here I thought you were going to kiss me before we went in there." Her back is to the wall, and I'm standing in front of her.

I lean in. "Do you want me to kiss you?"

"That would really give it away when my lip gloss is all over your lips."

"I'd go in there with red lipstick stained on my lips."

She playfully shakes her head. "Okay, well, I have to tell

them about Decker, I suppose. So, why don't we just tell them we're testing the waters?"

I groan. I don't love this whole "let's go slow" thing she's set on, but I get it. I don't like it, but I get it. There is still so much up in the air. My contract. Her job in New York. And all the bullshit drama from the past that we need to work past. So I understand why she wants to tiptoe into this thing. But I'm not idiot enough to let any of that stuff get in our way again. Not a goddamn chance.

Hell, I loved getting her to fall in love with me the first time, so I'm excited to do it all over again. Although I didn't have so many rules to work around the first time, and sex was already on the menu on day one.

"Okay. Testing the waters." I hold up my hands. "No hand holding."

I swear a flash of disappointment lines her face before she steps around me, opening the door to the diner.

"Tweetie," the hostess, Marla, greets me.

I stop, although I know where the gang is. "Hi, Marla, this is Tedi."

Marla purses her lips. "Hi, Tedi. They're in the back."

"Thanks." I move to grab Tedi's hand but stop myself. We start in, and I stop outside the glass window. "This is the pancake man. Bodhi's favorite." I search the area, but he's not one of the kids watching.

"Oh fun." She steps closer. "He does shapes." She points, and I laugh.

"Come on." I lead the way, and she follows. I'm going to have to work on this hand-holding rule. I don't love having her behind me without me guiding her. That, and I just want to keep touching her.

We reach the table, and the usual crew is in attendance, but I tilt my head when I see Easton and Decker there. What the hell?

"Hey, guys," Jade says. "So happy you could make it."

Bodhi climbs off his chair and heads right over to me. "Where have you been? The pancake man already made mine."

I ruffle his hair. "Sorry, I slept in."

The adults at the table laugh.

Tedi makes the rounds, saying hello to everyone, and slides into one of the only two seats left at the table. Conveniently right next to one another at the end, across from Decker and Easton.

"How are you?" Tedi asks Decker.

"I still have my vision." He eyes me. "I see you two have figured things out."

Easton laughs, rocking back on the two rear legs of his chair.

Bodhi runs back over to his seat when Henry tells him he needs to eat. Such a drill sergeant that man.

I stand at the end of the long line of tables. "Let's try not to make a big deal about this, but Tedi and I are..." I look down at her. "What are we doing again?"

"We're taking things slow. Testing the waters."

I nod. "Yeah. That. And we're not saying anything else. So carry on with breakfast."

I sit next to Tedi. I have no idea how I'm not going to put my hand on her leg or around her shoulders. How do I act as if the love of my life didn't just say yes to giving us another chance?

The waitress comes and takes our order.

"So, you move fast," Decker jokes to Tedi, and everyone at the table laughs.

She leans forward. "I'm assuming Decker told you all..."

Kyleigh shakes her head. "Easton was the tattletale. I do have to say, I called it. Right, Eloise?"

Eloise sips her coffee and nods. "Yeah. She called it at the game."

"You knew he was my fake boyfriend?" Tedi asks, sounding surprised.

"I would've done the same thing." Kyleigh kisses Rowan's cheek. "It was either that or Decker was a horrible boyfriend. He never showed you any affection."

Easton laughs again.

"What do you keep laughing at?" I ask him.

"My Grandma Dori would have been so proud of me."

"Explain," Tedi says.

"Decker told me before we ever went to the bar—"

Tedi's head whips in his direction. "Decker! That was our secret."

Decker shrugs. "You know I suck at keeping secrets, and I had to tell someone all the shit I was dealing with."

"My grandma was a notorious meddler and matchmaker. It was actually easier than I thought." Easton looks at the group. "Tweetie was staring at the two of them in the emergency room as if he wished the hot sauce had gotten in his eye so Tedi would kiss his boo boo. I just had to nudge him to consider that maybe they weren't a real couple—or at the very least, that they were having problems. And then in the middle of the waiting area, I thought Tweetie was going to pummel Decker to the floor for breaking Tedi's heart." Easton looks at Tedi. "He was willing to step aside if you were happy. Not every guy would do that." Easton raises his eyebrows and looks at me. "So, you can thank me by giving me your condo."

I laugh, and Tedi looks at me with those eyes again. Soft and warm like in the past when I did something sweet and unexpected. But there's no "I love you" sex coming my way this time. That's okay. She's worth waiting for.

"You want in The Nest?" Rowan asks. He flicks his gaze to

Kyleigh, and something passes between them. I don't like it. As if he's going out just like Henry and Jade.

"No. I don't want to move into The Nest. I want to move into one of your condos."

"No baseball players," Conor mumbles around his food. "Colts don't live in nests."

Easton rolls his eyes. "No shit, dumbass."

"Kid ears," Henry says.

"Sorry," Easton mumbles.

"Maybe you could call it The Barn," Henry says.

"Or The Stables," I add.

"No, The Pen," Rowan says with a laugh.

"Why don't you three move out and we move in?" Decker says.

"Then you'd miss that Mexican restaurant near you. It's so cute." Tedi looks at Decker.

I turn to her. "I thought it was fake?" I wave my finger between the two of them, eyebrows drawing down.

"It's been, what, two minutes, and he's already jealous again. Run, Tedi."

I throw a creamer pouch at Rowan, and he catches it.

"We met there when I asked him to be my fake boyfriend." She smiles at Decker.

"Remind me to talk to you later," I say to him.

Decker rolls his eyes. "Hey, I got so drunk I threw up. I took a puck in the face. And I got hot sauce in my eye. I think I was punished enough."

"No good deed goes unpunished," Easton says.

The whole table laughs.

"You really were a good sport. I would've backed out after the puck thing for sure," Henry says.

Our breakfast arrives, and as Tedi takes a knife and fork to her pancakes, a thought occurs to me. If I don't get another contract with Chicago, mornings like this are all over. It'll be another team and another found family I'll have to leave. Will I be able to handle it? Will I be able to not spiral again? For Tedi, I would, but I'd miss this. I'd miss them.

Tedi puts her hand on my thigh. "Aren't you going to eat?"

I take her hand and put it on her lap. "No touching, remember?"

She shakes her head with a smile and goes back to eating her pancakes, joining in the conversation with my friends as if she's been here since day one.

I finally realize only one thing matters. Wherever I go, Tedi has to be by my side. Everything else is just extra.

So I spend the rest of the breakfast thinking of ways to get us to that finish line.

forty-one

Tedi

THIS IS GOING TO BE SO MUCH HARDER THAN I thought. Especially since I'm around Tweetie the majority of my day since I still have to center the social media campaign around him.

I'm in the airport, waiting to board the plane. We're running behind since there's snow in Philadelphia, and we've been delayed for about an hour.

My brother's name flashes on my phone screen, so I get up and walk away from all the players. "Hey, Toby," I answer.

"Aunt Tedi!"

"Mason? Shouldn't you be getting ready for school?"

"Daddy's making me breakfast. Are you coming here?" The excitement in his voice warms my heart.

I asked if I could stay back one more day to spend it with my family and fly back the day after tomorrow, rather than with the team. Coach Buford said he was fine with whatever. I don't really ask Bud anything if I can avoid it. Thankfully, he never travels with us.

"I'm coming. Just waiting for the weather to clear up by you, then my plane is going to take off."

"Will you come to my school?" he asks.

"Buddy, we talked about this," Toby says in the background.

"I'll try. If this plane takes off, I'm there," I say.

"What about Tweetie?" Mason is in first grade, so he's too young to remember Tweetie and me as a couple, but it's been talked about enough around him that he's aware we had a relationship.

I lean against the wall and search out the man in question. He's sprawled out on one of the seats with his friends, talking and laughing. As if he can feel my gaze on him, he looks up, and our gazes collide. A slow smile tips the corners of his mouth.

Damn, I'm in so much trouble.

I quickly turn my back to him. "Oh, Mason, they have to get to the arena, and then they take a nap and then they play again. I'm sorry."

"After the game! Daddy said we're going, and I can miss school tomorrow."

I hate upsetting him. "They fly out right away. But you have me."

"Oh."

Toby laughs in the background. "Aunt Tedi is way more fun than Tweetie, trust me."

I cringe. I haven't brought my family up to speed on Tweetie, and they probably still hate him. Which would make it uncomfortable if I brought Tweetie to dinner tonight. I can just imagine my two brothers and dad with crossed arms, glaring all night.

"I told all my friends that I knew him and the other Falcons. Kyler said I was lying and said I was making up stories to be cool."

I close my eyes, hating to hear my poor nephew upset. "What's Kyler's last name?" I ask, the protective aunt coming out.

"Tedi," my brother sighs with a warning in his voice.

Whatever.

"Watson," Mason answers like the good kid he is.

I rack my brain for how I can make this up to him. "I'll tell you what. I'll try to get some autographs, okay? And you can show those off."

"Anyone can get autographs."

"Hey, Mason, let's thank Aunt Tedi. That's a big ask. Now eat your breakfast."

"I'm sorry..."

"Hey," Toby gets on the phone. "Don't worry about him. This Kyler is a real asshole. So are his parents."

"I wish I could help, but I don't think my bosses would appreciate me taking the team to a school instead of them resting before their game."

"Don't sweat it. You know he'll be really excited to see you when you come. So..."

"Oh god, I don't want to know." I find a corner to tuck myself into, really hoping my brother isn't about to give me bad news. There's always that so and a long pause right before he tells me something bad.

"Do I have to remind you that you're the older sister? You should be calling me with these things."

"It's not my fault someone messed with our birth order personalities."

It's a running joke that Toby is more like a firstborn and I'm more like the middle child. The only thing that worked out is that Theo is definitely the baby. If only by five minutes.

"Dad's got a girlfriend."

"Oh my god. You scared me. Good for him. What's she like?"

I've wanted my dad to find someone and be happy for years, but he struggled after my mom left. Raised us and spent the rest of his time keeping his business afloat. By the time we were all out of the house, Toby had Mason and needed help with babysitting. Dad's never taken any time for himself.

He blows out a breath. "She's okay. A little overbearing, always trying to give me advice on Mason. Like because I'm a single dad, I don't know what I'm doing. But she seems to make Dad happy. She's an artist."

"Sweet. Is she going to be at dinner?"

A big body presses against me from behind, and I look over my shoulder to see Tweetie. My eyes widen, and I step away, turning around and pushing him out of the small alcove I'm in. He laughs and doesn't allow me to move him. The big brute.

"Nah, Dad told her that you don't like new people."

"He did not!" I keep giving Tweetie the death glare. He just laughs.

"He did. So it sucks for you. You can't meet her."

"I'll change that."

Tweetie tilts his head toward the waiting area and does a plane motion.

"Hey, Toby, we're boarding, so I gotta go. I'll call you when I land and get to the hotel. You're picking me up, right?"

"Of course, I love taking the day off and being your chauffeur."

Tweetie still hasn't left, and I feel as though I'm half in and half out of this conversation with my brother.

"Please tell Mason I'm sorry again. I'll find some way of making it up to him."

Toby says something I don't catch because Tweetie has moved me into a corner, his big body blocking my way. His head is beside my neck as he inhales, then moans.

"What are you doing?" Toby asks.

"Sorry. Gotta go. Love you." I click End and push at Tweetie's chest.

He chuckles, stepping back a bit. "Hey, you never said I couldn't smell you."

"You're a beast."

A wicked grin crosses his face. "One kiss." He holds up his finger.

"Do I need to remind you of all the people out there? One being your coach, who I don't think would be too happy about me screwing one of his players. Oh my god, I just realized I'm actually everything I was afraid to hire. I've done exactly what I tell all my employees not to do."

"They'll understand." He inhales again and sighs. "I'm irresistible. You didn't stand a chance."

I shake my head, but I can't fight the smile on my face. God, this man. "You're sitting with your friends on the plane."

His eyebrows draw down, and he pouts. "Nope. We have social media things to talk about."

"No, we don't." I push him, and he stumbles back, still laughing.

"Half the trip I sit with you," he says, but I shake my head. "Counteroffer?" he whispers in my ear and steps in line with me as I walk us back into the terminal.

"You have fifteen minutes, and we use it to discuss an idea I have."

His head falls back. "I'll take what I can get. So... who is Mason, and why are you sorry?"

It's a reminder that although I feel as if no time has passed between us, it has. He doesn't even know that Toby had a kid.

"Mason is my nephew. Toby's son."

He blinks a couple times, seeming to realize the same thing I just did. "And you're sorry for?"

"I don't want to tell you because if I do, you're going to

try to make something work." I eye him. "Mostly to get in my pants."

"Hey now, I've been respectable. Now what is it?"

"Nothing, but do you think you and maybe the rest of the Trifecta and Conor could sign some merch when we get to the hotel?"

He quirks his eyebrow and nods. "Of course. For Mason?"

I nod, not about to tell him about the little shit named Kyler who made my hit list a few minutes ago.

"No problem. The guys won't care either. Mason will be at the game tonight, right?"

I nod and grab my bag, seeing the players lining up to get on the plane.

Tweetie walks over to his bag, and we fall in line as we walk toward the gate. I really hope people assume we're talking business, because I don't want news about us to get out until I can tell my boss, which I'm not about to do until I'm certain I'm prepared to give up this opportunity for Tweetie.

His hand falls to my lower back, and I circle around and give him a death glare, earning a laugh as always.

I don't have it in me to complain about how much he wants to touch me, and he's crazy if he thinks it's not just as hard for me not to take him into that bathroom and fuck his brains out.

forty-two

Tweetie

I WATCH TEDI GO TO HER USUAL SEAT ON THE PLANE as I plop down in mine. All three of my friends look at me. "What?"

They all laugh. "It's good to see you smiling again."

I nod, pulling out my phone and hoping that I get this handled before the plane takes off and I have to put it on Airplane Mode. Searching through my contacts, I find the right Toby. How do I know four Tobys? I really need to learn to put last names in my contact records.

Hey Toby, it's Tweetie.

The three dots appear, and I really hope it's not someone saying, "Toby who?" because he's changed his number.

I know.

He's just as much of a smartass as his sister.

I didn't know if you'd still have my number stored.

I debated, but lucky for you, you're a professional hockey player.

Thanks?

Tell me you're not texting me to ask for my sister's hand in marriage. Did my dad not respond or something?

"Who are you texting?" Rowan asks from across the aisle.

I glance at the window, seeing our plane is being de-iced again. Love flying in the fucking winter.

Why would you think that?

Because you two are demented, and now that she's with the Falcons, I'm sure you're going to give it a go again. Please tell me I'm wrong.

I think you should hear it from Tedi.

Don't make me have to kick your ass.

If I hurt her, you get five good shots.

Deal. But really...

I'll meet you today if you want to talk face-to-face. But I'm on limited time here. You have a son, huh?

You're on a time crunch but you want to know about my son and how I'm a single dad??

So he and Carrie didn't work out. I can't say I'm surprised.

She was so bossy and pushy. Their entire wedding, all she did was drag him around. He deserved better.

> Mason, right? What did he ask Tedi to do today?

The three dots appear, disappear, and appear again before disappearing again. I look out the window to clock how much time I might have.

"Seriously. Who are you texting? Because I can see her, and she's reading a book or something." Rowan glares at me as if I really would be messaging another woman.

I'm insulted until I realize that these guys have never seen me with Tedi. They've only seen the version of me after Tedi, when I tried to forget what it was like to be with the woman I loved. The guy who couldn't breathe without her. I'll prove it to them in time.

> Why do I feel as if we're both going to be put in a headlock?

> Stop with the dramatic childhood stories. What does Mason want?

> There's a boy at school...

> Toby...

> He told the kid he knew you, and the kid was a dick about it and told everyone Mason was lying. He asked Tedi if you could come to his school to prove him wrong. But he's fine. I'm about to get in the car to drive him to school. No worries. All good.

As much as I appreciate Tedi not committing me to something without asking, I was already upset that I couldn't stay with them for dinner tonight because I had to fly back with the team.

> Can I have Mason's school and address?

Tedi will strangle me if you guys lose your game.

> I'm not going to lose. Hello, it's me.

I can just see Toby rocking his head back in agony, wondering how he gets out of this and wishing we never exchanged phone numbers all those years ago.

> Still afraid of your older sister?

Laredo Grade School, 5874 Washington Street. Text me on your way, and I'll meet you.

> You'll be my favorite brother-in-law.

I see things haven't changed. Still driving in the fast lane.

I won't bore him with details of how his sister has put the brakes on us for a while.

The plane pulls back from the terminal.

> See you soon. Plane is taking off.

If the plane goes down, save my sister.

> I'll put on her oxygen mask before my own.

How sweet.

> Don't be jealous, you'll find your person soon.

(Gif with the middle finger)

I click my phone off and shove it in my pocket, noticing three pairs of eyes on me.

"What?" I sigh.

They all tilt their heads. As the plane's engines roar, I lean in and ask them to do me a really big solid, to which they all agree because they're my best friends and want me to win the girl.

I hate the ache that nestles into my chest that next year at this time, I probably won't be with them.

forty-three

Tedi

I STAND IN THE ENTRYWAY OF THE HOTEL, CHECKING my watch for the time. Where is Toby?

Suddenly, a huge pickup truck comes flying into the roundabout and skids to a stop. Seriously?

Theo honks the horn instead of getting out of his truck and greeting me, the man-child he is.

I walk out of the sliding doors and open the passenger door of his truck. "Why are you here?"

Theo smiles, his beard unkempt, his beanie covering what I'm sure is a mop of dark hair that's equally as messy as his beard. He smiles wide, and for a moment, I forgive him for never finding it within himself to grow up.

"Is that any way to say hello to your baby brother?" He pushes fast food bags out of the way onto the floor of the truck.

I grunt, put my bag on the seat, and accumulate the variety of fast food bags before going over to the trash and tossing them in. Then I grab my bag filled with the Falcons merchandise I was able to scrounge up in the small amount of time I had, climb up using the step, and sit my ass in what I assume is a filthy seat.

"Stop with the judgment. I just got it cleaned last week."

I look behind me in the back seat of the quad cab, see all the blueprints, and raise my eyebrows. There's crap everywhere. Before I have time to respond, he throws it in drive and peels away.

"Theo, do I have to remind you that there are people I work with at that hotel? And please tell me where Toby is?" Toby would have had his heated seats on for me. It would have smelled nice in his vehicle, and the mats would've been vacuumed.

"I'm offended." He turns the truck, and soon we're on the highway.

"You're taking me to Mason's school, right?"

"Those were my orders." He sits back in his seat, resting his hand on the lower part of the steering wheel, not concerned at all that the roads are shitty from the aftermath of a snowstorm.

From what the news says, another storm is headed this way. Not sure why we're putting our lives in jeopardy for a non-conference game.

"How have you been?" I ask.

"Not as good as you apparently." He glances over and waggles his eyebrows.

"What are you talking about?"

"Oh, nothing. You know I'm always kept in the dark. Except for this time." He waggles his eyebrows again.

"Theo!"

He laughs, putting his hand on my leg. "Loosen up. You're about to see our nephew."

"How is he?"

Theo's head moves side to side. "As good as can be

expected. I think we all know how he's feeling. We've been there." Theo's joking, always-ready-for-a-good-time personality sobers because he's right. We all know what it's like when your mom doesn't want you.

Toby's wife, Carrie, decided last year that she didn't want to be married or be a full-time mother. She gave Toby full custody, and she occasionally comes to visit. It's more than we ever got, and I'm on the fence over which one is easier. When your mom just disappears or when she sometimes has a hankering to see you to ease her guilty conscience, then disappears again.

"Did you hear Dad's getting laid again? It's really taken the grumpy old man out of him."

"Yeah, I messaged him that I want him to bring her to dinner."

"I guess I'm going to be Toby's favorite sibling again." Theo grins.

I check my phone because I thought Tweetie said he would call me when they were done with their morning skate, and I wonder if it went long. This is the problem. I already want just fifteen minutes alone with him before he goes to the game, and we're separated until I get back to Chicago.

"Toby said she's kind of overbearing?" Theo will give me all the dirt that Toby doesn't want to spread.

"She tries to mother Mason like she's already his grandmother. Toby's not having it. It's really funny to watch, though."

I frown because I want my dad to find someone who fits into our family, but maybe that's hopeful thinking. If he's happy, we need to stay out of it.

"Shit." He looks at his blind spot, checks his mirrors, and drives across three lanes to the exit. When he rushes toward the light at the end of the exit ramp and makes a hurried left, the blueprints on his dash all shift to the right and onto my lap.

"Theo!" I shout like I always have at him. I toss the blueprints back on his dash.

"I've been on autopilot at this job site lately. The man is driving me fucking insane. We'll decide on one thing, then he sees something online and wants to change it. I mean, he's paying for it, but he doesn't understand that every tweak has consequences."

I smile at my brother because he may always have a dirty car and probably an equally dirty house, but he is meticulous in his architectural designs.

He stops at a light, taking his hands off the wheel and digging into his center console for something. "So, we're ignoring the fact that you're working with JD?"

I blow out a breath. "I'm not discussing it with you."

"Okay, buzzkill."

"All right, let's talk about your women. Who's in your bed currently, Theo?" I cross my arms and raise my eyebrows at him, waiting.

"You know I don't kiss and tell." He pulls out a pack of gum and offers me a piece. I take one.

"Neither do I."

"So there's something to tell?" The light turns green, and again, my back slams into the back seat before he turns left.

"I didn't say that."

"You implied it."

"Okay, I'm done talking now, Theo."

"Jeez, nice big sister you are."

Thankfully, it's only two more minutes before he's pulling down a street, and we stop in front of the school we all attended when we were younger. Toby's not one for change, so of course he moved into the same district we lived in, only a mile away from our childhood home. Theo parks in the lot.

"You're coming?" I ask.

"I wouldn't miss this."

I scrunch my eyebrows, but whatever. I'm sure all the ladies in the front office will love seeing Theo Douglas again. The class clown who grew up to own an architectural firm with his brother.

I walk fast to the doors while Theo saunters behind me. It's freezing, and the snow is still coming down slow and steady. When we get in the doors, I shake the flakes out of my hair and off my coat. Theo rings the buzzer to get access through the next set of doors. He waves, and the door unlocks.

"Still sweet-talking the ladies, huh?" I laugh.

"Theo," Donna coos, standing and rounding the desk. "Toby's here, and I heard you were coming. Tedi!" She wraps us both in her arms. "How are you?"

We let her hug us, then she steps back.

"Oh, the Douglas kids." She gives us a soft smile.

This is what happens when you're the kids whose mom left them. Every staff member gives you extras, whether it's attention or cookies in the lunch line. They're doing it to be sweet, but it's just a constant reminder, honestly.

"You guys look good." She tugs on Theo's beard. "Except this. Shave."

Theo runs his hand down his full dark beard. "The ladies love it, Donna."

She rolls her eyes. "Always the ladies' man. Remember in the fourth grade when you and Foster Davis got in that fight over Carly Jacobs?"

Theo nods. How does Donna remember these things?

The sound of kids screaming draws our attention away from Donna.

"Is there an assembly or something?" I ask.

She smiles. "You don't know? I thought you were behind it."

I stare at my little bag with maybe enough merch for Mason's class. Please tell me that Mason didn't overpromise.

Donna rounds the desk. "Let me get you passes, then you can head on down. Tammy is supposed to come back and replace me, so I'll see you in there. So exciting, right?"

"Can't wait." Theo gives me a look I can't quite decipher.

"I'm sorry, Donna, but who is in the gym?" I lean forward as though it's a secret, when really, it seems as though maybe it's just a secret from me.

Theo swings his arm around my shoulders. "Shh... Donna, let it be a surprise."

Of course, Donna pretends to zip her lips and throw away the key. Seriously?

She hands us our passes, and Theo leads me down the hall. I think I would remember my way, and if I didn't, the kids cheering and yelling would have drawn me in the right direction.

We pass an entire case filled with Decker and Foster Davis accolades. I guess that's what happens when you play pro somewhere—your childhood school showcases you.

"Theo, what am I missing?"

"If I ruin this, I'm not gonna get out of this school without being beaten to a pulp, so humor me and just go to the gym." Theo continues leading while I drag my feet because I'm pretty sure Mason told someone I was coming, and everyone is going to assume all the Falcons will be joining me.

We're a few steps outside the gymnasium when Theo laughs, nudging me by the back to go first. I step into the elementary gym, so much more grown than the last time I was here, and I hear his voice before I see him.

My smile grows the farther I walk in until it probably takes up my entire face.

There in front of all the students are Tweetie, Rowan, Conor, and Henry. Mason is standing up there with them.

Theo pats me on the back and leans his shoulder against the wall, watching the tears well in my eyes.

"And the entire reason we're here is because Mason has a really cool aunt who does our social media." Tweetie taps Mason on the shoulder and points at me.

Mason sprints over, and I crouch, hugging him tightly. Tweetie's smile is just as big as mine. I mouth thank you over Mason's shoulder.

"You did it! Thank you, Aunt Tedi." He squeezes his arms around my neck. "I gotta go." Then he's off and back with the guys in the middle of the gym.

Tweetie gets back on the microphone. "We'll take some questions. Unfortunately, we weren't able to get merch here, but we've ordered T-shirts for everyone that will be delivered next week."

The kids cheer as Toby comes over and stands next to me. I must look like a blubbering fool. Why is this making me cry? I never would've asked Tweetie to do this, and here he is with his three best friends from the team, making my nephew king for the day.

"You just became the aunt of the century," Toby says.

"I can't believe he came."

Toby and Theo both give me a look, and Toby says, "Yeah, you can."

And he's right. Because even with all the bad that's happened with us, this is the Tweetie I fell in love with. The man who would do anything to make me happy.

forty-four

Tweetie

THANK THE UNIVERSE FOR SMALL FAVORS. IT'S AS though all the powers are on my side to win Tedi back.

We didn't get to play our non-conference game since the weather was so shitty and Philly couldn't get out of Toronto from their game the night before. The snowstorm is keeping us here for another night, so when Tedi suggested Rowan, Conor, Henry, and I come to her dad's house for dinner, she didn't have to ask me twice. It just sucked that the other three came with me. I wouldn't have minded the time alone with her.

We arrive at Tedi's childhood home with her since she waited for us while the rest of her family came back here. It's a three-bedroom ranch that's modest and well-kept. It sits on a nice piece of land. I haven't been here in years, and I really hope her dad is okay with me coming.

Tedi opens the door. "Hello!" she calls into the house.

"Hi!" Mason emerges from the kitchen area. He skids to a

stop and waves at the group of us. Tedi swoops him up, and he wiggles to get free. "Snow!"

He laughs as she shakes her hair, and all the flakes land on his face. She gives him a big kiss on the cheek and releases him.

"Do you want to see my daddy's old room?" he asks us guys.

"Let me introduce them first, then they're all yours." Tedi runs her fingers through Mason's hair, and I find myself admiring the way she is with him.

It's been a while since I've seen her with kids. She's probably like an aunt to Aiden and Saige's girls now. The thought that I missed seeing that happen makes my chest squeeze.

We all take off our shoes and coats in the entryway.

Tedi leads us through the family room and into the kitchen, where her dad and the woman I suspect is the new girlfriend are cooking. There's a pot of sauce on the stove and some pasta boiling. It's been a minute since I've had a home-cooked meal like this. Toby and Theo are at the table, each with a beer in hand.

"Okay, you guys already know Toby and Theo…"

Her dad looks over and doesn't smile. Great. I figured there would be some work to do here. I practiced my speech on Conor earlier in the hotel room.

"This is my dad, Derin." She puts her arm through her dad's and rests her cheek on his shoulder just like she used to do with me. Then she kisses his cheek, and he smiles for the first time.

"Rhonda, this is my daughter, Tedi."

Rhonda turns from the stove to face Tedi. I'm not sure how I would feel if my mom ever had a boyfriend. She's gone on dates, but no one seems to stick longer than a few months. Since I'm rarely home, I only hear about them from Georgia.

"Hi, Rhonda." Tedi puts her hand out with a welcoming smile.

"Sorry, dear." She shows Tedi how her hands have hot pads on them.

Tedi pulls back her hand, and her shoulders slump, which makes me hate Rhonda.

"Dad, you remember Tweetie." Tedi recovers quickly, she's dragging her dad across the kitchen by his arm.

"Yes, hello, JD" He puts his hand out, and I swear Conor coughs out a laugh.

"Thanks for having us, sir."

"You can still call me Derin."

I nod and don't say anything else, but Tedi's already moving him toward the others. She introduces him, and they're all polite and thank him for having them.

"What can I do to help?" I ask after all the introductions are over.

"Oh, that's not how Rhonda rolls." Theo tips his beer at me and takes a sip.

"I'll get you guys a drink. We've got beer, water..." Toby stands, and Tedi walks by me to join him in the garage to get the drinks.

I keep my feet cemented to the kitchen floor, so I don't tell Toby to forget it, I'll go with Tedi. The last time I came here, my tongue was down her throat before the door shut. What I wouldn't do for that to happen now.

Two small hands grab mine. "Come on. I want to show you my daddy's room," Mason whines.

"Go ahead, we have a few minutes before dinner's ready," Rhonda says.

I had plans on talking to Derin to let him know that his daughter is in good hands with me. That I'm not that guy I was when we broke up. But I allow Mason to drag me down the hall, and he stops me in the doorway of what I guess was Theo and Toby's bedroom as kids. There are two twin beds and a million trophies—mostly from hockey by the looks of it. Two dressers and two desks.

"My daddy played hockey too." He picks up a trophy and brings it to me.

"Want to see my room?" Tedi whispers behind me, winding her arm around my waist and holding a beer in front of me.

Mason takes the trophy and goes back over, stretching on his tiptoes to reach another one. "I'm gonna play this year."

I feel like a bad guy for not following his every word, but Tedi is distracting me with her tits pressed against my back.

"I hope you love it," I say.

"I'm gonna go show Rowan this one." He moves to slide by me in the doorway. "Excuse me."

Then Mason is gone. What would it be like to have that much energy?

Tedi takes me by the hand and leads me down the hallway.

"I thought hand holding wasn't approved?"

She looks over her shoulder but doesn't say anything. I step into her childhood room that's half gym, half bedroom. Last time I was here, it was still her room, and we slept in the bed together. Derin was a pretty chill guy, but I'm not taking my chances now. I stop, releasing her hand and placing my palms on the doorframe.

She turns around. "What are you doing?"

I look down the hall. "I'm not going in there."

She crooks her finger, and fuck, how much willpower does she think I possess?

I shake my head, and she tilts hers, teasing me. "I was going to loosen up a rule. I thought maybe a kiss in my old bedroom where I used to dream of kissing a hot hockey player."

"You fulfilled that dream years ago." I push back into the hallway, away from temptation.

"I'm starting to second-guess how much you want me." She tries to saunter past me, but I hook my arm around her waist and tug her to my chest before she can walk down the hall.

"If you said yes, I'd take you to that garage, make you place your hands on the wall, and sink into you," I say, and she giggles. "I'm trying to be respectful, and I need to talk to your dad before I leave here."

She circles out of my arms. "No, you don't."

"Yes, I do. I want him to know that I'm serious and I'm not going to hurt you again."

She inhales and studies me for at least a minute. "Tweetie."

"Jeez, lovebirds, get your asses in here for dinner," Theo shouts down the hall.

"You swore. You owe me a dollar," Mason says.

"Come on, let's just eat." She walks in front of me.

I'm not going to lie, all I can watch is her ass shift side to side as she walks. We get back into the kitchen, and Tedi might miss the way her dad is giving me the evil eye, but I'm not.

The table is set, and we all sit down to eat. Mason carries most of the conversation, consisting mostly of questions about hockey. We hear about Kyler Watkins and the bully he is to Mason. I think Kyler might get a visit from Tedi before we fly out tomorrow.

Rhonda doesn't say much, but when she does, it's to Mason about wiping his face or to stop talking while he's chewing, making Toby go more and more rigid in his seat.

Derin's head is down, focused on his plate almost the entire meal.

By the time dinner is over, the guys say they'll clean up, and Rhonda tries to tell them the steps to do it in and where things are. Toby's jaw clenches, and Theo laughs. So opposite those two. Because the guys are helping with clean-up duty, Mason is suddenly interested too.

I take my opportunity and approach Derin. "Do you have a minute to talk?"

He glances at Tedi behind me, then sighs. "Sure. I need a fresh beer anyway. Come on."

I follow him toward the garage door, and Tedi squeezes my hand when I pass her on the way.

Once the door shuts, Derin crosses his arms and stands in front of me. I'm taller by a head, but he's intimidating as all hell. "I'm doing this to appease my daughter, but I'm going to be honest, I don't like you."

I guess I have a lot more work than I thought.

forty-five

Tweetie

WHAT WAS THE SPEECH I PRACTICED WITH CONOR again? I can't remember a fucking word of it. "First, let me apologize. When we broke up, I was lost. It's no excuse because Tedi should've come first, but I took her for granted. I'm sorry. I know you trusted me with her, and I failed you both."

"I don't give a shit about me, JD."

I wince at the initials. It only makes me feel like my dad's genes did trickle down to me.

"You won't understand how I felt hearing the pain in her voice until you have a child of your own. Feeling as if you're to blame because you welcomed the man into your life, told your daughter he's a good one. You know what she's been through with her mom. Now..."

I open my mouth to respond, but he holds up his hand.

"I also understand I'm not in that relationship. That I'm an outsider and biased that my daughter is perfect. She's a grown adult. She can make her mistakes, and all I can do is be here to pick up the mess you leave. I picked it up once, and I don't want to pick it up again." He gives me a stern glare.

"I understand. And I know I could stand here and make promises and tell you I'm different. But those are empty words, so I'll prove it to you. Know that she's safe in my hands."

He stares at me, then turns and goes to the fridge. "You want one?" He holds up a beer.

"Sure." As if I would say no.

He gets one himself and pulls over a step stool, sitting on it. A few minutes of silence fills the cool room until he speaks again. "You seem to make her happy. Well, you do make her happy. I picked the wrong person once upon a time, and my kids got hurt from it. So, I'm always really protective of them. Hell, I'm about to break up with Rhonda if she says one more thing to Mason. Jesus Christ, woman." He shakes his head.

I bite my lip to not laugh. He's right. Give the kid a break. Toby's going to lose it at some point on her, and there'll be another host of problems.

"All that to say, I wanted to come out here and be a hardass, but I have a soft spot for my kids and what makes them happy. I heard what you did for Mason today. That Kyler is a real shithead and so are his parents. Thank you for going even though Tedi never asked you. You were always good to her, until you... well, I can understand when life keeps knocking you down. She had her own demons to conquer too."

"I wanted to conquer them for her."

He laughs before sipping his beer. "Do you know her at all?"

I chuckle and take a pull from the bottle.

"Something keeps bringing you two together, but you guys keep getting in the way of it. Tedi says you're taking things slow. I think that's a good idea, but I don't trust that it's going to happen. Maybe you two prove me wrong. No matter what, I'm giving you a pass here. Don't make me regret it." He tips his beer back again.

"I won't. You'll be dancing at our twenty-fifth wedding anniversary."

He chuckles. "God willing. You always did make me laugh."

He stands from the step stool, and I hold out my hand in front of him. "I'm really sorry for ever putting you in that position."

His hand slides in mine with a firm handshake. "I appreciate it. Now, I rarely see my daughter, so let's go enjoy the night." He puts his hand on my shoulder and squeezes.

"Can I ask you a favor, Derin?"

"Favors already? Jeez, kid. You're taking my precious daughter, what do you want now?" He chuckles.

"Would you mind calling me Tweetie? JD is just..." I'm not sure if Tedi's ever shared my past with him, but I really don't like anyone but my mom and sister calling me that, and only because it would be weird for them to call me by my hockey name.

He gives me a quick nod. "Sure."

"Thanks."

"Now when you go in there, I'd appreciate a few tears and cover your eye like I hit you." I'm not sure of the look I give him, but he laughs. "I'm kidding. Jeez, Tedi must run circles around you."

We go into the house, and Tedi's at the table with Mason and what looks like homework. She eyes me, then her dad.

"Well, his nuts are still intact, so maybe you'll have a cousin after all, Mason," Theo says from the couch.

"Cousin? I want a cousin!" Mason eyes Tedi's stomach.

She picks up a pencil and throws it at her brother. "That's how rumors start."

An hour later, Rowan, Conor, and Henry leave in an Uber, leaving me with the rental car. Toby and Mason leave soon after, much to Mason's displeasure. Theo sees Rhonda out and cleans off her car. Tedi and I stay for another two hours, talking with her dad.

When he gets up to go to the bathroom, I turn to her. "I want to give you some time alone with your dad, but I don't want you to go to the hotel by yourself."

She shakes her head. "I'm kind of beat from the early morning flight. You must be too."

I stretch because she's right. I'm exhausted.

Her dad returns. "I was about to kick you two out. You're young, you shouldn't be hanging out with an old man." He doesn't sit but remains standing and opens his arms.

Tedi stands and hugs him tightly. "Come visit me once in a while."

He kisses her cheek. "I will. It's just so busy." When I walk over and put my hand out, Derin shakes it. "It was nice seeing you again, Tweetie."

Tedi looks over her shoulder at me.

"Oh, get the hell out of my house." Derin shoos us with his hand.

We get our shoes and coats on and say one last goodbye.

The ride back to the hotel is uneventful except for the side streets the plows haven't gotten to yet. By the time I park the rental, drop the keys off at the front desk, and walk Tedi up to her room, I wish we were past this slow pace so I could crawl into bed with her. I miss the days when she'd come to games with Saige and I'd spend the night in her room.

"Thanks for everything today," she says with her back to the wall right by her door.

I step closer and rest my arm on the wall above her head. "You never have to thank me."

"I appreciate it. All of it."

"I know."

"And my dad? How was that?"

I lift one shoulder. "We're good."

She smiles and doesn't ask me any more questions because she knows I'm not going to tell her.

"Good night, Tedi." But I still don't move.

"Okay, one kiss won't kill us." She glances down either end of the hall, then grabs my jacket and tugs me to her, crashing her lips against mine.

Fuck yes.

I place my free hand on her hip, bringing her flush to me, my tongue diving in and seeking hers. She meets me with the same intensity. If she'd let me, I'd take her right here. Our mouths are hungry and unapologetic, taking what we want from the other. A voice whispers that if I don't do what she wants and take this slow, we'll never get to where I want us to be, so I reluctantly close the kiss. She whimpers but presses her back to the wall, touching her lips.

"Good night, Tedi." I step back. "Get into your room and lock up."

She looks as if she wants to second-guess her decision, as though she wants me to go into that room with her.

"I know, babe, but we're playing this the right way this time."

She smiles and places her keycard over the lock. "Sweet dreams, Tweetie."

"Oh, they'll be filthy, not sweet."

She laughs, and I wait for her door to shut before I head to the elevator, really wishing Conor wasn't sharing my room with me. I need to get rid of this pent-up sexual energy, and there is not a chance I'm jerking off when he's only one thin wall away.

forty-six

Tedi's Journal Entry
Present day
Philadelphia

To my older self,

We are so weak, Tedi! We so would have caved tonight after one hot kiss outside the hotel room. And the fact that Tweetie was the one who pulled back, reminding me that we need to take this slow if we're ever going to get where we want to be, only made it harder not to say screw it and drag him into my hotel room.
Patience.
Patience is all we need so we can have a lifetime with him.

Hopefully, he's the one next to you in bed when you reread this someday.

Hopefully, he's the one next to you in bed when you reread this someday.

forty-seven

Tweetie's Journal Entry
Present Day
Philadelphia

To my teenage self,

I'm so fucking proud of us, man. We walked away and did the right thing where Tedi is concerned for once in our fucking life. I just hope I can keep making us proud. This time, I promise you, I won't ruin our chance. We will get that happily ever after. You can count on me.

forty-eight

Tedi

I'M AT THE FALCONS PRACTICE. AGAIN, FLETCHER IS with me, getting some pictures and footage for me to use. I've decided to do an angle on Tweetie that highlights him as a leader and a captain on the team. So we're grabbing images of him with different teammates throughout practice. We get some pictures of him offering advice to Alvin, who is the left wing on the second line, along with a few of the other guys.

So many young kids look up to Tweetie, like my nephew, that I think it's important to showcase how he got this far in the league. Next week we're going to highlight his workouts. I pushed that one off a week because I'm not sure I can sit in a sweaty gym and watch him lift weights and train without me asking him to stretch out his hip flexors on me.

"Tedi, it's been a minute." Bud comes up behind me, and Fletcher lowers the camera, eyeing me.

Great. This is the last thing I want to deal with.

"It's come to my attention that Tweetie and some of the

others went to your nephew's school while they were in Philadelphia."

"Yes, it was spur of the moment." I force myself to smile.

He sits on the bench behind me, and I'd rather not have my ass in his face, so I step to the side and sit a little ways down from him.

"Good thing the game didn't happen. My starting line out doing press when they should be napping." Bud clucks his tongue.

I stare at the ice, not wanting to look at him for fear I'll say what I'm really thinking. My gaze catches Tweetie's, and he shifts his attention over to Bud, who's next to me.

I don't really know how to answer Bud. I want to say he's not really in charge of what they do during those hours between morning skate and the games. It's a bit of a gray area. They're grown adults, and he's not their mother. But I like my job and my paycheck more.

"They could have still napped. They weren't there long."

He stretches his arms out along the back of the bench and his fingers are too close to me, so I slyly inch over a little more. "How come there wasn't anything on our socials about it? Seems that would be a good way to promote the team, visiting a school." He clicks his tongue off the roof of his mouth again. "Oh yeah, it was at a Philadelphia school, not a Chicago one. And you weren't prepared, but I did okay a big box of T-shirts to be sent there. T-shirts that parents will probably throw away since they're for another team, not their hometown team."

I inhale, pushing back my snippy reply. "Regardless of the school, it was a nice thing to do. And I'm sorry about the whole spur-of-the-moment thing. They did a favor for me, and I take full responsibility for it."

"Is there anything I should know?" Bud asks, and my body tenses.

Tweetie starts to skate over, but I try to give him a look that says not now.

"Regarding?" I turn to face Bud, staring him in the eye to show him I'm not afraid. Even if my insides are clenching in concern that he's found out about Tweetie and me.

It's going to be inevitable that he finds out if this continues with us. I haven't investigated the rules and whether I can even have a relationship with a player, but at a minimum, it would be frowned upon. It's not lost on me that I'm doing the one thing I wanted to make sure the people who work under me didn't.

"It's nice that you've become friends with that whole group. How is Decker, by the way?"

"Good." It comes out as an automatic response when I probably could have just said we broke up.

"He's a quiet one, huh?"

Not the Decker I know.

I shrug. "I've known him most of my life, so not around me he's not."

Bud looks at the ice, where a drill's going on, but Tweetie's gaze keeps lingering on us. Fletcher distracts himself from our conversation and takes pictures again.

"So different from a guy like Tweetie." Bud turns to me, tilting his head.

Something inside me says he knows. He might not know everything, because Bud doesn't seem like someone who plays games, but maybe he knows about our past.

"Yes, they are very different."

He chuckles and stands. "Next time, Tedi, don't have the players do your personal favors on my time. I'd hate to make a call to the national office again. I like you."

My jaw clenches, and I watch him go, wanting to chase him, jump on his back, and pull out all those stupid hair implants.

"He's an ass, Tedi," Fletcher says. "Ignore him."

I nod and stand to go back to the job I've been hired to do by the national league and *not* Bud Caldron.

"Bud!" Tweetie calls, and Bud stops right before he's about to go to the tunnel.

"No, no, no." I don't even realize I'm talking out loud until Fletcher glances at me.

Tweetie says something to Bud. The conversation is short, but Tweetie's good humor isn't part of it, that much is clear. Bud looks in my direction and raises his eyebrows right before he walks through the tunnel.

I might as well call Mr. Herington myself.

forty-nine

Tweetie

AFTER PRACTICE IS DONE, I SKATE OVER TO TEDI TO find out exactly what Bud said to her. I saw her face, the way she paled and tried not to make eye contact with him. I'm sure it had something to do with Mason's school visit. I've been tagged in a lot of photos from parents and the school itself about it.

When he finally walked away and she rose to go back to Fletcher, I took my opportunity to make sure Bud knew the school visit was my idea and thanked him for signing off on the T-shirts for the school.

"How are the pictures, Fletch?" I ask, giving him a fist-bump. "You're welcome for having such a beautiful face that you don't have to do much editing."

Fletcher laughs and shakes his head. "Come on by when you're done," he says to Tedi, eyeing me.

"Walk with me?" I ask and skate along the boards until I get to the opening.

I deny myself the urge to touch her. To place my hand on

the small of her back to help her on the ice or lean in to kiss her on the nape of her neck.

"What did he say?" I ask.

She sighs. "You can't be my protector. Not here."

The rest of the team is already in the locker room, so we have a little privacy to at least talk.

"It's instinctual. I know you're all badass and can take care of yourself, but I'm an alpha, babe, you know that."

She rolls her eyes, but a smile still plays at her lips. One of my favorite expressions on her. "I think he suspects or knows about our past. He wasn't happy about the visit to the school. But whatever, I can handle him." She looks down the hallway. "But, Tweetie, I'm not ready to out us here. There are repercussions for me that I have to consider."

I understand it would be far worse for her than me. Decisions will have to be made.

"Do we know the rules?" I ask, hoping she's already looked them up.

She shakes her head. "No. I'm not sure how to call HR and be like, 'Hey, if I fall in love with one of these hockey guys, what's my chance of keeping my job?'"

"One, I'm not just one of these hockey guys, and two, if you fall in love?" I step an inch closer, my skates making me so much taller than her now.

"I would like to at least show them how successful I can make this program before I cause problems. Bud is sniffing around, and I wouldn't be surprised if he's asked some people—"

"We're getting ahead of ourselves. So far, we aren't even a couple."

"But we've already—"

"No one knows that." I look around to make sure we're still alone. "Only you and I were there that night."

I can't wait for so many more nights just like that with

her. I can't wait until we share the same home, the same bedroom. When we're back to being his and hers. But I also know how important her job is to her, and I'd never want to be the reason she loses that. Decisions will have to be made, but it'd be great if we could delay them until after this season, until after we're official and have some time under our belt.

"I know I'm getting ahead of myself." She leans her back against the wall, staring at the floor.

"I really want to hold you right now," I whisper.

Her gaze lifts to meet mine, and I hate seeing the pain there. "I want you to hold me."

She lowers her arms, and I take the opportunity to graze her fingers with mine. It would be easy to retreat if anyone came out. "Come home with me. Take a nap with me."

"That's not exactly going to keep me in the good graces of Bud Caldron. I need to work here. Make you look all alpha and leaderly."

"Man, your job is easy." I laugh, and a door opens down the hall.

Both of us glance to see who might be coming, but no one does.

"Hey, um..."

Her eyes narrow when she hears the hesitance in my voice.

"My mom and Georgia are coming to the game tonight." I cringe.

She smacks me in the stomach. "Why didn't you tell me sooner?"

"I forgot. It's been planned for a while, and you distract me. My mom called me this morning to tell me when they're flying in and where they're staying. But they'll be seated right by you, and I wanted to warn you before you... I'm assuming you're going to the game tonight, right?"

She laughs. "Do you want me to come to your game?"

"Since you started going, I've had some pretty awesome games."

"And that's the only reason? Because it makes you play better?" Her eyebrows lift.

I inch closer, my fingers running down the length of hers. "No." I shake my head. "It's more selfish than that."

She tilts her head.

"It calms me when you're there," I say.

"Why?"

My fingers tighten around hers and the side of my body leans into hers. "Because seeing you in the stands reminds me that the best thing in my life isn't the game—it's you."

"Tweetie!" She pushes me with her free hand, and I stumble back until I catch myself.

"What?" I hold up my hands.

"You can't say stuff like that. Not yet."

I wish no one was around so I could grab her hand and tug her into my chest and tell her we can take this slow, but it's the truth. After she was no longer in the stands, I'd find myself looking to where she used to sit, and I realized I'd thought hockey was my number one, but it turned out it was my number two. I'd sacrificed my first love for my second. I was just too dense to see it.

"Sorry?" My tone suggests I'm anything but.

She narrows her eyes. "Go shower and sleep. I have to go get this handled with Fletcher." She shakes her head as she walks ahead of me down the tunnel.

"Only if you do that again."

She swivels around, walking backward. "What?"

"I hate it when you walk away from me, but I still enjoy the view."

She continues to shake her head, and when she gets to the end of the hall, she glances both ways before bringing her hand to her lips and blowing me a kiss.

Fuck, I love that girl.

fifty

Tedi

I'M IN THE STANDS WITH ALL THE USUALS—KYLEIGH, her dad, Eloise, Jade, and Bodhi. The guys are in the middle of their warm-ups, and I'm fairly sure Tweetie has positioned himself right in front of me because he knows how hot I get when he does that. The few sly looks he's given me over his shoulder when he changes positions confirm my suspicions. But I have a little surprise of my own for him.

I might not be able to wear his jersey to the game, but I have on a T-shirt with his name and number under my sweater. I made sure to take a picture and send it to him before the game. Hopefully he checks his phone after warm-ups, before he comes out to play.

"Tedi," a woman says, and a smile comes to my lips.

"Melody." I stand, and Tweetie's mom's arms are already out and ready to embrace me.

She's taller than me, her hair more gray than blonde. With a kind smile, she pulls me into a warm, welcoming hug. "I missed you. And I'm not the only one."

"I missed you too." We pull away from one another, but she continues to hold my hands. "How have you been?" I ask.

There's a knock on the glass, and we both look to find Tweetie there. His smile is big and wide because he loves his mom and his sister.

"Tedi," Georgia says, and we hug. "I see he still keeps tabs on you." She laughs.

Melody goes to the glass and tells him to have a great game.

I lift my phone to signal to him to make sure he checks his, and he nods, skating away.

"Let me introduce you, unless…" I walk them over to all the girlfriends and wives of Tweetie's best friends.

"Kyleigh. Jade," Melody says.

Her words are like the quick sting from a whip, reminding me of our time apart. Of course Melody and Georgia know Kyleigh and Jade.

Eloise gets up out of her seat and holds out her hand. "Hi, I'm Eloise, Conor's wife."

"Wife?" Georgia says. "That boy moves as fast as my brother." She eyes me. Her similarities to her brother always surprise me. There's no denying they're siblings.

Melody moves down the line, hugging Conor's dad hello. Was that hug a little long to be a friendly one? I think so.

Everyone catches up with each other as I finally sit down in my seat. Georgia is next to me, and it appears we lost Melody to Conor's dad. She's decided to sit at his end, and everyone slides over one.

"So…" Georgia elbows me.

"What?"

She crosses her legs and arms, waiting for me to tell her.

"Did you talk to your brother?" I ask.

"I did, and he's about as tight-lipped as you're being, but I take it as a good sign that you're here."

"I'm here for work. Social media thing." I ease past the other stuff that Georgia really wants to know about.

"And now you're in the first row of the wives and girl-friends section, telling my brother to check his phone when he gets into the locker room?" Her perfectly sculpted eyebrows raise.

"I hate that you're a cop."

"Detective," she says. "Which gives me a lot of resources, so either you give me the dirt, or I search it up on my own."

"And here I was excited to see you."

She laughs. "I was pretty damn excited when Tweetie brought up your name."

"So he warned you ahead of time?" I ask, the lights going dark, which means they're about to announce the teams and start the game.

We both stand, and she leans over and whispers in my ear, "I heard your name before you ever landed in Chicago."

I must give her a look, because she takes my hand. "You were always his one, and after the first breakup, he needed a confidant." She raises her hand. "That was me. Which prob-ably wasn't great since I was going through a divorce." She shrugs. "But I'll tell you one thing, and I don't say this so you take my brother back, but he never stopped."

My forehead wrinkles. "Stopped what?"

The announcer comes on the microphone, and the crowd cheers.

"Loving you, silly. He was just too hurt and too proud to chase. I'll give you a little warning. That doesn't hold true anymore." She wraps her arm around my shoulder and pulls me into her side. "Welcome back into the family."

She laughs just like Tweetie does, and when they announce his name, she jumps and hollers, cheering on her brother as tears well in my eyes. God, since when do I cry so much?

When the third period comes around, the score is tied.

The clock is winding down, and my stomach twists, unable to shake the fear that they might actually lose. And his mom and sister are in the stands.

"I absolutely hate this part," Eloise mutters, gripping the edge of her seat.

St. Louis gains possession on a breakaway. I almost want to close my eyes—Conor's an incredible goalie, but there's only so much one guy can do. Their center winds up for a shot. He shoots it hard and fast, but Conor blocks it and it flies to the right.

"Oh, thank God." Eloise exhales, pressing a hand to her chest.

But our relief is short-lived. The rebound lands right on the stick of St. Louis's right wing. He snaps a quick pass across to the left wing, who fires off another shot. Conor stretches, and it deflects off his shin pad. The puck pops into the air, and our defenseman tracks it, smacking it out of danger and down the ice.

Rowan gets it first, skating hard, but instead of taking the shot, he passes to Henry just before a St. Louis defender crunches him into the boards.

Jade winces. "I hate those hits."

The worries and nervousness from the women who love these men send me back to the game when Tweetie was injured the worst—on the ice, clutching his knee, his face twisted in pain, the trainers rushing out. The way he was carried off, unable to put weight on his leg. I shake away the memory.

Tweetie gets the puck, but two St. Louis players pin him to the boards. He battles, fighting for space, but he's trapped. Rowan loops around, wedging in, his stick joining the other three. He digs the puck free and passes it to Henry, who's waiting.

St. Louis is on them, though, giving them no clearance for

a shot. They pass and move, trying to shake the defense. Rowan, Tweetie, and Henry weave in and out, circling the net. I can see Tweetie's mouth moving, no doubt chirping to someone on the ice and living up to his nickname.

"Come on, guys," Georgia urges, her voice tight.

I glance at the Jumbotron to see that there are less than twenty seconds left.

Finally, Rowan shoots, but their goalie is just as good as Conor, and he blocks it. The crowd groans, thinking it's over, but Tweetie rebounds the puck. The goalie can't recover fast enough before the puck goes in, and the buzzer sounds right before the timer runs out.

We all jump and cheer and hug one another.

"I have no idea how you do this all the time." Georgia has a hand to her chest.

"I'm pretty sure you're in more danger on a day-to-day basis being a detective." I wind my arm through hers. "Let's get you to the family room and wait for Tweetie to come out. You can calm your heart down."

Right before we turn to the stairs, I glance over my shoulder to see Tweetie still celebrating, but his eyes are on me as one of the St. Louis players talks to him. Both of us smile. I forgot how much I loved it when he sought me out when he should be enjoying the moment.

"You're coming to dinner with us, right?" Georgia asks when we reach the elevator to take us down to the restricted area.

"If I'm invited."

Another rule lined out. I'm not being very good at adhering to my own damn rules.

"My brother didn't invite you?"

"In his defense, I told him dinners were off the table. We're supposed to be taking this slow."

She laughs and laughs and laughs until we're off the elevator. "You two. Someone should write a book about you guys. You're both so naively funny."

"Gee, thanks, Georgia."

"I'm just saying, when is enough enough? You guys have been through so much shit, and here you are again." She puts her hand on my arm, stopping us in the hallway. "Just be happy and live. It doesn't need to be more complicated than that."

Melody comes by, and Georgia walks with her. I stand there for a moment and contemplate Georgia's point. There's just a lot to the equation of us that we need to figure out.

"Great game, huh?" Bud walks by me on his way to the media room or the locker room, maybe. "Come, walk with me."

I fall in line with him. "Amazing win."

"He just promotes himself."

"Does that mean that you're signing him again?" How could they not?

He glances at me, and we come to the point where I go into the family area to wait, and he continues on. "Why don't we each stick to our own jobs, Tedi?"

Without a goodbye or telling me whatever it was he wanted me to walk with him for, he continues down the hall. I want to take off my shoe and throw it at the back of his head. He's a fool to not sign him, and I hate that he's acting as if there's some other left wing who's better than Tweetie. He not only has the best but also a player who will give his all and is a leader on the ice.

Bud's going to blow it, but what kills me is that Tweetie will be the one who's hurt most.

fifty-one

Tweetie

I'M LYING IN MY BED ALONE AFTER OUR DINNER WITH my mom and Georgia. I'm meeting them for breakfast tomorrow before they head back to Colorado.

I pull up Tedi's contact and hammer out a text.

> Were you trying to kill me before the game?

I study the picture she sent me again. Her tits straining the number—*my* number across her chest. I'm not sure there's a hockey player alive who doesn't want his girl to wear his jersey to a game. It's as if it's ingrained in us to want to show off what's ours, and I feel no different. I want her decked out in the number eight like she used to be. I want to look at her through the glass and see my number on her because it's a sense of belonging. To her.

> That was the point.

> I almost followed you home.

That's stalker behavior.

> Can you blame me? I want to see you in that T-shirt and nothing else.

That can be arranged.

At a later date.

> I'm staring at this picture like I'm thirteen again. Your tits look amazing.

I did perk them up a little. Age...

> They are still one of my favorite parts of you.

So are we going to keep up this texting thing all night? I think you might need a free hand soon.

I pull the phone away and press on her number.

She answers on the first ring. "I wondered how long you'd wait to use my number."

"I was giving you space." It's the truth. I went to call her a couple times, but I didn't want to infiltrate her life too fast. "I'm trying to be a good boy."

"Not even a finger touched my thigh under the table tonight. Kudos to you."

"Did you not see my napkin in shreds when we left?"

She laughs, so I ask for one more favor, hoping she'll indulge me.

"Tedi..."

"Yeah?"

"Can we FaceTime? I just want to see you." I know I'm

showing how vulnerable I am, how much she undoes me, but I don't give a shit anymore.

"You just saw me. We spent dinner together."

"Is that a no?"

"No, it's not."

The words are barely out of her mouth before I'm turning my phone back toward me and pressing the FaceTime button. Her face lights up my screen, and there's a little too much flesh to expect my dick not to perk up.

"Gorgeous," I say.

A slight blush pinkens her cheeks. "Handsome."

"This was a bad idea." The urge inside me to flee my condo and cross the city to get to her apartment is almost impossible to control. "I want to be with you even worse now."

"Me too. I kind of wanted to take your sister and mom to the hotel and have us go home together. Like old times."

Relief washes through me that she wants the same thing as me. That we're on the same page.

"What were you doing before I called?" I change the subject, needing to make sure I don't actually ambush her and show up at her door. She'd let me in, even though she shouldn't.

"I was writing in my journal." She flashes it on screen.

"You still do that, huh?"

She flashes her pen, her fancy colored pen she always used when writing to her older self. Her grandma had dementia, and she'd written in journals that they would read to her. Tedi wants the same thing if it happens to her.

"I do. How about you?"

I nod. "Not as often, but sometimes. Gotta keep that shit-head teenager up to date about our wins and our fuckups."

Once I started therapy, my therapist thought it would be a

good exercise for me to write to my younger self about what I've done and accomplished. He thought it was a way for me to forgive myself for the things I did in the past as well as work through some of the pain from my relationship with my father. It's kind of worked, so I can't say he was wrong, but at first it felt impossible to put pen to paper and write about how I felt.

"Your teenage self would love who he became."

"You think?" I lean back with my arm under my head on my pillow. "I think he'd kick me in the nuts for losing you."

"Well, then I guess senior citizen Tedi and young buck Tweetie would beat the shit out of both of us for what we allowed to happen." She pauses, looking contemplative. "Your sister brought up a good point to me today."

"Yeah?"

My sister is always giving advice when she's not asked. She practically forced me to tell her everything that went down with Tedi. She was relentless in her calls and her visits. I blamed it on her divorce and needing a situation or person to fix since she couldn't fix her own life. I'm not sure I would've made it through that dark time without her, though. I'm lucky to have Georgia, and I loved every time I looked into the stands and saw her and Tedi laughing together tonight. I'm not sure why my mom was sitting by Conor's dad, but that's a problem for another day.

"Your sister asked me when enough is enough. That maybe we need to stop punishing ourselves and just live. Stop overcomplicating things."

"Don't you just hate her and her free advice?"

Tedi laughs at my obvious joke. Georgia's told me the same thing many times before, but it's a hard thing to do.

"It's the worst." I watch her lie down and rest her head on her pillow.

"I wish I was next to you right now," I say, feeling my dick swell under my sheets.

"What would you do, Tweetie?" Her voice is soft and seductive, so I tread about as lightly as I usually do. Which is to say, not at all.

"Ask you to blow me?"

She shakes her head, a smile teasing her lips.

"Before I can answer that, I need to see what you're wearing. Will you show me?" I bring my hand down and stroke myself.

She pans the camera down her body.

"Slower," I say, enjoying the cami tank top that's snug against her bare tits, her nipples hard and poking against the fabric. The waistband is something plaid. I assume it's flannel pants, but she surprises me with shorts that showcase her smooth legs. "You kill me, woman."

She brings the camera up to her face again.

"What would you do if you were next to me right now, Tweetie?" There's that voice again.

"I'd inch over to you and start by kissing your shoulder."

"Sounds nice."

"I'd slide my finger under the strap of your cami and lower it away from your collarbone as my lips continued their journey up your neck to your jaw. I'd hover over you, my lips millimeters from yours. I'd tell you how beautiful you are and how I can't believe you're mine."

"Am I?" she asks, a desperation in her voice.

"Yes, Tedi, you're mine. Always have been."

"Go on."

"I'd place my lips to yours and slide my tongue along the seam of your lips, hoping and praying that you'd open for me."

"I would," she whispers.

"I'd slip my tongue in and seek yours out."

"My tongue would meet yours, and my fingers would weave through the hair at the back of your head, those beautiful blonde strands, just to make sure you deepened the kiss. You'd groan or growl or moan."

"I'd groan."

"I'd slide my arm out of my cami, and you'd remove the strap on the other side."

"My knee would nudge your legs."

"And I'd open them, giving you room to fall between them. Your hard bulge would press to my center."

"Then you'd get wet with the feel of my hard cock."

"I was already wet. I was wet from you just being next to me."

"God, I wouldn't want to stop kissing you, but there's more of you I have to touch, have to suck, have to lick. So my mouth would trail kisses along your flesh."

"Goose bumps would rise along my skin, chasing your tongue," she says.

"I'd nudge down the top of your cami until your tits popped free. I almost nut myself, but I glance up at you right as I open my mouth..."

"And suck. I arch my back, inviting you to take me."

"I wouldn't leave the other one out. I'd have to give it the pleasure of my mouth."

She giggles, and I tug on my dick harder.

"My other tit thanks you."

"By the time I'm done, your cami would be bunched around your stomach, and I'd be heading down to my second favorite part of your body."

"What's your first?" she asks.

"Focus on my fingers pulling back the front of those flannel boxer shorts and finding you wearing..."

"Nothing. I'm bare."

I growl, my dick so hard I'm not going to make it much longer. "Fuck."

"I thought you'd like that."

"My fingers would hook along the sides of your boxers, and I'd gradually tease you by sliding them down your legs until I free them and toss them far away. Your skin would pinken like it always does."

"It does?"

I chuckle. "Yeah, and it's fucking stunning. Watching your skin almost glow with the anticipation of what I'm going to do to you. Now, let me finish because I'm just getting to the good part."

"Well, excuse me then."

"Where is your hand, Tedi?" I ask. "Slide it under the waistband of those shorts."

"Yes, sir."

"You feel how swollen your clit is, how wet you are? Slide your finger inside and coat your whole pussy with your arousal. I want to hear it slip and slide through your folds." My dick twitches in my hand as I watch her slide her hand under the waistband of her shorts.

"God," she says, panting.

"Yeah, that's me, babe. Those are my fingers, exploring and teasing you. I'm right between your legs, and I'm staring up at you to make sure I'm doing exactly what you like. Listening to your breathing, looking for your reactions. Your head rocks back on the pillow and your back arches off the mattress because it feels too good. I bring my mouth to your clit..."

"Tweetie..."

"I suck, and I place my finger at your entrance, but I don't push it in. I rim your opening, warming you up, getting you so needy that you feel like you'll die if I don't give you what you want."

"Keep going..."

I tug harder on my dick now. Faster. "Your hands fly into my hair, making sure I don't have any crazy ideas of stopping. I love the tug you give my hair. As my finger slides and arches inside you, you grind along my face, taking what you want. You're so close to the edge."

"I am." She moans.

"Take it, babe, suffocate me with your pussy."

"Oh shit!" She drops the phone, and I'm left staring at her ceiling, but the sound alone makes me tighten my grip on my shaft.

"Show me. Show me your fingers," I beg.

She brings them to the phone and places them in her mouth, sucking her arousal off her fingers. That's all I need before I come so hard I drop the phone too. Tedi laughs, and it only makes me come harder.

After, I fall back on the mattress, spent but not exhausted. If she were with me, I could really get a workout and tire myself out.

"Your turn," she says after we've recovered our breath.

"What?"

"Swipe a finger and taste yourself."

I glance at the lashing of cum all over my stomach. "Would that get you all hot again?"

She laughs. "No."

We each put our phones on the bed and clean up before we're back to FaceTiming.

"I'll see you at the airport?" she asks.

"Yeah, I wish I was picking you up."

"I wish a lot of things, but soon. Now I still have to write in my journal and get my beauty sleep."

"You don't need any of that. You're beautiful."

"Night," she says.

"Night." But neither of us hangs up.

We both laugh.

"Hey, what is your favorite part of my body? I'll try to showcase it tomorrow for you," she says.

"That'll be hard."

"Why?"

"It's your heart, Tedi. My favorite part of your body is your heart."

She sighs, and her head falls to her pillow. "Good night, Tweetie. I have to go before I send an Uber for you. See you tomorrow."

I'm still laughing as she cuts off the video.

I lie in bed and think about what my sister said about leaving the past where it is. She's right, and an idea of a way we might finally be able to move on pops in my head. I hope it works.

fifty-two

Tedi's Journal Entry
Present Day
Chicago

To my older self,

Well, we're about to throw in the towel. He just gave us one helluva orgasm via phone sex. And he's saying so many sweet things. I'm starting to feel like I'm just wasting time that we could have together. Pretty soon, you're going to be reading that it's over, we lost the battle. Then again, we wouldn't lose because we'd have him, and that was the goal in the first place. He's really matured these last few years. I'm going to chance our heart this one last time. I hope you're not shaking your head reading this because I made a foolish decision. I hope you want to beat my head in because I did waste all this time without him. And I really hope that he's across from you right now as you read this.

fifty-three

Tweetie's Journal Entry
Present Day
Chicago

To my teenage self,

I know our journals are sacred. That we said we'd never share them with anyone. But she has to know. She has to read our thoughts for herself. It's the only way to heal us. To stitch up the wound from the past and move forward to a new future. Sorry, buddy, but I promise you, we can trust her.

fifty-four

Tedi

As we often do now, Tweetie and I make up some excuse to sneak off before boarding the plane. One of us grabs a snack, and the other one goes to the bathroom, or some version of that. No matter what, we're usually the last ones to get on the plane. Tweetie usually leads us down the jetway with his hand on my back. The best is when he places his hand low and his fingers cover my ass.

After we had phone sex, the line I'm trying to draw in the sand is getting washed away. Not that I'm crazy for sex, but more because I want to be with him. I crave being able to go up to him whenever I want and touch him, kiss him. Sex is just a really big added bonus.

I continue down the plane aisle as he slides into his normal seat with Conor, Henry, and Rowan. I'm just getting situated when Conor comes over and hands me a box. "Eloise wanted me to give you this. She said it was meant for you."

I take the small box. "Thanks. I'll send her a quick text to thank her."

"Oh, um… she's with a really big client, so maybe wait until we land." He's jittery, but I just smile and thank him again.

The nice thing about where I sit is that there usually isn't anyone across from me. Sometimes we have extra people like press or staff who don't always go to games, but the space gave me privacy to interview the other players who, thanks to Bud, aren't getting any publicity on the team.

The box isn't wrapped in paper, but it's a designer box with a ribbon around it. I hope Eloise didn't spend a fortune on something for me. I untie the bow and place the ribbon on the seat next to me before lifting the lid to the box.

Pushing through the red tissue paper, I see two journals. Tweetie's journals. The ones I gave him for Christmas the year before we broke up. He'd always used those black-and-white composition ones, and I'd make fun of him for it, while he'd joke about my fancy journals and colored pens.

My hand runs over the worn leather with a small heart in the bottom right corner. I wasn't going to put his initials on it, and it felt weird putting my name on it, so I settled on a small embossed heart.

I pick it up out of the box. There's no note or anything. I open it, and the first entry is dated the day I declined his proposal. I shut it and pull out my phone since we haven't pulled away from the gate yet.

I can't.

You said no flowers.

I took it back.

Please?

This is private.

> Nothing is private when it comes to you.

The plane pushes back from the gate.

> Tweetie...

> Please. I love you, Tedi, and I want you to read it.

> It's a long flight.

> Okay.

We're on our way to Anaheim, and he's right, we have a long flight.

As the plane barrels down the runway, I take a deep breath and open his journal. I'm not sure if my stomach dropping is from the plane or the words at the top of the page.

To my teenage self,

Our worst nightmare just came true, and I'm not sure where we go from here.

I knew he wrote to his younger self, but reading it makes me feel Tweetie's pain. The way he's almost telling his younger self, like, "Hey, look at us and what a fuckup we are." The disappointment Tweetie feels when writing, how he made a mistake or messed up is soul-crushing. He's told me stories about his dad and how messed up of a teenager he was. That if it wasn't for hockey, he never would've gotten his life together.

Tears fill my eyes as I read how much he hurt just like me in those days and weeks and months after our breakup. How he fought himself from coming after me. Telling himself he didn't deserve me, that he loved me enough not to drag me back into the fucked-up world of him being in professional sports and all that came with it. And then at some point, there's a shift, and he seems to come out of his grief enough to see that he has to move forward.

If he didn't play hockey, what else could he do? He never finished college, didn't have a degree, so how would he support himself? With hockey, he could give his mom the life she'd always deserved.

It was the last entry before he seemed to turn things around that made a fresh set of tears fall down my cheeks.

I have to trust that the universe isn't done with us yet—that Tedi isn't just a memory, but a part of my story still being written. Maybe we're just caught in some in-between, a pause instead of an ending. And one day, when the timing is finally right, she'll be mine again.

Until that day comes, I'll wait. And as I wait, I'll become the man she deserves—the best version of myself, for her.

I pick up the other journal, stuffing the one I've read in my bag.

The pilot announces that we're landing, so I put the second journal in my bag and pack up the rest of my stuff. I have no idea how I'll face him now or on the bus. All I want to do is get to my hotel room and read the rest of his journal.

The plane lands, and I don't have to worry because Tweetie doesn't try to interact with me. I end up talking to one of the trainers on the bus. By the time I get in the lobby, I hear Conor tell Tweetie what room they're in as they walk to the elevator.

Is he embarrassed or just giving me space? I have no idea.

I don't unpack or even take off my jacket before I throw myself in the chair in my room and pull out the second journal to continue reading.

This one starts off as he's working to make his spot on the team. Most of the entries talk about making "them" eat their words, and I'm pretty sure he's talking about Jana and Kane. How he's going to make the biggest comeback and fuck everyone who didn't believe in him. They're anger-filled entries, and I don't recognize Tweetie in any of them. I underestimated the chip on his shoulder—it was more like a chunk.

I freeze when I see the entry from the morning after Ford's retirement party.

We had her for one perfect night before a choice I made a year ago came back to destroy our chance. One impulsive decision was made because I couldn't handle the questions, because I thought erasing the past would help me move forward. Instead, it was the final nail in the coffin. The moment I removed that tattoo, I severed something I didn't even realize was still holding us together.

I get it now. It was more than ink—it was a promise. And now she's gone, buddy. That future we dared to hope for? It vanished the second she walked away. And she's never coming back. I feel numb and stupid and so goddamn pissed at myself.

I'm sorry. I really am. But love just isn't in the cards for us, not in this lifetime. We're not built for fairy tales, for that ride-off-into-the-sunset kind of love.

The hurt will fade. It has to. Because if it doesn't,
I don't know how we'll survive.

I read some more entries through the years that passed, though there aren't many. Most of them talk about how numb he feels, how he tries to mask it around other people so they only see the fun-loving, charming man he wants them to.

Then I reach an entry that's dated a few months back, when I first arrived in Chicago.

It's been three years, and she's just as breath-taking as the last time we saw her. I swore I'd never write her name in these pages again, but here I am—because Tedi Douglas is back in our life. And the second I saw her, I swear my heart remembered how to beat. The numbness faded. and color bled into my vision again.

It took every ounce of control not to pull her into my arms, not to drown in the scent that feels like home. She's the same sharp-witted, impossible woman we fell for. Fate, the universe, god, someone keeps throwing us back together, and I don't know why. But I do know that I'd be a fool to waste this chance.

I have no idea how to make her mine again, no way of undoing the past. But if I don't try, I'll regret it for the rest of our life. A future without her isn't a future at all. So wish me luck, buddy, because I'm going all in. One last shot at our one and only love.

What am I doing taking it slow and waiting? He loves me, and I love him. And sure, at points, that wasn't enough, but we're not who we were then. And all his painful words confirm to me that trying to convince myself I never mattered to him was misguided.

I pick up both journals, leave my room, and take the stairs one flight up, going to the room I heard Conor tell him they were assigned.

I knock, a lump in my throat and hope in my chest.

We're going to make it this time.

fifty-five

Tedi

Conor opens the door.

He smiles and reaches for his jacket. "I'll be in Rowan and Henry's room," he says over his shoulder, sliding past me. "My bed isn't part of your jungle gym."

The door starts to shut when Conor leaves, and I press my palm on it to keep it open.

The bathroom door opens, steam escaping. Tweetie is fresh out of the shower with a towel low on his hips, his chin-length blond hair still dripping, beads of water trailing down those mouthwatering abs. "Where did you say—"

He stands there, big blue eyes full of vulnerability, waiting for me to say something first.

For a second, my brain shuts down, and I forget all the things I wanted to say in my rush here. My heart hammers against my ribs until it's all I can hear.

Say it, Tedi. Just say it. Release all that hurt from years gone by. Start fresh.

"I love you." The words burst out of me like a shaken soda can exploding.

His expression doesn't change, but his eyes soften. He looks at me as though he already knew. Because he did.

And that's when I realize.

Of course he knew I loved him.

"You." I blink at him, my breath catching. I push the journals into his chest. "You about killed me with these."

The corner of his mouth twitches. "That was the point."

My jaw drops. "To kill me? Because if you killed me, then all those second chances you wrote about wouldn't be happening."

He leans against the doorframe, completely unfazed, as if my grand, dramatic sprint here to declare my love is just like any other day. "I wanted you to know what was going on in my head, how much you mean to me. That this isn't something I take lightly. I love you, Tedi. And I understand why you wanted to go slow."

I put my finger to his lips. "That's just it. I don't want to."

His eyes soften even more. "You don't want to go slow?"

My heart clenches, everything inside me unraveling at once. Then I shake my head. "I choose us." My voice shakes, but I push through all the worry and fear because he never purposely tried to hurt us. He was just trying to survive. "And I swear, if you try to tell me that I was right and we need to take our time, I will—"

"I wasn't." His lips twitch. This beautiful, frustrating man who always looks at me as if I'm his favorite puzzle to solve.

"Well... good." I step farther into the room, and he follows.

He wraps his arms around my waist, nuzzling his head into the crook of my neck. Just like old times.

"You're getting me wet," I say.

"I like it when you're wet."

I place my hands on his arms. "I believe in us."

"So no more fake boyfriends?"

I circle in his arms and jab him in the stomach. He feigns hurt, his chest shaking with laughter.

"I'm yours if you'll have me."

One beat of silence, then he just stares into my eyes.

"Oh my god, are you trying to play hard to get now?" I'm ready to jab him in the stomach again, but his fingers slide into my hair, pulling me toward him.

"Didn't you know?" he murmurs, his breath warm against my lips. "You've always been mine."

He kisses me. It's not a careful, hesitant kiss. It's years of longing and missed chances coming out to play. His lips crush mine, stealing my breath, while his hands grip my waist as if he's terrified I might change my mind and try to run out of here.

I rise on my toes, my fingers tangling in his wet hair, the heat of his bare skin searing the skin through my blouse. Nothing else in the world exists except for him... me... *us*. He lifts me effortlessly, and I wrap my legs around his waist.

"You know I'm never letting you go now," he murmurs against my lips, walking us backward.

"Me either," I pant.

"There are no takebacks."

"Then I sure hope you aren't defective." I playfully roll my eyes.

He chuckles, but the laughter fades into something deeper, something raw, as he lays me on the bed and hovers over me. His eyes are dark and hungry. "You really love me?"

I cup his face, my thumb brushing his cheek. "Would you like me to pinch you, so you know you're not dreaming?"

"I'm not really into pinching, but I'll take some sucking."

Tweetie's lips are on mine before I can make a smartass comment back.

There's no space left between us, no room for doubt. His hands slide into my hair, angling my head as he deepens our kiss. I clutch at his shoulders, his bare skin warm and solid beneath my fingertips. The scent of soap and him swims around us while his mouth explores and claims me.

A soft moan escapes me, and his grip tightens.

"Tedi," he murmurs, his forehead pressing to mine, his breath ragged. "Do you have any idea how many times I thought this would never happen again?"

I smile against his lips, my fingers tracing the sharp line of his jaw. "Yeah, you gave me your journals. But this doesn't mean I'm giving you mine. You know that, right?"

He groans. "I would never ask."

"Well, maybe one or two. I'm a sharer."

"No, you're not."

I draw back and act offended.

"So, you want to have a threesome? Share me with some other woman?"

Red veils my vision, and he laughs.

"I thought so."

I press my lips to his. This time, I take control, my hands sliding along his shoulder blades, remembering the dip and curve of every muscle.

He exhales sharply. "Tedi—"

"You talk too much," I murmur against his skin, letting my lips trail down his neck.

His head tilts back slightly, a quiet curse slipping past his lips as I kiss the spot just below his ear. He lowers me to the floor, and his hands trace the curve of my waist. I take his face in my hands, looking into his beautiful blue eyes—the eyes that are only filled with love for me.

His fingers go to my blouse, resting on the first button. With every breath, another button flicks open until he pushes it off me, and it floats to the floor.

"I can't wait to taste every inch of you." His hands go to my pants, and he unbuttons and slides the zipper down until I help him by wiggling out, and they pool at my feet.

I step out of my pants, and he steps back, staring at me. Tweetie brings his thumb to his mouth, studying me as if I'm some art sculpture he's admiring. Wanting to keep his eyes on me, I reach back and unclasp my bra, sliding the straps down my arms until it joins my blouse and pants.

He bites his thumb and groans. "Fuck."

Continuing, I ease my panties down and off my hips, then my legs, kicking away the flimsy silk fabric. His gaze heats, and I imagine all the dirty things running through his mind. It only makes me feel more wanted.

"You're awfully far away." I turn around.

He steps closer and runs his thumb over his name tattooed on my ribcage. "I love seeing this."

Our eyes meet, and I see guilt in his.

"No. Don't." I put my hands on his face and force him to look at me. "Enjoy seeing your name on my skin. I love that you love it."

"But—"

I shake my head. "It's in the past. Leave it there." I push a finger between his abs and his towel, tugging it off of him. "My job was much easier."

"God, Tedi," he says before he's on me. Neither of us can keep things slow and languid.

Our kiss is crazy and messy, and our hands are everywhere all at once. As if a timer's been set and once the buzzer goes off, we're done.

"You drive me insane," he mutters, stripping his mouth off mine, only to push me down on the bed.

"Good."

I watch his lips curl as he goes to his bag, digs out a

condom, and pulls it out of the package. I admire him running it down his thick length.

Then he's crawling up the bed, his knees pushing my legs apart. He lowers his body, the weight of him pressing me into the soft mattress. "Thank you."

"For what?" I run my hands through his hair.

"For loving me."

I bring his lips to mine, and our kiss slows, and our hands explore slower, savoring a moment we've both been waiting for. This isn't just sex. This is us promising each other a future together.

He wedges his hand between us and positions himself at my opening, sliding in.

As our bodies move together, heat curling between us, Tweetie whispers sweet things in my ear. How much he missed me, how much I mean to him, and how much he loves me. And I tell him the same as our lips drag across each other's heated skin. We share promises of a future because this time, neither of us is letting go.

I come on a cry, my back arching into him, and he swallows my moan before he comes on a grunt and a curse.

After we're finished, neither of us rushes to get up, not ready to face anything outside of the two of us.

fifty-six

Tweetie

TEDI'S AT THE DOOR, AND I'M KISSING HER GOODBYE when someone clears their throat behind her. Tedi and I look over, surprised, since when we looked in the hall, we didn't see anyone.

"Can I go into my room now?" Conor asks.

I step aside, holding the door open, and he slips by me.

"Just so we're clear, this was a one-time gift to you. Use Tedi's room from now on." He walks in. "Jesus, it smells like sex. If I get home and Eloise thinks I cheated, your ass is mine, Tweetie."

"Good luck tonight," Tedi whispers, both of us ignoring Conor's bitching.

"You gonna wear that T-shirt?"

She laughs but nods. I lean in for another kiss, but a door opens down the hall, and she steps back. "Sounds like a great plan. Can't wait to work on this angle. Good luck tonight, Conor and Tweetie." She waves and walks away.

I wait in the doorway and hear her say hello to Simon, one of the Chipmunks.

I shut the door and rest my hand on it, lowering my head, still surprised and elated over everything going on in my life.

"So, you're a taken man?" Conor asks.

I push off the door and walk over to my bag to pull out some clothes before I shower all over again. "Yeah, but we're not telling anyone."

He quirks an eyebrow.

I shrug. "Her job. We need to figure that out."

"Well, you know I won't tell anyone, but you better do a better job than what you just did now. Anyone could have seen you two." Conor sits on the edge of his bed, toeing out of his shoes. "And if I play like shit, I'm gonna be upset."

I walk toward the bathroom but stop. "Thanks. I really appreciate it. Giving up the room. It would've been a buzzkill if I was like 'let's go to your room.'"

"You're lucky I'm a romantic at heart. And I like the dramatic flair."

I laugh because he's the one who stopped a wedding to win his girl.

Closing the door to the bathroom, I'm waiting for the water to heat up when I get a text message.

> Thanks for a great time… Stud.

> Who is this?

> Oh, shit I thought this was the guy I just met in the elevator.

> Not funny.

> Neither was yours.

> Touché.

This is for proof later.

She sends a picture of her wearing my shirt, but I can clearly see she's not wearing a bra since her nipples are poking out.

If you win, I'll wear only this tonight when you get to my hotel room.

Deal.

Now go shower, and you better not be late to your game.

Yes, Master.

I love you.

Not as much as I love you.

It's probably a little sick how much we've been telling each other that, but I don't give a shit. We're making up for all the years we felt it but couldn't tell each other.

I think about taking a picture of me in the mirror and sending it to her, but my thumb stops on the picture I took of Tedi's tattoo earlier. Black lettering of my name rests along her ribcage, just beneath her breast. I kissed it and traced my thumb over it countless times today. The guilt still lingers, but I'll make things right—eventually. I just wish there was a way to show the world she's mine.

Then a notification pops up on my screen, and I know exactly what to do.

I upload the picture I took of her in black and white, and obscure it enough that no one will recognize her. This is the perfect way to tell the women slipping into my DMs that I'm off the market. My own quiet declaration to everyone following me that I'm in love with a woman who loves me so much, she inked my name onto her skin.

After I post, I set my phone on the bathroom counter and step into the shower, only thinking about having Tedi again tonight as the warm water sprays over my shoulders. A shoulder I wish still had her initials on it.

fifty-seven

Tedi

WE FLEW HOME THE NEXT MORNING, WHICH WAS nice since I got an entire night with Tweetie.

Here we are, back at the arena. Not that I'm complaining, but I'm biding my time until we can have a little reprieve to enjoy each other now that we're together.

"So, tell us?" Eloise puts her elbow on the armrest and her chin in her palm.

Bodhi isn't at the game tonight. He's spending the night at a friend's house, and it's weird not to have him here. Even the players seem a little lost that he's not here for them to high-five. But Jade actually has a drink in her hand, so maybe she needs a little break too.

"What do you mean?"

Kyleigh leans forward. Her dad isn't here either, so it's just the four of us and a few empty seats. "You tattooed his name?"

"Years ago. When we were in Florida."

"That's sweet." Eloise gives me puppy dog eyes.

No surprise. I've seen Conor's finger, and I'm not sure if her wrist tattoo has a meaning, but I'm assuming so.

"But you guys are, like, together now, right?" Jade asks before sipping her beer.

I glance around to make sure there aren't any eyes on us. "Yeah."

"I get there's a lot of history, and that can be hard to work through. Speaking as another second-chance love match, you learn from your mistakes, and I just know you guys are going to do great. You learn to appreciate each other more." Jade smiles at me.

"Eloise, you want to go sit by ourselves in the insta-love section and let these two second-chancers keep droning on?" Kyleigh jokes. She rests her back against the glass so she's standing in front of us and can hear us easier.

"I didn't mean any offense," Jade says.

"In truth, Tweetie and I were an insta-love connection, but we lost our way." I place my hand on Jade's. "Thank you for your words of encouragement. I hope we're as great at this as you and Henry."

"You will be."

"And we're super happy he chose you. I can't even imagine if we didn't like the person Tweetie ended up with," Kyleigh says, as though she was scared for a moment. "We have a pretty kickass girl squad going."

I know I'm not nearly as close to them as they all seem to be, especially since Jade and Eloise were friends long before they met their men, but I do feel a friendship growing. Hopefully Tweetie gets signed with Chicago again and he can stay here. Although I need to figure out what I'm going to do. We can't keep this a secret forever.

"You're going to the gala, right?" Eloise asks. "Because we're all going dress shopping."

"Eloise dresses us," Kyleigh says.

"I haven't talked to Tweetie about it. I mean, I'm not sure we can go together." I look around again. "But I'd love to go shopping with you. Even if I'm going solo."

The gala is in two weeks, and it's for a charity that the Falcons' owners, the Gershwin family, supports. Florida is in town for the annual outdoor game, so the Fury bought two tables, and everyone is coming up. I haven't seen Saige in a while, so I'm excited.

"Great!" Eloise gives me a big smile.

Someone clears their throat, and Kyleigh looks up behind us. "Hi, Mr. Caldron."

"Call me Bud, Kyleigh," he says, and my stomach sours.

She smiles, and he says hi to all the other women before sitting next to me. He doesn't fully relax, and something in my gut tells me he sought me out.

The guys are off the ice now, waiting until the game starts to come back out.

"Hi, Bud," I say. "I didn't know you sat down here?"

"I don't." He looks around as though he's disgusted. "I sit in the suite. So, what do you know about this post on Tweetie's socials?"

I knew this was going to be a problem and told Tweetie he should take it down. But if you know him, that wasn't going to happen. He's been bombarded with questions about who the woman in the picture is and women saying they have broken hearts and blah, blah, blah.

"I don't," I lie. "I don't manage his social media. Not his personal account anyway."

"You used to though, right?"

His question throws me for a second, but I managed a lot of athletes' accounts back in the day when I worked with Saige.

"Years ago."

"You know, Tedi, I don't care much for things happening

on my watch that I don't know about. Now, I am thankful that Nick Herington sent you down here, but I feel as if we're constantly butting heads."

How can he think that when I've done everything he's asked? "The entire campaign is on Tweetie. I've showcased him as the player he is for you. I thought that's what you wanted?"

His eyes never leave the ice, and his hands steeple in front of him. "I wanted you to show a man in his last year. I wanted to show the insecurity, the wins, and the grit it takes to be an older player in this league."

I turn toward him, and I know Eloise is listening, but I don't really care. "I'm sorry, Bud, but what does this have to do with the picture Tweetie put up on his socials?"

He sighs and looks up at the Jumbotron, then back down at me. "A taken player doesn't get the same attention as a single one. No one wants to see the man they want in their bed loving on someone else. You should know that. And honestly, I feel like all you've done is highlight him so another team will want him."

His thoughts are all over the place, but he's not wrong. Still though, I did center my campaign around Tweetie as he asked.

"I did tell you that we should focus on the entire team. If you don't sign Tweetie for another contract, you might just lose those fans as a result. I really wish you would've trusted me."

He laughs, a condescending cackle that makes my fists clench. "I've been in this business a long time, and I'm gonna be honest, I think this is Tweetie's last year."

Eloise sucks in a breath and makes a mouse-like whimper beside me.

"I think you're wrong," I say.

"That's your opinion." He pauses, and I'm hoping he gets

up and leaves. "I suggest you tell him to take down the picture of the tattooed girl and be back to the single Tweetie that everyone loves. The playboy sells, not the boring married man. If people aren't going to care about him, why would I resign him at his age? Now, I've given you some leeway on this since Nick said you were the best, but we're going to start doing what I want."

"Which is what exactly?" I hear the snap in my voice, and I try to rear it back.

"I want to see his faults as well as his accolades. No one likes a perfect man, Tedi. Women want a man they have to fix. Men want someone they can relate to. Do you think those guys at the bar are enthralled with how great you're making him look, as if he's a superhero? It just makes them feel shitty about their beer-bellied, shitty-job selves. You should realize that, since once upon a time, you tried to fix a broken man." He turns to me and cocks his eyebrow.

I open my mouth, but he puts up his hand. "Let me save you the excuses. I have eyes and ears all over this league. Again, Tedi, I like you, but you fight me too much. Start doing what I'm saying, or I'll make another call up to your boss."

He stands and walks away.

I slink down in my seat before I storm up the stairs, jump on his back, and throw him to the floor.

"I hate him," Eloise says. "And you don't think—"

"Can we keep it to ourselves right now?" I'm going to tell Tweetie, but he's not going to want anyone else to know about it.

"Of course." She nods, giving me a concerned look.

The lights dim, and the announcer comes on. I sit up straight, excited to see Tweetie play, but the entire time, I will myself to believe that this will not make him spiral. Whatever happens, wherever he ends up, we'll get through to the other side together this time.

fifty-eight

Tweetie

"I HAVE NO IDEA HOW YOU HAVE THE ENERGY FOR this, but I am not complaining," Tedi says, her fingernails digging into my shoulder blades harder with every one of my thrusts.

Her back is to the wall, and she's wearing my T-shirt. I made a mental note to get her my jersey even if she's just wearing it in private.

We didn't make it two steps into my condo before we were on each other, stripping one another out of our clothes. The only time we parted was when I ran to my bedroom to grab a condom.

"Fuck, Tweetie. It feels so good."

"You feel good." And she does. It was always different with Tedi. Still is.

The urgency, the feral need, the feeling of never getting enough of her—it's addicting, and I love every fucking minute of it.

She slides her hand down between us.

I groan. "Yeah, babe, touch yourself."

Her head hits the wall, and her free arm wraps around my neck. Both of us glance down. I watch her circle her clit while my cock drags in and out of her. I'm barely holding on.

"God, I'm so wet."

The only noise in my condo is our breathing and the sound of me driving into her. She's moaning and whimpering, and I don't relent, because she's close, and I can't wait to see her come apart around me.

She clenches around me, and her eyes shut, my name slipping from her lips, then her body goes limp in my arms for a moment.

Before she's fully recovered, she slips her hand out from between us and runs her arousal over my lips. I suck her fingers with a moan. The taste of her makes my balls draw tight, and with one final thrust, I still, unable to hold it back any longer. She tightens her legs, giving my arms a reprieve while I empty myself into the condom.

Tedi nuzzles her head into my neck, her labored breaths easing back to a normal rhythm. "I love you."

"I love you back." I run my hand up her side.

I'm still trying to believe that we're here. That Tedi's in my condo and we're making a go of this. A part of me still thinks I'm dreaming.

She loosens her legs, and I lower her to the floor.

"I'll be right back." I head to the bathroom to get rid of the condom.

When I drop it in the trash, she's at my back, her arms wrapping around my waist and her cheek on my shoulder blade. Perfection. This feels like perfection. As if she couldn't stay away from me for such a short amount of time, so she's joining me.

We stay like that for a minute, basking in the feeling of being here, together.

"Now, get out. I have to go to the bathroom so I don't get a UTI." She giggles, kissing my back before unwinding herself off me.

"Still shutting the door?" I ask, stepping around her to give her the bathroom.

"Yep." She pushes the door shut.

I grab our clothes off the floor by the front door, walk to my bedroom, and toss them on the bed. She's in the doorway moments later, watching me shove my legs into a pair of sweats.

"Do you have anything for me?" She steps in, stripping the T-shirt off her body.

"Are you kidding? What's mine is yours."

She goes to my dresser and opens a drawer.

"Fair warning though, I might go all caveman alpha male seeing you in my clothes."

She thumbs through the T-shirts, doesn't pull anything out, and shuts the drawer. Instead, she walks to my closet, and I hear her pushing aside the hangers, as if she's searching for something specific. I sit on the edge of the bed, watching her.

She sighs and pulls a sweatshirt off a hanger. Turning around, she holds it up to herself, and I laugh.

It's her favorite sweatshirt of mine. Old and worn and the one I toyed with getting rid of so many times but couldn't.

"Do you remember?" She tosses it over her head and saunters across the room to me.

"I do." I give her a warm smile.

We were on vacation and got stuck in a rainstorm. Running into the nearest store, we bought two sweatshirts. Then we got back to where we were staying and used the excuse of getting warm to strip and slide under the blankets for some skin-to-skin contact. It's one of my favorite memories with her and one of the reasons that sweatshirt still hangs in my closet.

Tedi claimed both of them as hers after that. I wasn't complaining.

She drops one leg on the right of my hip and the other one on my left, straddling my lap.

"Are you hungry?" My hands find her ass, tugging her the rest of the way to me.

"Yeah, but nothing crazy. What's with this Chicago pizza I keep hearing about?"

"It's deep dish, and it's so good. And you have to try it."

She nods, kisses me, and crawls off my lap, situating herself beside me against the headboard. "I like your place. Right next to Colts' stadium, huh?"

I eye her, and she laughs. Fucking Decker Davis. I'm not sure I can ever look at him the same. Then I grab my phone from the pocket of my jeans and pull up the pizza place I usually order from.

"Hey, someone came to see me in the stands today."

I glance from my phone to her. "You sound hesitant. Did someone hit on you?"

"God, no." She acts as if the idea is ludicrous, but I catch guys checking her out all the time. "It was Bud."

I roll my eyes, click the order button, and toss my phone on the bed.

She brings the sweatshirt over her legs and crosses her ankles. "I don't want to ruin tonight, but I think you need to know."

"Okkaayy..."

"Bud is upset about the post you made. The one with—"

"I know which one." Anger is the first emotion that arises because I'm not letting hockey dictate my life anymore.

She scoots closer to me, taking my hand. "He has a point." I open my mouth to argue, but she puts up her hand. "I'm not saying you have to delete it, but I want you to know what you're up against if you don't."

I trust Tedi, I always have. She's probably the reason I'm such a popular player. She taught me how to show people the person I am through my posts. It's the only reason I started doing it myself after I lost her. "Go ahead."

"Bud isn't set on signing you next year. He's almost throwing it around like if you want a contract, you play by his rules."

I slide my hand out of hers, both of my hands going into my hair. "He's holding that over my head?"

"I know. He's a controlling asshole. He's not happy with the way I'm showcasing you either. He said you seem too perfect and people can't relate." She shrugs. "I'm biased, and maybe I've been doing that without realizing it, but I do have some ideas that might help him be happy. What it comes down to is that he's threatening both of our jobs. He says if I don't do what he wants, he's calling my boss, and if you don't delete the post, he might not give you a contract."

I whip my head around and steady my gaze on her. "I'm not deleting it."

She nods. "I figured. But—"

"I don't care. I'm not going to let Bud Caldron bully me. Fuck him. Another team will want me if he doesn't." I'm not going to let anyone come between us again. My job will not affect us, but damn, I'm gonna miss Chicago and the guys.

"I don't understand him. You've gotten a lot of fans who are happy with that post. I'm not sure why... well..."

"What?"

She blows out a breath. "All publicity is good publicity. And although you've never been the bad boy who's going out and doing illegal shit, you are... were... the guy who got them publicity for just being you. You're always around the city. Not a homebody. You're accessible to your fans."

"That's exactly what we did in Florida to get my name out there, remember?"

"I know, but Bud believes he needs you single, and apparently he wants you to show your age."

My face contorts with disgust. "What?"

She nods. I can tell from how many deep breaths she's taking that she doesn't want to tell me any of this. "He wants me to show you struggling more. As if you're toying with retirement because you're falling short." She bites her lips. "I'd never do that. Plus, it's bullshit. You're the strongest one out there. The best player."

I quirk my eyebrow. "You're definitely biased."

"I am, but everyone loves you, Tweetie. And the post thing is your decision. I'm not going to be upset if you take it down. I don't need you to publicly claim me." She shakes her head. "But for the campaign, I have other ideas to make you more relatable that don't involve any of the shit Bud wants. I just wanted to run it by you first because if you want me to do what Bud wants and go that way, I will. If staying in Chicago is that important to you and you want that contract, I'll make it happen."

"Fuck that. I don't give a shit about Bud. And yeah, I love Chicago. I love these guys." I grab her hand and pull her onto my lap. "But I want this more than anything." I wave my finger between us. "Maybe I'll retire, move to New York with you."

She studies me for a beat. "There's one more thing."

I rock my head back. "Whhaattt?"

"We can't go to the gala together. We have to go separately. Bud seems to know something is up."

I frown. "Why do you think that?"

"He's sniffing around. Mentioned how I used to do your social media back in Florida. I don't know, just a feeling I have." She takes my hands, lifting them and entwining her fingers through mine. She watches our hands move together for a second before her gaze meets mine again. "I want us out there, but I have to tell my boss first, and I'd rather be the one in charge of your campaign. If we have any shot of you staying in Chicago, I need to be here running this for you."

"Tedi, I—"

"I know, Tweetie. I know I'm more important, but you playing where you want is more important to *me*. I love you so much, I want this for you." She leans forward. "Secrets can be fun." She kisses me on the neck. "Sneaking around." She kisses my jaw, then her lips are millimeters from mine. "We know what we have. We don't need to share it with the world to know it's true." She presses her lips to mine, then draws back, waiting for my answer.

And fuck, of course I want to stay in Chicago. Especially if we win the Cup. I want the last years of my career to count.

"Okay," I agree, but I remind myself if this goes south, I'm tugging Tedi into a life raft and we're getting the hell out of Dodge.

This time, I'll save us before anything touches us.

fifty-nine

Tedi

THERE'S A KNOCK ON MY DOOR, SO I STOP IN MY second bedroom and peek my head in. "Are you ready?"

"Just grabbing my lip gloss," Lyric says with a smile. She looks beautiful in the dress that Eloise picked out when I told her Lyric was flying in from New York to be Tweetie's date to the gala.

"You look great. I'll get the door." My heels hang off my fingers as I pad across my apartment and open the door.

The girls all thought I was crazy when I first mentioned Lyric being Tweetie's date. Tweetie isn't exactly on board either, but he needs some kind of cover after he put that picture of my tattoo on his socials. And Lyric is my best friend in New York, and I trust her implicitly. She knows my past with Tweetie, and I've filled her in on everything going on. She's more than happy to help us.

I swing the door open and have to hold back a gasp. Tweetie looks so handsome in his tuxedo. His normally wild tresses have been slicked back off his face. He takes his time taking me in, his eyes slowly roaming over my body and back up.

Then his smile drops. "I don't like this." He steps into my apartment.

I look down at my dress. "That wasn't exactly the reaction I was going for." I blow out a breath, shutting the door before a hand pops out and stops it.

"He made me wait down the hall because, to quote him, 'I wasn't gonna see his hot-ass girlfriend before him.'" Decker steps into my apartment, shoving his hands into his pockets.

"Thank you again for doing this," I say to Decker, then eye Tweetie, who shakes his head. His mouth is a tight line.

"Sure, and don't worry, I was already given the rules on the way up," Decker says.

"What rules?" I ask, looking at Tweetie again.

"No dancing. No touching. Definitely no kissing. Not even on the cheek. Honestly, I'm pretty sure I'm supposed to act like we're two awkward teenagers at a church retreat." Decker looks at Tweetie. "Did I cover it?"

"Tedi," Tweetie whines.

I walk over to him and wind my arms around his neck. "You look very handsome." I kiss him.

Tweetie unwinds my arms, taking my hand, and tugs me down the hall. He doesn't give an explanation to Decker as he leads me to my bedroom, shutting the door behind us. He sits on the edge of my bed. "I don't like this."

I sit next to him and place my hand on his thigh. "It's one night, and it's not like we're not going to be together. We can be the foursome who are stuck together like glue."

"Do you really expect me not to touch you?" His eyes narrow. "And seriously, look at what you're wearing. My dick is already at half salute."

I giggle, and he growls. "It's kind of a turn-on when you get all broody. I think it's because you're usually not like that."

He stands and shakes his head. "Please, Tedi, let's just say fuck all this and run away together."

I meet him in the middle of the room. Picking up his hands, I place them on my hips and fiddle with his tie. "I'm yours. Just remember that tonight. I'm coming home with you. You're going to be the one who unzips this dress. The one who watches it fall to the floor. The only one who will know what my skimpy black thong looks like. You'll be the one who gets to kiss every inch of my skin." I rise on my toes and kiss him. "Only you."

He blows out a breath and seems to calm a little.

"Now, how do I look?" I do a little twirl.

"Breathtaking."

I smile and tilt my head. "There you go. Thank you. Come on. Let's just get this thing over with so we can come back here."

"How skimpy is the thong?" he asks when I open the door.

"Would you rather I go without?"

"Fuck no, because then I'll out us before we even get into the venue."

I laugh and take his hand, pulling him across my apartment.

Lyric is already out of the bedroom. She and Decker stand awkwardly by the kitchen island.

"Okay, Tweetie, here's your date and my friend, Lyric." I bring Tweetie to my side and display my hands like Vanna White. "Lyric, Tweetie Sorenson."

Tweetie gives her a nod. "Don't touch me tonight."

"Well, this is going to be fun." She eyes Decker before grabbing her coat off the hook by the front door. "At least I got a great dress out of it." She shoots me a reassuring smile.

I gave her the whole lowdown of how Tweetie's not really

on board with this fake date thing so she could be understanding when his rare bear side emerges.

I slip my shoes on, and Tweetie grabs my coat, holding it out for me. "Thanks." I give him a smile.

The entire time walking out of my apartment and climbing into the car Tweetie ordered for us tonight, Tweetie is tense. His back is straight, and he's not nearly the charming guy he normally is.

Part of me feels guilty. "If you'd rather not do this—"

He holds up his hand. "It's fine. You're not going to lose your job because of me," he grumbles.

"I'd rather lose my job than make you this uncomfortable."

He takes my hand and squeezes it. "It's one night."

I look at Decker. "Keep Lyric company if this one abandons her"—I nod in Tweetie's direction—"and I get pulled off to chat about something work-related, okay?" I don't want her to have a shitty time. Plus, maybe Decker and Lyric will hit it off.

Decker nods, a half-smile forming as though he might like that idea.

We pull up to the venue, and I give Tweetie one more long kiss, then rub my lipstick from his lips. "I love you."

I move to get out of the car, but Tweetie tightens his grip on me. I turn around and he releases a long breath, then lets go of my hand. "I love you so much."

"I know," I say.

The door opens, and I accept a hand from the driver and step out of the limo. Decker steps out after me, and I hook my arm through his, the two of us walking into the venue.

We manage to get through the doors and check our coats before someone grabs my hand and turns me around.

"Saige!" I smile at my oldest friend and look around, noticing the rest of our friends from Florida.

She tugs me away from the group. "Yeah, yeah, you can say your hellos after you tell me what the hell is going on."

"Tweetie!" the Florida guys all shout.

I take one glimpse over my shoulder to see he's left Lyric with Decker, and he's being swarmed by all of his old teammates. Then my gaze snags on Kane and Jana, standing off to the side and watching it all. I really hope they can mend this rift at some point.

Saige tugs me away from the group. "What is going on? Please explain to me why Tweetie is posting a picture of your tattoo. Are you guys back together? I'm assuming no since he showed up with some blonde on his arm?" She crosses her arms, her eyes spitting fire.

"You look gorgeous," I say.

She nods, then glares. "Start talking."

I laugh and tell her we're back together and everything that happened to get us there. Then I explain the Bud thing and how I don't want to lose my job.

I don't bring up the fact that if Tweetie continues to play, there's really only one way we can be together. I might have a tough decision to make. There's no way I'm doing long distance again.

"I cannot believe you made him bring a date." Saige rolls her eyes. "Tedi, all that shit that you went through."

I shake my head. "I know. But honestly, I can't explain it. Maybe I've matured, or maybe it's because there's been all this time..." I would never betray Tweetie and tell anyone about his past or his journals. But that was a huge part of why I'm okay with this plan. I don't think he'd ever jeopardize us. "I think this is it for us. It's our time. I don't have those insecurities anymore. I know that man is as committed to me as I am to him. We just have some things we have to figure out before we can tell the world."

She pulls me into an embrace.

"You're going to mess up my hair." I tighten my arms around her, and we hold one another for a minute.

"I'm so happy for you. I'm happy for him. I'm happy for both of you." She pulls back, tears in her eyes.

Someone clears their throat next to us.

We both turn to see Tweetie.

sixty

Tweetie

I SAY HELLO TO ALL MY FRIENDS, BUT MY GAZE tracks Tedi. Saige pulled her away the minute we got in here.

"So, finally, huh?" Aiden punches me in the shoulder.

"I think it's great. She was always your one." Imogen's hand runs down my arm as her husband, Warner, puts his hand out for me to shake.

"Is that how you're still so fucking good on the ice?" Warner asks.

I look around the area, but no one from the Falcons is here, and I trust my old teammates to not say anything.

"It's kind of under wraps," I say.

"Hence the blonde and her showing up with Decker Davis?" Aiden asks, eyebrow raised.

I nod. I hate this, and I feel bad for leaving Lyric. She was nice enough to do this for us, and I'm definitely making the whole situation uncomfortable.

I meant what I said in the car—Tedi's not going to lose her job because of my bullshit. So I'll play the part she wants me to as long as I'm the one who takes her home and I'm the one who holds her tonight.

Saige squeals, and she and Tedi hug. I hope that means she's on board with us, but there are a few things I need to straighten out while I'm here with the Fury. And the first one is with Saige.

"I'll catch you guys in there?" I nod toward the ballroom.

Aiden nods, a smile playing at his lips because he probably knows what I'm about to do. "Her bark is worse than her bite." He pats me on the shoulder.

I walk toward Tedi and Saige and clear my throat to get their attention because the two of them act as if they're in a goddamn bubble all the time. As if no one else is in the vicinity. They turn toward me, and Tedi's grin is enough for me to know she's falling a little deeper in love with me right now, knowing I'm here to talk to her best friend.

"Hey, handsome. Are you here with anyone?" Tedi asks, pretending to flirt with me.

"Not the person I want to be with."

She giggles and reaches her hand out but retracts it. That anger boils a little more inside me.

"Don't worry, the one you want will be in your bed tonight," she says.

"Do I have to stay here to pretend like we're all in this conversation together? Because I have my own husband I need to flirt with since we have no kids with us this trip." Saige thumbs in the direction I just came.

"Actually, I came over here to talk to you," I say, turning to her.

"I'll leave you guys to it." Tedi walks by me, her finger discreetly running against my arm.

"And I'd really appreciate it if you didn't go dancing with Davis or anything," I say over my shoulder.

Tedi giggles, not telling me she won't. Then Imogen giggles, and I see the two of them hugging.

Saige crosses her arms and stares at me as though she's waiting for me to fall to my knees and beg her to accept us. I'm ready to do it, but then she laughs. "It's about fucking time you got your head out of your ass."

"You don't need me to convince you?"

Her arms loosen, and she tilts her head. "Tweetie, I know the kind of guy you are. You're the same guy who made my best friend fall in love with him all those years ago. Now, I don't love everything that went down, but if she's ready to move on, which she seems to be, then I'm good."

"Seriously?" I arch an eyebrow.

"What did you expect? That I'd put up a fight? I've always loved you, Tweetie."

I shrug. "I just thought I'd have to do more convincing."

She laughs. "You're too hard on yourself." She touches my forearm. "But you are aware that if things go south and it's your fault, I'm not going to be so nice."

"I know, Saige." I chuckle.

"But that's not going to happen. I have a great feeling about you two this time around. She seems..." She looks over to where Tedi is talking with Kane and Jana. "I don't know. Maybe she's done all this growth these last few years, and I didn't see it because I'm such a big part of her life, but..."

I don't say anything because Saige is right. There's something different with Tedi now. The old Tedi would have never orchestrated this night. She would have never been able to handle seeing another woman on my arm. It's sexy as fuck that she's so confident in us, in me. All this shit with Bud and my contract doesn't mean anything. Maybe it's time to hang up my skates and just be done with it all and focus all my attention on what means the most to me.

"Yeah. I know what you're saying."

"I can't wait to see you two really together." Saige gives me a big, cheesy grin, then squeezes my arm. "Now excuse me, I have to go seduce my husband."

But Aiden's already on his way toward us.

"I love her," I say. "I know those are simple words, but the feeling that goes along with them isn't. I have no way to convey how strongly I feel for her."

She nods. "Those of us who know, know. You don't have to explain."

Then she walks away, and Aiden smiles at me over her shoulder. He whispers something in her ear, and she laughs.

Tedi is still talking to Imogen, head tossed back in a laugh. Fuck, we've been here, like, fifteen minutes, and I already want her in my arms.

But I'm a man on a mission, and I'm going to make this time count. We may not be able to act as though we're a couple, but I can still solidify our future. So I head across the room to the next people I need to make amends with.

Jana stiffens and taps Kane's arm when she clocks my approach.

"Tweetie." Kane puts his hand out between us.

I shake it and move my attention to Jana. "How are you guys?" I ask, hating the awkwardness between us.

"We're good," Kane answers, and Jana's silence doesn't go unnoticed. "Busy with the kids."

"I'm sure. Listen." I look over my shoulder. "I just wanted to say, I'm sorry."

Jana sucks in a breath.

"Tweetie, you don't have to—" Kane begins, but I interrupt.

"I do. I acted like an asshole. It hurt, it did, but I understand that you had a business to run. At the time, I was pissed, and I was hurt, but mostly I felt betrayed by you guys because we were friends. When it all went down with Tedi, I think...

no, I know I blamed you both. Thought you ruined my future —my career and with Tedi. And I've held that blame and resentment all these years. I just wanted to come over here and say I'm sorry."

"It was such a hard decision for us. I don't want you to think we went into it lightly," Jana says.

"Honestly, looking back now, I'm not sure you would've soared with us like you have. Warner's still there, and you aren't the kind of guy who wants to play second line his entire career. You're too good for that." Kane runs his hands through his long hair. "Look at you now. You're a force to reckon with. You, Aiden, and Warner are the final three left from that dynasty. Cory, but he's still got age on his side. All that to say, I think you ended up right where you should have. The star on a team. An integral part of the team. Fucking Jagger Kale with his Trifecta." He rolls his eyes.

"Jealous?" I grin.

"Fuck yeah, you guys are unbeatable this season," Kane says.

Jana steps up to me. "I'm going to let you guys talk, and I'm going to find the other women." She looks me in the eyes. "Thank you for the apology, and I want to say I'm sorry too. We've had a lot of regrets, and letting you go was at the top of our list. Which was why we tried to get you back." She glances at her husband. "Unsuccessfully. But I heard a rumor, and I'm happy to see all the stars are aligning again. And when you're on that bus with the Cup in your hand and your girl on your side, just remember... you have me and Kane to thank." She laughs. "Just kidding. Good luck for the rest of the season, and this better mean you're coming down to Florida to visit. Payton and Axton still talk about you at Ford's retirement party and how you got the whole room to dance." She hugs me.

"You can count on it. Thank you."

She kisses Kane on the cheek. "Now I need some girl time. See you, boys."

Aiden and Warner come over, and we talk hockey, life, and all of their stories involving kids and wives and trips make me excited for the adventures Tedi and I are going to have.

Finally, I feel as though I'm on track to have the life I've always wanted.

sixty-one

Tedi

I TUCK MYSELF INTO A CORNER NEAR A LARGE potted plant and send a text to Tweetie.

He's across the room with Aiden, Warner, Rowan, and Henry. At first, I felt bad for Lyric. Other than dinner, neither of us has really talked to our dates. But Decker's taken the responsibility of getting her a drink and keeping her entertained. I was ready to send her to an expensive spa and give her the works, but she's been chatting with Decker since Tweetie and I left the table separately. Maybe I made a love connection.

Tweetie pulls his phone out of the inside of his tuxedo jacket, and I watch the small smile crease his lips when he reads my message. He searches the room, and when his gaze lands on me, butterflies flutter in my tummy from his knowing smile.

He tucks his phone back into his pocket and excuses himself, disappearing through the doors into the hallway.

I follow a short distance behind. When I reach it, the door to the coatroom is barely open, so I look both ways. Not seeing anyone, I slide in, shutting the door behind me.

I'm not more than two feet inside before an arm hooks me around my waist and pulls me between two rows of coats. My back lands against the wall, and Tweetie's body cages me in.

"That was sexy," I whisper.

He waggles his eyebrows in the dim light. "I've got moves better than that."

"I know you do."

I kind of love the fact he hasn't even tried to kiss me yet. That he's just happy to have me alone in a room.

"You've been like a politician the way you're working the room tonight."

He rests his forehead against mine, breathing me in. "I've been a horrible date."

"I think Decker's probably thankful for that."

He draws back, and I nod.

"Does that mean I get you alone in the car on the ride home?" His fingers roam over my ribcage, his thumbs close to the bottom of my breasts. It only makes me grow hotter for him as my nipples pebble.

"We do have to keep up appearances, but if we outstay everyone, I can't see why not."

"Thank fuck, 'cause I have plans."

"Oh, what kind of plans?"

"My hand sliding up your dress." He bunches the fabric, pulling it up, and his knuckles drag up my thigh.

My breath hitches. "I like the sound of that."

"We'd have to be quiet because the driver does not get to see any part of you."

"Keep going..."

His fingers find my panties, and he slides a finger under the elastic. I close my eyes, and he buries his head in my neck.

"I love the way you smell." He sucks my earlobe into his mouth, then nips at it. Pushing the wet silk fabric to the side, he runs the tip of his finger through my folds. "I want to fuck you right here. You have no idea the restraint it's taking to not turn you around and take you like a rutting animal from behind."

I rub the bulge in his pants, wanting him to do just that. He positions his body so it's easier access for both of us, and I use the space to pull at the end of his belt, opening it. His finger continues its exploration, and his thumb rubs the lightest circles over my clit.

Somehow, I get his belt free, his pants unbuttoned, and his zipper down while he's driving me to the edge with his fingers. I tuck my hand down the front of his boxer briefs and find him hot and hard in my palm. He sucks in a breath, cursing.

I tighten my fist with the amount of pressure I know he loves. The one good thing about being with someone so long is the fact that you know how to get them there fast.

Just when I'm about to fall to my knees to take him in my mouth, the door opens and a woman giggles.

"What about your wife?" a woman says.

Both of us freeze. Then we scramble to get ourselves presentable, except we're already found no matter who it is. Tweetie zips up his pants, and I shove my dress back down.

"Don't worry about her."

Tweetie and I look at one another with open mouths.

Bud Caldron.

As if I didn't already know he's a slimy prick—but his wife is in the other room. Maybe she's aware of his philandering, maybe she's not. Regardless, hooking up when she's in the other room is a new low, even for Bud.

Tweetie's hand finds mine, and he moves to leave as soon as we have an opening. I really hope they take another spot in the coatroom and we can sneak out.

As we're sliding along the wall, the coats push apart, and Bud emerges with a girl who's way too young behind him.

And she's not even the same girl from the dinner. So he's a habitual cheater, not just in love with someone who's not his wife.

Laughter erupts out of him, and he releases the girl's hand. "Well, well, well. Look who we have here."

I want to punch the smug look off his face.

Tweetie's hand tightens around mine, and he steps forward, positioning me behind him.

Oh no, he doesn't. I step up to his side. Tweetie glances at me but says nothing, concentrating his attention on Bud.

"You're like two defective magnets," he says, shaking his head.

"And who's your guest?" I ask.

Bud cuts his gaze to me. "It's none of your business. She doesn't work for the national league or any other hockey organization. What I'm doing isn't against the rules. Can you say the same?"

"So marriage vows don't matter?" Tweetie asks, obviously seething.

Bud laughs. "Give me a fucking break. Your old flame comes back to town, and you decide you're all about monogamy? You'll dump her the minute she goes back to New York and be back to your philandering ways."

I've had about enough of this man. I release Tweetie's hand and step in front of him, poking my finger in Bud's chest. "You're a piece of shit. You don't know me. You don't know Tweetie, and you know nothing about our relationship." I lean around him to look at the girl. "And seriously, have a little respect for yourself and his wife. I'm not sure what he told you to get you to come in here, but it's not worth compromising your dignity."

The girl starts crying and runs out of the coatroom without saying a word.

"You're done," Bud says with a slimy grin. "I'm calling Mr. Herington. Fraternizing with the players? You'll never come back from this. Say goodbye to your career, Tedi. Or is that how you got as high up as you did? Did you fuck your way to the top? And now you don't care because you hitched your wagon to Tweetie?"

Tweetie's hands land on my hips, and he practically picks me up and sets me down behind him. Then he cocks his fist back and punches Bud in the face. "Watch what you say to my woman."

I gasp, and my hands fly up to cover my mouth while Bud cowers, his hands up until Tweetie backs off.

Once it's clear that Tweetie isn't going to punch him again, he points at Tweetie with a scowl. "And now you're done. Enjoy each other, you two, you just torched your careers."

"The hell I did. I'll find another team. You want to play games with my contract? Do you think you're going to tell me what I can post on my social media? Try to peg me as a certain person that you think the people want? All that should matter to you is how I perform on the ice. And that I fill that fucking arena for you. So fuck you, Bud, I'll find another organization that appreciates me."

He shakes his head, smirk still intact. "Not when I'm done making phone calls."

Tweetie leans in. "Try it. I'll have fun seeing you in court."

Bud just smiles but thankfully keeps his mouth shut.

Tweetie takes my hand, but I stop, wanting to get in the last word. "Have fun explaining to Mr. Gershwin how you just lost the best player on your team. I'd hate to be in your shoes."

Tweetie pulls me out of the coatroom, and there are a lot of eyes lingering on us. We must have been louder than I thought. Regardless, Tweetie stops us, pushes me against a pillar, and smashes his lips to mine.

He claims me without a care in the world of who might see, making me fall in love with him even more—which I thought was impossible.

sixty-two

Tweetie

WE WENT TO TEDI'S AFTER THE GALA, AND SHE packed a bag, then we came back to my place.

I ran out this morning and got us bagels. She's still sleeping when I get home, and I watch her for a moment, loving the image of her sleeping in my bed. Her dark hair is strewn across the pillow, her arms tucked underneath. I love the fact she's naked under that sheet because of our incessant need to touch one another as if each of us still can't believe the other one is really there. Those light touches led to a lot more several times throughout the night.

I lean down and kiss her shoulder, but she pushes me away with her hand.

"Not yet," she groans.

After last night, I'm not sure what to expect, other than that she's going to lose her job, and I'm more than likely either getting traded or retiring. One thing is for certain—with Bud as the GM, Chicago is no longer an option for me.

My phone blew up last night in my guys' text message

thread—both Chicago and Florida—but I ignored them, just wanting to be with Tedi. We need to figure out this next step together without anyone else's opinions or advice.

I go into the kitchen and put the bagels with cream cheese on two plates. I pour two cups of coffee and walk back to my bedroom, figuring I'll take my time admiring her, waiting for her to wake up. She stirs, sliding over when she feels me climb into bed, and wraps her arm around my waist while placing her head on my side.

She moans and wraps one of her legs around mine. "Ew, sweatpants."

I laugh, and she kicks my legs as she tries to get comfortable. I push her dark hair away from her face.

She peeks one eye up at me. "Time to face the real world?"

"I got you bagels."

She lays her head back down. "I've been spoiled the last couple of years." After a kiss on my stomach, she sits up, and when the sheet falls to her waist, I admire her tits out for my viewing pleasure. "That's the first place we're going when you visit New York. We're getting bagels."

"Visit?" I raise an eyebrow.

She gets out of bed, wrapping her arms around her body as if she's cold, and tiptoes to my closet. She grabs a sweatshirt and puts it on before crawling back into bed.

"I don't want to be presumptuous," she says, sitting against the headboard, crossing her legs, and grabbing her plate to bring it closer.

"Be presumptuous, Tedi."

She glances at me, then back at the bagel, taking off the paper. "Then I would say when *we* visit together. A weekend trip maybe."

I tilt my head, not understanding.

She sighs and concentrates on getting her bagel free of the parchment paper. "I don't think I can do long distance." She slowly lowers the bagel to the plate and places it on the night-stand. Swiveling, she faces me but doesn't look me in the eye. "I made my decision when I agreed to start us back up. And I don't want you to fight it. This is what I want, and it has nothing to do with what happened... well, that's not true." She grows quiet again.

"Tedi, you can tell me anything." I place my hand in hers, and she cups her other hand over mine. "I want us to do this together. Make these decisions together because we come first."

"I'm going to resign."

"No." I shake my head, and she tilts hers.

"I told you that you couldn't fight it, and I don't have a lot of choice. I'm probably going to be fired if I don't anyway."

"Fuck, Tedi, I hate this."

She picks up my plate, reaches over me to put it on the nightstand, and climbs into my lap. "Listen, the minute I went to your hotel room in Anaheim, I knew a decision had to be made with my job. When I was reading your journal, I saw how stupid I was for not going to Nashville. I was so hell-bent on being independent and not needing anyone that I just threw us to the wayside, expecting us to survive. There's no reason I couldn't have found another job. I'm a talented woman."

I laugh, and she does too.

"And the same applies now. I found my love of working in the hockey industry because of you, doing your social media and all the Florida Fury players. So it was a natural progression for me to get to the national office, but I can find another job in a different market. You can't. You have a few years left, maybe more if you keep working out like you are."

I smirk, my hands falling to her hips.

"So, I'm going to follow you. That is, if you want me to." She raises her eyebrows.

My hands glide up her body until they're cradling her cheeks. "I don't want you to have to make that sacrifice."

"I'm not. You trump it all. I want this more than I want anything else. And I'm confident I'll find my footing and the place I'm supposed to be. But I don't want any of that if I don't have you."

"I'm prepared to retire," I admit, and I am.

She laughs and shakes her head. "And I would never be able to live with myself. Plus, I'm invested now. I'd like nothing more than for Bud Caldron to eat his fucking words."

Fuck, how did I ever get so lucky to get her?

"Are you sure?"

She inches forward on my lap, and even through my sweatpants, I feel the heat of her bare center. "I'm positive. Now, kiss me so I can go eat my mediocre bagel. And don't take that as I don't appreciate you getting it for me. You'll understand when you have a New York bagel."

I'm not an idiot, so I do what she says, and I seal our future with a kiss.

sixty-three

Tedi's Journal Entry
Present day
Chicago

To my older self,

Well, we're unemployed. I sure hope you're reading this and saying it was the best decision we ever made. Although I'm not worried. Jobs will come and go, but Tweetie is our forever. Tell him hi from past me. LOL! Mr. Herington did offer to let me finish out the season, but I didn't want all the politics and bullshit, so I declined. I'm ready for our new adventure anyway. I think maybe I'm ready to leave sports and venture into another area entirely. Maybe help small businesses. Who knows?

Now we just have to figure out where Tweetie will land, but there's still a lot of the season left. Tell him he better have won the Cup because I want to shove that trophy down Bud Caldron's big mouth.

sixty-four

Tweetie's Journal Entry
Present day
Chicago

To my teenage self,

We're winning at life, buddy. Sure, our hockey career is up in the air, but I don't care. We have Tedi and that's all that matters.

sixty-five

Tweetie

I'VE SHOWERED AND AM CHANGING IN THE LOCKER room after practice when Coach Buford calls out to me. The guys all look at me, and I can see the uncertainty in their eyes. I'm annoyed at all the gossip going around. Everyone suspects I won't be in Chicago next year, and they're right, I won't, because I won't play for Bud Caldron. Period.

I set my bag back down and head into his office. I'm about to sit down, but he shakes his hand and points at the door.

"Come with me."

I follow him out the door and down the hall toward the elevator, knowing instinctively that we're heading up to the offices.

"Am I being let go?" I ask. "Fuck, he traded me?"

Trade deadlines are approaching, and I thought I was in the clear. How did I not even consider that Bud might trade me just to fuck with me?

"Mr. Gershwin wants to talk to both of us," Coach says.

We step into the elevator, and my anxiety racks up.

"Coach, the other night... did you talk to them? I mean, we're so cohesive together."

I don't care where I end up, but I don't want my team to suffer because of my decision. I was prepared to help the Falcons win the Cup and then leave. Not leave them in the lurch.

He doesn't show any reaction. "Let's just see what he wants, then we'll go from there."

I blow out a breath, and he steps off the elevator. I follow him down the hallway of the management offices. We reach our destination, and Mr. Gershwin's assistant tells us he's expecting us and to go right in.

Coach looks at me, and I want to throw up, but most of all, I want to call Tedi.

Mr. Gershwin's office is a reflection of the man. It's more like an old library with dark wood bookshelves, a big mahogany desk that sits in front of the window, and brown leather couches and two leather chairs.

"Chris. Tweetie. Have a seat." He rises from his chair and walks around his desk, signaling with his hand that we should head over to the couches.

The Gershwin family has owned the Falcons forever, and I wonder who will be next in line to take over. I've noticed for a while that Mr. Gershwin struggles to walk a little and hasn't been down to see the team as much as he used to. I'm pretty sure they have four daughters. Maybe it will be like Jana taking over the Fury from her dad.

He sits in a chair, and we both sit on the couch. "Do you guys want a drink?"

We shake our heads.

He laughs. "You guys seem terribly nervous. Tweetie, your leg."

I look down to see it bouncing up and down. I press my hand on my thigh to stop it.

"I don't get a thrill from scaring people, so let's get right into it. I heard about the other night, Tweetie. You and Miss Douglas in the coatroom." He tilts his head down and looks at me from under his bushy gray eyebrows.

I open my mouth, ready to out Bud, but I shut it. That's not the point. I'm not going to be one of those people who points fingers. "I apologize for that, Mr. Gershwin. It was poor judgment on our part. And—"

"I heard she resigned," he interrupts.

I nod. "She did."

Coach Buford whips his head in my direction. "She did? Jesus, who will they send us now?" he whines, dropping his chin to his chest.

"Well, that's the second issue. The first issue I want to discuss is the fact that I fired Bud Caldron this morning. Effective immediately."

Coach Buford and I gawk at Mr. Gershwin.

"Oh," Coach says, eyeing me, not being discreet at all.

That sourness in my stomach lifts.

"He thinks he has eyes everywhere? Well, this is my organization and my team. I've been watching him for a while. I haven't liked a lot of things he's done when it comes to the players and some of his other decisions as of late, but you were my final straw. Tweetie, you're what I want this team to represent. My daughter showed me some of the social media posts where you went to the school in Philly. The school sent us a thank you note with a picture of all the kids wearing our T-shirts." He smiles. "It was really cute. And you didn't do it because someone made you. You did it on your own."

"Actually." I cringe. "Tedi... Miss Douglas..."

He waves me off. "You did it for the girl?"

"Well, partly, but had I heard the story from someone else, I would've done it just the same."

"You know, Tweetie, I'm old-school. Maybe I'm getting

old, but I think people get better with age. And I'm not about to replace my older players just because they're old with new shiny kids that will come with a media storm. I've watched you mature, and now you've found yourself a woman you love. And who must love you since she resigned in order to be with you."

I could go on and on about Tedi and me. I have no idea if he knows about our past or not.

"I wanted to call you up here to tell you that whether we win the Cup or not at the end of this season, we want to resign you. I hope you still want to be a Falcon."

Coach smiles at me and pats my knee.

"I do." I nod eagerly.

"Good. Bud is an idiot. A line like you guys comes around once in a career, and he would have blown that up for reasons I'll never understand." He shakes his head. "Oh, and my daughter also showed me your declaration post of that picture of the tattoo. I'll never understand why people tattoo each other's names on their bodies, but I think a lot of Chicago will be happy to see you so happy. Back in my day, you held your cards close to the vest. You kids just put it all out there. It's refreshing." He presses a button on the phone on the table next to him. "Shirley, make a reservation at that new Italian restaurant and call Glenda and tell her I'm picking her up at six for a date."

Shirley says okay, and his finger releases the button.

"Now you're making me a romantic," he says.

"Thank you, Mr. Gershwin. I really appreciate the opportunity to play for you."

"You don't have to thank me. You earned your spot." He looks at Coach. "Scared you, huh?"

Coach nods. "I didn't know what I was going to do."

Mr. Gershwin laughs and puts up his fingers, a little space

between his pointer and thumb. "Okay, I like to scare a little bit. It's fun." He shrugs.

To him maybe.

"You said the second issue was who is going to replace Tedi?" I prod.

"Oh yes, I wanted to mention my daughter. She's the one up on all this social media stuff. She said she liked Tedi's angles on your campaigns and would like to talk to her." He takes a card out of his pocket and slides it across the table. "I just hate the idea of her being out of a job because she found love. What kind of happy ending is that? Tell her to call my daughter. She has her hands in a lot of companies. I can never keep them straight. It's some clothing company she's been trying to get off the ground."

I pick up the card. "Thank you. I feel like I need to promise you I'll win the Cup. This is all so generous."

He shrugs. "You don't have to guarantee the Cup, but it would be nice. I love a girl who gave up her dream to marry me and raise our kids. She says she's never regretted it, but I think had she been able to have a career *and* be a mother, she would've preferred that. Her overinvolvement in my kids' schooling and extracurriculars says she'd probably be better at running this organization than me. It was different times then, though. Anyway, I guess when you have four daughters and never want to see them sacrifice anything, it changes your way of thinking."

I pocket the card. "Thank you again."

"You're welcome... again. Now go tell the girl." He points toward the door.

I stand and shake Mr. Gershwin's hand, and when I try to say thank you again, he shoos me out of the room.

I go back down to the locker room, grab my bag, and order my rideshare, eager to get back to tell Tedi that we have a home base. A place to start the next chapter of our life together.

sixty-six

Tedi

I BLINK. THEN BLINK AGAIN. THERE'S NO WAY I'M seeing what I think I am.

I bought the pregnancy test just to make sure since I enjoy a drink now and then. My nipples have been extra sensitive lately, and I'm late by two weeks. Regardless, I really didn't think I was pregnant.

But I'm pretty sure those are two pink lines.

I bring the stick up to my face and squint just in case I'm seeing things.

Yep, two lines.

I bring the stick closer to the light because maybe it's fainter than I think.

Nope, bright pink.

Well, shit. He knocked me up the first time I had sex with him. Go fucking figure. Only us, I swear.

Get ready, Tweetie Sorenson. You're gonna be a dad.

sixty-seven

Tweetie

THERE'RE SO MANY CHOICES, AND THE LADY IS growing impatient with me, but it has to be perfect. Especially since she'll be wearing it for the rest of her life.

All the diamonds sparkle under the overhead lights, and I ask the lady to take out another one. I inspect one closer, bringing it up to my eye, making sure there aren't any flaws.

Yep, it's perfect.

I bring it to the light to make sure it sparkles enough.

Yep, super bright.

It's the one. This ring was made for her, so I tell the lady to wrap it up.

Get ready, Tedi Douglas. You're gonna be a wife.

sixty-eight

Tedi

I HAD TO GET OUT OF TWEETIE'S CONDO, SO I WENT to the coffee shop that everyone loves, got a tea, and people-watched for a few hours. Tweetie texted to tell me he was delayed after practice, so he wouldn't be home for a while anyway.

I have no worries over whether Tweetie will be happy about this baby, but I wanted to be by myself to come to grips with it and what it all means.

What will our life be like with a baby? We don't even know where we're going to live at this point. And being pregnant and then a new mother is going to make it more difficult to get a new venture off the ground.

My hand falls to my stomach, and I rub my still-flat belly. I admire the families walking by the window, some looking a little frazzled or tired.

The longer I sit here, the more I feel ready to conquer this next step of my life. Especially with Tweetie. Sure, we haven't had a lot of time on our own since we've gotten back together, but we have years behind us where we traveled and had time alone.

My phone dings on the table, and I pick it up, seeing a text from Tweetie.

> Where are you? I'm home, and you're not. :(

I laugh and type out a quick response.

> Right around the corner. Do you want a coffee?

> Just you.

My insides flutter.

> On my way.

> Hurry.

I take one last sip of my tea, dump it in the trash, and leave the coffee shop.

When I get to The Nest, I type in the security code, not even bothering to tear down the handwritten sign. Let those girls think they have a chance. What's wrong with a little hope?

I climb the stairs, wondering what this will be like with a baby carrier. Probably not ideal.

I open the condo door and don't see Tweetie in the main room. "For someone who says they missed me and wanted me to hurry, where are you?"

"In here. Sorry." Tweetie steps out of the doorway of his bedroom, and he's wearing that mischievous smirk I love.

My stomach drops as I wonder if he found the test. But I stashed it way in the back of the cabinet under the sink. There's no way he found it.

"What's going on?" I narrow my eyes.

"What? I can't be excited to see my girlfriend?" He breaks the distance and hugs me, tucking his face in my neck and inhaling. "I missed you."

"I missed you too."

He kisses the hollow of my neck and tugs me by my hand into the bedroom. "So I got you a gift," he says, and I see a wrapped box on the bed.

"Oh, how nice." I pick it up and sit on the bed. "Do you want me to open it now?"

"Yes." His blue eyes are wide and expectant.

My head tilts. "You're acting weird. Is this some prank or something?"

"No. It's just something I'm excited to give you."

I study him for a few seconds, then tear off the paper. "A journal."

He grabs a similar one from the dresser. "It's a matching one to mine. Brand-new ones to start our brand-new life together." He hands me his, putting it on top of the one he got me. "I got you some fancy pens too."

I smile. "I love them." I go to hand his journal back, but he straightens and takes a step back from me.

"Flip through it, make sure you like mine before you rip open the cellophane on yours."

"I'm sure I'm going to love it," I say.

"Make sure." He nods toward his, so I do what he says.

I thumb through it, but I notice writing on the first page, so I stop and open it fully.

It has today's date on the page.

Today, I asked her to marry me...

. . .

I lift my eyes off the journal and find Tweetie on bended knee, a ring box in his hands.

"No," I say, shaking my head.

He draws back, hurt flashing across his face. "What?"

"You found out?" I don't know how he found the pregnancy test, but he doesn't have to do this just because we're having a baby.

He lowers the box and sits back on his heels. "Found out what?"

"Oh, you didn't? You don't know?" Excitement builds inside me, like fireflies sparking to life when it gets dark.

He blows out a breath, forehead creased. "Know what, Tedi?"

I wave my hand. "Nothing. Carry on." I cross my legs and wait with a smile and joy in my heart, but Tweetie just stares at me. "Here, let's start over." I pick up the journal. "A journal, I love it. Oh, you want me to read yours. I'd love to." I put my journal down and pick up his, opening it to the first page with his handwriting on it. "Oh, Tweetie, you didn't..."

He doesn't move, just staring at me.

"This is where you're on bended knee with the ring." I motion to him with my hand.

"This isn't a play, Tedi. Tell me what's going on."

I rock my head back and my shoulders slump. "I just ruined your entire proposal."

"You're dodging. What piece of the puzzle am I missing?"

I cover my mouth and stand, overcome with excitement. "Hold on, let me get something." I walk out of the room but come back and point at the bed. "You sit."

"So now I'm a dog. Great."

I go to the bathroom, and of course the pregnancy stick is still where I shoved it. He never saw it. I'm the worst girlfriend ever.

When I walk back into the room, Tweetie is sitting with

the ring box clasped in his hands, his eyebrows raised all the way to his hairline.

"What is going on?" he asks with exasperation.

I walk up to him, and he opens his legs, letting me slip in between them. "Are you ready?"

"Tedi," he seethes.

I bring the pregnancy stick out from around my back and put it right in front of him.

The ring box drops to the floor with a thud, and Tweetie looks from the stick to me, then back to the stick. "This is yours?"

I nod.

"How?"

I shrug.

"When?"

"I'm pretty sure it was that first time when you came to my apartment."

"How long have you known?"

"A couple hours. I took the test today."

He takes the stick from my hands and stares at it. "A baby?"

"Yeah." Tears well in my eyes. "Which explains why I've been so emotional lately..."

He winds his arms around my waist and brings me toward him, hugging me hard and kissing my stomach.

I brush his hair away from his face. "You okay with it?"

He picks up his head and rests his chin on my stomach, those baby blues glittering with unshed tears. "Are you kidding? I couldn't ask for anything better."

"Good." I kiss his forehead.

"You thought I knew this and that's why I was proposing to you?"

I shrug. "Not the entire reason, but..."

He reaches between us, and I back up to allow him to pick

up the ring box. "No reason to replay the scene." He pats his lap, and I sit.

"It was really cute. I loved it."

He shakes his head. "I had a whole speech about the first time I saw you, but honestly, I'm so thankful that you made that fuck-it bucket list because had you not, we might not be right here, together. So, please marry me because I really want to sit by your side when you tell our grandkids how you met their grandpa."

"Tweetie!" I smack his shoulder, and he laughs, popping open the box.

"You still have to answer."

"Yes!"

He chuckles. A beautiful cushion-cut diamond on a silver band sits in the middle of the black velvet box. "I was going to have my number engraved, but..."

I hold out my left ring finger, and he takes it out of the box. "I wouldn't have minded."

I hold up my hand and admire the way the ring sparkles under the lights.

"One last question," he says.

"What?"

"What do you think of Chicago?"

I turn to him and tilt my head.

"Turns out Bud Caldron got fired and they still want your boy."

"Really!"

He nods, and I squeal, tackling him to the bed. My lips fall to his, and I kiss the only man I've ever loved.

"Whoa, the baby." He slides me off him.

Oh boy. It's going to be a long nine months.

But I'd have it no other way.

epilogue

Tweetie

I WAIT FOR TEDI TO GET ON THE BUS FIRST.

"You can just sit," I tell her, and she glares at me over her shoulder.

I've been getting plenty of glares and huffs and overall annoyance from her, but she's carrying our baby. What does she expect?

"I'm not going to sit." She runs her hands over her small swollen belly. She's just started showing. "I'm going to celebrate along with Chicago."

We get to the top of the bus with all of our closest friends.

The four of us guys stand on top of the championship parade bus, the Stanley Cup raised high above Conor's head. The sun reflects off the silver surface, nearly blinding me, but hell if I care. The deafening roar of the crowd fills my ears, and I lean forward, putting my hands on Tedi's stomach. She swats me off and rolls her eyes at our friends.

I stare at the tens of thousands of fans packed onto the streets, a sea of blue jerseys below.

Rowan and Henry lean over, cheering with the fans and egging them on to make more noise. This moment—this feeling—is everything. Years of grinding, sacrifices, pain, and passion have given us this moment. Conor passes the Cup to me. I held it in Florida and again in Nashville, but this feeling never gets old.

I scan the crowd of fans, all the ones who rode out this year with us. My heart swells at the look of pride beaming from their faces. Henry takes the Cup from me, and I pound my chest and point at the crowd, letting them know this is as much theirs as it is ours.

A microphone lands in my hand. The crowd quiets slightly, waiting.

I take a deep breath, then let it out in a victorious roar. "THIS ONE'S FOR YOU! LET'S GO!"

I move Tedi in front of me, holding her close as the crowd erupts. The bus keeps rolling, confetti swirling in the air, and for this one perfect day, I am on top of the hockey world with my girl at my side. Life can't get any better than this.

One month later...

We're down at Peeper's Alley, in our private room, for what's probably our last time because after tonight, this room isn't ours anymore.

"I don't think you have to take all of our stuff down," I say to Ruby, who's replacing some of the Falcons stuff with Colts paraphernalia.

"What do you care? You're leaving me."

"Ah, Rubes, we'll be back."

"Nah." She waves at Conor. "You're not going to hang out

at a bar. You'll be meeting at some kids' restaurant now, griping about playdates and helicopter moms."

I run my hand over Tedi's stomach, and she places her hand over mine.

We all knew it was time we left The Nest. Tedi and I wanted more room for the baby, and Kyleigh said she was growing tired of all the girls loitering around. Eloise and Conor have some bucket list items they want to check off.

But the kicker was that the same developer Jade and Henry are working with had just bought three houses on their street.

"You guys are really moving onto the same street?" Ruby asks.

We all look at one another. "Yeah," we say in unison.

She shakes her head. "Thank God you're leaving then, because I don't want your crazy to rub off on me."

She walks out of the room, and two large bodies walk in.

Easton holds out his hand. "Keys please."

Ruby walks back in and points at Easton. "This one is going to be a problem."

We all laugh.

"I'm good people. I'm from Alaska." Easton sounds legit offended.

Ruby stares at him as though he's crazy too. "Exactly, you're not used to women. What's the ratio between men and women up there? This room is sacred."

Easton looks from her to us. "What did you tell her about me?"

"Tell them the rules, boys." She shuts the door when she leaves.

Easton and Decker sit, looking after Ruby as though maybe they're a little afraid of her.

"Are you sure you're ready for this?" I ask them both.

Conor, Henry, and Rowan all laugh.

"What's so funny?" Decker asks, he and Easton sharing a look.

I stand and hold out a hand for Tedi. "Just send us an invite, okay?"

Everyone else stands and gets ready to leave.

"To what?" Decker looks us all over.

"Your weddings." I wink at them.

The eight of us—well, ten if you include the two little ones in their mommies' bellies—walk out the door, leaving Peeper's Alley for the new generation.

Hopefully, they do it right and end up where we are... living our happily ever afters.

You clearly know what's coming next? Who do you think gets the first book?

The End

also by piper rayne

Chicago Colts

The Hotshot

Book #2

Book #3

Book #4

The Nest

Mr. Heartbreaker

Mr. Broody

Mr. Swoony

Mr. Charming

Kingsmen Football Stars

False Start (Free Prequel)

You Had Your Chance, Lee Burrows

You Can't Kiss the Nanny, Brady Banks

Over My Brother's Dead Body, Chase Andrews

Chicago Grizzlies

On the Defense (Free Prequel)

Something like Hate

Something like Lust

Something like Love

Plain Daisy Ranch

One Last Summer

The One I Left Behind

The One I Stood Beside

The One I Didn't See Coming

The Baileys

Lessons from a One-Night Stand (FREE)

Advice from a Jilted Bride

Birth of a Baby Daddy

Operation Bailey Wedding (Novella)

Falling for My Brother's Best Friend

Demise of a Self-Centered Playboy

Confessions of a Naughty Nanny

Operation Bailey Babies (Novella)

Secrets of the World's Worst Matchmaker

Winning my Best Friend's Girl

Rules for Dating Your Ex

Operation Bailey Birthday (Novella)

The Greene Family

My Twist of Fortune (Free Prequel)

My Beautiful Neighbor (FREE)

My Almost Ex

My Vegas Groom

A Greene Family Summer Bash (Novella)

My Sister's Flirty Friend

My Unexpected Surprise

My Famous Frenemy

A Greene Family Vacation (Novella)

My Scorned Best Friend

My Fake Fiancé

My Brother's Forbidden Friend

A Greene Family Christmas (Novella)

Lake Starlight

The Problem with Second Chances

The Issue with Bad Boy Roommates

The Trouble with Runaway Brides

The Drawback of Single Dads

Modern Love

Charmed by the Bartender

Hooked by the Boxer

Mad about the Banker

Single Dads Club

Real Deal

Dirty Talker

Sexy Beast

Hollywood Hearts

Mister Mom

Animal Attraction

Domestic Bliss

Bedroom Games

Cold as Ice

On Thin Ice

Break the Ice

Chicago Law

Smitten with the Best Man

Tempted by my Ex-Husband

Seduced by my Ex's Divorce Attorney

Blue Collar Brothers

Flirting with Fire

Crushing on the Cop

Engaged to the EMT

White Collar Brothers

Sexy Filthy Boss

Dirty Flirty Enemy

Wild Steamy Hook-up

The Rooftop Crew

My Bestie's Ex

A Royal Mistake

The Rival Roomies

Our Star-Crossed Kiss

The Do-Over

A Co-Workers Crush

Hockey Hotties

Countdown to a Kiss (Free Prequel)

My Lucky #13 (FREE)

The Trouble with #9

Faking it with #41

Tropical Hat Trick (Novella)

Sneaking around with #34

Second Shot with #76

Offside with #55

Holiday Romances

Single and Ready to Jingle

Claus and Effect

Merry Kissmas

cockamamie unicorn ramblings

You got them! After all these years, we finally gave you Tweetie and Tedi's book (if you're new us, these two first appeared in our Hockey Hotties series, which is where most of the flashbacks happened).

As usual, the pressure is intense when we make you wait a long time for a couple's story. We weren't sure when we left these two open ended in Offside with #55, when or if we'd ever get back to them. But readers kept asking for their story so when we plotted The Nest series, we figured it was our best opportunity to bring in Tweetie before he got too old, but of course we made you wait until the final book in the series. He's not the kind of hero who can be a book one boyfriend, he has to grow on you a bit and make you want to figure out what's behind the façade.

We did feel a lot of pressure to deliver an amazing story for our long-time readers. Tweetie was so much fun to dig into and figure out, as was Tedi. Their dynamic together surprised us back when we first wrote them in My Lucky #13, and it was no different in their own book.

What changed from our original concept to us writing the book? So many things. Let's see...

He was going to retire to win her back (but we felt Tedi wouldn't want that in the end. That she'd want him to have his final years in the league). He was going to be traded (this ended up being a whole timeline problem, and we wanted him to win the cup with the rest of The Nest). The pregnancy was decided in about a day before our editing deadline (but they deserve a big happily ever after with a red bow). Tedi was going to be in a relationship when the book started (we didn't want the OM drama, plus we got to bring in a character from our new series (although that was decided mid book as well). By far the worst thing that didn't get in this book because we just couldn't make it work was a hate fuck between them (when we got to the point when it would happen it just didn't seem right. Not for them at least). Crossing our fingers that we can add a hate fuck into another book soon! LOL

As always, we have a lot of people to thank for getting this book into your hands...

Nina and the entire Valentine PR team. The organization, the promotion, the way you keep us on point with deadlines. We appreciate you SO much!

Cassie from Joy Editing for line edits who once again accepted chapters after the deadline- one of these days we won't have to email you a week before with the subject line - Question!

Ellie from My Brother's Editor for line edits and proofing. We give you barely any time, but you always come through.

Hang Le for the discreet cover and branding for the entire series, which is always top tier. Your talent and eye are unmatched.

Simone at Buerosued for our illustrated cover. Your work

is amazing and we're so happy to be working with you on this series. We love Tweetie and Tedi's pose! It was so perfect and led to many scenes in their book.

All the bloggers who choose to read us when you have so many options out there. We're appreciative and honored to be on your list of must-reads and love reading all your reviews, edits, and more.

All the Piper Rayne Unicorns who support us every day, all day. We'd be lost without you answering our polls and telling us what you love and hate. We strive to give you the best Piper Rayne experience, and we can't say much else except that you're fantastic and unmatched!

You, the reader, reading this now in real time, who has an abundance of books to choose from—thank you for picking up one of ours. Readers threw so much support behind this series, *especially* the audio versions, and we can't say thank you enough. Word of mouth is always the best form of advertising, and we appreciate you sharing your love for this series with the romance community!

We're sure you see the set up... we're staying in Chicago, we're keeping Ruby and Peeper's Alley, but we're shifting gears to baseball. We're popping our baseball sports romance cherry, and we're excited to do a little something different in familiar surroundings. See you at The Barn in 2026. Or The Stable, or something else. At the moment it's The Barn, but have you met us? We change our minds a lot! LOL

xo,
Piper & Rayne

about piper & rayne

Piper Rayne is a *USA Today* Bestselling Author duo who write "heartwarming humor with a side of sizzle" about families, whether that be blood or found. They both have e-readers full of one-clickable books, they're married to husbands who drive them to drink, and they're both chauffeurs to their kids. Most of all, they love hot heroes and quirky heroines who make them laugh, and they hope you do, too!